BALLAD OF THE HIRED BLADES

THE DEADLY EXAM

J.D. RAJOTTE

authorHOUSE®

AuthorHouse™
1663 Liberty Drive
Bloomington, IN 47403
www.authorhouse.com
Phone: 833-262-8899

Published by AuthorHouse 11/17/2022

ISBN: 978-1-6655-7178-4 (sc)
ISBN: 978-1-6655-7179-1 (e)

Library of Congress Control Number: 2022917857

Print information available on the last page.

Any people depicted in stock imagery provided by Getty Images are models, and such images are being used for illustrative purposes only.
Certain stock imagery © Getty Images.

This book is printed on acid-free paper.

I'd like to thank my beautiful fiancé, for supporting me throughout this process, my family for always believing in me, and my amazing son, for teaching me how to be a better man with every passing day...

CONTENTS

PROLOGUE

In the year 2097, a mysterious plague befalls the world of Giganus. Unwitting creatures both big and small, begin to fall victim to a mysterious, mind-altering affliction. The culprit? A new breed of parasite with an appetite for mischief and destruction, a fiend they call "The Wurm". The unfortunate hosts targeted by this mysterious new threat? Animals; birds, fish, mammals, and any creature that inhabits the planet save for humankind. Once infected by this menace, hosts become ruthless, gifted with unnatural speed, power, and a hunger for flesh and violence. As Wurm-infected insurgents begin terrorizing towns and villages, the people call upon the world's most powerful and respected group of mercenaries, The Hired Blades Association. Notorious for their skill in the fray, the members of The Hired Blades Association start fighting back the ranks of the unwelcome parasite. Sharing what knowledge they earn in battle with the world government, the two begin working in tandem to dig deeper towards the source of the fearsome threat. But as the Wurm forces continue to fall to the Blades, more questions begin to arise than the answers they receive. After nearly twenty years pass by, the mysterious Wurm threat steadily becomes largely under control by the efforts of The Hired Blades. But suddenly in the past six months, a significant surge of Wurm activity is felt throughout Giganus; prompting the Hired Blades to take a new stance on their elusive foe. Specialized teams, focused on zeroing in on the heart of the Wurm menace; and learned, Veteran Blade recruiters tasked with gathering them. One such Veteran makes his home in the trees outside a meek mountain village, awaiting the arrival of his next target.....

CHAPTER ONE

The Veteran Blade

It was dark, the air riddled with the smell of gunsmoke. One hundred bandits gather in ragtag huddles, planning their assault. In the distance, a lone mercenary hides, nestled in the trees. Readying his rifle; a dark blue, 7mm Arcane Pierce, he studies its various clips and cartridges. His nest nuzzled in between two mighty oaks yields the perfect cover to accomplish his deadly task.

As the bandits drunkenly cackle about their plans to raid the humble village of Macorin, the mercenary laughs to himself. For only he knows the soon-to-be fate of these marauders. Tonight they do not raid a village, a treasure trove, or a bank vault. Tonight, they raid only the gates of hell.

The Sniper takes aim toward his first victim, the largest goon to be seen with the meanest mug.

Krrrackk *Pew*

He fires. A vibrant projectile of light finds its way to the base of the target's skull, exiting through the front of his forehead. The bandit drops his frothy, half-full glass of mead and falls to his knees. He lets out a wheeze as the air escapes his now lifeless lungs, then collapses with a resounding thud. The entire camp falls silent, not a sound but the ominous wind whistling through the wispy oaks to be heard. Then, a more courageous bandit speaks out.

"Who was it! Who killed Patrice?!?!"

No one can speak, for they do not know. He speaks again, his raspy voice bellowing through the silent encampment.

"I know you're out there!!" he turns to his bandit peers. "What are you fools doing?! Clearly, we have guests! Let's give 'em a warm Piranha Gang welcome!!"

The disheveled Group starts to sober up.

"Yeah! Get the bastards! They took our mate!!"

"Let's skin 'em alive!!"

The rowdy bandit leader retorts.

"Get to the weapons shack! Let's flush the bastards out...

Pew. Sizzle. Fizz.

The mercenary marks his second victim. The bandit leader falls to the ground, a singed hole burned through his eye socket. The thugs relent.

"Oh God! Chief!"

"Get those weapons!"

The Sniper grins. He lifts a detonator towards his ear and presses a shining green button. *KABOOM* An explosion goes off inside the bandits' artillery shack, blowing their heavy weaponry to smithereens.

"Shit! What's going on?!"

"We still have our rifles! Get to the tents!"

The Sniper takes aim and picks off several more thugs as they scramble to the barracks for cover. Barreling through the door, the bandits swiftly begin to arm themselves. They hurriedly grasp at pistols, rifles, knives, swords, and anything they can get a hold of to defend their lives from the unseen assailant. As the last of the bandits make it to their tents, the mercenary prepares the next phase of his plan. He chants a mysterious incantation, as an eagle tattoo on the inside of his left forearm starts to glow a golden hue.

"Nubibus autem oleum." Said the Sniper.

A nimbostratus cloud formation appears over the perimeter. From it begins to rain a grease-like substance. The bandits revel in this freakish occurrence.

"God wants us dead!"

"What the hell is happening?!"

"Wait... This smells like gasoline!!"

The Sniper follows up his Arcane combination.

"Ignis Sagitta!" He mutters.

He points his index and middle finger towards the now saturated tents full of bandits. Brilliant arrows of pure flame shoot from his fingertips, striking the tents and setting them ablaze in an instant.

"OooOOAAaaAAAHHH!!!!"

"AAGH!! HELP ME I'M BURNING!!!"

Several bandits catch fire, running from the tents and crying out for help before suffocating to death. A number of them flee the tent unscathed, scrambling to get their wits about them. The Mercenary continues his chant.

"Disseminabunt. Sequitur quod venari!"

The rain stops as the nimbostratus separates into smaller formations. The miniature clouds follow the escapees directly overhead.

The Sniper whispers. "Fulmen."

Each small cloud releases a lightning bolt to the top of the target's head. *Thud* They fall to the ground, frozen and lifeless. Smoke billows from their singed hair.

Some raiders cry out. "We're all gonna die!!"

"I have a son!! This can't be happening!!"

The Sniper's arm begins to tremble. He digresses.

"Uggh, oh stop you! We're almost finished here. Just one more..."

He raises his arm.

"Obice Tenebris!"

An Indigo dome of impenetrable light surrounds the encampment. The bandits watch in horror as they are locked inside the blazing forest. The lone mercenary readies his Arcane Pierce.

"Alright, time to earn your keep."

He begins to pick off bandit after bandit. Skillfully landing a finishing blow with each shot. Some unwitting foes take to hiding behind a pile of mead barrels.

"Hmm, this calls for a trick shot." Said The Sniper.

He selects a different clip loading it into his weapon with swift finesse.

Aiming with great care, he takes a precise shot at the trunk of a tree adjacent to the hiding bandits.

Pfew *Fwishh*

The bullet pops like a paintball on impact, separating into a barrage of light beams which bounce off of the tree and riddle holes into the hiding bandits with ease.

Nearly 10 feet away, a surviving bandit catches a glimpse of the Sniper's beam projectile trail.

"Hey! I saw where that came from! Let's go! We can't let this bastard kill us like this!"

Some half dozen or so remaining bandits gather their wits and run for the Sniper's nest, not but 100 yards down. The Sniper relents his position.

"Hmm... I should not have trapped myself in the barrier this time. Welp, guess it can't be helped."

The Mercenary puts down his rifle and pulls a black metal spearhead and a baton-like object from his rucksack. As he pushes a button on the baton, it extends into a five-and-a-half-foot pole. He then fastens the spearhead on top with a resounding *clink*.

Vrrrrzz

The edges glow a bright orange hue, as a mirage-like heat emanates from the blade.

"It's been a while, huh? Since I've done it up close..."

As the bandits draw near, the Sniper drops from his nest to the ground below. He lands on a pile of leaves.

Pfffsssst

As the leaves scatter, the Sniper hoists himself up; gathering an olive-colored fedora he was wearing and his glowing spear. A devilish grin and cold dead eyes plastered across his face. The first bandit approaches.

"You! *Panting* you Goddamned swine! We got you now! Any last words pissant?!"

The bandits ready knives and energy pistols as they try to catch their breath. The Sniper replies.

"Good evening gentleman! Before we get started, allow me to introduce myself. My name is Faxion, and I'm here to inform you that you've chosen the wrong village to pillage." The Sniper pulls a terribly folded document from his back pocket. "The village of Macorin has employed the Hired

Blades Association for protection from one "Piranha Gang". It states here that you fellows seem to have been imposing a harsh tax on the village people to live on this side of the mountain. A mountain, which if I'm not mistaken, is under Hired Blade jurisdiction. No?"

"Where's the rest of ya!" A bandit cries. "The whole camp is in ruins!! My mates are all burnt to cinders!! I know there are more of you, come out and we promise to make it fast!"

Faxion refolds the document and stores it away inside his olive trench coat.

"Nope, sorry." Said Faxion. "Just me! Doesn't take a whole lot of us for a job like you."

"Oh yeah?! Bullshit!" Said the brash bandit. "You expect us to believe our whole Gang got wiped out by a single guy?!"

Another bandit cries out.

"Alright well either way, you're going to suffer! You're gonna wish you brought more of your Blade buddies to help you out, shit head."

"Fair enough..." Said Faxion. He raises his wrist, a large, LED glowing watch begins to whistle.

Whiisssss

An electromagnetic pulse fires in the bandits' direction. The startled bandits fire their weapons at will.

"DIE BITCH!!!! GRRAAAAHH"

Tchk *Tchk* *Tchk*

But as they furiously pump the triggers of their weapons, the guns don't fire.

"You know, funny thing about energy-based weaponry." Said Faxion. "With the proper frequency, they're rendered completely useless..."

The bandits look down at their now lifeless, fully automated Lazer pistols. It was at this moment they knew they were dealing with an individual beyond their capabilities. A look of sheer hopelessness runs across all of their faces. Any bandits with bladed weapons charged forward. Those without grab rocks, sticks, anything that their hands could grasp.

Faxion's hand glows yellow as he mutters "Callous." and taps his chest with his palm. A golden protective light covers his skin. He leaps into the fray, whirling his weapon like a wheel of flame in the night.

Krisshh *Fshiiing* *Krissshhh*

The spear effortlessly cleaves arms and legs, cauterizing and searing flesh as it passes through.

"AAAGH!"

"OUGH!"

"NGGAAH!!"

The blazing dance of the Mercenary continues, as scattered body parts fly through the air. As The Hired Blade leaps from bandit to bandit, one gets close behind and jams his knife into Faxion's side.

Ksssshh

But to no avail, as the blade scrapes along him as if hitting concrete and then snaps. The bandit backs away in horror.

"What... What are you?" Said the frightened bandit.

Faxion turns to him and grins. "There are things in this world that you do not understand. As long as you follow this path, you never will."

The scared bandit collapses in disbelief. He watches as his brethren are hopelessly cleaved and skewered. In a matter of moments, Faxion fells the last one right before his eyes. Shaking his head in bewilderment, the desperate bandit staggers to his feet and charges forward. Faxion scoffs. He plants his spear in the ground, takes a rooted fighting posture, and fires a spinning kick to the young bandit's face.

Crrackk *Thud*

Faxion's heel lands a direct hit to the bandit's chin. On impact, the young criminal crumples to the ground, barely conscious. Faxion balls his left hand into a fist causing his eagle tattoo to glow. As he releases his hand the magic dome comes undone.

Fzzz

He walks over and squats down to the bandit's level.

"You never ran, that's good. There's fight in you... Do you have a family?"

"...Yeah, three sisters and a Mom..." Said the young bandit.

"Ahh, so you're the man of the house. Go, be the man of the house. Be the man your family needs you to be. Put this life away and make something of yourself. I've killed enough sons, fathers, and brothers today."

Disheveled, the shaken bandit staggers to his feet.

"Fffreakin', wwhatever you say man yeah. I'm outta here!"

The lone bandit runs off into the woods, stumbling awkwardly over stones and tree roots along the way.

Maw of the Unbound

As the flames of the burning encampment crackle and roar around him, the Veteran Blade leaps down from his Sniper's nest with a duffle bag of his deadly goodies in hand. Readying himself for departure, the mercenary begins to pack the rest of his belongings neatly into the bag. But whilst disassembling his Arcane Peirce, Faxion begins to hear the sound of a mysterious, low growl. The strange noise echoes from within a nearby burning tent.

Grrrrrrrrrrrrrrrr

"What the devil?..." He said, pulling his infrared spear from the ground in caution.

Warily, the Hired Blade marches toward the blazing tent. As he approaches the front flaps of the entrance, the growl steadily increases in volume; a sinister, phlegmy rasp in its tone. He whirls his spear like a windmill, slicing the blazing flaps of the tent like fine paper.

Shick Shick

As the curtain of flame falls to the earth; Faxion is greeted by the sight of three monstrous wolves, tied by burning rope to steaks in the ground. Each one's fur a different shade of bluish-purple, with strange cerulean patterns glowing across their bodies. Their physique is impressive, easily twice the size of a typical wolf. Their eyes glow a ghoulish violet, as the manged canines tug and bite at the burning rope tied around their necks.

Faxion looks on in lament, a far more serious glint in his eye.

"I see... They were keeping Wurm stricken wolves..." He glances down at the burning rope holding them in place. "And Wormwood rope, they hate the stuff. It's no wonder such mighty beasts couldn't break free..."

But as Faxion assesses the new level of threat, the first Wurm wolf successfully relieves itself from its constraints, as the rope gives way in a burning pyre. Almost immediately, the beast sees the wandering mercenary standing at the tent's entrance. In an instant the wolf lunges forward toward Faxion, closing the gap between the two in the blink of an eye.

AWOOOOOO Cries the wolf, dashing towards its prey with reckless abandon.

"Shit!" Exclaimed Faxion. He swiftly dodge-rolls away, just in the nick of time.

As the wolf misses its target, it nimbly pivots around and dashes forth yet again.

Grasping at his infrared spear, the mercenary blocks the incoming jaws of the monstrous wolf with haste.

KSHHH

"Tch, and here I thought this job would be easy..." He said, as the vicious canine gnaws away at the metal spear handle.

Snap *AWOOOOH*

The next wolf's rope gives way, as the singed monster dashes forth from the blazing tent. Faxion firmly kicks the first wolf in the chest, knocking it back as its jaw releases from his trusted weapon. He back handsprings away, drawing his trusted Stinger plasma pistol and firing at the Wurm-infected wolves with deadly precision.

POP POP POP POP

But the nimble creatures dash to and fro, deftly dodging the azure heat from the projectile. They circle around and lunge with swiping claws and snapping jaws, each attack coming dangerously closer and closer to the Hired Blade. As Faxion narrowly dodges and parries the onslaught of the vicious Wolves, he's shocked by a sudden clamping down on his right calf.

Grrrrrrrrr Growls the third Wurm wolf, locking its jaw onto Faxion as the remains of the wormwood noose burns off from around its neck.

Pinned by the mighty beast, Faxion's "Callous" armor begins to slightly crack under the power of the Wurm wolf's jaws and teeth.

My God. He thought. *They're small Wurms, maybe only pawns. Yet they hold this much power.*

Suddenly the other two wolves close the distance, latching onto Faxion's arms and biting down with all of their might. Unable to raise his clamped appendages, he struggles in futility to maneuver his infrared spear.

Krsshhhick

Layers of Faxion's arcane armor begin to crack and shatter, nearly leaving the mercenary's flesh exposed.

Faxion sighs.

Well this simply won't do, will it... He thought. He glances at the eagle tattoo on his arm, shaking his head in disdain. *I'm sure this will cost me, but here goes...*

Faxion balls his fist and shouts an incantation.

"Ignis, Tempestas!"

The eagle tattoo on his arm begins to glimmer brightly, as Faxion's entire body begins to radiate a crimson energy.

FWOOOSH

Suddenly, a blazing tempest of flame bursts forth from the aura encasing his body; searing the three Wurm wolves in a huge blazing sphere until each one is burnt to a fiery crisp.

Faxion stands to his feet, brushing the ash of the wolves off of his shoulder. He shakes out the arm with the eagle tattoo, pulsing his fist open and closed in pain. It takes a moment, but the strong sensation of numbness and tingling begins to fade away.

"Ugh, I'm sorry. I've overused you today..."

The weary mercenary takes a deep breath, letting out a sigh of relief as he scans the area once more for any potential threats. The blazing forest yields no sign of resistance, as looks down and taps away at the touchscreen of his bulky watch. The ring of an outgoing call chimes for a moment, before a bald, muscular old man in a sharp gray suit appears on the screen. His face, covered in exotic tattoos; with a long gray goatee and an "X" shaped scar running along his left cheekbone.

"Chairman Yang?" Said Faxion.

The man replies.

"Fax! What took ya so long? I was beginning to worry those savages had skinned you alive already! I mean this is a big job to undertake alone."

Faxion chuckles. "Hahaha, come now, you know a few low-level bandits can't stop me. I'll let the people of Macorin know their Piranha problem is over in the morning, and I'll be on my way."

"Very good Fax, you've done an exceptional job as always." Said Chairman Yang. "The money will be transferred to your account immediately, that's $13,647.99 aurem. I'll call the clean-up crew to take care of the bodies, and whatever miscellaneous damages were caused by your rampage as always. We'll keep you posted on any new jobs in your current area."

Faxion sighs in relief. "Thank God, I have to pay off repairs on the Rhino by Friday. Until then I'm stuck taking the metro across the countryside. Well, if that's all sir I'll be taking my leave."

Chairman Yang lifts a beige folder from his desk, he opens it and flips through the pages.

"Faxion, before you leave I have a proposition to make. The rising threat of the Wurm species is becoming a real problem, we've discovered a pattern in their activity that suggests they're growing in number and are planning something big. The Board and I have decided to take action. We're making a new position for Veterans like yourself, to raise a fresh crop of Hired Blades to hunt the Wurm. Pay can be discussed later, but I assure you it's far better than taking these miscellaneous Hitman jobs. So, what do you say?"

Faxion takes a moment to ponder. He brushes the stubble on his chin between his thumb and index finger. The Veteran Blade comes to an answer.

"Sir, if the Association is in need you know I'm here to help. I gladly accept! Keep me posted on the details."

"Ha! I knew I could count on you Deadeye." Said Chairman Yang. "Happy to have you on board Fax, I foresee great things to come. Over and out."

Chairman Yang hangs up the telecommunicator. Faxion adjusts the settings on his watch, puts his hand on his hips and takes a pause.

"Alright, well I guess I just became a recruiter! This should be *quite* fun..."

Faxion hoists his rucksack over his shoulder, pulls his spear from the Earth and starts his walk towards Macorin village. Leaving a burning wasteland of wreckage behind him, with a devilish smirk across his face.

CHAPTER

TWO

Plight of the Young Dreamer

Chamboree, a quiet town sitting at the peak of the windy mountain of Minego. The breeze rushes past giant rock formations as the sun casts a stone-shaped shadow on the mountainside. It was noon, a young man works a small fruit stand at the bazaar in the town square. His hair buzzed like the fuzz of a peach, about 5'9 in stature with eyes mauve as a clematis. He wipes a bead of sweat from his coarse brow as he chops and dices the produce for famished customers to devour.

"Shit." Said the young man. "I'm so damn hot I feel like a tray of biscuits in an oven. And where the hell is everyone? This place is like a ghost town today. There's no one to buy grandpa's damned fruit and I'm over here working for peanuts, frying like an egg as usual."

Suddenly a pair of voices are heard in the distance.

"Yo Pilet!"

A pair of teens draw near. One boy, large and a bit round in shape. Sporting a thick, dark mustache. The other a young girl in a scarlet and black plaid shirt, ripped and tattered blue jeans and hazel, attentive eyes, liken to a hawk. The boy speaks

"Where were you today? *YOUR* ass is never going to graduate if you keep this up, we only had a half day and you still cut class?"

Pilet responds.

"Oh *this* fool, what's up James? I thought you were busy stealing booze for the party on Friday, with your nasty mustache trying to look all old and shit. Oh, and hey Nivia."

"Hey Pilet." Replied Nivia. "We missed you today, Mrs. Mena says you owe her more homework in history class now. I could help with that if you'd like…"

James interrupts.

"You mean *you* missed him today, right? I could care less what Mr. Pretty eyes here does in his free time, or lack thereof."

James laughs. A blushing Nivia punches James's arm.

"Shut UP James." Snaps Nivia.

Pilet raises one eyebrow and looks at the two confoundedly.

"Right…" Said Pilet. "Well anyway, you could tell Mrs. Mena to expect that homework when I feel like doing it, which is never… So basically she can expect it never. Or never expect it? I don't know, tell her I died or something!" Pilet brushes his face with his palms in frustration. "I'm tired of going to that stupid school, with those half-assed teachers and that grimey, two-faced principal. I'm tired of this town, I mean it's so boring! All we do is catch snakes and skip stones in the river! And dude how many times can someone window shop at a mini-mall!"

James interjects.

"Psssh what?! I love killing snakes! It makes me feel like a badass, and the mayor pays us for the heads of all the poisonous ones."

"I mean I love the mini-mall." Said Nivia. "But I definitely understand what you mean, Pilet." Said Nivia. "There's not much to do in this town as a high schooler…"

"See she knows!" Replied Pilet. "Thanks Nivia, you're the only cool one around here."

Nivia blushes. James retorts.

"Alright bro, well it's better to be bored in class than bored under a bridge when your homeless ass has no diploma in 10 years. Get it together man, I kinda miss shooting spitballs at Clarence together."

Pilet replies.

"Man whatever, I'm saving up to leave this dump. That's why I'm always at this dinky fruit stand. I'm gonna go see the world! There's so much cool shit out there! That's why I want to be a Hired Blade. I'm gonna take the Blades exam and be a certified badass."

Nivia gasps.

"A Hired Blade? Are you crazy?? They do really dangerous things! I heard on the news that a group of them got attacked by a dinosaur the other day! It's so scary Pilet, don't join such a crazy Association!"

"Haha yea, and besides you probably couldn't make the cut!" Adds James. "Most of those dudes have a background in some kind of violence. I heard a few days ago there was a super tough Blade that saved Macorin from like, a hundred bandits. By himself! The guy left body parts lying around everywhere... And here you are making fruit baskets in the middle of the bazaar, not the best skill set to be a badass mercenary."

Pilet interjects.

"First of all they didn't get attacked by dinosaurs, they were hunting them. The government pays Hired Blades to capture or kill rogue Fossil creatures. I also don't care that I don't have crazy training, I'm a natural athlete! I'm easily the fastest kid on the track team."

James corrects Pilet.

"You mean the track team you got kicked off of for skipping school? *That* track team?" James laughs as Pilet shrugs his criticism. Pilet retorts.

"At least I made the team, fatass! Hahahahaha!"

James starts to become visibly angered, his face becomes flush as he puffs out his chest. He bellows.

"Alright douchebag, well we can't say we didn't try! Come on Nivia, let's leave fruit boy to his apple stand or whatever."

Pilet replies.

"They're cotton candy fruit! Man whatever, leave then. You're taking up all my oxygen standing there."

James flips Pilet the middle finger with both his unkempt hands as he walks away. Nivia stays a moment to lament with Pilet.

"I don't know what happened..." She said. "You guys were best friends until last year? It really is a shame Pilet, I know he doesn't like to say it but James misses you. Ever since you started running track you two have fallen apart."

Pilet replies.

"Tch, It's not my fault. James is jealous because I made the team and he couldn't run from his bed to the fridge in the time it takes me to make a mile."

"And yet here he is reaching out to you when all your track friends forgot you existed." Nivia adds. "Just try to come back, Pilet. We've known you forever and we miss you."

Pilet replies.

"Yea whatever, well thanks I guess but I have a job to do."

Nivia shoots Pilet a disappointed look as she turns to depart. She leaves with a parting message. "Please take care of yourself, Pilet..."

Pilet falls silent. He stares off in the distance with a look of chagrin as Nivia slowly leaves the bazaar.

The Mysterious Miner

Some hours pass, as very few customers have made their way through the square to purchase Pilet's wares. The sun sets on the square as the miscellaneous vendors close up shop. By now Pilet is all that's left, stubbornly waiting for a potential customer. As the night's chill starts to settle into the mountain, Pilet finally decides to close the stand. He takes his chef's knife and pushes the excess fruit from the cutting board into the trash receptacle to the side of his stand. As he cleans the fruit from the table, he hears a voice several feet away.

"You know, in some countries that could feed a whole family for a night."

Pilet turns toward the sudden voice. He sees a middle-aged man. Hair a dark brown with gray patches miscellaneously peppered in. His physique, unimpressive but clearly in shape. A warm look in his navy blue eyes and a soft tone in his voice. His stance relaxed, with a subtle bend in the knees. Under his olive trench coat, Pilet can clearly see high-tech LED-lit shin guards. Pilet responds.

"Hey, what's up man? Can I help you?"

The man speaks.

"Well, I'm just passing through town straight off the metro. I figured I'd stop by the local grocery to grab a bite. You see I've had a long trip, and I'm starving! But by the looks of it, I guess I'm a bit late to the party."

Pilet responds.

"Yeah, most everyone's closed up here when the sun goes down. People around these parts are scared of the dark."

"Hmmm, and you are not?" replies the man.

"Man, I could give a damn less." Said Pilet. "I have to make money to get out of this boring town. Besides, if anyone gives me trouble I've got a rack of razor-sharp cutlery here with their name on it! Say, you seem like a guy who knows what's up out there. Know anything about a group called, "The Hired Blades Association"?"

The man's eyebrows slightly raise.

"Hmm. Yes, I might know a thing or two. Why do you ask?"

"Because," said Pilet "I'm gonna be one! I'm saving up to take the exam, I hear Blades get all the best jobs and tons of benefits. I'm sure it's not as hard as everyone makes it seem."

A subtle grin creeps onto the stranger's face.

"Right... Well I might be able to make something happen, I know some people. Allow me to introduce myself. My name is Faxion, I'm a traveling... erm..." Uncertain of the young man's intentions, Faxion decides it's best to withhold his identity. He sees a pickaxe leaning on the corner of a building. "Miner! I'm a traveling miner. I travel and find nice places to mine, and then I mine them!"

Pilet looks puzzled.

Oh, ok... What do you like, mine for?"

"Fossils!" Replied Faxion. "Fossils are a hot commodity right now. Lots of folks digging them up and selling them to those high-end science labs you know."

There is an awkward silence.

"Well, ok then." Replied Pilet. "Good for you dude. So like, do you want to buy some fruit?"

"I would appreciate that, thank you." Faxion replied. "While we're at it, can you point me in the direction of the nearest inn? It's a bit late to continue my travels and I could use a hot bath."

"Yeah man sure." Pilet points down the road. "My Grandpa actually owns the village Inn, and this fruit stand... Which he makes me run! He's basically a slave owner."

Faxion chuckles in response.

"Hahaha, sounds like a good man. Teaching you the value of hard work is his job, and your father's of course."

Pilet scoffs, looking off in the distance.

"Nah, don't have one of those."

"Oh I'm sorry to hear that." Said Faxion.

"Don't be. My Mom died giving birth to me, and I guess he thought that was as good a reason as any to take a hike. The guy dumped me on my Grandparents. They're actually pretty cool, but my Grandpa just makes me work a lot. Whatever, money is money."

The two make a monetary transaction and Pilet hands Faxion a plastic tub of his freshest cut fruit. Faxion swiftly opens the tub and pops a piece into his mouth.

"This is really exceptional!" Said Faxion, licking his lips in delight. "What kind of fruit is this?"

"Cotton candy fruit. It grows locally around here, the only place in the world too. Melts in your mouth don't it."

Faxion puts the tub in a large gray duffel bag around his shoulder.

"That it does. So how far is this Inn?"

"It's literally around the corner, here let me close up and I'll take you." Replied Pilet.

Pilet takes a few minutes to clean and sanitize his workspace. The two set off to the Inn down the road.

Casually strolling through Chamboree village in the darkness of nightfall, the two pass by the various cozy cottages and aging houses of the mountaintop. Warmly lit dining room windows show local families sitting down for home-cooked dinners, as the smell of freshly baked bread and sauteed beef wafts through the air. As Pilet and Faxion continue down the weathered red brick road, The sight of a large, two-story building of mandarin orange brick can be seen in the distance. Brown, shale tiles layer themselves between the first and second floor, as well as forming the roof of the establishment in a stark, wedged angle. Pilet points attentively towards the building.

"That's it right there." He said. "Home, *sweet* home..." As the two approach the Inn, Pilet begins to open up about his curiosity for the Hired Blades Association. "So dude, I was wondering about the Blades. You said you know someone involved with them, right?

Faxion nods.

"Yes, I did say that. He's a very skilled Blade actually. A revered member of the association."

Pilet's eyebrows raise.

"Oh shit, really? Nice! So how can I contact this guy? Does he have like, an email or something?"

The pair reach the front door of the inn, a finely crafted set of dark, cherrywood double doors with brass doorknobs; as they faintly make out the sound of an elderly woman hollering.

"Oh great, not this again." Said Pilet, facepalming in embarrassment.

"Whah?" Replied Faxion curiously, as he walks up and reaches for the doorknob.

"Don't stand there!" Pilet exclaims.

THUD

Suddenly, the front door flies open and slams Faxion in the face, swiftly sending him falling flat on his back. The aforementioned elderly woman storms out, her hands balled into fists.

"Shit, too late. Sorry man." Said Pilet.

The elderly woman begins to shout from outside the open door of the inn.

"You never listen to me Milo you old bastard! I'm leaving this time for real!" She turns to see Pilet standing in the doorway. "Oh hello Pilet my baby, how was school today?"

"I didn't go Grandma, I hate that shithole."

"Aw baby, that's great! Don't forget to do your homework. Also remember to take out the trash, because your Grandfather is being an immature son of a bitch again!" She turns to Milo. "I HATE YOU!" She briskly walks into the night.

"HAH!" Milo retorts. "Oh Tecia, my Tecia. You'll be back you old crohn. And if not? GOOD! Finally gives me a chance to relax, for once in my Goddamn life! Oh, Pilet buddy! How's it going?! Hey, who's your friend?!"

Faxion gets up off the ground, brushing the dirt off of his back. He gives his nose a wiggle to make sure it's not broken.

"Well alright then!" Said Faxion. "That was unpleasant." He turns to

Milo. "Hello sir! Allow me to introduce myself. My name is Faxion, I hear you own and operate this establishment?"

"Well that would be correct, would you like to rent a room?" Said Milo. He sees Faxion's red nose and dirt-stained coat from the door incident seconds prior. "Your clothes look like they could use a good washing, and is it cold outside? Your nose tells the tale! We here at Dreams of Chamboree have the best washing machines this side of, well, Chamboree! Only $2 Aurum per cycle. A ration of detergent is complimentary with your stay!"

Faxion smirks, the man clearly has no idea of the unintended battering just given by his wife.

"Well that sounds wonderful, I would love to wash and hang up for the night. The road is long. And while beautiful, these mountains are not easy to traverse. I must have wrestled with at least 3 filthy goats on the way here!"

Milo's eyes widen as he makes an engaging, quite hilarious face.

"There's a good chance that goat was my brother!"

"By God you're right, I can see the resemblance!" Both men let out a bellowing, deep belly laugh that could easily wake each guest on either two floors. Pilet shakes his head in disdain.

"What the hell am I watching..." He muttered.

"Well mister Faxion." Said Milo. "Or, Fax. Can I call you Fax?"

"I'd be appalled if you didn't!" Replied Faxion.

"Haha good show! So one night's stay comes to about $75 aurum including all amenities."

"Sir, I'll gladly take it!"

As they shake hands and close on their transaction, Milo motions to Pilet.

"Pilet my buddy! Why don't you show our friend to his suite? It's room number 207. The linens are fresh and the mini-fridge is stocked to the brim. Please help yourself Mr. Fax!"

"freak! Grandpa c'mon I just got home!" Exclaimed Pilet. "I worked all day at that God damned fruit stand. I wanna chill for a second!"

"Oh yes!" Said Milo. "How was the stand today? How much did we bring in? Did you wash the cutlery?"

"You know what, forget it... Just give me a second, I'll take him upstairs."

Faxion giggles to himself as he watches the interaction unfold.

Pilet motions to Faxion.

"Alright man let's go, 207's on the second floor, follow me."

The two make their way up the rickety staircase. The worn birch handrails and the noisy floorboards speak of the years of service this Inn has provided. The carpeted flooring a subtle tint of emerald, with walls a dark shade of mandarin orange. Scattered across the walls of the hallway hang portraits of vast landscapes and monuments around the world. As they pass the portraits, Pilet inquires to Faxion.

"Ever visit any of these places?"

"Yes, I have." Faxion points to one behind them. "That jungle kingdom we just passed? It's called Prehistoria. It's actually a sanctuary to many a dinosaur that had been brought to life by fossil restoration these past few years. The King is a cool guy, maybe one day you'll meet him if you become a Hired Blade."

Pilet sassily retorts.

"That's WHEN I become a Blade. Nothing's gonna get in the way of my dream."

Faxion's eye's narrow as he ponders the resolve of the young prospect.

"I hope so boy, I hope so."

The pair reach the end of the hallway, as they approach the door to Faxion's site.

Pilet tosses Faxion a white card key.

"Room 207, here ya go. Like the old man said, the room's stocked. Bed is made. just try not to run up the AC, it gets noisy and wakes people up sometimes. Anyway enjoy your stay, hopefully we can talk before you leave."

Faxion inserts the key card into the electronic lock. The door opens as the mechanism glows green. Faxion puts a hand on Pilet's shoulder.

"We could talk right now if you'd like. I have the time."

"Oh, you do?" Responds Pilet. "Ok, that's cool..."

As the two walk into the freshly flipped room, Pilet's mind races back and forth about the illustrious organization Faxion has contact with. The two take a seat at a small coffee table in the corner. Pilet speaks.

"So listen man, how does a guy become a Hired Blade?"

Faxion walks over to a coffee maker nearby, starting a fresh pot for himself and his young guest.

"Hah! Well it's great to hear someone so enthusiastic about this. Such a powerful organization is not easy to enter, that's for sure. First of all, do you have any form of combative experience? Martial arts training, shooting, security jobs and the like? Have you ever even been in a fight?"

Pilet thinks for a moment. He responds.

"Well I wrestled and ran track in 9th and 10th grade, but my grades were too low so I got kicked off the teams. Me and my friend used to shoot the neighborhood snakes with BB guns, but I could never hit 'em! So I would just end up smashing the damn things with the gun like a club. Never did any martial arts, but I'm real good with a knife. I've been cutting fruit and skinning snakes for years.

Faxion interrupts.

"Well that's not a bad resume, most kids your age have more experience with a video game controller than a blade."

Pilet continues.

"As far as fights go, I've seen my fair share of little scrapes. Nothing to write home about though."

"Well just the same, the Hired Blades exam is no joke. Entrants are required to pass both a written and physical exam, but that's the easy part..." Faxion begins to pour the fresh coffee into a pair of mugs. "The Final test calls for participants to traverse a dangerous terrain, the likes of which changes every year. Entrants have to then reach a pre-determined landmark and obtain a "special artifact"."

"Ok, so... That's it? What's it like a hike in the woods to a secret cave? Man, these guys watch too many movies. I'm not worried, if anything that sounds kind of fun!"

Faxion grins. He opens a mini fridge below the coffee maker and pulls out a carton of milk, pouring some into both cups.

"That's the spirit! I like your style, kid." He takes a seat, handing Pilet one of the mugs as he stirs some sugar packets in. "Now, one thing that's been on my mind is this. You're young, what like 18? While I'm not saying it's a bad idea to be a Blade, you'd have to leave home on almost any job you take! I mean, most blades spend 9 months out of the year traveling on their journey. Your grandparents seem quite fond of you being around, and you're under your grandfather's employ on multiple duties. I would think that leaving would pose a bit of an issue right about now, no?"

Pilet takes a sip.

"Nah, my grandpa has tons of employees. He just had me working so much to teach me "hard work and discipline" or whatever. Since I don't have a Dad I think it's this thing he always has in his mind. Like a job he feels like only he could do. But at the end of the day, he knows I'm my own man, I do my own thing."

"Sounds like a good man." Added Faxion. "Well ok. At any rate, if that's your choice then no one can stop you."

Pilet scratches his head.

"Alright man now I have a question. How do you know all this shit? I mean... who are you?"

"Hahahaha I thought you'd never ask! Well it's safe to say I'm no fossil Miner. I'm actually a Veteran Hired Blade, Faxion the Deadeye. I'm just coming off a job in Macorin and I thought I'd pass through the highest town in the Minegogue mountain range."

Pilet takes a second to gather his thoughts. His mouth agape and his eyes widened in shock.

"Macorin... Are you... Are you the bandit killer?"

Faxion chuckles at his new nickname.

"Hah! Word sure travels fast, yes that would be me."

Pilet can't believe his eyes as he realizes he's sitting in front of a trained, seasoned killer.

"Holy shit. Hey man I could talk to my uncle about room and board, I mean you don't have to pay."

"Oh stop now, I'm a normal human just like you and I won't have special treatment. So tell me, are you still interested in joining our ranks?"

Pilet fervently slams his palms to the table, as Faxion comically lifts the mugs from the table.

"Oh my." Said Faxion. "You'll spill my Joe..."

"Yeah of course I'm still interested! It's my dream, I'm not gonna quit til I make the cut!"

Faxion sips his coffee, putting the mugs back down onto the table.

"You very well might have to take a life, or two. Are you ok with that? " . . ."

Pilet falls silent for a moment.

"I don't really know. I've killed a lot of snakes."

"People aren't snakes." Replied Faxion.

"No, no they're not."

After a tense pause, Faxion cracks his knuckles in excitement.

"Well that's as good an answer as I could've hoped. You see, no one ever knows if they can. That is, until the very moment that they have to, and by then your body makes the choice for you." He takes the fedora off of his head, hanging it on a standing coat rack by the door. "But I wouldn't worry about that right now, that's a good way to halt your progress."

Pilet sighs in both relief and disappointment. Faxion continues.

"Now listen, I happen to be tasked with recruiting for the Blades. I could train you if you'd like."

"Really?!" Exclaimed Pilet. "That would be amazing! I mean like you don't have to... But HELL YEA!!"

"Hahahahaha! That's the spirit! We're going to have loads of fun. There's so much to learn and so little time! Now, why don't you rest up and we'll talk to your grandparents in the morning."

Pilet grabs his coffee and gets ready to leave Faxion to his sleep. As he walks to the door, he turns once more to the Veteran Blade.

"Thanks man, I promise I'm gonna turn this world on its head."

Faxion goes for a handshake, but Pilet instead clasps hands and bumps Fax in the shoulder.

"I guess that's how the young people shake hands?" Said Faxion "Looks like we're going to be teaching each other."

The two part ways for the night. As Faxion kicks off his combat boots and hangs his olive trench coat, he falls face-first into his pillow.

"Some rest at last, thank the Lord."

He slowly begins to drift off to sleep, nodding in and out as he shuts off the bedside lamp with a *clink*. As nightfall envelopes Chamboree, the many crickets of the woods orchestrate a melodic symphony of a lullaby. The wind rustles through the leaves and trees, as a tranquil ambiance settles over the night sky. That is, until a sinister aura creeps through the brush of the woods with mal intent. In a desolate corner of the woods outside Chamboree, a devilish, glowing pair of violet eyes pierce the darkness like a predator from hell, lying in wait of its prey..."

Enter: The Fiery Prospect!

The morning comes. The light of the rising sun peeks through the curtains and hits Faxion in the eyes, as the crisp morning air wafts beneath his nose.

CRASH

"HELP!!"

He abruptly awakens to the sounds of hysterical screaming in the bazaar. Grabbing his rucksack, Faxion runs out to the window to assess the commotion.

"GUUUAAAAAAAHHHHH!!!!!"

An ear-shattering cry can be heard, far too menacing to come from a human being.

Peering out of the window with haste, Faxion sees what looks to be a massive purple gorilla, rampaging through the plaza. Flipping over vendors' tables and chasing civilians, the beast poses an immediate threat to the defenseless people down below. He reaches for his rifle case, assembling his Arcane Pierce with record speed. But as he takes aim for the heated Gorilla, he struggles to lock onto a good shot, as the beast leaps speedily to-and-fro in a reckless manner. Seeing the numerous people running for cover in the bustling bazaar, he realizes that the crowded area is full of too much liability.

"Shit. There are too many damned people out there. One wrong move could cause massive collateral."

Suddenly, there is an abrupt knocking at the door.

"Fax! Hey It's Pilet, open up! There's a BIG, crazy monkey outside and it's attacking people!!!"

Faxion unbolts and opens the door.

"There's no time to waste, follow me."

Pilet nods.

"Right."

The two run down the stairs and out the door to the perilous plaza.

As they approach the square, the gorilla lets out a bellowing roar. A terrifying sight, it stands near 8 feet tall, with dark cerulean stripes in miscellaneous patterns across Its body. Its eyes glow a bright, ghoulish violet hue. Faxion turns to Pilet.

"These people know you, try to calm them down and get them away from the square. I'll hold off the Gorilla."

"I want to help too!" Exclaims Pilet, stomping his feet in protest. "Come on man, that thing's no bandit, it's the size of a truck!"

"This is not a debate!" Shouts Faxion. "You have potential but zero training. You'll be more useful helping others escape. Now go!"

Pilet scoffs and runs toward the nearest civilians.

"Don't die before you teach me shit dude!"

Faxion makes his way toward the Gorilla. He casts "Callous" on his skin and readies his infrared spear.

Vrrrrrrrrr

The ominous hum of the superheated edge can be heard throughout the plaza, as the glowing red edges shine brightly, even in daylight.

Faxion then takes a low squatting posture. "Fleetfoot." The soles of his shoes glow a light yellow, granting him an arcane agility.

Fwish

In an instant, He nimbly bolts toward his opponent. But the Gorilla's reflexes are too fast. It swats Faxion out of the air, sending the Veteran Blade flying into a nearby window. As the glass shatters, he lands in the living room of a family of five, all hiding behind various pieces of furniture.

"My apologies, you should see the other guy!..." They stand there, mouths wide open and unable to speak. He continues. "Well then, good day!"

Faxion nimbly leaps from one end of the room to the other and then out of the broken window, once again meeting his enemy in the square.

"GRAAWR!"

The Gorilla beats his chest and smashes a fish stand, raining tuna and halibut from the sky. Faxion twirls his infrared spear with dextrous skill, slashing and slicing through the falling fish in mid-air.

"I've heard of cats and dogs but this is ridiculous!"

As the two race toward each other, the Gorilla starts beating the ground in front of him like a rolling drum. The earth trembles, sending jagged debris flying right towards Faxion.

Kching *Twang*

He dodges and parries with his spear, knocking the debris away from him like a spinning baton. As he closes in on the Gorilla, he leaps for a high overhead slash. But it was a feint. As the Gorilla blocks high, Faxion smoothly slides down low and swipes his blade across its exposed underbelly.

"GWAAAGHAAH" The beast lets out a seething scream. "GAH HOOAGH!"

Faxion backflips and side steps nimbly out of the creature's range, as it readies its wits about it. The beast smashes the Earth, lifts a massive tile from the ground and hurls it at Faxion. Without time to evade, Faxion whirls his infrared spear to generate force.

Kashiiinnnnng *THUD*

The spear slices the massive projectile in half like butter, as the two halves of tile fall to the floor, singed from the heat right down the middle.

The riled beast turns around, soon seeing a frightened little girl hiding behind an overturned produce cart. It swings its massive forearm and crumbles a statue on a huge water fountain in the center of the square.

THWACK

As the statue falls to the ground, the beast musters all of its strength to raise the giant object and hurls it towards the girl.

"GUUUUAAAAAAAHHHHHH!!!!!!!!"

In the split second before the projectile lands, Faxion darts forward and pushes the girl out of harm's way, getting smashed against a nearby building in the process.

"AAGH!!"

The arcane armor of his "Callous" technique took the brunt of the hit, but the jolt was enough to knock him unconscious.

Having successfully evacuated most of the townspeople, Pilet turns his attention toward the action at the sound of Faxion's yell. Seeing the Deadeye pinned by the statue, Pilet immediately darts toward the scene.

"Shit!!"

Scanning the area in a panic, he sees his mentor's open rucksack on the ground, with two high-tech-looking knives peeking out. He lifts the blades, taking a quick gaze at the sleek design. Broad and one-edged, much like the chef's knives used to cut fruit at the stand. A smooth, black leather grip twirled meticulously around the handle, with a metal handguard across the knuckles and a curved prong likened to a pitchfork on the back to catch an incoming weapon. Pilet presses a pair of red buttons on the side of either blade's handle.

Vrrrrr

To his amazement, The blade becomes extremely hot, emanating mirage-like heat waves from the edges as they glow a wicked orange. With no time to spare, he tightly grips the knives and bolts toward the Gorilla as fast as he can.

"Ugh... Whah?...." Groans the frightened little girl.

Staggering to her feet, she looks up in horror as the angry behemoth draws near. The beast lifts its massive forearms, readying a ruthless downward strike to the quivering child. But just as it's about to pummel its victim, the fiery, knife-wielding prospect closes the distance.

"GRAAAAAAAAAAAAAAHHHHH!!!!!!!!" Screams Pilet.

With a heated determination in his eyes, Pilet lets out a Savage roar as he leaps on the beast's back and drives his blades through Its coarse flesh.

"RRRAAAAAAAAAAGHH!!!!"

The Gorilla lets out a surprised and desperate cry.

Pilet quickly works his way up the beast's back with the knives, stabbing into its flesh and proceeding to scale the gorilla like a rock climbing wall. As he makes his way to the top of the head, Pilet raises the blades for a finishing blow. But just before he can, the monster reaches up and grabs him, squeezing the young prospect with viscous force.

"Nggah!"

The gorilla tosses Pilet off with a labored wheeze, feeling the effects of its wounds.

Crash *Crush* Clang* *Crash*

Pilet takes a tumble into a massive jewelry stand, flying hopelessly through the various glass cases. The sound of shattered glass brings Faxion back to consciousness. He foggily makes out the young warrior in the jewelry case.

"Gguhhh. P, Pilet?..."

As Pilet gets up, he pulls shards of glass from his forearms and back. Blood starts pouring down his body, staining his once stark white tank top into a dark crimson.

"Ugh, shit!" Shouts Pilet in agony, as he rips jagged glass from his flesh.

"Alright asshole, you came to the wrong town." He brandishes the glowing knives, holding them up towards the face of the gorilla. "Let's go!!"

Pilet shakes the rest of the shattered glass off of his shirt, again darting towards the bloodthirsty beast.

"GOOOOOAAAAARRRGHH!!" Shouts the gorilla, as it meets Pilet mid-dash with a terrifying uppercut.

But Pilet manages to sidestep quick enough to leave the beast's vast rack of ribs exposed.

"You won't need these anymore!"

Shhiing

Pilet dexterously slices his blades across the monster's body, carving meat from in-between bone. The gorilla lets out the most terrifying, bellowing scream Pilet has ever heard.

"KRRAAAAAAAAGGGHHHHH!!!!!"

The yell startles Pilet enough for the beast to land a desperate counterattack with the back of its forearm.

Thwack

"UFFGH!"

Pilet bounces off the massive arm and into the corner of a building ten feet away. He writhes in pain, desperately staggering to his knees.

"Ggguuhh... *Cough*" The young standout begins to spit up dark blood. "No. I won't let you win. How am I *cough* gonna be a God-damned Hired Blade if I can't beat one stupid ugly monkey."

He struggles laboredly to his feet, clanging the knives loudly together in protest.

"This is it... THIS IS IT! I'M TIRED OF BEING A NOBODY!! My Dad didn't want me. I don't have a Mom. No one in this town gives a shit about me! I'm gonna be somebody! I'm gonna be a Hired Blade!!!"

The veins on Pilet's head begin to throb as his temperature reaches feverish levels. His skin turns brick red with heat, as steam starts billowing from every pore of his skin. Suddenly his wounds begin to seal up and his muscles swell, becoming increasingly vascular with each heaving breath. His mauve eyes begin to glow vibrantly as a shining, amethyst pattern presents itself across his body.

"GRAAAAH!!!"

Shing *Shing* *Shing* *Shing* *Shing* *Shing* *Shing* *Shing* *Shing* *Shing*

He pounces at the behemoth with blinding speed, mercilessly unloading a barrage of stabs into its belly.

"Brrrnnghh"

The monster vomits dark blood past Pilet's ear in an attempt to bite, but Pilet nimbly back steps three feet away. In a lastish effort, the weakened beast reaches with outstretched hands toward the speeding knife wielder.

Kssh *Kssh* *Ksshing*

In an instant, Pilet swiftly cleaves and chops each individual finger off, as they fly deftly into the air. Without a second of hesitation, he lunges forth; plunging his blades into the nose of the Gorilla and then slicing outward from the base of the skull.

Kssshlick *Shinnggg*

Pilet leaps back from the mutilated belly of the beast, landing several feet away while fingers still rain from the sky.

Lifeless from the vicious onslaught of the fiery prospect, the beast drops to the earth with a resounding *thud*. The fall of the gorilla's body shakes the very ground, causing more broken glass and jewelry to fall to the earth with the quake.

"*Gasp* *wheeze* *wheeze* Ffax, Faxion..."

Pilet's body returns to normal, his wounds fully healed but muscles and tendons completely exhausted. Unbeknownst to him, a mysterious purple aura emerges from the Gorilla and begins sinking into Pilet's body. He looks around for Faxion, all the while trying desperately to catch his breath. Suddenly, Pilet hears his mentor's voice calling out to him.

"Hnnng! Hey kid! Get me out from behind this thing!"

Faxion comes to, struggling to pull himself out of the vice he's been trapped in.

"Oh, oh shit. When I saw you get hit honestly I thought you were dead! How are you alive right now?!?"

Pilet heaves and grunts as the two struggle to move the statue. All of a sudden, the aforementioned purple aura begins to overtake Pilet. His eyes begin to glow as his arms become extremely muscular, and covered in purple fur-like hair. With this newfound strength, he shifts the statue just enough for Faxion to slide his body out.

"Phew, many thanks!" Said Faxion. "Don't worry about me, that "Callous" technique I cast onto my skin has protected me from much worse."

Pilet scratches his head in confusion.

"What the hell's a "Callous"? You mean like when you spend all day shoveling snow and the skin on your hands gets rough?"

Faxion shakes his head.

"If you're to be a Hired Blade you'll have to know this sooner or later. "Callous" is a special technique. It comes from a high-level skill known as "Auracast", which utilizes the energy or "Aura" of the world around us to cast arcane techniques and achieve supernatural feats. All Blades are required to learn this skill, but don't fret! It's not hard to pick up... Just think of it like casting a magic spell!"

Faxion staggers to his feet. He shakes his head and blinks rapidly, collecting his wits about him.

"Now while Callous protects the body from outward harm, it unfortunately doesn't protect my brain. So I can still get K.O.ed from time to time... Keeps me pretty though!"

Pilet scoffs.

"Tch. You're a funny guy. I guess that's how you managed to move around so quickly too. Well either way I'm glad you're ok."

Faxion tips his hat.

"Now *you* on the other hand, you are an interesting guy. I came to around the time you took a spill trying to steal necklaces over there. You were pretty ripped up, and now you're completely unscathed! You moved faster than my "Fleetfoot" cast! There's a lot you don't know yet. Let's make sure everyone is safe and talk to the local authorities first."

"Yeah, yeah that was crazy... Huh?"

The crowds of people hiding from the gorilla start to come out in the open.

"Wow, did you see that?"

"He's so strong!"

"I didn't know that kid could move like that!"

"Mmm, who is that handsome man in the fedora!"

One or two people begin to clap, then five or six. Before long the crowd breaks out into thunderous applause.

Clapclapclapclapclap

"Woohoo!"

"Go Pilet!"

"You really showed 'em kid!"

"Thank you!!"

Pilet can't believe his eyes. He looks down in embarrassment, but Faxion quickly leans his elbow on Pilet's shoulder in a relaxed posture.

"Hey hey!! Thank you thank you, you're far too kind! C'mon kid lighten up, there're lots of cute girls in the audience you know."

Out of the crowd comes Pilet's friends James and Nivia, completely astonished at what they just saw.

"Dude, you just shish kabobbed that big ape. Like, anything I said about you not being a Blade I take back 200%."

Nivia peeks out from behind.

"That was really scary Pilet, I'm happy you came out ok. It looks like you didn't even get a mark on you too, but you're covered in blood!"

"That's the monkey's blood Nivia, don't be so naive! Pilet jacked him up good, that's what happens when you get down 'n dirty. I remember when we used to kill snakes, I would be covered in that shit. Tomato soup everywhere."

Pilet responds.

"Thanks guys, I'm glad you two are ok too. You should get home though, I don't know if that thing had buddies still roaming around."

"Oh ok, well you be safe too." Said Nivia. "I couldn't take it if you got hurt from one of those things. I mean! You know, you're one of my best friends..."

Intrigued, Faxion chimes in.

"You guys have one hell of a friend here. I'm a Hired Blade of over twenty years and I've never seen a civilian take it to a monster like that."

James and Nivia are even more awestruck.

"Woah, holy shit he's a Blade?" Said James.

"Oh wow, that's amazing!" Replied Nivia.

Pilet responds.

"His name's Fax, he's a master and he's gonna teach me stuff so I can take the Blades exam and be a Hired Blade. I told you guys I was gonna make it one day."

"That's really great Pilet." Said Nivia. "I'm glad you found a teacher that really knows his stuff. Now we don't have to worry about you going out there and getting hurt on your own. I know you're going to do great!"

"Thanks Nivia, you're still the coolest kid in town."

Nivia begins to blush, as James snarkily retorts.

"You know another kid from this town is standing right here, right? Like, right here. Punk."

"Oh I know fatass, that's why I said it."

Faxion and Nivia stand there awkwardly as the two young men glare at each other. Faxion breaks the tension.

"Yes, well just the same. It's not safe for you guys to be out right now. Let's all get home in case more angry beasts are out and about."

The kids say their goodbyes to Pilet as they head back to their homes.

As Pilet and Faxion gather their belongings, the local police make their way to the scene. Parking and stepping out of their squad cars, two officers meet them at the center of the square. Before they can speak Faxion pulls out an official Hired Blades Association badge. The Gold badge glints dazzlingly in the morning sun. Showcasing the symbol of the Hired Blades Association, a series of five double-edged swords surrounding a large cracked diamond. The officers appear stunned for a moment, then don a more serious expression as they immediately understand the situation.

"Hello Master Blade, we got a report that there was a dangerous animal causing trouble in the vicinity. Do you know anything about this?"

"Why hello gentlemen, yes I do." Said Faxion, as he candidly pockets his badge. "The beast was infected with "the Wurm". It bore the characteristic markings and aggression of a Wurm pawn, however this one was far larger than normal. I believe you have yourself the region's Wurm *King*, it must have wandered into town and panicked at the sight of so many humans. Now that the King is dead, its pawn underlings should sense its demise and flee the region. Congratulations! You're now Wurm free."

The officers let out a sigh of relief.

"You have no idea how long we've been searching for this King. We've all been fearing the day when it would finally show up, who'd have thought it would end up here by accident? We appreciate your work Master Blade."

One of the officers does a double take, as he spots Pilet packing Faxion's bag behind him.

"Pilet? What are you doing here kid? Not causing trouble are you?"

"Nah officer you know me, this monkey started the fight. I just finished it."

Faxion clarifies.

"I'm guessing you've met. Pilet here escorted the town to safety, and when I was in trouble he sprang into action! He's actually responsible for the bloody, furry mess you see here."

"Wow kid, I'm impressed!" Said one officer. "You've come a long way from skipping school and biting ankles." He then turns to Faxion. "Mr. Blade..."

"It's Faxion sir."

"Mr. Faxion, we'd appreciate it if you could follow us to the precinct for a full report of the events that happened today."

"I'd be happy to! Pilet, you should go back to your grandparents and explain the situation, maybe talk to them about your plans for the future while you're at it."

"Alright man, don't take too long. I'm stoked to learn some cool shit."

"Haha don't worry, the day is young yet! Alright boys, let's get a move on."

The officers lead Faxion to the squad car, where they head to the precinct. Pilet takes a look at the messy square. Ambulances everywhere escorting the injured, and clean-up crews covering the gorilla's body with a tarp at the scene. He picks up the two knives from earlier.

"I forgot to give these back..."

He hangs them on his belt and makes his way back to his grandparent's Inn, taking one last look back at the carnage he just took part in.

"There's nothing more we've ever wanted for you in this world."

Some hours have passed and Pilet has explained the town square situation to his grandparents. By this time he's begun opening up about his desire to become a Blade, and the identity of his friend Faxion. Tecia opens up.

"God Pilet we were worried sick about you! First we hear there's some kind of giant ape running a muck in the square, and then to find out that our little boy was galavanting around playing superhero with it! And this idea of leaving to fight more monsters?! Are you mad?!"

"Grandma, relax." Said Pilet. "First of all, Fax did most of the fighting while I helped the people get away. Second, I'm leaving to take the Blades exam and there's nothing anyone can do about it! Grandpa, you know I've wanted to do this for years, talk to her!"

Milo takes a moment to gather his thoughts.

"You know Pilet, ever since your mother passed away we've taken it upon ourselves to raise you like our own son. My daughter thought she met the man she loved, but he disappeared the night you were born. Men like that unfortunately never settle down. They roam the earth, wandering and planting their seed wherever they go."

Milo lets out a distressed sigh.

"I knew from that moment that you were going to be the same. Unable to be tied down, unable to be rooted for too long. I can't stop you from leaving home, I don't have the right."

He pats his fist to his chest with gusto.

"You're a man now, and there's no need to lie. We know you fought the Gorilla in the square, The police called and filled us in. You're a hero! It's because of you that dozens of innocent people are safe. If you're old enough to kill a monster like that, you're old enough to make your own decisions."

"Grandpa. I..."

"All I ask is two things." Said Milo "Number one. If you meet a woman you love and you have a child, you raise that child. I'm not saying things have to work out between you and your mate, but you owe it to that child to be there when they need you. There's nothing more shameful than a man who can't face the gravity of their own decisions."

Pilet swallows tensely, pondering about his own father.

"Agreed." He said.

Milo continues.

"Number two. Stay in touch! We love you Pilet, we've raised you the best we could. All we want is to know how you're doing from time to time."

Tecia gives Pilet a vicious glare.

"You'd better answer when I call you, boy..."

"Tch, alright Grandma." Said Pilet, looking away tensely.

"Now I can't speak for this Faxion character since I don't really know him. But from what I've seen and what you've told us, I'm confident he can show you the way to reach your dreams." *Milo chokes back tears* "And there's nothing more we've ever wanted for you in this world."

Tecia begins crying and runs into Milo's embrace. She turns to Pilet.

"Baby we love you! Make sure to brush your teeth and do everything mister Faxion says, he knows best!"

Suddenly, a voice echoes from a distance.

"Rest assured ma'am he's in good hands." Faxion walks through the door, a folder of fresh police documents in hand. "I'm sorry I'm late. The HBA, or Hired Blades Association, works closely with the Federal government on matters regarding monsters like this. I promise you, no decisions about the boy were to be made until first discussing with you."

Tecia and Milo give Faxion a warm smile. Tecia responds.

"Mr. Faxion, we appreciate everything you've done for our little Pilet today. We understand he wants to learn from you and will not take no for an answer, no matter how hard I try!"

Milo, Tecia and Faxion laugh. Milo then chimes in.

"We only ask that you take good care of him sir, It's come to my understanding that you have quite the credentials! I'm sure that if there's anyone capable of keeping him in line, it's you."

Pilet speaks.

"You guys act like I just signed a death warrant. I'm gonna be fine! I just killed a giant Gorilla! There's nothing in this world that can stop me!"

Faxion laughs and puts a hand on his shoulder.

"Well you heard it here first. I'm sure I'm going to have an easy job."

Milo wipes the tears from his cheeks.

"That's the spirit my boy! There's nothing in the world that you can't handle! I believe in you!"

Tecia begins to smile and hugs Pilet.

"We love you so much, honey. Take care of yourself and be happy and free. If you need money you let us know and we'll happily take care of you."

Pilet chokes back tears of his own, taking a deep breath before sighing out heavily.

"Thanks Grandma, I love you too. I think I'm gonna be fine, I've saved plenty by cutting all that damn fruit in the square!"

Everyone shares a good laugh, as the setting sun begins to recede over the skies of Chamboree.

The morning comes, bringing with it an unshakable feeling of nostalgic inception. Birds begin to melodically sing, echoing in the dawn as Pilet and Faxion prepare to leave for Grand Titanus City, the capital of their home continent Kettlena. It's the home of the Hired Blades Association and the first section of the Blades exam. Pilet makes his way to Faxion's room with a full suitcase. He knocks on the door.

"Hey Fax it's me, are you good?"

The door opens to Faxion curiously peeking at Pilet with a mouth full of toothpaste. He brushes vigorously while standing there looking Pilet directly in the eye.

"Yrrp erm erll srrt!"...

Pilet can't help but crack a smile and break out laughing.

"Bahahaha! Stop being weird dude we gotta go!"

Faxion starts cracking up too. He spits, gargles, rinses and repeats.

"I said, "Yup I'm all set!""

Pilet reaches into a backpack on his back, pulling out the two high-tech knives he fought with yesterday.

"Hey man, I forgot to give these back. Sorry about that, I gotta say they're wicked cool though. Definitely came in handy."

Faxion pushes Pilet's hands back to him.

"They're going to come in handy for many more days to come, those are yours now."

Pilet looks surprised.

"Oh... for real!? Are you sure?"

Faxion nods.

"Of course! I saw the way you handled those things, you looked like a damn assassin! As a Veteran Blade I'm mailed the latest weapons and technology every month, last month were those. They're a form of infrared long knives, the Dragonfly model."

Pilet shoots a confused look to Faxion.

"Infrawhat?"

"Infrared! Hahaha, like the tip of my spear. Infrared technology is kind of like... the red hot coils in your toaster. It uses infrared radiation waves to emit heat from the edges of a blade. It's hot enough to cut through pretty much anything that's not heat-treated to specifically defend against it. So basically, those knives cut through stuff like butter!"

He rummages through his rucksack.

"Here, here's the scabbard. Put those things to good use!" Faxion hands the Dragonfly scabbard to Pilet, as he ties it to his right thigh. "Now let's get moving. Hope you said your goodbyes, it's a long trip by train to Grand Titanus from here."

The two make their way past the reception desk towards the entrance. They open the door and are met with thunderous applause.

"Yaaaaay!"

"Hooray!!!"

Someone had recorded the entire battle in the square, which was sold and broadcast on local television. Many of the townsfolk recognized Pilet and called his Grandparents that afternoon, who then set up a goodbye celebration. Faxion smiles and gives the crowd two thumbs up and a bow. Pilet, overcome with emotion, hangs his head yet again. He gathers himself and looks up to his townsfolk, yelling a short but sweet message to them all.

"Thank you!!"

They continue to applaud as Pilet and Faxion make their way past and head toward the train station at the end of town. Once there, he's met by his grandparents and his two young friends. Tecia starts.

"Have fun baby! Remember to brush your teeth and floss damn it!"

Pilet hangs his chin forward in embarrassment.

"Grandma chill!"

Milo gives him a bear hug.

"We'll miss you boy. Stay safe and give 'em hell. Ya hear?"

"I will, Grandpa. I will."

Peeking out from behind Tecia, Nivia shyly walks over to Pilet. She bashfully hands him a little white envelope.

"Open it later, I just wanted you to know how I felt before you left. I'm gonna miss you Pilet." She smiles warmly at her treasured friend. "Have fun out there in the world!"

Pilet grins, gently nudging Nivia on the arm.

"You know, you believed in me when no one else cared. I just want you to know I'm always going to remember that. I'll come back, and when I do you'd better be ready to hang out. The one thing I regret is that we never really got to chill together, you're such a cool chick."

Nivia's cheeks turn beet red. She responds.

"I, I definitely will. I'll keep my calendar open."

James interjects, tactlessly stepping between the two.

"Here." He said, handing Pilet an old bowie knife. The edges jagged, with a worn, brown leather handle. "From when we used to kill snakes together."

Pilet takes the knife and looks at James with remorse.

"What happened to us man?"

"Tch, I got jealous." James replied. "We got older, you got on the track team, the wrestling team. I never could. You had talent, physique, ladies talked about you. And then you just, *threw* it all away to sell bullshit fruit all day... You've got so much going for you man. Just make use of it, *ok?* Sorry I've been a dick."

"It's all good." Said Pilet, holding out his hand to shake. The two clasp hands and bump shoulders. "I'm sorry I've been a dick too. Don't worry, you're a smart guy. Go make something of yourself. Talk to my grandpa about business. Brains and greed are a good combo for success."

James lightly pushes Pilet.

"Piss off." He said, as the two share a genuine chuckle.

As Pilet and Faxion board the metro, Pilet looks back at his family and friends. They all wave and shout their goodbyes to him from a distance, as the train's horn begins to blow loudly signaling their imminent departure. Slowly but surely, the locomotion puts distance between them and Chamboree, as the rural mountain peak village grows smaller and smaller. Before they get too far, Pilet smiles and gives his family a nod, and one simple wave. Finally, the fiery prospect and his Veteran mentor take their seats, as the pair disembark on a journey that would be talked about for ages to come.

CHAPTER

THREE

The Capital

The screeching of the rails and the rumbling of the train car lulls Pilet to sleep, as his mentor sits directly across him. The Veteran Blade gazes through the window, into the colorful mountain range as the train whizzes by. He reflects on the recent events that took place at the center of Chamboree.

When he was enraged, Those markings on his body... Thought Faxion, as he looks over to a sleeping Pilet. *I've never seen a human move like that without auracast. Is there something I'm not seeing?*

As Faxion ponders his conundrum, the rocky hills of Minegogue begin to blend with the lush, grassy fields surrounding the Capital City. They pass a vast lake with dozens of tourists fishing, kayaking, and taking photos. Some moments later the train descends on Grand Titanus Station, a bustling mecca for inter-regional transportation. Droves of civilians pack the marble platforms, eagerly awaiting their chance to board their respective trains.

Faxion shakes the fatigue from his eyes, as the train's conductor makes his way through his section.

"Tickets please! Last stop, Grand Titanus Station!"

Faxion gives Pilet a shake.

"Hey, hey you. Wipe the crust off your eyes, we've got work to do! The day's just getting started.

Pilet slowly comes to. Mouth agape with saliva running down one side of his face. His eyes rapidly flutter open.

"Nguh. Hnng... What. What? Oh, oh shit ok... Where's my ticket?"

He furrows through his rucksack, rummaging until he finds a crumpled, off-white train ticket.

"Ok buddy, here you go."

Pilet hands the ticket to the conductor, as does Faxion. The conductor shoots a grimaced look at Pilet's disheveled face as he takes their tickets.

"Oooh boy, you need a mirror son. Thank you gentlemen, I'll take these. Please enjoy your stay at the Capital! No but seriously young'n, you're going to need this."

The conductor hands Pilet a handkerchief from his shirt pocket and motions to wipe his face. A confused, half-asleep Pilet takes it and looks over to Faxion.

"Hahahaha! He's right you know. You're a mess if I've ever seen one!"

Pilet shoots him an unamused glare and clears the dried drool from his cheek. He goes to hand it back to the conductor.

"Uhh, yeah... You can keep that. Good day boys." The Conductor walks off to continue taking tickets.

Faxion stands up to reach for his rucksack on the overhead shelf.

"Alright Lad, let's get going. The City is massive and it's important to know how to navigate, I wouldn't want you to get lost in Dragon's Alley after dark."

"Dragon's what? Well anyway, this is totally exciting! I've read about Grand Titanus City in the magazines my Grandpa's always taking to the toilet."

The two ready their belongings and make their way off the train, squeezing and wriggling through crowds of weary passengers. As they exit the station, mighty skyscrapers tower over the horizon; reflecting the beautiful, blue skies and white fluffy clouds surrounding Titanus in their windows. Flying, chrome vending machines offering various goods zoom by; stopping for any pedestrians flashing their Titan Vending Co. membership cards. Waves of hover cars, floating inches off the ground; accompanied by their older, four-wheeled counterparts pack the streets in uneven rows. A separate lane in between cars and pedestrians gives way to taxi carts, pushed by varying species of speaking dinosaurs. The sight of this baffles Pilet.

"Fax, that's a velociraptor... It's like, right there... What's that all about?!"

"Dinosaurs need jobs too, you know." Replied Faxion with a sarcastic undertone.

Pilet stops in his tracks, stomping his feet in confused frustration.

"Dinosaurs work here?? What?!? How? Why?!"

"All in due time." Said Faxion, continuing to walk by. "We'll get to all matters of fossil creatures before the day is done. You must not leave Chamboree often, do you lad."

"Wait, you're just gonna leave me here wondering why there's talking dinosaurs wheeling people around right now?" Said Pilet. "You can't just, I mean... Alright, whatever..."

The sidewalks are filled with booths and tables of peddlers, trying to profit off of tourist naivety. One such turns his eye to an unsuspecting Pilet.

"Dude, this place is wild!" Exclaimed Pilet in elation. "There are so many lights, and the food smells amazing! Look! There are more hovercars than I've ever seen in my life!"

Faxion chuckles.

"I'm glad you like it! To be honest, after a while it gets old. Between standstill traffic and the occasional mugging attempt, I'm basically over it. I'd say the only reason I stay is that number one; Hired Blades Headquarters is here, and number two; I do love the view of the skyline from my apartment."

As they walk by, a peddler puts his arm out against Pilet's torso, blocking him from advancing.

"Brother, let me get your attention real quick. I got these watches and they are *hot*! These are going for like $150 each at Joe's Ice shack! But I'll get you 2 for $30 aurum, It's a deal you're not getting anywhere!"

Pilet guides the peddler's hand off of his chest.

"Nah my man I'm good. Good luck with the hustle though, I know that life." Pilet and Faxion continue forward.

The Peddler doesn't seem too thrilled at this answer. He walks in front of Pilet as they try to pass.

"Woah there cool guy, you're just gonna walk by me like that? What, you think walking away from people is funny? Me and my friends don't"

Some of the Peddlers get up from their booths and surround Pilet and Faxion.

"What's up, fool?"

"You think you're *bad*?"

"This is our side of Titanus tough guy, you must be lost."

Pilet's eyes fix on the first peddler. His nostrils flare and his upper lip raises to one side, revealing his canine. He begins to reach for the Dragonfly knives tucked into his inner Jean Jacket pocket.

Just then, Faxion puts a hand on his shoulder. He mutters "We don't do it like that around here." in Pilet's ear. He then addresses the peddlers. "Excuse me gentlemen, can we help you?"

A peddler to his right flank answers. "Ain't no *gentle* men here. You could help us by peeling that wallet from your pocket."

"And If I refuse?" Said Faxion.

Each of the peddlers reach into their jackets to briefly reveal hidden pistols, before quietly tucking them back in. Pilet's eyebrows raise at the new level of danger.

"We've got ways of being very persuasive. Don't be stupid, that wallet ain't worth your life." Said the first peddler.

"In broad daylight? I'd be hard-pressed to think so. But I'm curious. Please, persuade me." Said Faxion

A bead of sweat runs down Pilet's forehead. He looks at Faxion through the corner of his eye.

"What are we doing man?" He mumbles. "I'm fast, but I can't deflect bullets..."

Faxion gestures an arm out, with his palm face down to Pilet.

The peddlers pause without a word. Knowing full well that a firefight would draw unnecessary police attention to their operation; they glare at Faxion in frustration.

"I figured as much. As you were..." Said Faxion. He nudges Pilet forward as they continue walking.

"Hey! Wait bastard!" Shouts the original peddler, gripping Faxion's arm as he passes.

Faxion swiftly breaks the grip, twists his hand at an unnatural angle, and folds his wrist at the joint; locking it at a painful leverage.

"Agggh! What the hell is this?!" said the Peddler, falling to his knees in pain.

As the thugs advance to help their friend, Faxion flashes a hidden dagger in his sleeve and points it toward the peddler's neck.

"Let's not be hasty boys, your friend's life ain't worth it, yeah?"

They slowly put their hands in the air in response.

"Listen man, we're just trying to sell these watches. That's our bad, let's just relax buddy. Didn't know we were messing with some secret agent guy."

Faxion retracts the blade and shoves the peddler towards his buddies.

"Have a nice day gentlemen." He motions a speechless Pilet to follow as they finally take their leave.

Sometime later...

"So what was that? *We don't do it like that around here.*" Nonsense?" Said Pilet. "You'd rather stand *unarmed* in the middle of a bunch of guys with guns?"

"We're not in a small mountain village with a lazy, slow responding police force anymore." Replied Faxion. "If you visibly pull out a deadly weapon, people are going to scream and call the cops; who can be found patrolling every other block. Those thugs never would have pulled a gun. There were too many witnesses, and they don't want prison time."

Faxion shrugs his shoulders apathetically.

"They're just trying to make a buck, sometimes they get carried away but none of them have the guts to pull the trigger. Lesson number one: Never start a fight you don't plan to finish."

"Yeah, Noted. I guess pulling out big, fiery knives in front of a crowd would've been a problem. Anyway... Where can a guy get a cup of coffee around here? I need a boost, especially after *that* shit."

The Sisters Sierro

The two head to a nearby coffee shop.

The Lava Bean Cafe; a chain of stores offering a variety of caffeinated beverages. Lava Bean's world-famous coffee beans come from Magma Mountain, an active volcanic mountain range that runs directly parallel to that of Minego.

Pilet and Faxion arrive at the spotless, double-glass doors of The Lava Bean. As they enter the cafe, the smell of freshly brewed coffee wafts through the air. The shelves are lined with bags of retail coffee grinds and colorful mugs. Upon the face of each product lies the characteristic symbol of the "Magma bean"; a pitch black, stubble-covered bean with vibrant red streaks running across the outer coating. Miscellaneous cafe-goers sit at tables and booths scattered throughout, reading books and typing away on laptops.

As Pilet approaches the counter, the attending Barista greets him with a smile.

"Hello sir, how can I help you?"

"Hey, how's it going? I'm gonna get a medium iced Magma Mocha. Fax you getting anything? I'm buying."

"Why thank you sir! Alright, well I'll take a small Cocoa Soot latte with almond milk, steamed at children's temperature. With a little extra Soot on top."

The Barista inputs the order. "Can I get a name for the cups?"

"It's Pilet, that's P. I. L. E. T."

"Ok thank you. That'll be $8.49 aurum please, your drinks will be ready at the end of the counter momentarily."

Pilet hands the barista his debit card. The Barista swipes and returns it to Pilet with a receipt. "Have a nice day!"

Pilet and Faxion begin to walk towards the end of the counter, but as they do so Faxion spots something that makes him stop in his tracks. Oblivious to this, Pilet keeps walking and talking without him.

"So children's temperature huh? Ha! What's that all about? Is your tongue starting to get too sensitive with age? ... Fax?"

Pilet turns to see Faxion walking towards two young women sitting in the lounge.

One of them, fair skinned with warm, ginger hair in a ponytail. Tall with dark-rimmed glasses and a forest green pea coat. She clutches a very old, green leather-bound book; covered in a mysterious, foreign text.

The other slightly shorter, with platinum blonde hair flowing down past her shoulders. Draped in a beige knit sweater and covered with vibrant crystal jewelry.

"Oh, this should be great. One second the guy's pulling a knife on a hustler, and the next he's hitting on two chicks. But Mister manly can't handle coffee when it's too hot?"

Pilet walks over to meet Faxion with the two young women. As he gets closer, he starts overhearing their conversation.

"And then I said *"Let's not be hasty boys, your friend's life ain't worth it, yeah?"*, And the guys just crumpled! The girl's eyes widened in astonishment at Faxions story.

Standing behind Faxion, Pilet clears his throat.

"Ahem..."

"Oh, Pilet!" Exclaims Faxion. "Ladies, meet my young friend! This is Pilet Whydah, he's my newest project. I mean prospect? Well, there's not much difference I suppose, he's still pretty green under the gills. Now Pilet, I'd like to introduce you to some friends of mine. Meet Faith and Yuuna Sierro, two sisters from the forest village of Miantha! It's actually due south of your home on Mt. Minego, small world huh?"

Faith's index finger re-aligns her glasses as she reaches out to Pilet for a handshake. "Hello Pilet, I'm Faith. This is my little sister Yuuna, we're pleased to meet you! You're very lucky to have a friend like Faxion, he's helped us both countless times."

Yuuna does the same.

"Hi Pilet, It's so nice to meet you! I'm glad you're ok after what Fax told us about this morning, that's really scary! Thank God you're not hurt! You have to be super careful around these parts with peddlers, they're so persistent it's annoying."

Pilet shakes their hands and responds. "Uh hey guys, happy to meet you too. Yuuna, those are really cool gems on your necklace."

"Thanks! I use them to cast spells and keep evil away."

"Oh that's, nice..." *I fought a purple gorilla with like, space age knives yesterday, at this point nothing should surprise me.* Thought Pilet. "Yeah, those guys are horrible salesmen. Good thing Fax has such good people skills... If you could call it that. So what brings you two to Grand Titanus from Miantha?"

Faith responds. "We're getting ready to take the Hired Blades Exam, both of us have been training to become Licensed Hired Blades for the past two years. It's really a pleasant surprise to see Faxion here, considering he was the one who inspired us to do so."

"No way, so am I!" Said Pilet "Fax is helping me get ready for the exam, although two years is a lot more time than the two weeks I have. I guess I'll really need to cram if I want to pass."

"Oh." Said Faith. "Two weeks? Like, the two weeks til the exam? I mean you've started *some* training, right?"

"Nah, but how hard can it be? Where there's a will there's a way right?!"

The girls look at each other, then back to Pilet. They cringe as they both respond with a, "Sure..."

"Well, I believe you can do it Pilet!" Said Yuuna. "If anyone can help you it's Fax! Speaking of."

The girls grin and fall silent for a moment, looking behind Pilet. Pilet raises one eyebrow puzzledly in response.

"Hey, where *is* Fax?" Just then he feels a cold sensation on the back of his neck. "Gaah!"

Pilet jumps forward crashing into the girls who inherently catch him. He turns around to see Faxion holding his iced Magma Mocha in the air where his neck was but a moment ago. Pilet glares at Faxion for a moment while he regains his composure. He tries to look serious but he can't hide a quivering lip and a grin. Then all four of them burst into laughter.

"They called our order, but I guess you don't answer to "Pilot," or ''Peelot''. Oh that tricky, silent "T" you have there. They must not train baristas to spell *made-up* names. Just the same, it's what you get for drinking *iced* coffee you monster!"

Yuuna retorts. "Hey, I like iced coffee!"

"Well, that must reflect your frozen heart doesn't it, hmm?" Said Faxion

"This guy's one to talk, mister children's temperature! You're like 80 dude you outgrew that drink when dinosaurs walked the earth *the first time*!"

Faxion digressed. "Hey stop that, I'm only 46, and I've very sensitive taste buds you know…"

For the next few minutes, the four enjoy their morning coffee and chat. When they are finished they part ways to continue their daily activities.

"Have a wonderful day friends!" Said Yuuna. "Please be safe and steer clear of the peddlers!"

"Yeah and good luck Pilet, I hope you do well and become a Blade." Said Faith.

"Thanks guys, good luck to you too. I'll see *you* in the winners' circle!" Exclaimed Pilet.

Faxion grins and tips his hat. "Ladies, good day."

The Stoic, Island Swordsmen

Pilet and Faxion leave The Lava Bean Cafe and continue to trek across the expansive city; passing massive lit billboards, huge skyscrapers, and dozens of exotic food trucks.

Eventually, they come to a series of side streets with vibrantly lit adornments strewn across from building to building. Fierce-looking Dragon statues, varying in colors and patterns, stand guard at every doorstep. Shops selling everything from foreign food and clothing to discounted state-of-the-art technology line the walls. Directly above each first-floor shop lies apartments, housing the store owners and miscellaneous renters.

Faxion stops Pilet and points to the entrance. "Welcome to Dragon's Alley, try not to get lost."

"Oh. So this is the place I'm not supposed to get lost at. Why's that?"

"Well there's an immense network of confusing side streets that make up this area, many tourists lose their way and end up wandering for hours. Now, Dragon's Alley is a haven for people from countries outside of Kettlena to reconnect with their culture. You see, some native Kettlenians have a negative opinion of outsiders, and they mistreat them discriminatively. Because of this, the residents of Dragon's Alley have taken to the Serpent Dragon; a universal symbol of strength and peace. Each alley-goer paints a dragon statue with the colors of their native flag and places it at the entrance of their store or home. This is as if to say, "Keep your pride, but leave your prejudice at the door."."

"And all the stores? They can't just *live* here and rent storefronts *elsewhere*? I mean it's beautiful, but a bit cramped if you ask me."

"Some of these people are not here legally, they make a living off of the native goods they sell. It's not uncommon for a family to sell merchandise without a permit on the first floor and reside in the second. Risky, but not a bad deal if you think about it."

The two begin to stroll through the neighborhood, taking note of some interesting stores they find. They happen upon a storefront with exotic weaponry lining the windows and walls.

"There! We gotta go there Fax. Look at those swords!" Pilet points to a series of decorative sheathed longswords in the window."

They enter and take a look around. The store is filled to the brim with older modeled weaponry and equipment. Some excavated bronze daggers and oaken clubs occupy ornamental glass cases, most of which have been salvaged from indigenous peoples overseas. Pilet and Faxion sift through trinkets of the past in a large chest on the floor.

"Dude look at this bronze knife, it's got like a winged snake carved into it. And its just $4 aurum! What a steal!"

Faxion begins to speak "That snake is--"

"It's a cloud viper." A young man interjects. "The ancient symbol of nobility on the island of Hachidori." Short and stocky. His complexion is a warm, chestnut brown. Extremely muscular, with five o'clock shadow. His hair, long and braided, with a colorful shade of yellow running through a single braid on the right. He's fully suited in gunmetal black, half-plated lamellar armor; to which a yellow gem adorns the center of the chest plate. Two elegant-yet deadly, one-edged longswords cling to his left hip.

"Oh, why yes!" Said Faxion. "Yes it is."

"Max. It's impolite to interrupt." A middle-aged man of similar stature and skin tone approaches. Although not as lean with a slight pot belly, his built frame and pulsating muscles draw respect from the eyes of passersby. Sporting braids with four yellow stripes across the top and a scar through his right eyebrow.

"My apologies Father." Said Max.

The man extends a hand to Faxion and Pilet. "Kenzo Quinn, and this is my son Max Quinn. Please pardon our intrusion. You've found a good piece there; it's a ceremonial sacrifice dagger, I'm sure many a goat has fallen to it."

Max offers a slight bow to Pilet and Faxion in repentance. The four exchange handshakes.

"Faxion Deadeye, pleasure to make your acquaintance!"

"I'm Pilet, how's it going."

Max's eyebrows raise as his jaw drops slightly. He turns to Kenzo and mutters. "Father... Faxion of the Deadeye..."

Faxion grins and tips his fedora.

"I take it you've heard of me?"

"Of course, it's an honor to meet you, brother." Said Kenzo. "It's not every day you get to meet a "Veteran" Hired Blade, a true expert of warfare. As one of the heads of the Sanda clan of Hachidori, I work together with the Hired Blades Association to help contain the spread of the Wurm on our Island home."

"I figured as such." Said Faxion. "It's hard to mistake those yellow stripes, and the honor is all mine. It's not every day you get to meet a fourth-degree Sanda Master and his first-degree prodigy."

Pilet looks lost. Not sure what anyone is talking about, he wanders some feet away and begins to spin and finesse with the Hachidorinese dagger. Max takes note of his technique.

"You have skills, yes?" Said Max. "I see you're very dexterous with a weapon, I assume your father has taught you his Hired Blade ways."

Pilet, caught off guard, immediately drops the dagger.

"What?! Father?! No no no. He's just my friend dude, you got it all wrong. He teaches me stuff but that's about it. My Dad's a deadbeat, with no balls! Only thing he taught me was to run from responsibility, and I never took to that lesson."

Max is stunned by this blatant lack of respect for his father.

"How could you speak about your father like that? You lack discipline! I would be beaten black and blue for uttering those words. He gave you life!"

"HAH!" Exclaimed Pilet, doubling over in laughter. "Look buddy, the only thing my old man gave me was a headache anytime someone brought him up. I've been flying solo since I was born, he left my Mom the second he found out she was pregnant. I've got no need for his help or lessons."

"I apologize, I did not realize your situation. Well, that's very sad. I'm sorry for your predicament, but I'm glad you found a Master to take his place."

"No problem buddy, all part of being a bastard."

Faxion and Kenzo draw near.

"Pilet, did you know that Max here is training for the exam too? It's exciting, you've already made friends with three candidates!"

Pilet speaks. "Oh, no way! Alright cool man, can't wait to see you on the field."

"Thank you, you as well. I've trained my whole life for this moment. There is nothing that can stand in my way of becoming a member of the Hired Blades Association, my trusted Lacerates will make sure of that."

Max pats his hand on two beautifully crafted, sheathed longswords affixed magnetically to his hip. The M7 Lacerate; thin, lightweight, and remarkably durable. Each one made of the world's strongest metal, "Lacerate Steel". Able to swiftly slice through the hardest of materials with ease, these swords are a traditional favorite of the warriors of Hachidori. Having been heavily modified over centuries to complement each clan's fighting style, Lacerates come in different shapes and sizes.

"He's ready" said Kenzo as he looks to Faxion. "It's time for my son to learn the secrets of warfare this world has to offer, and bring this knowledge back to our people. So is the way of the Hachidori. Becoming a Blade and traveling the globe will allow him this."

Faxion nods and replies. "Exciting, I'll be eagerly awaiting your performance during the Exam friend! I'm sure a warrior of your pedigree won't disappoint."

"Thank you sir." Said Max. "It's an honor coming from one of your caliber, and I wish the best of luck to you too Pilet. Maybe we'll see each other out there. If so, you have an ally in me."

Pilet pats Max on the shoulder. "Thanks buddy! Glad to hear it, same here!" He turns to Faxion and whispers. "*Let's get out of here Fax, the lemon-headed kid is weird.*"

The four part ways. Pilet purchases the Hachidorinese dagger and stashes it in his rucksack. As Pilet and Faxion continue their path down

Dragon's Alley; they eat garlic roasted flarepheasant from Zardenia, drink screechergoat's milk from the mountains on Mudona, and watch Itedonian belly dancers perform to the songs of their homeland.

The Prehistoric Pugilists

After enjoying what the Alley has to offer, Pilet and Faxion emerge into the bustling big city streets yet again; this time finding themselves in front of a massive building with rows of stone pillars surrounding it. A lush courtyard sits in front, erecting a massive fossilized recreation of a Brachiosaurus, towering over the flowing crowds. Across the top of the building runs bold print reading *"Tales from the past predict the future.".* Below this, just above the set of four adjacent doors leading into the facility, reads "Grand Titanus Museum of Paleontology".

"And here we are, the piece de resistance." Said Faxion. This museum is where you'll learn of fossil creatures that have been resurrected in recent years."

"Oh, ok. Cool! Let's do it!" Pilet hoists his rucksack over his shoulder as the two head for the entrance. They get to the doors and are greeted by the admission desk.

"Good day sir, how can I help you?"

Faxion flashes his Hired Blades Association badge. "I'd like two spectator tickets for the day please."

The receptionist's eyebrows raise, her mouth agape. "Oh! Why yes Mr. Blade give me one moment to ready your tickets please."

"Please, take your time."

The tickets print as the receptionist hands them to Faxion, still warm from the machine. "Thank you, and enjoy your visit to the Museum of Paleontology and Prehistoric Preserve!"

"Why thank you very much Ma'am." Faxion hands one to Pilet.

"Dude, what was that? Blades get free shit around here??" Said Pilet.

"Of course! Silly child. Being a Blade comes with all sorts of benefits, one of which being free admission to Museums around the globe! After all, it's our perilous exploits that are responsible for a large portion of the recovered artifacts stored here. I've actually worked hand in hand to protect archeologists responsible for finding several pieces on this site alone. Hell, I've excavated some of these pieces myself, by hand!"

As they step inside they are met by the wails and screeches of assorted baby Dinosaurs, playing with children in a huge petting zoo by the lobby. Reinforced glass cases filled with fossilized bones and teeth line the walls. Mini electronic tablets lay beside each exhibit, informing museum-goers of their contents.

One exhibit showcases a pair of pachycephalosaurus; thick-skulled, pugilistic herbivores, butting heads in a caged sandpit. A sign reads, *"Pach fighting training grounds. Home of the Grand Titanus Crasher Kings. "*.

One of the Pachs sports vibrant green scales and a reinforced black neck brace. The other, covered in radiant yellow scales, with ankle braces on either foot. As the pachycephalosaurus exchange glancing blows, shockingly, they begin mocking each other in human speech.

The green Pach lowers his head and tries to ram yellow in his left flank, but yellow nimbly sidesteps and clotheslines green with his tail on the way out.

"Hah! Is that all you got, Mortimer?" Jeers the yellow Pach fighter. "My grandma butts faster than that and she died 65 million years ago!"

Mortimer collects himself and wipes the sand off of his beak.

"Always running like a bitch, huh Dunn? Stand your ground for once!"

Faxion and Pilet approach the cage door leading to the training pit. Faxion clears his throat.

"Ahem, good day boys!"

The two dinos pause and turn at the familiar voice. Upon seeing Faxion they both exclaim, "Fax!"

"Where ya been?" Said Dunn. "Some of the other Blades stopped by the other day. They were raving about some ass-kicking you gave the Piranha gang in Macorin, the whole Museum fight crew was cheering!"

"Hell yeah we were!" Said Mortimer. "Most of us were pretty drunk at the time. To be honest we all thought we dreamed it in the morning, until we saw the news story speaking of a "Hired Blade in an Olive green Fedora". Everyone knows who that is! We were so Goddamn excited that *our man* blasted those posers. Good shit Fax, no one likes those stuck-up thieving pricks."

"Hahahaha! Ah, I appreciate it guys, to think word spread that fast!

Now, I want you to meet a very special friend of mine." Faxion grabs Pilet by the shoulder and pulls him around to meet the two Fighters.

Standing upright, the Dinos dwarf Pilet by the height of another adult human. He looks up at them, speechless at the sight of speaking Dinosaurs. Faxion continues.

"This is Pilet, my new friend! He's a gifted prospect trying for the Blades Exam in two weeks. He's already killed a Gorilla Wurm King bigger than both of you!"

Pilet begins to sweat at the mention of their size, in comparison to his kill. He nudges Faxion with his elbow and mutters, "Chill dude, chill." The Dinos respond to Faxion.

"Oh damn, alright. This kid's no joke huh?" Said Mortimer. "What's up my man, the name's Mortimer. Any friend of Fax is a friend of mine." Mortimer reaches a reptilian claw out for a handshake, Pilet quickly meets it with his hand. Dunn does the same.

"Sup little dude, I'm Dunn; Dunn the matador, fastest Pach this side of Kettlena! If Fax says you're tough then I believe it. Maybe one day we'll spar if you're up to it. You Blades are always a fun time."

Pilet gulps deeply at the thought of a 1 ton, Dinosaur prize fighter chasing him down the street. Fanning the nervous sweat from under his tank top collar, he quickly changes the subject.

"Hah, yeah... What's up guys, glad to meet you. Those are cool braces you're both wearing, what's that all about?"

Mortimer scratches his neck under the athletic brace.

"Damn thing looks cool but it itches to high hell after a while, it's just added support. My fight name's Mortimer the Enforcer. I'm heavy-headed; I like to ram into anything that pisses me off. To fight like that you need more support than just your spine. Same with Dunn and the ankles, he's a bitch that likes to dance around instead of fight, so he needs to protect those feet from all that running he does."

Dunn lets out a bellowing laugh.

"You say that buddy, but your face tells a different story." Dunn points at a red, tail-shaped line on Mortimer's face from the whipping he received moments ago. "This guy's mad because he's been shooting blanks all morning, not my fault he's a one-dimensional fighter."

The two face each other in a crouching position, beginning a low growl. Faxion interjects.

"Come now, we all know you're both *exceptional* in your own right." Faxion grins. "But I know what those *exceptions* are."

The fighters smirk and halt their intimidating dance. Mortimer speaks.

"This guy, he's always gotta go there. We got a little outta line *one time* and I ended up airborne!"

"Yeah, kid." Said Dunn. "Just so you know, don't get on Fax's bad side. The dude *acts* all nice, but he'll whip your ass in a second no matter how big or bad you are."

"Yeah, I've noticed." Said Pilet. "The guy almost shanked a peddler this morning for selling watches."

"Ha! Again?" Said Dunn. "That's like number four this year! Just learn to walk away old man!"

"Never!" Faxion grins. "I have to show these bastards who's boss! They walk my streets forgetting their manners, I won't have it! I simply won't stop until I've paddled every peddling ass in Titanus!"

The Fighting Dinos break into hysterical laughter.

"Classic Fax." Said Mortimer. "You're a damn goofball of an old geezer, and *that's* coming from a literal fossil. Anyway buddy it's great seeing you again. As always the team seriously appreciates your contribution. Fightin' ain't cheap you know kid, your buddy here was one of the first Big-Wig Blades that helped the Crasher Kings get off the ground. When Pach fighting first became legal, Fax sponsored us with gear and funding."

Dunn adds. "Yeah, and his fighting tips helped get us to the top. I'm fighting the Champion in my weight class next month with some of the moves he's been using on me! No one puts you on the ground quite like Faxion of the Deadeye."

"It's all about leverage, and redirection. Don't forget it when you're giving 'ol Stinger Logan a Thrashing next month! Remember, less is more. Minimum effort and maximum efficiency is the key."

"Yeah yeah I got it..." Dunn whispers to Pilet. "This guy likes the sound of his own voice."

Pilet smiles and whispers back.

"I know, he's a real mansplainer. His parents probably never listened to him."

Faxion shoots them both a sharp, subtle glare.

"You're both hilarious...Anyway, my young companion has much to see yet. It's about time we explored the rest of the museum. Best of luck to the Crashers in the PF1 Grand Prix!"

"Yeah, it was great meeting you guys." Said Pilet. "Hope you smash the other guy and snatch that belt! Go make those big bucks as the Champ, just don't forget about us at the top!"

"Hah!" Said Mortimer. "Fax, I like this kid's style! Go get that Blades License Pilet, and don't take shit from *nobody* along the way!"

"Yeah kid! Break a leg!" Said Dunn.

The Veteran Blade tips his fedora to the fighting Pachs, continuing on his tour of the illustrious Museum.

Origins: Fossil resurrection

The duo encounter schools of children and teens on field trips, making funny faces at docile fossil creatures grazing behind the exhibit glass. Pterodactyls with messenger bags soar freely above the crowds. The massive flying reptiles perch on thick, artificial branches scattered high on the walls of each floor. They place packages ordered from the gift shop via the Museum's app into designated dropboxes, as a clear tube transports them to waiting museum goers down below.

As Pilet and Faxion reach the second floor, they come to an exhibit showcasing three colorful and vibrant crystals of varying heights.

One crimson red crystal, 7 inches in length Labeled, *"Refractor piece Alpha, RepCo North"*. The second, an emerald green; 11 inches long, labeled, *"Refractor piece Beta, RepCo East"*. The third and final crystal glows a marvelous violet, 9 inches long, *"Refractor piece Gamma, Repco West"*.

To the side of the crystals lie three, small model buildings in succession under the words *"RepCo Fossil Restoration Laboratories"*. A fleshed-out timeline reaches across the wall of the exhibit, documenting various dates of note within the past seven years. A large, wall-mounted tablet sits before the crystals; displaying information on all that is shown. Pilet walks over and touches the red crystal. He gazes at the iridescence before him, lost in the subtle cracks and waves.

"What... is this?..."

"Beautiful isn't it." Said Faxion. "And it's a replica too, not even the genuine article."

"What?! You mean this isn't even a real stone? Why would they put it here then?"

Faxion strokes his chin, pondering how to respond. He grins

"Rather than run the risk of "Man-splaining" any longer; why don't you read the tablet over there? Use that *quality education* you received on the few days you actually went to class at Chamboree High."

"Oh, a real funny guy we got here!" Said Pilet. "Alright fine, where's this stupid tablet..." Pilet wanders for a moment, eventually finding the information tablet and begins to read...

"The history of fossil creature restoration:

In the year 2103: Famed paleontologist and Scientist, Doctor "Eroll Nashorn" discovers a revolutionary technique for the restoration of soft tissue within fossilized remains. While this breakthrough in technology shakes the scientific world, Dr. Nashorn is dissatisfied. Although scientists are now able to recreate entire fossil creatures organically, they cannot give life to their creations. The lifeless corpses decay, with no ability to think and breathe for themselves.

In 2107: A troupe of archaeologists accompanied by Licensed Hired Blades discover a unique crystal, in the ruins of a pyramid in the Devil's Tongue Desert. They call it; Refractor Alpha. The Hired Blades on staff quickly identify the latent properties of aura lying within the crystal and recommend it be sent to a laboratory for testing.

While running diagnostics on Refractor Alpha, a laboratory technician wearing an ammonite fossil necklace was struck by a rogue wave of aura emitted by the crystal. Thankfully unscathed, the lab tech reported a frantic squirming feeling across their chest. The Ammonite had come back to life! However, the fossil creature perished moments later as it was merely reanimated skeletal remains. Armed with this new knowledge, Dr. Nashorn leads a scientific movement to uncover the secrets within Refractor Alpha.

2108: Dr. Nashorn succeeds in resurrecting the first, live and healthy fossil creature; a trilobite named Zuerst! Expeditions begin scavenging the lost ruins of Devil's Tongue in search of ancient technology similar to Refractor Alpha.

2110: A group succeeds in locating a second, life-giving crystal; "Refractor Beta". Two months later, the third crystal; "Refractor Gamma" is unearthed.

2111: Three separate lab facilities are constructed for the sole purpose of fossil restoration study, and at the heart of each lies one of the precious Refractor siblings necessary for reanimation. These facilities; RepCo North, East, and West, have proven instrumental for advancing our knowledge of the past..."

Pilet sighs.

"Wow, that's the most I've read all year. So this all started like fourteen years ago... Back in 2103?" Pilet shrugs his shoulders. "It's news to me. I remember going on a field trip to RepCo West a few years back, but me and James were too busy stealing ammonite rocks to listen to the history lesson. Which reminds me, I knew dinosaurs were alive now, but I've never seen one talk like those guys. When did *that* become a thing?"

"Well." Said Faxion. "The first few years of fossil resurrection saw Nashorn simply reviving creatures *exactly* according to their base DNA, but like most men of science, he became curious. Before long he had begun genetically modifying and enhancing his creations in an unnatural way. Vibrantly colored scales, extra talons, miniature versions of colossal

Dinosaurs, and even humongous forms of naturally smaller ones! It became more a game of playing God than a means of learning about the past..."

"Oh, alright." Said Pilet. "I guess that explains the flashy colors on your punch-drunk friends downstairs."

"Precisely!" Replied Faxion. "It's around that time that the Doctor started using the Refractors to enhance their IQ. Their brains grew to the level of humans, so he started programming them with the knowledge of our languages. It's a mixed bag, what kind of fossil creature you'll meet when you see one? Some might growl at you and eat leaves, others might recite mathematical equations. It's an interesting world we're living in today."

"Damn, dude." Said Pilet. "I'm glad they're cool then. Especially the Crasher King's, I wouldn't want to get on *their* bad side."

"So this is important Pilet, remember this when you meet a dinosaur. The correct term they prefer is "Fossil creature", as dinosaur seems to have become a derogatory term for an old person."

"Oh..." Replied Pilet.

"Also, The Crashers are HFFCs, or "High Functioning Fossil Creatures". They're held to the same behavioral laws as humans. Don't worry about them, they know better than to start trouble. The Fossil creatures that do not speak are called "LFFCs" or "Low Functioning Fossil Creatures.""

"Waaait wait wait... "Low functioning"? They don't get offended by *that?*"

"It's a term that the FC officials *themselves* came up with to differentiate. We simply honor their wishes."

"Got it, well I better remember that then. Wouldn't want to piss off a dinosaur- I mean, Fossil creature."

The two spend the afternoon reading and examining ancient finds and learning about various prehistoric species. Once they've had their fill of the Museum, they find their way out and make way for Faxion's high-rise condo to settle in for the night.

"You are, to say the least, completely terrible at most aspects of Bladesmanship."

After walking several blocks, they arrive at "The Free Enterprise"; a grandiose, 35-floor condominium skyscraper. The setting sun reflects off of the countless, winding windows.

"Wow, high roller!" Exclaims Pilet. "Fax this place is *serious*. Can't say I'm surprised; you being a loaded, badass Blade and all... But damn! This place makes Dreams of Chamboree look like a bigger pile of dogshit than it already is!"

Faxion chuckles.

"I mean, I'm not one to *brag*. But that place *has seen* better days."

Pilet and Faxion enter and make their way past the reception desk. Faxion flashes his Hired Blades badge.

"Good evening Derryl."

"Why, good evening! Welcome back Master Deadeye! Your room is freshly flipped, as well as the extra room you requested for the next two weeks. Here is the key to room 3205."

Derryl hands Faxion a card key in a Free Enterprise pamphlet, which Faxion immediately passes to Pilet.

"You found me a place to stay when I needed it." Said Faxion. "Allow me to return the favor."

Stunned, Pilet takes it and brushes his buzzed head.

"Aw man... Fax, you shouldn't have. I could've slept on a couch, or like a futon or something. I'm not picky."

Some moments later the two arrive at Pilet's room. Pilet taps the card key to an automated touchscreen. *Clunk* A green light flashes as the door unlocks. They walk into the sight of a lavish suite with multiple chambers. A mini cafe, a bedroom with a massive TV, a study, even a hot tub.

Pilet stands in the doorway in awe, arms hanging down limp in front of him, his mouth agape and eyes lost in a daze.

"So". Said Faxion. "Still want to sleep on a futon?"

"Ta hell with that!" Exclaimed Pilet. "This is what it's all about! Look at this!" Pilet rushes past Faxion to the hot tub and turns on the water. "Do you see this shit?! Hot water! And it could probably last for like, a whole hour! And this!"

He rushes past Faxion again to the bedroom, grabs the remote, and leaps four feet in the air. He lands on the bed, arms folded behind his head in a relaxed posture.

"There's probably like, freaking, a hundred channels on this bad boy! Oh, and this!" He rushes past Faxion *again* to the espresso machine in the cafe chamber. The cabinets, full of Lava Bean brand coffee products. "I can be a God-damned barista master. Look at all this caffeine, I'll be wired for days!"

"Well, I'd certainly hope not." Said Faxion. "You're going to need solid nutrition and good rest from now on. You see, this is where the vacation comes to an end. Starting tomorrow, we're going to begin a serious training regimen for the next two weeks straight. You've a lot to learn and, to be quite honest, almost no time to learn it."

"Oh, ok..." Pilet's face becomes attentive, he calms down and takes a seat at a booth-styled coffee table by the espresso machine. Faxion joins him.

"Yeah, please." Said Pilet. "What do I need to know? I've been wondering in the back of my mind what kind of craziness is in store..."

"Well, there's much to know." Said Faxion. "But in your case, we're going to learn the bare minimum required to pass on a *general* level. The most important thing is to focus on your strengths and use them to your advantage, to get you through the *rough* stuff. Here's a schedule I've made for the course of your training." Faxion pulls a sheet of paper from his trench coat pocket. Pilet looks it over. It reads.

Basic Blades Conditioning.

1. 6am: Jog 20mins at the track
2. 6:25am: 40mins kickboxing
3. 7:15am: 40mins grappling
4. 8:05am: 40mins weapons fighting
5. 45 min break/shower
6. 9:30am: 60mins Shooting range/gun knowledge
7. 10:40am: 60 mins Auracast training
8. 11:40am: Done.

"Wow!" Said Pilet. "This is cool. I'm going to learn weapons fighting? And Auracast? Whatever that is. And this is all done by mid-day? That's not a raw deal!"

"It's not." Said Faxion. "But it *will be* difficult. The idea is not to overload or overstress you. You need to be in a good mindset to pass. And it'd be a damn shame if you had no time to enjoy the city while you're here. So take that time to relax here, or journey out there. Just keep yourself out of trouble please. My room is right next door, 3204. Just holler if you need something. Now, I had room service gather some of my books for you and leave them on the shelves of your study. There's a written test before the practical exam and if you fail that, well you're shit out of luck from the get-go."

"A written exam, *great*. I'd have actually gone to school if I knew you needed to read to be a Hired Blade. I thought it was all about kicking ass. I just want to hit stuff!"

"Only thing you'll be hitting is the books and some pads for a while, so make a MagmaMocha and get comfortable. Now, there's something absolutely imperative that needs to be done before we continue any further. A tradition passed down to every Hired Blade in the world."

Faxion takes a deep breath, exhales slowly, and brings his fingertips to meet before his chest, fingers spread apart. The room grows a bit cold on the inhale, then warm on the exhale. He continues this process as a small marble of blue light begins to form in the space between his hands.

The marble grows larger as electricity surges around it. Faxion compresses the now baseball-width orb down to the size of a pea. Pilet sits in silence, unsure of what is to come from this ritual. Faxion takes one final deep breath, and on the exhale, suddenly shoots the minuscule light projectile directly into Pilet's solar plexus.

KSHOOM

The projectile knocks Pilet back into his seat. In shock, he screeches painfully.

"UUNNGH!! AAAAGH!!"

A surge of pain and spasm rushes through Pilet's entire body as he gasps for air. All of his muscles uncontrollably contract, forcing him into a tight fetal position. He sits there, violently seizing, with veins bulging from his neck, forehead, and temples. His skin becomes red, as he begins to sweat profusely.

"NGGAAAAAAAHH!!!"

Just then, a shockwave of purple aura erupts from Pilet, knocking back Faxion as well as everything not bolted to the floor. Pilet's eyes glow violet as the pattern from his showdown with the gorilla returns to his skin.

"Ffaxx, whhatss ggoing onnn!?"

Faxion's palm begins to emit a light blue aura. He cultivates this energy and sends it toward Pilet. The Aura envelopes Pilet, coursing through his subtle energy systems. It brings a cooling effect to his entire body and numbs the pain of the ritualistic aura bolt.

"What a powerful reaction, I knew it! Look!" Faxion holds a mirror up to Pilet as he sees the effects of the Auracast. "This happened to you when you fought that Wurm King! You're very special my friend, I've never seen anything like this in my life!"

Pilet gasps as he collects himself.

"Wwhat, what was that!? And what is this!?"

"That was an "Aurabreak", a technique used by experienced Auracasters to unlock the natural barriers in someone's energy field, thus allowing for much greater use of Aura. It seems you have immense amounts of latent Aura stored within you, the kind inherited at birth. One or both of your parents must have been very powerful."

"And these glowy tattoos??" Said Pilet.

"Honestly? I have no idea. As I said, this is new to me. I'm incredibly intrigued. Now, take some aspirin for the aches because tomorrow we start *all cylinders firing*."

Faxion takes his hat and coat off and heads for his room.

Pilet finally gathers his wits about him. As he calms himself the patterns begin to disappear into his skin, and his eyes return to their typical mauve.

"Wait, Fax."

Faxion stops and turns his head inquisitively.

"Hmm?"

"Thanks. I still can't believe I'm really going to take the exam... It's insane. I've never wanted anything more in my life." He takes a deep breath, settling down from the auric beating he just took. "I just wanted you to know I appreciate it. I'm used to getting the short end of the stick... All my life. So this is kind of a breath of fresh air."

Faxion grins. He puts his hat on just to tip it at Pilet.

"It's only up from here Lad. It's *only up* from here." He turns and makes his way out the door.

Books lie scattered all over the floor, Pilet picks one up by the binding. A maroon cover, adorned with miscellaneous mandalas. Across the top it reads, *"Auracast for the simple-minded"*.

Pilet scoffs. "This guy..."

Over the course of the next two weeks, Pilet works tirelessly toward his goal. Many hours of Faxion, mercilessly beating the life out of him in sparring sessions, sharpens his reflexes. Dozens of fencing matches teach him how to lunge and riposte with a blade. Multiple trips to the shooting range give him the skills to handle a firearm. Several trips to the hospital show him how *not* to auracast fireballs. Before long, Pilet begins to show the true colors of a mercenary; multi-talented, lethal, and swift.

Two weeks later, he emerges the training grounds; confident in his newfound abilities. But, will it be enough to pass the notorious, ever-evolving Hired Blades Exam? The Sun sets on the horizon over Grand Titanus City, as the would-be Blade and his seasoned coach take a seat at a rickety bench overlooking Lake Titanus.

Pilet gazes meditatively into his reflection, holding a glass cola bottle below his lips as he takes a swig. His fingers covered in supportive athletic tape, a bandage runs across the bridge of his nose. Darkened, black and blue bruises lay beneath his left eye.

"Fax..." Said Pilet. "...Do you think I'm ready?"

"Honestly? No." Said Faxion. "Absolutely not at all."

"WHAT?!" Pilet stomps his feet and Chuck's the cola bottle over his shoulder, knocking an unsuspecting pigeon out of the air in the process. "What the hell do you have me doing all this shit for then?!" Yells Pilet, oblivious to the cloud of gray feathers falling from the sky behind him.

Faxion reaches into his trenchcoat and brandishes a cigar. He lights it, takes a puff, and exhales.

"You are, to say the least, completely terrible at most aspects of Bladesmanship." Faxion pauses. He takes another puff. "But what skills *you do* possess, *far* outweigh the gravity of your inabilities." He flips closed his lighter. *Shink*

"I believe you to be the dark horse of this year's exam. Not many know of you my friend but rest assured they will, and it will be for no other reason than for your performance. So, do I think you're ready?" Faxion pauses to fiddle with his cigar. "I think that you'll be ready when the time comes, and not a moment sooner. You have what many lack; adaptability and heart, and what a great combination of qualities to have..."

Pilet takes a moment to reflect on his mentor's answer. He sits down on the bench and rests his chin on his palm. "Well, guess I'm ready as I'll ever be..."

The two watch the sunset over the horizon, drinking a cola and smoking a cigar......

FOUR

The Hired Blades Exam

Room 3205, The Free Enterprise. The open window welcomes the crisp morning air into the suite. A gentle breeze flows through the bedroom, past an open laptop, over a stuffed duffle bag and into the room's cafe; where it settles itself into the lungs of Pilet Whydah. He takes a deep breath, slowly inhaling the fresh gift of the city skies. The sound of coffee pouring from the espresso machine into a porcelain mug fills the room. Pilet takes the last of his creamer from the mini fridge. He opens the cap and pours what's left into the mug, watching it fall, drip by frothy drip.

"Damn, I hate it black..."

He grabs his laptop and takes a seat at the coffee table. As Pilet opens up his emails, he re-reads messages from the past week.

"Sunday, October third: Hello! Congratulations candidate. Your request to participate in the 127th Hired Blades Licensing Exam has been approved! The test will take place at The Hired Blades Association Headquarters in Grand Titanus City. It will be held Monday, October 8th, at approximately 9:00 AM. Please make sure to prepare adequately with a No.2 pencil, Combative equipment of your choosing and a change of clothing. The duration of the Exam will last anywhere from 2 hours to several days, depending solely on the performance of each individual candidate. There will be a written portion before the physical examination; after which, eligible candidates will be transported to an undisclosed location for further testing. While the location changes every year, what we can say is to dress for dry hot weather, it's going to be a scorcher! Below is a copy of the waiver of liability, please read and electronically sign before arrival. Best of luck!"

Pilet closes the laptop. He plops on the bed and begins to stuff clothing and toiletries inside. While packing a pair of socks, he knocks over the jean jacket worn the day of his departure from Chamboree. Contents of the inside pocket spill out; some chewing gum, loose change, the bowie knife given by his friend James, and the letter handed to him by Nivia. Pilet picks up the parting gifts. He unsheathes the knife and stares at the dull, jagged edge.

"Phew, you really need a sharpening. Not much use to me like this, but just for old times sake..." Pilet takes Nivia's unopened letter and begins to rip at the seal with the sharpest edge he can find.

"I can't believe this was here the whole time, poor Nivia probably thinks I forgot all about her."

Pilet manages to open the envelope and unfolds the letter. It's written in magenta ink. With it is a printed photo of a young Pilet and Nivia, smiling together by a mountain stream. It brings him back to a time when the two had spent the morning gathering smooth stones to decorate a class project.

The letter reads,

"Dear Pilet,

I'm excited that you're finally able to chase your dreams. As long as I've known you, it's been plain to see that you want more from life than what Chamboree has to offer. I'll be worried about you, I know the Hired Blades go on scary missions and put their lives on the line for our safety. I think it's an amazing opportunity and I know you can do it, it's the job you were made for! Don't forget to call or write, it's going to be lonely here with just James. Um, there's something I've been wanting to tell you for a long time. I've always been afraid to tell you because I didn't want to ruin our friendship or get in your way but, well... I love you Pilet. I've had feelings for you ever since we were little and you fought the upperclassmen who stole my lunch money. You always stood up for me when the bully jocks or mean girls made fun of me. You never joined in on their cliquey behavior, I'm sure that's why you left all the sports teams. You have a really good heart, Pilet. And you're so brave. You always try to help those in need, no matter what the cost. When things get really tough just remember there's one person who appreciates your efforts. You are a hero Pilet. Go out there and make the world a better place, one dangerous mission at a time."

"- Love, Nivia -"

The letter floats to the ground as Pilet's shuddering hands release it. He sits there in silence, gazing at the blank wall in front of him.

"..."

A few minutes pass by as Pilet finally collects himself. He rubs his face vigorously, looking down at the floor in disbelief. A thousand thoughts rush through his head in an instant.

"This whole time, I had no idea... All those years of her coming to help me out at the stand, or playing referee between me and James. She would text me every time I cut class to make sure I was ok, every time! And she would *always* get me a present on my birthday. I thought she was just being a good friend. How could I be such an idiot..."

After a moment's pause he rubs his knees, pushes off the bed and stands to his feet. He stretches his shoulders and neck, readying himself for departure.

"This is it." Said Pilet. "I can't fail now, it's just not an option. I have people waiting for me to come back with that badge. I have to make things right by them. And Nivia..."

He looks down at the letter one more time.

"I love you Pilet."

Pilet re-seals the letter into its envelope. He readies the rest of his belongings, shuts the window and makes for the door. As he exits he takes a look back at the room that housed him for the past two weeks.

"So long Free Enterprise. Next stop; Adventure..."

As he closes the door to his suite, a familiar voice takes Pilet by surprise.

"Talking to yourself now? What took you so long??" Said Faxion, peering from over Pilet's shoulder.

The unexpected voice shocks Pilet. He leaps into the air as his belongings go flying.

"AAH! You freaking stalker!" Pilet picks up his bag. "Never any warning with you huh? I get it mister stealth assassin, you're *cool*. Can I just have a moment's peace? Psychopath."

A smug grin runs across Faxion's face.

"Nonsense!" He wraps his arm around Pilet's neck and whispers in his ear. "The time for peace is over, this is the dawn of war..."

Pilet pushes him off and scoffs.

"Crazy old man. If I die today it'll be a heart attack from the stress of living with you!"

HBA Headquarters

The pair take the elevator to the first floor and exit through the lobby. On their way out Faxion tips his fedora to the receptionist.

"Good day Derryl!" Said Faxion.

Pilet tips an invisible hat in towe.

"Good day Derryl!" Said Pilet, in the best impression of his mentor to date.

Derryl stores away some miscellaneous paperwork and greets the duo.

"Why Master Deadeye and Master Whydah, have a wonderful day! And Master Whydah, I wish you good luck and fortune on your big day. Under Master Deadeye's tutelage you're certain to be victorious."

"Thanks a bunch D." Said Pilet. "Tune in later to watch me smoke the competition."

The two exit the lobby and begin their walk towards Hired Blades HQ. Faxion flags down an FC-Taxi to hitch a quick ride. A 12 foot long

Huayangosaurus with a multi-seated saddle on it's back comes to Faxion's call. The 5 foot tall spiked reptile pulls around the curb to its side.

"Hey boss, where to?" Said the Huayangosaurus.

"Hired Blades Headquarters please." Said Faxion. "And I must say what immense shoulder spikes you have!"

"Thanks chief, the lady likes 'em. She won't let me shave 'em down you know? I keep getting 'em caught in stuff, but what are you gonna do. *Sigh* The things I do for love."

Not long after, Faxion and Pilet arrive at their destination. They dismount from the spiny reptile and tip him generously.

"Thanks boss, good luck gettin' that badge kid." Said the Huayangosaurus.

"No, thank *you*." Said Pilet. "Give the wife and kids a squeeze for me."

"Will do." Said the FC taxi, as he continues his arduous traffic route.

The duo turns to face their destination. Hired Blades HQ, a Massive building with the symbol of The Hired Blades Association plastered across the facade. Five, double-edged swords side by side, behind a large diamond that's been cracked down the center. Before the building lies a lavish courtyard with shrubbery trimmed in the shape of diamonds. Beyond this sits a large set of staircases with handrails, leading up to Blades HQ. As they walk through the courtyard they pass scattered groups of candidates, muttering to themselves in small droves.

"Hey look, that's the Kingkiller from Chamboree."

"He took out a Wurm King on his own? But he's so scrawny..."

"Nah he must be super strong!"

"A Veteran Blade was there too, he probably did most of the work for him. Kill stealer..."

In the past two weeks news has spread throughout the Blades community, of Pilet and Faxion's battle in Chamboree. Assorted candidates come to shake Pilet's hand, and congratulate him on a job well done. Others skeptically mock from a distance. Pilet and Faxion greet the candidates in passing and continue up the steps to the entrance.

"Damn!" Said Pilet. "They're calling me the King Killer now huh? This is nice, people know who I am! Gotta say I could get used to this treatment."

"Word to the wise, don't." Said Faxion. "You shouldn't let that battle get to your head. It's great that you beat a King, but that's only a fraction of what you're about to see today. And besides, you had to use your "Ace in the hole" to even put a scratch on it. You remember this terminology, yes? It may be in the written exam."

"Yeah yeah. "Ace in the hole: Any technique used by a Blade that greatly enhances their combat capabilities and/or fighting style. These skills should be used sparingly or as a last resort, due to the heavy strain they tend to put on the user." God, you know how many times I had to memorize that?"

"Good. Hopefully you won't need it next time. Remember, manage your aura wisely. Just because you have a lot, doesn't mean you won't run low. Wouldn't want to be stuck dead in the water against a horde of Wurm coyotes now would you?..."

They reach the top and enter the revolving doors. Inside they are met with marble halls, beautiful cut gems adorned on pedestals and portraits of prominent Blades past and present along the wall. They pass a Lava Bean Cafe, built into the lobby. Pilet spies Faith and Yuuna standing on a long line of candidates and Blades, waiting to place their order. Pilet and Faxion walk over. As Pilet taps Faith on the shoulder, she inquisitively turns her head.

"Hey, long time no see!" Said Pilet. "You guys excited for the test?"

"Pilet! Hi!" Said Yuuna.

"What a pleasant surprise." Said Faith. "It looks like all of Faxion's candidates are addicted to coffee."

"Faxion's candidates?" Said Pilet. "You guys are getting sponsored by Fax too?"

"Yup!" Said Yuuna. "He's a real pal! We couldn't have entered without the *ok* from someone as notable as him, seeing as neither of us trained at the academy."

The Blades have several academies worldwide, responsible for the training of potential candidates. Those who aspire to take the exam without academic training are called prospects, and are required the sponsorship of a qualified individual to participate. It is notoriously difficult for prospects to pass...

Faxion tips his hat.

"Anytime girls. Your parents would be proud of how far you've come. I'm just happy to have helped get you there."

Just then; the sound of a row of mugs shattering on the floor echoes throughout the Cafe.

Crash *Thud*

Two young men get in a scuffle on the ground. The one on top, a spiky haired platinum blonde. Very muscular with a full set of white, state of the art plate armor. The bottom man sports a black tank top reading "Funk" across a blue monkey with shuttered sunglasses. He wears a brunette mohawk with indigo tips.

"Get your big ass off me you tool!" Yells the mohawked man. "I'll kick the shit outta you I swear! It's not like I'm lying, everyone knows you're still sucking on your Dad's taint you spoiled punkass bitch!"

The armored man starts raining down punches on his grounded opponent, who begins covering his face.

"Oh yeah? Is that so, band geek?! When are you going to kick the shit out of me hmm?!? I'm waiting!!"

A group of other candidates on either side rush to the fight. A Hachidorinese warrior with two blue stripes in his corn-rowed hair pulls the armored assailant off of the mohawked man. His armor, the same as that of Max; but with blue trim and a blue chest gem instead of gold.

"Lazlow, chill chill." Said the interloper. "We got bigger bones to break. These guys are small time, don't waste your energy."

"Let go Arturo!" Said Lazlow. "These third rate losers think they actually stand a chance this year, it pisses me off! The lot of them don't deserve to step foot on the testing ground!"

Two young men help the mohawked candidate off of the ground, both wearing t-shirts with the same logo as him. One man, tall with long ginger hair and a beard. The other; average in height, with a goatee and jet black, medium length wavy hair. They both carry guitars on their backs.

"You ok Lukah?" Said the goateed musician. "Me and Svenn got your back if pretty boy wants trouble, ya know? These guys don't know what the Funk Munkeys are made of, ya know??"

Svenn just flips his hair and nods.

"Mhmm..."

Lukah collects himself and tries to lunge at Lazlow, only to be stopped by his friends.

"Let me at 'em Clint! I'm not done with this self absorbed prick!" Said Lukah. "I just told him what everyone else is thinking, he's a piece of shit riding his old man's coat-tails to success. If he doesn't like to hear it then he should get off his high-ass horse!"

"Enough brother. We gotta save our energy for the big day."

A fourth Funk Munkey approaches. Clearly at least a decade older than his crew, bags under his eyes and brown, matted dreadlocks down past his elbows. His mocha skin, covered in tattoos. His raspy, deep voice beckons.

"Lazlow The Gavel." Your reputation precedes you. We're not lookin' for trouble. But if you are, we're not gonna be backin' down."

He pulls an old wooden drumstick out of his back pocket, carved with runic symbols. As he inhales a deep breath and rubs the instrument with his thumb, a dagger sized blade of pure yellow aura extends from the tip.

"Danba The Witch Doctor." Said Lazlow. "I'm not scared of your ridiculous folk castery, go back to Dragon's Alley with that nonsense! A foreigner like you could never stack up to an authentic Kettlenian Elite like myself! I'm 270 pounds of pure, blind justice. You're just a lightweight in charge of a band of incompetent baboons."

Danba's shoots Lazlow an offended, slightly puzzled look. He turns to Arturo.

"How are you gonna rep a damn fool like this? You come from outta town yourself, no?"

Arturo replies. "*My* father is a warrior chief, not a Zardenian peasant. You just worry about yourself, drummer boy."

Two figures emerge silently, from shadows cast on the ground by the guitarists. Assassins in matching stealth garbs and cloth masks that cover the lower face. One female, adorned in maroon and a long, scarlet three strand braid. The other male, dressed in turquoise. His teal hair, short with a gelled-flip in the front.

"Starting trouble again Laz?.." Said the turquoise assassin. "The day just started, we can't take our eyes off of you for a second can we."

Taken by surprise, the guitarists reach for their sidearms; Blade standard issue Stinger pistols. But as they frantically clutch their holsters, they quickly realize their weapons are missing.

"Looking for these?" Said the maroon assassin.

The two each hold up a Funk Monkey's Stinger, displaying the skill of their sleight of hand. They toss them to the side and both fold their arms in authoritative fashion. She continues.

"You guys are out of your league. You might as well drop out of the Exam *now*. I'd like to say no one would judge you, but we will. Still, it's better to exit with your life while you can..."

The confused and frustrated guitarists pull their guitars over their shoulders and begin to strum. Aura starts to emit from the instruments. The assassin's eyebrows raise.

"How unwise." Said the turquoise assassin. "I guess it can't be helped. Dabria, I'm feeling a code: Blossoming death lotus for these two. What do you say?"

"Sounds good to me, Asger." Replies Dabria. She turns to face the musicians. "A word of advice boys, me and my brother are about to annihilate you. You should probably close your eyes and imagine a peaceful, happy place. Wouldn't want your decapitated head to be frozen in an unsavory facial expression."

"Hmmf!"

Svenn scoffs and flips his hair. His bass guitar begins cultivating more aura.

"*You* don't know what you're getting yourselves into, ya know?!" Said Clint.

Arturo takes a ready, crouching stance and puts his hand on the hilt of his M8 Shred longsword. The serrated edge of the blade peeks out for a moment as he prepares to draw.

Lukah pulls a chrome microphone from his messenger bag and begins clearing his throat. A bead of sweat drops from his forehead.

Danba keeps his drumstick dagger trained on Lazlow as the armored Kettlenian exclaims.

"This is gonna be fun."

Some fifteen feet away, Pilet and his group spectate the action. Faxion begins to prepare himself for intervention.

"No no, this simply won't do..."

As he takes a step toward the altercation, he is met with a muscular forearm across his chest; halting him from proceeding. A massive man with a white set of plate armor similar to Lazlow's stands beside him.

The armored man mutters, "My boy, my problem.".

Surprised, Faxion turns and immediately recognises the man.

"Well now, look who it is..."

Faxion stays with his group as the large man approaches the scuffle. As he draws near, he pulls his Hired Blades badge from a compartment in his armor and flashes it to the battle-ready group.

"This is Lazlow the Vice speaking, Enforcer of the Hired Blades Association. Would the Emissaries to each group involved in this altercation please step forth."

The candidates lower their weapons and release any stored aura. Lazlow the Gavel and Danba the Witch Doctor step forward.

"Lazlow the Gavel reporting father, I mean sir." Said Lazlow Jr.

"Danba the Witch Doctor reportin' sir." Said Danba.

"Which one of you is responsible for this mess?" Replied Lazlow Sr.

"The Funk Monkeys sir!" Said Lazlow Jr. "I was berated by one of their members, he insulted you as well!"

"Is this true Danba?" Said Lazlow Sr.

"It is true sir, I gotta apologise for my young friend Lukah. He's a good boy at heart but he can be a bit brash. However, The Gavel is the first one to get physical here. I'm just tryin' to keep the peace in this situation. The Reaper Elite have gotten involved in a way that incited a riot among my associates. We just responded in a protective manner"

"Like *you* could've protected yourselves from us..." Muttered Lazlow Jr.

"Enough boy." Said Sr. "Today is the day of the Exam, you're not even Blades yet and you're already acting like a bunch of children! I don't want to hear of another issue until you're on the battlefield, then *by all means* you can kill each other for all I care. You are dismissed."

The two emissaries turn toward their crews. Lazlow Sr. grabs Jr. by the bicep and whispers to him.

"And next time drop a few elbows *before* someone breaks it up. It's perfectly legal in self defense, and it leaves a scar they'll never forget for crossing us."

Jr. grins. He replies, "Will do sir. Will do..."

The Prospects Unite!

Over at the bar, a barista mops the floor of spilled coffee. He bends over to pick up one of the few mugs left intact, and as he gets up he slips and falls on a wet patch. Flailing about, he sends the mug flying towards Pilet and company. The mug soars through the air as it nears an unsuspecting Faith from behind, picking up speed. A unanimous gasp resounds throughout the Cafe. Faith turns her head and notices the dense ceramic mug headed straight for her face.

Shing

The sound of a blade being drawn is the last thing she hears before the mug is sliced clean in half, mid-flight. The two pieces fly past either side of her, missing by inches. Not but 2 feet away stands Max Quinn, slowly re-sheathing his M7 Lacerate longsword.

"Oooh." "Aaah."

Miscellaneous cafe goers applaud the quick swordsmanship skills of the young Sanda warrior.

Still stunned by the sudden action, Faith is speechless. She shakes her head to wake up and offers a hand to Max.

"Wow, thank you!" Said Faith. "That mug almost took my eye out. How did you move so fast?"

Max replies. "You're very welcome, the Sanda tribe are known for our lightning style. The speed of our draw is unparalleled among the warrior people of Hachidori. Just glad I could be of assistance."

A Lava Bean shift manager walks over to the group and addresses Max.

"Sir, you're going to need to pay for that. It was a 19.98 aurem mug." She said.

"Oh, oh my..." Said Max. "My apologies, let me take care of that." He looks back and forth awkwardly and reaches for his wallet. Faxion puts a hand on his shoulder.

"Please, let me." Faxion flashes the manager his Blades badge. "Put it on my tab."

"Sure thing." Said the manager. "Just keep that thing sheathed in here..."

The girls shoot her a disgusted look. Pilet slaps Max on the arm.

"Dude, that was wild shit! I had no idea you could handle a blade like that. I take back everything I said about you being weird." Said Pilet.

"I, well... Thank you?" Said Max.

"The nerve of that woman." Said Faith. "It was their fault the mug went airborne anyway! You know what..."

Faith motions to follow the manager but is stopped by her sister.

"Just let it go sis, Fax took care of it." Said Yuuna.

"Fine." Said Faith. "I should make a call to corporate for that crap... Anyway, what's your name, friend?"

"Max, Max Quinn. I was just passing through to get a drink for my father when I caught the tail-end of that altercation. I noticed Pilet and Mr. Faxion so I figured I'd ask what happened, that's when the cafe worker took a spill..."

"Well, we were hoping to recruit some candidates at this cafe for our team. Would you like to join? And while we're at it, Pilet! You should join us too!" Said Faith.

"Team?" Said Pilet. "What team? I didn't know we needed to team up for the exam."

"It's really highly recommended." Said Yuuna. "Most of the graduates of Blades academy have already teamed up by the time the Exam rolls around, but us prospects usually have to make teams the day of when we get here. It's really dangerous to go in without a group, there's so many challenges that could kill you at the testing grounds."

"That's what those two groups were." Said Faith. "The Funk Monkeys and The Reaper Elite. It looks like they got into some sort of disagreement, but lucky for them when you're part of a team your friends have your back! It's so much better than going alone."

"Well I'm in!" Said Pilet. "Let's get this Blades License, the four of us together are sure to pass!"

"It would be my pleasure." Said Max. "I am a prospect as well. I had not considered teaming with other candidates as I'm familiar with no one. I'm sure with our combined effort this exam will be no challenge at all!"

"Then it's decided!" Said Faxion. "A full team of prospects, what a glorious occasion! And how uncommon."

"Yay! Welcome to the team guys." Said Yuuna.

"Awesome!" Said Faith. "Pilet, The King Killer is on our side! And we could really use those sword skills Max, I'm counting on you."

"And don't forget his sick braids!" Said Pilet. He brushes his own buzzed head. "We got to show these other punks which team has the best hair around here."

Max feels the top of his head as he releases a bellowing laugh. Faith and Yuuna look at each other, then back to the Sanda warrior and giggle. A booming voice echoes throughout Blades HQ from the sound system.

"Good morning candidates, and welcome to the 127th Hired Blades Association Licensing Exam. Please check in at the admission desks as soon as possible as the Exam will be starting in approximately 20 minutes. There will be a holding area for your belongings at the door to the Written exam room. Please enter with only your No.2 pencil, no unnecessary electronics will be permitted past the holding area. Thank you and best of luck."

Kenzo Quinn approaches and plops his hand on his son's shoulder.

"What's the holdup on that tea my boy, your test is starting soon! Wouldn't want to be falling asleep in the middle of your history portion now would we?"

"Father!" Said Max. "I've been invited to join Pilet and his friends team for the exam! I will do my best to represent the Sanda with Honor."

Kenzo's hands slap his head in excitement. "Excellent! I was hoping you'd make yourself some friends boy! I hear the exam is particularly difficult when braved alone, still the Sanda are no strangers to being outnumbered."

Faxion mutters to Pilet. "Did he really think Max could do it by himself?"

Pilet replies. "You're one to talk buddy, you sent me out here without the heads up about teams."

"Oh posh." Said Faxion. "As the girls' sponsor I would've asked for you to join them if they hadn't invited you first. Regardless, maybe it would've been good training to be mauled by a giant desert scorpion by yourself."

"A desert what!?" Said Pilet.

"Oop, I've said too much." replied Faxion. "Now ladies this is Kenzo Quinn, Max's father and a Fourth degree Sanda master."

"Oh hello sir." Said Faith. "It's a pleasure to meet you, my name's Faith. Your son just saved me from an evil coffee mug! He's quite the swordsman."

"Hi Mr. Quinn!" Said Yuuna. "We're really excited to have Max helping us out!"

"What's up Kenzo." Said Pilet. "Happy Max is tagging along, just in case an army of teacups shows up to avenge their friend."

Kenzo shoots Pilet a puzzled look.

"It's a long story, father." Said Max.

"Right... Well I'm ecstatic for you all!" Said Kenzo. "I'm sure my son will do a fine job aiding you to victory. I'll be rooting for you from the sidelines! And master Faxion! What a surprise seeing you again!"

"That it is my friend." Replies Faxion. "I'm very happy to have Max join my sponsored bunch. When this is all over we *must* have a celebration! Let's not jinx it though." Faxion turns to the team of prospects. "For now keep your heads in the game, the real test has yet to begin. Let's head to the proctoring grounds for further instruction."

"Goodbye father." Said Max. "The next time you see me I'll have the proud badge of the Blades."

Kenzo bearhugs Max and lifts him into the air, squeezing so hard their armor makes a clanging sound. Max wheezes as Kenzo releases him.

"Good luck son. Go out there and make the Sanda proud."

The group says their goodbyes to Kenzo as they make their way to the written exam portion. Each candidate checks in with admission and leaves their belongings at the holding area. They enter a large auditorium-styled room filled to the brim with small, white writing desks. Each desk is spaced apart to maintain a 3 foot distance between. As Pilet, Yuuna, Max and Faith enter; Faxion stops at the door.

"This is as far as I go folks. Do your best, I know this sheet of paper isn't enough to stop you from becoming the toughest Blades in history." Faxion grabs Pilet by the shoulder. "And Pilet, remember everything we went over. Trust me, you've got this. But also... Don't muck it up."

Pilet grins. "Beat it old man, I'm plenty smart enough for this. You'll see. I'll be like, the first one out of their seat."

"Yeah, to use the bathroom for your nerves." Said Faith. She gives Pilet a mischievous smile. "Let's see how smart you got in two weeks."

Pilet gives Faith a contemptuous side-eye. "Hmmph. I'll ace this. Just because I don't carry around a dusty, beat up book like you doesn't mean I can't."

A Written Fiasco

The candidates enter and begin to take their seats in the massive auditorium. The exam proctor walks onto the stage in the front of the room. Wearing a black leather jacket and blue Jean's. His sleeves are rolled up showcasing a pair of thick, lit up high-tech vambraces around his wrists. A navy blue headband holds down his dirty blonde, slicked back hair, revealing a serious look plastered across his brow.

"Good morning candidates." Says the proctor. "My name is Caffo Gilwick, I will be your Proctor for the 127th Hired Blades Blades Licensing Exam. Today's written examination will be composed of four sections; Hired Blades history, knowledge of combat, geography and Wurm theory. Any candidates caught looking at their neighbors papers will be promptly escorted out of the exam with no opportunity for refund. Also, it goes without saying that the use of aura cast during your exam is expressly forbidden under punishment of disqualification. You have exactly 90 minutes to complete this exam. Please have your No.2 pencils ready. The time is now 9:00AM, you may begin."

Caffo takes a seat at a desk placed specifically for him at the center of the stage. Several Hired Blades strategically placed around the room take authoritative postures, watching the candidates actions intently. Pilet opens his test booklet.

"Section one: Hired Blades History. #1.What year did Dennis Rundham defeat the Mountain dragon Sindro to free the people of West Minnow?"

"Oh what?" Said Pilet. "It's not multiple choice? I suck at dates, shit uh... 2044? Let's go with that. I know it was in the 40's..."

As Pilet continues to haphazardly answer his questions, the clock ticks on. Minutes pass by as assorted candidates nervously tap their pencils and bite their nails to the root. In the distance a candidate begins to sweat profusely in frustration. He mutters to himself in fear.

"I, I can't do this... How was I supposed to know *why* the Blades symbol has a cracked diamond on it?! I wasn't even alive when they were formed!"

Faith is positioned one seat staggered in front of him. Quietly breezing through the exam. The frantic candidate leans his neck to peek at her paper.

"She seems smart, she has to know... Just one small gander..."

He leans a bit too far, as two Hired Blade proctors instantly appear in front of him. Frightened by the blinding speed of the Blades, the candidate frantically falls out of his seat.

"Oh shit! Wait! I was just... I had a wedgie! I just had to pick at it!!"

The Blades lift him up off of the floor and begin walking him out as the crowd turns.

"NO! You can't! I spent every dime I had to take this exam today! I need to be a Blade! My Dad paid for my schooling, he's going to kill me!" Said the Candidate.

"You should have thought about that before cheating." Said the Blade on his left.

He is escorted out of the room, leaving a sinking feeling in the belly of the remaining candidates. Caffo speaks.

"There were 348 of you this morning, now there are 347. If that worries you, then you're applying for the wrong career. Prepare for that number to continue to decrease."

Phew

Faith lets out a sigh of relief as she returns to her paper.

"I thought I had done something wrong when those two showed up behind me, guess I'm so good I inspire cheaters."

As Pilet returns to his test, he too reaches the question about the symbol of the Hired Blades.

"#22. Why does the Hired Blades symbol feature a large cracked diamond behind five, double edged swords?"

He recounts a moment on the train ride from Chamboree, when he asked Faxion about his Hired Blades badge.

"Hey Fax." Said Pilet. "What's the deal with the Blades badge? I saw it when you showed the cops, the thing looks more like a pro wrestling championship belt to me."

Faxion laughs. He pulls the badge from his pocket and brandishes it.

"Well. These five swords represent the first five Hired Blades to ever exist. You see in 2031, Kettlena's president Rodney Petersin had an incredible run in office. He worked together with the people of Kettlena to solve major issues in

*hunger, poverty and illness. But, while on a campaign against discrimination;
Rodney began to notice a shift in the morale of his supporters. Fearing a military
coup was brewing, he enlisted the aid of five, highly regarded ex-military
generals as his personal bodyguards. The five defended president Petersin from
waves of contract killers on the night of his famous Grand Titanus address.
While succeeding in their efforts, all but one general fell in battle that night.
His name was Gregory Galant. After the incident, the president worked
hand in hand with Galant to create an elite group separated from the state to
undertake dangerous tasks. Thus, The Hired Blades Association was born."*

"That's cool. Damn, God only knows what those guys went through that
night. So that explains the swords, what about the diamond?"

"Well, traditionally each president elect of Kettlena is given a priceless
diamond ring to signify their position as head of government. However after
realizing the attack on his life was set up by his peers, president Petersin
punched a stone wall in frustration. This broke his knuckle and chipped the
diamond ring something fierce. Obviously, a diamond can't be cracked straight
down the middle, but the visual of a chip just didn't have the same effect you
know? Anyway, he then sold the ring and donated the proceeds to General
Galant as a token of partnership, renouncing the corrupt politicians who
had once backed him. Galant used the money to craft the first airship fleet of
the Hired Blades Association, as well as build Hired Blades HQ. It was this
"cracked" diamond that allowed the first batch of fresh Blades to get off the
ground and become the organization we are today...

Pilet picks up his pencil and begins to scratch a makeshift answer.

"*The president punched a wall, broke his special ring and sold it to make
the Blades. The swords represent five badass dead generals.*" Perfect. It was
something like that, I'm sure they'll get the point."

As time passes the candidates zoom through the exam. The fear of
failing causes miscellaneous rumbling stomachs to be heard throughout
the auditorium. Question after question, Pilet answers to the best of his
ability.

"#37: When engaged in swordplay, what is the proper technique to
parry a lunging stab. #56: What is the name of the city, home to Kettlena's
largest Coliseum. #71: What is the reason for the recent concern of the
Wurm threat spanning across the globe."

As the clock strikes 10:30AM, Caffo Gilwick stands and approaches the front of the stage.

"Time's up, candidates. Drop your pencils and flip your exams face down. A Licensed Hired Blade will come to each section to retrieve them. Once your exam has been taken, you may take a seat in the lounge right outside. It should take approximately thirty minutes to finish grading each test."

The candidates have their tests taken by roaming Blades Proctors. Once relieved of their tests, candidates begin forming single file lines in the aisles and start making their way out of the auditorium, and into the lounge. Pilet, who's last name is Whydah, leaves his seat in the "W" section towards the end of the room.

The Lone Archeologist

As one of the last candidates to exit, he looks pensively for his new group of companions. He enters a massive lounge, filled with several sets of couches and chairs setup by wall mounted televisions. To the side lies a bar with a wide variety of drink selections on tap and a rerun of a recent Pachycephalosaurus fight playing on the TV. As Pilet passes by he recognizes a familiar green dinosaur on the screen to be Mortimer the Enforcer, walloping his adversary. He pauses and takes a seat at the bar to witness the festivities.

"Give it to 'em, big green." Muttered Pilet.

A candidate sitting on the stool next to him mistakes Pilet's cheering for an insult. A tan skinned man of average build. He wears a green plaid button-up, well worn and faded. Sporting beige, well fitting pants and a wire wrapped white and black crystal around his neck. A silver watch on one wrist and a bracelet of cherrywood beads on the other. He holds a cigarette in between his index and middle finger, tapping on the countertop. His hair a dark brown, short around the sides with some length to the top.

"Excuse me?" Said the man in plaid. "I'm not big, and who am I giving what to?"

Very confused, Pilet turns to the man in green and quickly realizes his fault.

"Oh, my bad buddy. I meant the green Dino, dishing out the beating up there."

Pilet points towards the mounted TV screen.

"I met that guy, he's pretty chill. Scary as hell though... Not going to lie I almost shit my pants when I saw him. Wouldn't want to be on the other side of the cage with *his* big scaly ass."

"Right... Ok, well never mind then. My mistake." He motions for the bartender. "Hey, I'll have another pumpkin scotch over here."

The bartender takes an orange bottle of liquor from the middle shelf. He pours it in a fresh glass for the man in plaid.

"How'd you fare on the written?" Said the stranger as he lifts his glass toward his face to take a swig.

"Honestly, meh. I feel like I did enough to pass, just not with flying colors. Initially I thought I'd do awesome. But I guess studying for like, 15 minutes a night didn't pay off too well. Good thing my sponsor likes to talk so much or I'd really be worried. Yourself?"

"I feel like I did alright. The name's Bhujanga by the way, Bhujanga Garuda. I'm an archeologist so the geography and history sections were a cinch. The auracast questions didn't give me too much trouble either, considering I've been casting since I was 5. The combat questions gave me some trouble though, don't use guns or swords all that much so I don't have a world of experience to draw from."

Pilet's eyebrows raise in surprise.

"I'm Pilet, Pilet Whydah. Did you say you're an archeologist? Dude you must be making serious cash *already*, why go through the pain of being a Blade? You could like, die... Archeologists can just hire *us* to protect them from all the scary stuff that goes "bump" in the darkness of an ancient ruin."

Bhujanga takes a drag of his cigarette, the flame on the tip glows an emerald green. He exhales dark indigo smoke.

"I work best alone. Don't need anyone to protect me, they usually end up getting in the way regardless. Plus when you're part of a team you need to distribute the pay, which I'd rather not. The only reason I'm here is so that I can legally protect myself on excavations, this way I'll be able to work without hiring an archeologist crew or other Blades. That's why

I'm taking this exam solo, without joining any team. It's good practice for what's to come."

"Shit." Said Pilet. "I mean I'm pretty confident in my own abilities, but you're on a whole different level aren't you. Gotta admire that fighting spirit!"

Pilet calls the bartender over and orders a round on him.

"Not many candidates around trying to take this exam by themselves." Said Pilet. *This guys going to be dead by the morning, he's gonna need this drink.* He thought. "I hope you do well buddy! Here's to you."

Pilet raises his glass. Bhujanga's brow slants in surprise at the kind gesture. After a brief pause of reflection, Bhujanga meets Pilet's glass with his own. The drinks clang together.

"I appreciate it..." Said Bhujanga "Hope I see you at the finish line. Friend..."

The two finish their drinks just in time for the results of the exam to be displayed across the various monitors in the lounge. Caffo Gilwick's voice echoes over the PA system.

"Good day candidates, your results will now be released for your viewing. They will be displayed as follows: Each candidate's full name will be listed in alphabetical order, side by side with either a red "X" or a green Check mark. Check means pass, X is fail. Those receiving a Checkmark may proceed to the gymnasium across the hall for further testing. To any given a red X, we appreciate your interest in joining the Hired Blades Association. Please exit through the double doors past the bar, study hard and try again in two years. Thank you for your contribution in the 127th Hired Blades Exam."

Pilet looks up and studies the many names listed on the screen. Every few seconds the listing rotates to the next set of names displayed in alphabetical order. The first name he recognizes appears. "Bhujanga Garuda, Check."

"Oh hey buddy, you made the cut!"

He turns to see an empty barstool beside him where Bhujanga sat moments ago.

"Oh, strange guy..."

He continues to read as his allies' names begin to appear in the listing. The first pops up "Max Quinn, Check.".

Pilet sighs in relief.

"Nice, that's one teammate still in this."

"Faith Sierro, Check.", "Yuuna Sierro, Check."

"Good good... Now, just me...."

As the screen continues to cycle through listings, mere seconds begin to feel like hours in Pilet's mind. A warm uncomfortable gurgle greets his stomach, as a bead of sweat pours down his brow. He pinches the front of his shirt and begins to fan the perspiration accumulating across his chest. The "W" section finally appears. He intently scans the list to discover his fate.

"Waldridge, Wannya, Wes, Wendigo, Why are there so many W's?!?"

His eyes finally lock onto his name. "Pilet Whydah, Check.".

"YES!!" Shouts Pilet as he slams his empty glass down on the table.

Taking the rag off of his shoulder to clean a freshly washed wine glass, the bartender glares at him from a distance.

"Congrats, don't break the merchandise kid." Said the bartender.

Pilet awkwardly places the glass to the side and flashes the bartender a bashful smile. He looks around as some candidates jump for joy while others hang their heads in defeat. By the looks of it, about one third of the applicants have failed the exam. They make their way out of the lounge, past the bar and through the double doored exit. Miscellaneous failing candidates complain about their experience.

"This test was bullshit. I'm becoming a plumber, if I'm going to deal with shit I might as well get paid."

"It's not fair! Once that guy got thrown out I got so nervous. I couldn't even spell my name right!"

"I can't believe I studied the wrong year's material. Why does the library carry books from two tests prior?..."

Unable to make out his teammates in the crowd, Pilet begins to cut through waves of excited entrants across the lounge. Beneath one large monitor lies a set of scarlett, hand carved doors, leading down a beautiful marble hallway. The walls are lined with assorted high tech weaponry and armor, as well as artifacts radiating ancient aura. As Pilet reaches the end of the display hall; he enters a vast gymnasium, filled with anxious exam goers.

The Physical Begins: Birth of The Hidden Blades!

Bleachers surround the perimeter, seating many a spectator to the testing process. The softwood flooring offers a nice give to the joints of athletes performing across the room. Lines separating different zones have been set down with black tape. On one end of the gymnasium lies a sizable shooting range, allowing about a dozen candidates to fire at a time. Adjacent to this are two cages side-by-side to test candidates' martial arts skill. Next to that lies a set of squares for fencing matches; lined with training sabers, fencing foils and all other manner of dueling weapons.

As Pilet leaves the hall he's greeted with the Voice of various exam Proctors, coordinating with Caffo Gilwick over what candidates are going where first. Caffo pulls the mic on his headset close to his mouth and begins to speak to the approaching entrants.

"Candidates, welcome to the Gymnasium of The Hired Blades Headquarters. The next phase of the exam will see you tested on your various physical fitness and combative skills, to determine whether or not you are eligible for the demanding nature of being a Licensed Hired Blade. For this portion you will now meet with your teams and report back to these team registration desks in 10 minutes. Please have your team name ready with the full names of each of your members, as well as each team's emissary decided."

Pilet looks around pensively for his comrades. Off to the left standing by the fighting cages he sees Max, methodically practicing a martial arts form. He then turns to the right, noticing Yuuna and Faith doing isometric exercises in a lunging posture.

"Finally!" Said Pilet.

He first heads over to Max. Again cutting through the crowds of entrants blocking his path. After some finagling he reaches his swordsman teammate.

"Max!" Said Pilet. "What's up dude?! Sorry to interrupt your dance, but we gotta get the crew together and make a name for ourselves. Caffo says we're gonna be teamed up for the rest of the exam."

Max halts his technique and meditatively bows. He replies.

"It's the "Waves of Harmony" form. Performing this ritual is said to grant the practitioner balance and serenity within the subtle energy systems. Also, I can see our friends over by the fencing racks. It seems they are doing training of their own."

The two spot Yuuna and Faith on the far right of the gymnasium. The girls are warming up with some light stretching and isometric postures. Lunging down while reaching overhead, breathing slowly and mindfully. As Pilet and Max approach them, the girls finish their routine with hands clasped at their chest. As they see the boys draw near, Yuuna reacts.

"Hey guys! Fancy meeting you here!"

"Yo!" Said Pilet. "Glad we all passed the written test in the first place."

"It's about time to officially form our team right?" Said Faith.

"Yes ma'am" Said Max. "What an exciting endeavor. Caffo says we need an emissary and a team name. Any suggestions?"

The group takes a pause, each of the members ponders the possible combinations in their head. Yunna breaks the silence.

"Well, I nominate Pilet for team emissary! He's seen and fought a real life Wurm King, so he's the only one who's made a name for himself between us. I haven't stopped hearing other candidates talking about him all day. Plus every emissary needs a Title, which Pilet has! "The King Killer" sounds *super* fierce. The rest of us might not generate any respect as unknown prospects, but he sure will!"

"Oh hell yeah!" Exclaims Pilet. "Well I second that! If anyone gives us trouble I'll make sure they know they've made a mistake."

Max and Faith look at each other skeptically, imagining a hot-headed Pilet representing their crew in front of the Blades Committee.

"Hold that thought." Said Faith.

Faith takes Max to the side for a moment to speak in private.

"So..." Said Faith. "What's your take on that? He can be a little brash, and I'm not sure if that's a good look for the rest of us towards the proctors and examiners."

"I agree." Said Max. "I have my doubts as well, but I do have to say your sister has a point. On paper he's got more experience than us, and it's been broadcasted clearly across channel 6 news. No one knows me and you, he's the famous one."

Max makes a cringey face.

"At the very least, if he causes trouble he'll have to answer for himself. Could you imagine being an emissary and having to take responsibility for every mistake he makes? I mean we saw it with The Funk Munkeys, that Mohawked boy probably gives The Witch Doctor a lot of trouble. As emissary, at least that fool from The Reaper Elite can take the fall for his own antics."

Faith's expression becomes a mix between that of someone who has just seen a ghost and a war veteran seeing horrible flashbacks of battle.

Her eyebrows lift as she smacks her lips together and mutters, "Yeah... Good point. Alright, it's decided then..."

The two turn back around to face Pilet and Yuuna. Faith and Max point at Pilet and agree in unison. "He's emissary."

"Awesome!" Said Pilet.

"The poor boy has no idea what he's agreed to." Whispered Max to Faith.

"It's ok." Muttered Faith. "Better him than us." She clasps her hands and turns to the others. "So ok, now that we have our Emissary sorted out... We need a team name. Any ideas?" "Ooh ooh! I know! Let's go with, "The Starchild". Said Yuuna.

"Starchild is singular" Said Max. "There's more than one of us..."

"Starchilds?" Said Yuuna. "Or wait. Starchildren! Let's be born of the cosmos..."

"I'm sorry but I'm not doing that." Said Pilet. "The other guys are going to laugh at us, and eventually someone's going to try to steal my lunch money. You know how long I've been saving this lunch money? I cut class in school for like... Three years!"

"Hmmph!" Pouts Yuuna. "Don't be mean. Do *you* have any bright ideas??"

"Pilet relax, no one's taking your lunch money." Said Faith. "First of all, I'm sorry Yuuna but I'm also not doing that. You could make that your title though, since neither of us have one yet. As for our name, I think "The Arcane Assailants" sounds nice. Rolls off of the tongue nicely, no?"

"Hah." "No?" Said Pilet, in his best Faxion impression. He tips an invisible fedora on his head. "You sound like Fax now, no? "Starchilds" sounded better, no? I don't think it's a good fit. Not sure what you guys' fighting style is like but I don't use auracast all that much. I like to run around and stab things, not very "Arcane" of me."

"I agree" Said Max. "Of course we're all skilled in the arcane arts to some degree, but I personally prefer the blade over the spell. As far as a team name goes, I'm good with anything that encompasses each of us on a general level. Maybe something more neutral. What's a common ground we all share? How about the fact that we're all attempting to become Hired Blades? Let's start with that. Not that we have much time to decide..."

As the group ponders this question, Pilet thinks about what encompasses a Licensed Hired Blade. The first thing to come to mind is Faxion, the only real blueprint for a Hired Blade that he has. He recounts the time in Grand Titanus with the street peddlers, and the discretion his mentor used to diffuse the situation.

Pilet speaks on his revelations.

"I've got it." Said Pilet. "How about, "The Hidden Blades"?"

"Hmm, interesting." Said Faith.

"Yeah." Said Pilet. "I don't know about you guys, but the only Hired Blade I know is Fax. The guy might be corny as hell, but he's also a legendary Blade. He's not the kind of guy who rushes in without a plan, you know? The dude's probably a *beast* at poker, because he keeps his hand hidden until he basically knows what everyone else has."

Pilet strokes his chin, trying to find the words to describe his decision.

"He's tricky, always has something up his sleeve; and it's gotten him this far in his career without dying, so I trust it. And we're at an advantage here as prospects, no one knows our skills yet. Well, aside from what I did to that monkey in Chamboree... But in this exam, we're the dark horse. We are "The Hidden Blades" of this competition. I don't know, I think it works well enough..."

"No no, it's great!" Said Yuuna. "I totally agree Pilet. We are *hidden* and we hope to be *Blades*. So fitting!"

"Wow." Said Max. "I couldn't think of a better name if I tried, I third this motion."

"Then it's decided." Said Faith. "I agree as well, from this point on we are "The Hidden Blades"."

A familiar voice is heard peeking out from behind Pilet.

"Well now, glad to know I inspire such greatness!"

Pilet's shoulders hike up as he leaps in surprise.

"Bastard!! Stop!! Stop doing that! Why me? Why always me?!?" Said Pilet.

The Hidden Blades crew break into hysterical laughter at their emissaries expense. Pilet stands, hands down and fists clenched with a blank, unamused expression on his face.

"Dicks…"

Caffo Gilwick's voice is heard booming over the PA system of the gymnasium.

"All candidates please make your way to the team registration tables. The physical portion of the Hired Blades Licensing Exam will now commence."

"That's your cue folks." Says Faxion. "Take no prisoners! I can't wait to see you all at the winner's circle."

"Thanks Fax." Said Pilet. "Don't blink, I'm gonna score better than all these other chumps. I'm the King Killer!"

Faith folds her arms in contempt.

"Oh boy…"

Pilet flashes Faxion a fist bumb, Faith and Yuuna give him a group hug and Max bows in reverence as the four leave the Veteran Blade by the bleachers to continue with their exam.

A Deadshot trained by a Deadeye

They reach the registration desks, as Faith does the honors of inputting the teams information. She grins and giggles quietly, as she lists Pilet "The King Killer" Whydah in the Emissary box. Caffo begins to explain the next phase of the exam over the microphone.

"In this portion of the exam you may retrieve your belongings, including all combat equipment, from the designated holding station. For the physical examination there will be four main sections; Shooting, Mixed martial arts, Weapons fighting and Auracast. The shooting portion will see entrants firing down range at moving and stationary targets utilizing standard issue firearms. Mixed martial arts matches will test the hand to hand combat skill of each entrant in randomized match ups with each other. Weapons fighting will see you tested by a proctor in a one on one duel, using various forms of close combat weaponry, all safe and training level equipment so don't worry. As for Auracast, that will be explained in the courtyard when the time comes… Now, the monitors across either side of the gym will now post the order in which your teams are to report to each station and when to do so."

The large monitors on either side of the gymnasium display the names of the various teams and their corresponding sections. The Hidden Blades find themselves located at the shooting range first, alongside a team called "The Mystic Marauders". They retrieve their equipment from the holding station, meticulously affixing weapons and armor taken from storage bins. As the freshly equipped Hidden Blades make their way to the shooting range, they happen to walk alongside a group one could only assume to be The Mystic Marauders.

Much like Pilet's group they are a full team of four; two women and two men.

One of the men, fair skinned, easily one of the largest humans within a 10 mile radius. He stands at about 6'6, at least 315 pounds of all muscle with a jet black chinstrap goatee. His massive armor set, a gunmetal gray and white mix, with bulky gauntlets that appear to shift and change at will.

One woman, skin tanned a caramel shade with long, wavy, dark brunette hair. Her wrists and ankles are covered with bangles that make a jingling sound whenever she moves an inch. Her long magenta and pearl colored dress slit down the side revealing her right leg, with a Stinger pistol and a retracted papercut longsword holstered around her thigh.

The other woman sports a crimson combo of a sports bra and fitted athletic shorts. Her blonde ponytail tied back tight, and a 9mm, blood red Arcane Pierce around her shoulder.

The second man, shorter than the first but still tall and lanky. Wearing a deep blue bandana on top of his head. This covers his slicked back, light brown hair matching his tanned leather vest. Shirtless beneath the open vest, revealing a chiseled six pack abs. He too holsters a Stinger pistol and Papercut longsword on his right thigh, over black cargo pants tucked into his black boots. A dark tattoo of a jellyfish surrounded by runes covers the back of his left hand.

The Hidden Blades and The Mystic Marauders inadvertently begin walking parallel to each other towards the shooting range. Tension building, each adjacent member silently eyes each other up and down.

Yuuna and the bangled woman share a subtle, warm smile while Faith and the blonde sniper exchange cold, serious expressions. The massive warrior looks at Max and lightly pounds his chest with his right arm, Max responds with a slight bow. In front of Max is Pilet, walking alongside the man with the jellyfish tattoo. Pilet stiffens his brow and flares his nostrils, looking straight forward. The tattooed man glances at Pilet through the corner of his eye for a moment, then fixes his gaze toward the shooting range and continues his silent march.

The groups stop at the range, each individual firing lane separated by a sturdy divider for safety. The proctors on site instruct Pilet's group to spread out, staggered between members of The Mystic Marauders. Hung on each lane's divider walls are a standard issue Stinger pistol and a 7mm "Pilum Beam Rifle", two commonly used Hired Blade firearms.

"Hello candidates." Said one proctor. "Your objective is to simply pick up each firearm, fire until finishing your clip, and reload your weapon with the extra magazine provided. Do this for both the Stinger and Pilum Beam, and your accuracy will be graded accordingly."

Pilet is stood side by side with the bandana wearing Marauder, who after picking up his Pilum Beam begins to speak.

"So, The Hidden Blades huh?..." Said the Marauder. "You guys must be new around here, never heard of you."

"Yeah, we are." Said Pilet. "And don't worry, it won't be long before you're wishing you'd *stop* hearing about us."

The man grins as he fires a beam shot at his target.

"Hah, gotta love that spirit. The name's Puerto, they call me "The Man o' War" from Port Lyso." He pops off another beam shot. "I'm the Marauders Emissary. The big guy is Cornelius, the girl with the noisey jewelry is Dunya, and the Sniper's Wendy." He takes aim and fires again.

Pilet begins firing aimlessly. "I'm Pilet, Pilet Whydah. The quiet, awkward looking swordsman is Max, the short buggy eyed one is Yuuna, and her sister Faith is the pretentious looking amazon."

Surprised at the lack of respect for his team, as well as his terrible aim, Puerto covers his mouth trying not to laugh at Pilet.

"Wow, you guys must be a banger at parties. Sounds like you deeply appreciate each other." Said Puerto.

"Oh for sure." Said Pilet sarcastically as he continues to fire at will. "We're like soul mates. True blue best buds forever."

While overlooking the other candidates, the two proctors turn their heads at the sound of the haphazard marksmanship of The King Killer. They look puzzledly at Pilet, then back to each other. The proctors begin scribbling in their clipboards, shaking their heads in disbelief.

"That one's their Emissary." Said one proctor.

The other proctor takes a deep breath. "Lord help them. Hope we never get stuck on a mission with that guy. He'll shoot us both in the ass."

Pilet finishes the clip on his Pilum Beam rifle, attempts to reload and fails miserably. He looks over at the proctors who are preoccupied with Cornelius, who's broad shoulders have gotten him stuck in between the two dividers. The proctors recruit Max to assist them, as the three begin pulling with all their might.

"They don't pay me enough for this shit." Says one proctor. "This year's crop has me seriously worried."

"What are they feeding you boy?!?" Exclaimed the other proctor.

Taking this golden opportunity to cheat, Pilet whispers to Puerto.

"Shh, shh. Hey man, how do you reload this thing??"

"... Are you kidding me?" Said Puerto. "You're supposed to be a mercenary, explain to me how you can't even reload a rifle? What, were you hoping you'd just kill everything in one magazine? Not with shooting like that..."

"Hush, quiet! Are you trying to get me freakin' kicked out?? Bro please just show me how to reload this thing!" Said Pilet.

Sigh "Fine, ok look." Puerto fires his last few shots. "Take out the empty magazine, that part you seem to have down. Then just insert the new one, and pull back on the bolt to reload the chamber. That's it."

Pilet takes his advice and reloads the Pilum Beam rifle.

"Oh man, thanks a bunch buddy! Alright, didn't do so well on the first go 'round but with the Stinger I'm gonna nail it for sure."

Pilet hangs the Pilum Beam back on the divider wall and readies the designated Stinger. He trains his eye on the target and continues where he left off, which was not well...

Puerto mutters to himself. "Shit, I can't believe I thought this guy was a threat..."

Some ten feet away, Max and the proctors finally free Cornelius from the divider wall. However they pull too hard as he's released, causing the

300 plus pound man to fall directly on top of the three. As they lie there struggling, none of the other entrants bat an eye or attempt to help. Except Yuuna of course, she merely giggles in the background.

About 10 minutes later, all of the candidates have finished their magazines and reloaded for the next troupe. By this time the proctors have already scored their efforts.

"Ok folks." Said the first proctor. He cracks his back, wincing from the squashing he took moments ago. "Ugh. Ok, your scores have been submitted. Just make your way to the next designated section via the monitors." He starts to talk under his breath. "The sooner these screwups are out of my sight the better..."

Pilet turns to Puerto and offers a handshake. Puerto looks at the outstretched hand, pauses for a moment, and decides to shake hands.

"It's better to make friends than enemies right?" Said Puerto. *Even if they're useless in a firefight.* He thought.

"For sure buddy. Really appreciate the tip back there, I owe you one!" Said Pilet.

Puerto relents this statement...

"No! No you don't! I mean... It's fine, don't mention it... Really. Forget about it..."

The rest of the Hidden Blades and The Mystic Marauders approach their Emissaries, having seemingly bonded over blaster fire.

"It was great meeting you guys, really!" Said Yuuna. "I hope we see each other again soon!"

Puerto gulps and takes a deep breath.

"I do not hope that at all." He mutters to himself.

Dunya replies. "You too lovey, it was a pleasure darling really it was. Be safe out there, we'll be rooting for you."

Wendy motions to Faith.

"You're no slouch with a firearm homegirl! I honestly hope I *don't* see you on the battlefield." Said Wendy.

"Believe me." Said Faith. "I'm not looking forward to that either. I knew you were a deadshot when I saw that Arcane pierce. As per usual I was right. You take care of yourself out there!"

Max and Cornelius approach, commending each other on their skills.

"You really are an incredible shot." Said Max. "To have the forearm strength to stabilize firing a pistol in one hand and a rifle in the other, at the same time! It's astounding how close they were to the target."

"No you are the incredible one my friend." Said Cornelius. "I am not a small man, and for you to be able to lift me off of those *useless* proctors like that, it's no small feat. I'm actually frightened that there are warriors of your calibur taking the exam this year!"

As the two teams say their goodbyes, they congregate in their respective groups again to continue the testing.

"How was meeting their Emissary Pilet?" Asked Yuuna.

Pilet responds. "It was great! The guy taught me how to reload a gun! Good thing the big dude fell on Max or the proctors would've noticed him giving me advice. So thanks for that buddy."

The three look at Pilet, concerned, but not surprised.

Faith responds. "You didn't know how to…"

She looks at his target, not a single shot fired near the bull's eye. Very few landed on the target at all. Just a mess of scorched, blaster fire miscellaneously scattered across the background.

"You know what. Nevermind. Just glad you didn't hurt yourself." Said Faith.

"Or anyone else." Adds Max.

The group looks up to the nearest monitor and sees their next destination: The fighting cage.

The Beatdown in the Cage

Marching across the crowds of fellow candidates, they enter the waiting area on the sidelines of the cage. The first MMA proctor they see sports dark brown, corn-rowed hair. He wears a pair of black and gold trunks, black fingerless sparring gloves and a wooden necklace charm of a stingray. His bare back; covered by the tattoo of a bloodied panther, standing stoically atop a savannah cliff. He sees Pilet's group and begins instruction.

"Alright guys, which group are you?" Said the Proctor.

"The Hidden Blades." Answers Pilet.

"I'm Rexmere, the head MMA proctor for today's exam. We're gonna match you up against another team chosen at random. Matches consist of four, one-on-one fights. Three person or smaller teams have to choose members to fight multiple times. Of course since you have a full team of four all of you can fight just once. You're all going to be graded on your individual performance in the cage, win or lose. Any questions?"

The gang shakes their heads in a unanimous "No".

"Good. Just wait over there until I call your group.".

Rexmere points to a row of folding chairs, behind a black-taped line outside of the cage. The gang takes their seats to spectate some of the matches.

As Mentioned by Rexmere; most entrants only have to fight once and do well in order to secure their place in the MMA portion, considering most teams are composed of at least 3 to 4 members. However, it *is possible* to register yourself alone as a team of one. One bold entrant has shown to employ this method, and so far it has been proven effective for them.

As The Hidden Blades take their seat on the sidelines, they are greeted by the awestruck gasps of the spectating audience. The crowd falls silent as a blood soaked Bhujanga Garuda exits the cage, leaving four beaten and battered members of his opposing team strewn across the floor. As Bhujanga takes his leave, he passes by Pilet sitting beside the cage door. Speechless, Pilet simply waves.

"Oh hey, good luck out there. Thanks for the scotch." Said Bhujanga.

"Ha...Yeah. Uh, don't mention it..." Said Pilet.

Faith, equally awestruck, inquires to Pilet.

"You know that guy? Who is he?!"

"We met at the bar after the written exam." Said Pilet. "He said he was an archeologist. But, I've never seen an archeologist do *that* to anyone... Shit, makes me wonder what kind of people *we'll* have to contend with out here."

Shocked by the speed of this brutal thrashing, Rexmere leaves Pilet's group and rushes to the proctor in charge of Bhujanga's match.

"What's going on here?!" Exclaimed Rexmere. "These fights are supposed to be one-on-one, you know that!"

"I'm sorry Rex." Replied the proctor. "He's a solo candidate, he registered himself as a team of one! He said he could take the four of them at once to save time."

"And what made you think letting that happen was a good idea?"

"Well, his opponents were the Hammerhead Thrashers from Maximal City. I mean, you know everyone from *there* is a top level martial artist! I was so surprised by his arrogance that I allowed it, I just figured I'd stop the match as soon as he started getting his ass kicked. But, he was just so fast... I honestly wouldn't want to be in the cage with him."

"That doesn't mean you let the kid go *cowboy* just because he has an ego!" Said Rexmere. "Rules are rules. These fights are one-on-one so that we can see all the action and act when we need to. With so many bodies flying around, how do you expect to see an eye poke or a low blow?? Don't let it happen again."

"Will do Rex, will do."

"Alright, good. I have a team ready to fight in the blue corner, call themselves "The Hidden Blades". Who's ready on your end?" Said Rexmere.

"The Cobalt Killers. I hope these "Hidden Blades" are ready for war, their opponents are all convicted murderers. I have a feeling those poor kids don't stand a chance. "

"Really?... Now that's interesting." Said Rexmere. "Well we're just going to have to see. You can never count a Blade out. They have Blade in their name already, now let's see them earn it. Go get the red corner ready, I'll prep the blue corner."

As Pilet and company speak about the beating Bhujanga just dished out, Rexmere approaches with a large duffle bag filled with fight gear. He tosses it to the ground before The Hidden Blades.

"In there you'll find gloves, headgear, trunks, sports bras and mouthpieces of different sizes." Said Rexmere. He points to several porta-potties behind them. "Changing room's that way. The match starts in five minutes, don't be late."

The team starts rummaging through the duffle bag for matching equipment. Max and Yuuna find their sets and head to the changing stations. At this time Faith recounts with Pilet the catastrophe that was his target practice.

"You know, you should really make a solid effort to pass this portion." Said Faith. "I saw your target at the shooting range. I mean, you can't seriously think you got a good grade with that accuracy, right?"

Pilet looks peeved.

"What?! I did fine! I hit the target plenty of times, just not the center part. What if I was fighting multiple opponents? They would've all been taking dirt naps!"

"If you were fighting multiple opponents, you would've had multiple targets." Said Faith. "Just try to do well this time, ok? I really don't want to see you fail because you weren't trying, none of us do."

She draws a pair of gloves from the duffle bag, slipping them onto her hands and tightening the wrist wraps.

"I used to be scared to try too, when I was younger. I figured if I never tried I couldn't fail and no one would laugh at me. But then my parents died, and I made a promise to them that I would make them proud one day. I know they'll never see the fruits of my effort among the living. But if there *is* a heaven, I believe they're smiling down on me with every step I take toward the future."

Pilet pauses, uncertain of how to respond to the testament of his teammate.

"Look, my folks are gone too." He said. "My mom died when I was born, and my dad split as soon as he found out she was pregnant. Crazy thing is as much as I hate him for that, I still want to see him. Some part of me wants to show him what I've become, without his help. I want my mom to be proud too."

Pilet releases a tense sigh.

"I'm kind of scared though. If I mess this up, I'll just be another burnout degenerate from Chamboree. I guess I haven't found a way to deal with that yet."

"Well just remember, you have what it takes to be here! You killed a Wurm King, if there's anyone here with the credentials to become a Hired Blade it's you! But from this moment on you have to be on point. No more half-assedness. Whoever we're about to fight, you need to put the fighting spirit of your mother as she brought you into this world all over their face! Don't let her sacrifice be in vain."

Pilet wells up with conviction. He simply nods, trying not to tear up at the thought of his mother's final moments.

The two find appropriate fight gear and change. As The Hidden Blades exit the changing stations, they meet back at the sidelines to await instruction. Rexmere comes over with a clipboard and begins to assign opponents.

"Alright, "Hidden Blades"." Said Rexmere. "Your opponents will be chosen from a team named "The Cobalt Killers".

"I see... This should be intriguing." Said Max. "I've heard about them. They're a group of ex-cons. I'm eager to see what they bring to the table."

Yuuna gasps and hides behind the row of folding chairs.

"No! What?!" Said Yuuna. "I hate fighting... And you mean to tell me of all the people, it's *killers* we have to fight?!"

"Sis, relax." Said Faith. "Just do what I showed you and you'll be fine."

"You can't promise that!" Said Yuuna. "Didn't you see what that one guy did to four people at once?! Why can't we go in together, mister Rexmere?"

"That was a fluke." Said Rexmere. "My associate made an error in judgment, won't happen again. Nobody is dying in that cage today as long as I'm on duty. But if you want to forfeit you have every right. You *will* however be forfeiting your right to continue with today's exam."

"I apologise Yuuna." Said Max. "I did not intend to scare you with the knowledge I shared. However if you are to be a Hired Blade, courage in the face of danger is a paramount virtue. We'll be right here cheering for you. Just do your best in there. If you feel the need to forfeit, at least you'll have done so with dignity."

Wiping tears from her face, Yuuna hugs Max.

"Thanks Max. I always knew I'd need to be stronger to be a Hired Blade. Knowing you guys are here really helps."

Max awkwardly reciprocates Yuuna's affection.

"Uh. Yes. Well, glad I could help." Said Max.

"Right..." Said Rexmere. "Well at any rate. Yuuna Sierro, ironically you're up first. Your opponent is Medhi Balma. After that; it's Max Quinn v.s. Samantha Wendigo, Faith Sierro v.s. Martin Monroe and Pilet Whydah v.s. Kenny Brown."

Rexmere lowers the clipboard from his gaze and addresses The Hidden Blades directly.

"The rules are simple; No eye gouging, groin shots, headbutts, fish hooks, biting, hair pulling, throat strikes or finger and toe twisting. Ok? Fight ends when either fighter taps out or if I jump in to stop it. Good luck candidates. Keep your hands up, and defend yourselves appropriately."

Across the cage the Hidden Blades eye their adversaries, standing side-by-side in menacing poses. Their faces covered in scar tissue, with murderous intent strewn across their brow. Yuuna hesitantly steps into the cage.

"You'll be fine." Said Faith from the outside.

"I hope so..." Yuuna replied.

Her opponent, 6 foot 1 and 200lbs, makes his way into the arena. His long hair is ponytailed back, showcasing barbed wire tattooed across his hairline.

"Hey pretty lady." Says Medhi. "Whaddya say we meet up after this for a nice, Itedonian flake roll. I promise to be nice if you say yes."

Yuuna looks disgusted. Her nostrils flare as she brandishes a small, smooth black stone from her pocket. She closes her eyes and meditates on the stone for a moment. It begins to emit an ominous black fog with the stench of sulfur. Medhi, weary of this motions to the proctor.

"Uh, yo ref! No one said we could bring weapons in with us?! I think she's gearin' up to throw stones! Well too bad for you missy, I'm not a glass house."

Concerned and confused, Rexmere comes closer to take a look. But as he grows near, the black stone sinks into Yuuna's chest revealing nothing but her empty hands making a praying gesture.

"Making excuses this early in the fight huh?" Says Rexmere. "Big scary killer trying to get the little girl disqualified. Just shut up and fight."

Medhi Balma looks perplexed.

"Alright whatever. It's a shame though girly. We could've had something special, now I've gotta kill ya!"

Yuuna takes a deep breath. As she exhales, she opens her eyes revealing them to be completely pitch black. She grins devilishly as she replies.

"Let's have a date in hell!" Said Yuuna, her voice clearly much raspier and hoarse.

She dashes for Medhi in an instant, taking him down with an abnormal display of strength. As she puts him on his back, she begins to drop elbow after elbow onto Medhi's face. Blood begins to trickle down his brow as he struggles to hold her down.

"What?! How the hell are you doing this?! Who are you!!" Said Medhi.

Faith shakes her head in disapproval.

"She'll never learn." Said Faith. "The damn crystals won't always do the job for her. She has to find strength in herself one of these days. Her codependency is astounding."

Absolutely befuddled, Max and Pilet turn to Faith in disbelief.

"What are you talking about?!" Said Pilet. "She's crushing it out there!! That guy looks like a cereal killer and she's making him look like a scared puppy that just took a shit on the carpet!"

"I've never seen anything like this." Said Max. "I'm so pleased my words of encouragement were able to help her!"

"Sorry Max." Said Faith. "But your words of encouragement have nothing to do with this. She used a crystal with auric properties. It's called Black Onix, and this *particular* one harbors the evil spirit of an ancient murderous sorcerer named Besmith. My parents kept it sealed in a blessed palo santo box, but the damn thing kept talking to her from inside. She kept opening it and getting possessed by him."

Faith grins, folding her arms in a mix of contempt and pride.

"But her aura is so strong that she would always stave him off and put him back after a few minutes, he's really more of a mischievous nuisance than anything."

"Oh..." Said Max. "Well then... I mean, should we be concerned?"

"Yeah, seriously." Said Pilet. "That's like, straight out of a horror movie I saw once... What if that thing tries to possess one of us??"

"It won't." Said Faith. "He likes her too much, plus she knows how to draw him out of people and re-seal him in the stone. His constant vying for control has caused her aura to increase immensely over the years, simply by always fighting him off. It's like a heavy weighted vest for auracasters."

"Well isn't that something." Said Max. "What an excellent work ethic, I must push my training to greater heights around the likes of you all."

"Well whatever he is, he's doing a damn good job in that cage." Said Pilet. "The poor Medhi guy looks like a butcher's block. Eww, shit. Oh, oh God damn. That looks like it hurts."

"DIE DIE DIE!" Said Besmith via Yuuna. "I'LL SEND YOU TO THE AFTERLIFE WITH ME!"

Besmith continues to batter Medhi with elbows over his guard. Medhi somehow manages to get to his knees and tries to stand up, but Besmith jumps on his back and wraps Yuuna's legs around Medhi's waist. Besmith proceeds to punch Medhi in the ear until he blocks with one of his hands, leaving his left neck wide open.

"Hehehehehe." Laughs Besmith maniacally. "You know nothing of death, you amature."

Besmith snakes Yuuna's arm across Medhi's throat and sinks in a choke from behind. As Besmith begins to crank the choke, Medhi claws at Yuuna's arm in desperation.

"Hnnnggg!!" Struggles Medhi, gurgling and choking in despair.

Slowly but surely, Medhi begins to fade from consciousness. His hands stop grasping at Yuuna's arms, floating lifelessly to the floor. Seeing this, Rexmere rushes to the scene and pulls Besmith off of Medhi.

"Enough fighter, stop! Fight's over, fight's over!" Said Rexmere.

Besmith releases Medhi and begins laughing maniacally.

"HAHAHAHA!!" Said Besmith. "FALL ON YOUR KNEES TO THE MIGHTY BESM..."

With Rexmere's back turned, Yuuna's head begins to shake violently as her eyes return to normal. The Black Onix creeps back out of her chest and falls into her hand, where she tucks it into her bra.

Rexmere suspiciously turns his head to Yuuna, and is met with a sinfully innocent smile. Skeptically, he turns back to Medhi and elevates his feet. As Medhi returns to consciousness, Rexmere stands the two up in the middle of the cage and raises Yuuna's hand.

"Winner, Yuuna Sierro!"

Pilet and Max cheer joyously for their teammate.

"Woohoo! Go Yuuna! You smashed 'em!!" Said Pilet.

"You're a true warrior Yuuna!! I admire your heart!" Said Max.

Yuuna jumps for joy and grins from ear to ear. But her celebrations are cut short when she sees Faith, standing with her arms folded in contempt. Yuuna exits the cage to a group bear hug from Pilet and Max.

"Eek!" Said Yuuna. "You're squeezing so hard guys!"

The three laugh as Max and Pilet release Yuuna.

"Tell Besmith he did great..." Said Faith, as she walks away.

"Man." Said Pilet. "She's so fickle. Well hey, whatever works right?"

Yuuna pouts and takes a seat.

Rexmere takes the center of the cage with his clipboard.

"Next up. Max Quinn v.s. Samantha Wendigo. Fighters, enter the cage."

Max walks up the steel, mini-stairs through the cage door. He prances around the perimeter, to gauge room for movement. After a lap he takes his place in the Blue corner, patiently awaiting his opponent. Just then, in walks an immense, muscular woman with various tattoos all over her body. Her hair is tied in a bun atop her head, revealing her thick, tree trunk-shaped neck. As she looks at Max she flexes her biceps, kissing each one and leaving scarlett lipstick stains across either. Unphased, Max simply bows in respect.

"Please forgive me." Said Max. "I apologize in advance for what happens next."

"No need to be sorry." Said Samantha. "I'm the Emissary of The Cobalt Killers. What happens next I can more than handle."

Off to the side Pilet strokes his chin.

"That's the Emissary huh? This is gonna be good." Said Pilet.

Rexmere raises his arm in the middle of the cage.

"Ready?" Said Rexmere. He lowers his arm in a flash. "Begin!"

The fighters start to advance. Max begins to bounce on the balls of his feet in a sideways stance. His rear hand up protecting his face, the lead hand relaxed stealthily at his side. He dances around the cage maintaining distance from his opponent.

Samantha slowly creeps toward Max with a menacing boxing posture. Hands up at her cheeks, swaying side to side like a viper.

As she gets within kicking range, Max punishes with a swift side kick. He sneakily lifts his lead leg and strikes with the blade of his foot, over and over maintaining a healthy distance. From time to time Samantha gets too close for comfort, Max answers with a straight right hand and cuts an angle to escape. He continues probing with the sidekick. To the ribs, then the knee, the face, knee, ribs, ribs, face. Before long Samantha's body becomes reddened by the strikes.

"Why does Max keep jumping back and forth like that?" Said Pilet. "Shouldn't he just stand and punch with her? I mean, it looks cool but it's hardly a fight if he keeps running away..."

"It's the squirrel style Pilet!" Said Yuuna.

"The what?" Said Pilet.

"It's called the Risu technique." Said Faith. "It's a traditional Hachidorinese fighting style where the user bounces buoyantly to avoid taking damage. It's evasive and very tricky on the vision. Often practitioners are able to land stealthy strikes on unwitting opponents. Hachidori has many exotic martial arts, I have a feeling Max has more than this up his sleeve."

As the fight continues Samantha becomes visibly frustrated with the direction it is taking. Seeking to shift the momentum to her side, she stalks Max to the edge of the cage. In the moment he's backed up against it, she explodes in; landing a right cross as he's taken off guard by the barrier behind him.

The crowd gasps "OOH!"

The punch lands squarely to his chin, sending a dazed Max crumbling to the canvas. Samantha follows him down and starts pouring down punches. Guarding himself while flat on his back, he tries to wrap his legs around Samantha. But to no avail, as she grabs his ankles and swings them to the side, exposing his back to her.

Things are not looking good for the young Sanda Warrior as Samantha Wendigo continues to shower him with punches to the side of the head. Somehow, Max stumbles to his feet; clinching in close to Samantha. Breathing heavy, with blood flowing down the side of his head, Max sneakily slides one of his arms around her waist. The other hand cups the back of her elbow as he scores a beautiful hip toss, landing her in a compromised position beneath him.

Angered by the radical shift in position, Samantha begins to flail violently on the ground. This proves to have been a fatal flaw, as she soon leaves an arm vulnerable to submission.

Max takes this opportunity and clamps down on the arm furthest from him. He interweaves his arms between hers and secures a vicious shoulder lock, putting tremendous pressure on her shoulder joint. With the lock secured Max pulls his hips over Samantha's head, acting as a vice to keep her in place. From here he proceeds to crank the lock until he's almost certain it's about to tear her shoulder.

"You should tap." Said Max. "It's over, there's no reason for you to suffer this. You've done well here, please tap."

Reluctantly, Samantha taps on the ground.

Rexmere runs to her aid and calls off the fight. He walks the two fighters to the center of the cage. Raising Max's hand he exclaims "Winner, Max Quinn!".

Max exchanges bows with Samantha before exiting the cage.

"Thank you." Said Samantha.

"For what?" Replied Max.

"You could have broken my shoulder, but you chose not to. You even talked me out of accepting the injury. You need not be so caring, and I appreciate that."

"Of course, such is the way of The Sanda Warrior. This is how we conduct ourselves. Thank you for a good fight." Said Max.

The on site medic comes to Max's aid as he walks down the steel stairs from the arena. The medic begins stitching together a laceration on Max's forehead. The rest of the Hidden Blades come to his side during treatment.

"Dude what a fight!" Said Pilet. "I got worried for a second, she rocked you pretty bad. But what a recovery! Nice shoulder lock too."

"You know this technique?" Said Max.

"Yea, it's one of Fax's favorites." Said Pilet. "Says he could do it in his sleep, and knowing him he probably has. It's no surprise he's single..."

"That was so amazing Max!" Said Yuuna. "What a good show of fighting spirit! I'm sure the other team is thinking the same thing."

"Yeah, I was literally on the edge of my seat!" Said Faith. "My sister had to catch me at one point."

"I saw that, while Samantha was pounding me. I was wondering how someone could fall out of a stationary chair." Said Max.

The group laughs. Finishing the stitches, the medic rubs his hands and takes a deep breath. He mutters "Mend.". His hands begin to glow a turquoise tinge as he floats them 4 inches above Max's cut. The wound seals remarkably fast, leaving the medic to simply remove the leftover stitches.

"Thank you sir." Said Max.

"You're very welcome." Said the medic.

He grabs his bag, taking his leave of the Hidden Blades. Max touches his head where the laceration once was. He feels nothing but soft skin where the stitches were.

"It's really something, what some simple auracast can do. Without it this would've taken weeks to heal, and it would've scarred." Said Max.

"It looks like the next guy could care less about scarring." Said Pilet.

He points to the next entrant, who has already made his way into the cage. About 5'10, round and very stocky, his face completely covered in miscellaneous battlescars. His bald head reflects the light from the ceiling toward the Hidden Blades. He strokes his thick, black goatee while awaiting his adversary. Standing in the center of the cage, Rexmere beckons.

"Faith Sierro, report to the arena."

Pilet puts his hand on Faith's shoulder.

"Good luck with that one. Hey, maybe if you run around with a box of doughnuts you'll tire him out."

Faith tightens her gloves and cracks her knuckles.

"I don't need luck." Said Faith. "Just this mouthpiece and someone to punch."

Faith pops in her mouthpiece and struts into the cage. She meets Her opponent, Martin Monroe at the center with Rexmere. Faith sways back-and-forth menacingly, with a scowl that could frighten a lion.

Martin scoffs.

"Why did I get stuck with one of the chicks." Said Martin, as he looks to Rexmere. "You couldn't have saved this one for Sam? I want the King Killer. This is bullshit."

Before Rexmere can respond, Faith interjects.

"You should focus on your fight." Said Faith. "Or else by the end of the day they'll be calling me "The Convict Killer"."

"Hmmph." Muttered Martin, unamused. "I thought I signed up for real fights when I entered this test. Guess I'll make this quick."

Rexmere shakes his head.

"If you two are finished, touch gloves and get back to your corners." Said Rexmere.

Neither fighter touches gloves as they backstep to their ends of the cage. Faith's eyes affix to Martin like piercing daggers.

Rexmere raises his hand.

"Ready? Fight!" He shouts as he swings his arm down.

The fighters swifty meet in the center.

Faith holds her hands up high, circling away from Martin's power hand in the rear. She begins to prick at him with a series of quick jabs, occasionally adding a right cross or a low roundhouse kick in combination.

Martin doesn't seem too phased by the offense of his opponent. He takes the shots and slowly walks forward, hands down at his sides. Undeterred, Faith continues with her steady probing. Some 3 punches later and Martin's nose and lip begin to bleed. Regardless of this, the man shows no signs of fatigue or pain.

Now frustrated by the lack of respect for her striking, Faith fires a high roundhouse to the face. She soon realizes her folly, as Martin eats the kick and catches her foot by the ankle in the process. He lifts her kicking leg to an unnatural height, causing Faith to fall on her butt. No sooner than her hitting the ground does she pop back up, backstepping to put distance between them.

"You're outta luck little girl." Said Martin. "Your shitty punches and kicks are like candy to me, I could eat them all day."

"Yeah, I see that." Said Faith. "It looks like you never stop eating."

Faith digs her back foot into the floor. She bites down on her mouthpiece and prepares for a fire fight.

"Get ready for a trip to candyland, shit head!" Exclaimed Faith.

Martin draws near as the two begin to slug it out in the middle of the cage. Faith bobs and weaves. Martin throws haymakers and uppercuts left and right. Faith blocks and dodges the best she can, countering some punches while receiving others to the cheek and side of the head. Whether a shot hits her or misses, she holds her ground in the center. She doesn't back up an inch as the onslaught continues.

Surprisingly, Martin begins to look dazed. Faith realizes that a stray uppercut must have landed flush for her, as a cut from the bottom of his chin opens up. Taking this opportunity Faith quickly backsteps, creating space to start teeing off with kicks. Slightly wobbled from the uppercut, Martin overextends a huge left hook. Faith leans back and sends an upkick to Martin's jaw.

Now Martin's hurt, and he's mad. Faith doesn't care. She lifts her knee imitating a front kick, but changes the angle at the last second and nails Martin with her signature question mark kick. Martin's massive body goes down with a resounding *thud* that shakes the cage floor.

Faith jumps on top of him, dropping blow after blow to the head. After three unanswered strikes, Rexmere decides he's seen enough and breaks Faith off of Martin, ending the fight.

As four medics laboeredly hoist an unconscious Martin away, Rexmere raises Faith's hand in the center of the cage.

"Winner, Faith Sierro!" Said Rexmere. "And good job out there, keep that up and you've got a real future in this business."

"Thanks." Said Faith. "That was just a fraction of what I can do."

Faith leaves the cage slightly dazed, with a fat lip and some blood running from her nose. The medic checks her for concussions, but determines she is ok and begins to cast "Mend". The team walks over.

"Holy shit." Said Pilet "You really didn't need luck out there, or a box of doughnuts."

Faith grins slightly as the medic ices her lip with a cold compress.

"No, but I could use one now." Said Faith. "I'm exhausted, and starving."

"What a stunning display of grit." Said Max. "I am without words at the determination you showed in battle."

Yuuna bashfully stands to the side, ashamed of the actions taken during her match. Seeing her sister fight her heart out against such a brute, she feels remorse to have succumbed to her fear of fighting. Noticing Yuuna's nervous energy, Faith calls off the medic.

"That's enough sir thank you, my sister can handle it from here." Said Faith.

Yuuna's eyes lit up with hope. The medic honors her wish.

"Very well." Said the Medic. "Good day to you."

As the medic leaves, Yuuna rubs her hands together and casts "Mend" hovering her hands before her sister.

"Hey sis, I'm really proud of what you did out there. Those guys are really scary and I know that must've been hard..." Said Yuuna.

"It was definitely difficult." Said Faith. "I'm glad you didn't get hurt in your match, not that it matters with your skill in healing auracast." Faith turns to Max and Pilet. "Hey guys, could you give me a second with my sister?"

"Yeah, sure." Said Pilet.

"As you wish." Said Max.

The boys take their seats on the sidelines as the next match is getting ready to begin. After a moment, Yuuna's superior skill with the Mend-cast fully heals her sister. As the auric glow leaves her sister's palms, Faith gently holds Yuuna's hands and laments.

"I'm sorry I was so hard on you earlier." Said Faith. "I know how you feel about confrontation. But I told you that becoming a Hired Blade was going to be dangerous and full of fighting, sometimes even killing. You know that one day you're going to have to learn to fight your own battles right?"

Yuuna sighs.

"I... I know. It's just something I'll have to work on... It's not easy, and it's not going to happen overnight. I need time Faith. Until then my crystals and auracast are going to have to carry me through..."

"Well, I'm not happy about it." Said Faith. "But I understand. We'll have to talk about this another time. Just know that I love you and I'm here for you. No matter what."

Faith and Yuuna embrace in a warm hug. A single tear falls from Yuuna's cheek.

"I love you too sis. I love you too..."

Pilet ties his fight trunks tight, as the final fight is announced.

"Pilet Whydah v.s. Kenny Brown. Will both fighters report to the center of the cage." Said Rexmere.

"Alright guys." Said Pilet. "Wish me luck..."

"You can do this, King Killer." Said Max. "Show them why you're emissary to The Hidden Blades."

Faith whispers in Max's ear.

"We both know killing that Wurm King wasn't the reason we picked him..."

Max quietly replies.

"Yes. Well. What he doesn't know can't hurt him. Right? It's just a vote of confidence."

"What are you guys mumbling about over there?" Said Pilet.

"Oh nothing!" Said Faith. "Do your best out there, remember your motivation." Faith looks Pilet in the eye. "She's looking down from above Pilet, she'll be proud of you no matter what. You just have to try."

A somber look creeps across Pilet's face. He turns to face the cage door. Suddenly he feels the weight of Yuuna hanging across his neck.

"Good luck Pilet! I know you can do it!!" Said Yuuna, as her hanging hug begins to strangle him.

Wheeze "Thanks, lighten up a bit though. You're gonna knock me out before the other guy gets a try."

As Pilet starts his walk to the cage, the voices of his friends and family begin to echo through his mind...

He remembers James' parting words to him.

"You've got so much going for you man. Just make use of it, ok?".

He walks up the steel steps and through the cage door. Kenny Brown stands across from him. Arms folded and chin high in the air. Tall and lean with long arms and legs, formidable traits for a fighter. Buzzed hair much like Pilet's, with a look of pure contempt in his eye.

"What up, King Killer." Said Kenny. He turns around and addresses the Cobalt Killers. "You guys lost to a bunch of murder virgins, at least mine popped his cherry." He turns back to Pilet. "Of course, Wurm King or not. It's nothing like the feeling of taking a human life."

Pilet cracks his knuckles. He recounts his Grandfather's advice.

"Stay safe and give 'em hell. Ya hear?"

Kenny continues.

"To know that you just sent one of your own kind to the afterlife, it leaves a sweet flavor in your soul. A feeling of total dominance over the spirit of another man. The power to let them stay on this plane of existence, or push them into the next one."

Nivia's letter floats through his thoughts.

"You are a hero Pilet. Go out there and make the world a better place, one dangerous mission at a time."

He flares his nostrils and begins to grit his teeth in his mouthpiece.

"And the frightened sounds they make, UGH." Said Kenny. "It's like sweet, heavenly music to my ears.

Faith's words of affirmation dance across his mind.

"Whoever we're about to fight, you need to put the fighting spirit of your mother as she brought you into this world all over their face!"

"Enough chit-chat." Said Rexmere. "Fighters, are you ready? Touch gloves if you wish and step back to your corners."

Both ignoring the glove touch, Kenny turns his back to Pilet on his way to his corner. Rexmere raises his arm. Pilet looks his vile opponent dead in the eye.

Rexmere thrusts his arm down. "Fight!"

"Don't let her sacrifice be in vain."

In that moment, Rexmere felt the wind rush across his face. Suddenly Pilet was across the cage, within arms reach of Kenny Brown. The young prospect had covered distance faster than anyone Rexmere had ever seen in his years as a Blade.

But Kenny is not without talent. With timing, reflexes and experience, Kenny fires a straight left hand right down the pipe. The fist of his lanky arm heads straight for Pilet's chin.

The words of his teacher ring throughout his soul.

"I think that you'll be ready when the time comes, and not a moment sooner. You have what many lack; adaptability and heart, and what a great combination of qualities to have..."

As if time itself slowed, Pilet visualizes the knuckles of his adversary coming for his consciousness. With the slightest tilt of the head, Pilet changes trajectory and slips past the punch. As Pilet eludes Kenny's fist, the two lock eyes; and with a cocked and loaded right hand, Pilet unleashes an undetected counter-cross directly from hell.

Ccrrraaacckk *Thud*

".................."

Rexmere shakes his head to wake up. With the speed of Pilet's advance, Rexmere didn't initially know where the fighters were in the cage. He turns to see the stiffened body of Kenny Brown, lying across the floor. Pilet stands about a foot away, facing the crowd. He looks at the knuckle side of his right glove.

"Guess I'm ready as I'll ever be..."

Rexmere collects himself and rushes to the fighters.

"HOLY SHIT!" Exclaimed Rexmere. "The fight's over!"

The spectating crowd begins to cheer uncontrollably at the lightning fast K.O. Bystanders and passersby puzzledly turn their heads to the cage, confused over the commotion. The Hidden Blades on the sidelines leap from their seats in unison.

"WHAT WAS THAT?!?!" Said Faith.

"My God!" Said Max. "Did that just happen??"

"What happened?" Said Yuuna. "I didn't see it! Did Pilet win?!?"

In the cage, Pilet looks up from his glove and sees Faxion sitting in the crowd. Arms folded, grinning ear to ear with his chin high. He tips his hat and gives Pilet a thumbs up. Pilet smiles and winks, pounding his fists together.

As the crowd continues to cheer, both monitors broadcast an instant replay of Pilet's match. Slowed down, the footage reveals not only the speed of his dash, but the skill of his technique. The moment Pilet's fist makes impact, the crowd unanimously jeers.

"OOH!"

Rexmere taps Pilet on the shoulder.

"You're gonna go far kid. You *and* your crew."

He raises Pilet's hand where they stand and parades him around the cage. After a moment Rexmere releases him. The two step out of the cage and approach the Hidden Blades.

"You guys have done an excellent job today." Said Rexmere. "Yours is the only four member group today to win all your matches. Even you little missy." He points to Yuuna's necklace of crystals. "I'll let it slide this time. I don't know what you did but whatever it was, I could sense it didn't affect your body, just your mind."

Yuuna's face resembles a dog caught red handed, eating Mom's fresh apple pie. She twiddles her thumbs tentatively.

"Oh um... I'm sorry..."

Rexmere continues.

"We're far more strict on the written than the physical. We understand candidates tend to specialize in certain areas when it comes to combat. Not everyone's good at everything. I myself am a terrible shot. But it doesn't matter when I get in your face with these hands."

Upon hearing this, Pilet turns to Faith and squints his eyes contemptuously. Faith shrugs her shoulders.

"I mean, my advice was still good." Said Faith.

"We all have strengths and weaknesses." Said Rexmere. "Us Proctors are just here to see if the culmination of these is enough for you to defend yourselves out there in the field. Anyway, I think it's time for you guys to head to the next section. But rest assured, I'd say you all passed the MMA portion today. The fight gear is yours to keep, we don't reuse gear here."

"Yuck! Thank God." Said Yuuna.

"That is good to hear." Said Max. "I too was wondering this, I guess the smell was just me..."

The gang looks at Max.

"What?.. I awoke late and was rushed before I could shower." Said Max. "Dude.... Say less." Muttered Pilet.

The girls bite their tongue, trying desperately not to embarrass their new friend.

A Fearsome Duel: The King Killer V.S. The Star of Menanois

After a few minutes the group changes clothes and heads towards the next section of the exam. Yuuna checks the monitor.

"It says we gotta go to theeee.... Weapons sparring section? I think it's that way."

Yuuna points to the far end of the gymnasium.

"Awesome, I finally get to stab someone..." Said Pilet.

"I don't think we're getting *live* Blades..." Said Faith. "I feel like there'd be way less candidates left alive by the end of the day. But then again who knows." Faith grins. "They let me beat the piss out of that goon in the cage."

Max and Pilet look at each other, then back to Faith, slightly concerned.

The gang reaches the Weapons sparring section, as a proctor approaches. His black hair combed flat to the right, shiny with styling product. His dark handlebar mustache bounces up and down as he walks. A thin, ball-tipped rapier on his left hip, a parrying dagger on his right. His navy blue, skin tight slacks rolled up over his brown loafers. He sports a spotless white button up with a red bowtie, and hung over his shoulder is a navy blazer. The Proctor speaks.

"Hello candidates, my name is Toste"

The group pauses.

"..."

There is unanimous silence. For whatever reason, Pilet grins devilishly. The Proctor continues.

"What is the name of your team?"

"..."

"Excuse me. It is extremely rude not to answer my simple question. Now, I will ask a second time. What is the assigned name of your group?" Said the Proctor flusteredly.

"... Your name is Toast?" Said Pilet.

"Yes!" Said Toste. "My name is Toste! Now, what is your team's name?!"

"Nah man holdup, we gotta talk about *this* first. Who named you Toast?? You should slap your Dad. What, was he hungry when you were born?" Said Pilet.

"Pilet stoppp!" Said Yunna.

Max and Faith are still speechless in disbelief.

Visibly triggered, Toste tightens his bowtie.

"EXCUSE ME! I'll have you know my father was one of the most celebrated swordsmen in Kettlena!" Exclaimed Toste.

"Oh yeah? What's *HIS* name, Jam? Butter?" Said Pilet.

Max interrupts.

"I apologize sir, we're the Hidden Blades. Please excuse my friend, he's just amazed at the uniqueness of your name." Said Max.

"And while we're at it." Said Pilet. "What's that sword for, *spreading* the jam? Or is that your knife's job. Kinda weird to be spreading your dad all over you, don't you think?"

Faith slaps Pilet firmly in the arm. "Shutup." Said Faith.

"Ow what the hell?" Said Pilet. He mumbles. "Not my fault the guy's named after his breakfast..."

"Mister Toast, what's to be expected of us in this section?" Said Faith, eluding the topic of his name.

"Ahem, yes, well. You are to be tested by one of the allotted swordsmanship Proctors here with a blunted weapon of your choice from the rack. As you can see there are more Proctors in this section because we test candidates individually, as opposed to in a group like the MMA portion." Said Toste.

"So it's a much quicker portion?" Said Max.

"Precisely." Said Toste. "You are to spar three, five minute rounds with a Proctor. The results of your performance here will reflect in your overall physical exam score. Simple enough, yes?"

"Yes, thank you." Said Max.

"Now who is your emissary?" Said Toste.

Max, Faith and Yuuna all point to Pilet.

"Yo! That's me." Said Pilet.

"How very interesting..." Toste replied. "You three, please wait on the sidelines for your next available Proctor. I will be testing Mister... What is your name?"

"Pilet, Pilet Whydah." Said Pilet.

"Oh the King Killer! This changes things..."

Toste takes the safety tip off of his rapier. Pilet fails to notice the devious grin, and nefarious glaze across his eyes.

"Well now, someone of your caliber certainly deserves a true test of skill." Said Toste. "Certainly it would be a disservice to use safety equipment against an opponent as powerful as you, right?"

"I, uh, well yeah of course!" Said Pilet. "Yeah... See this guy gets me! See that folks, even the proctor's are calling me strong. Ha! You guys picked the right emissary."

Catching on to the unforgiving tone in Toste's voice, the group looks toward Pilet with chagrin. Max pats him on the back.

"Well, good luck my friend. Have fun with *that*." Said Max.

The three take their leave and are soon met with Proctors of their own.

Some fifty feet away in the stands, Faxion exchanges words with Chairman Yang, the official head of The Hired Blades Association. The two are seated side-by-side on the top row.

Chairman Yang, a bald headed, older gentleman with a gray goatee, a bit on the longer and scruffy side. An "X" shaped scar runs high along his left cheekbone. Auric rune tattoos completely cover his body, his large muscular frame allowing for plenty of canvas space. One tattoo in particular on his left side of neck, showcases the symbol of the Hired Blades Association.

Chairman Yang takes a drag of a thick cigar.

"So Fax, the boy with the peach fuzz on his head, he's your recruit huh?"

"Yes sir." Said Faxion. "I came upon the lad on my way through the village of Chamboree. Not the sharpest blade on the rack, but the boy has a very unique set of skills, and the heart of a hungry wolverine in battle."

"That's good to hear. I have to be honest, with what I've been told of his performance so far, I was beginning to worry about your discernment. His written exam score was in the lowest percentile of passing grades, and he's actually done the worst of everyone today at the gun range. But after that 3 second knockout in the cage, the scoring judges have been reconsidering his future. They gave him the highest grade possible, an "S" rank in martial arts."

"Oh my, they gave him an "S" for that? That's wonderful! You know I too was worried, the boy has only had 2 weeks of Blades training, and how much can you learn in that brief period?"

"Well whatever you taught him with your fists worked out pretty damn well." Said Yang. "A knockout that fast without getting hit means the judges don't have much to judge. A shorter fight means less time to make mistakes. Plus the replay showed that he actually evaded a technique on the way in, a difficult maneuver while moving so fast. The only other cage fighting "S" rank was awarded to an archeologist kid who fought four people at once. The boy put them all in the hospital..."

"Well then!" Faxion shakes his head in disbelief. "What an interesting crop we have this year. I'm excited to see them in action during the next phase. I must say the location of this year's practical was an excellent choice. Putting the candidates in a place overrun with the wurm, forcing them to cull the local population. I see what you were going for with your decision."

"Haha, thank you Fax." Said Yang. "It's unusual, the rise in wurm activity there lately. We figured the best way to test the eligibility of this year's entrants would be to put them in the field, right out of the gate. The only way to see if they'll survive out there is to, well, literally see if they survive out there! Of course, *our* obvious benefit is population control of the region's wurm infestation. Now Fax about your fiery prospect, what the hell did you teach him with a gun? I don't know if you noticed but the boy basically hit everything *but* his target!"

Sigh "Yes I'm aware." Said Faxion. "Pilet lacks any skill with a ranged weapon, it's actually quite hilarious how bad he is. I spent a whole week trying to teach him how to aim, shoot and reload. I finally gave up when he almost shot me in the ass, I value my ability to walk and take comfortable shits too much... We decided to focus more on the skills he possesses than those he lacks. Trust me, he will more than make up for it I assure you."

"It's ironic isn't it." Said Yang. He grins and takes another long drag from his cigar. "Faxion of the Deadeye, raising a Hired Blade with dreadful aim. The boy might as well use his rifle as a club."

"Oh believe me sir. I've not stopped reveling in the irony of fate myself..."

Back on the testing floor, Toste readies Pilet for their sparring session.

"Ok boy." Said Toste. He glances at the Dragonfly knives holstered to Pilet's side. "It appears you fancy those Dragonflies on your waist. Refrain from engaging their infrared function, and they should fare fine in this bout, I shall permit their use. Now the rules are simple; try to hit me, and do not get hit. Easy, yes?"

"Yeah yeah got it, what happens when I hit you?" Said Pilet.

Toste scoffs.

"Well first of all, if *you* are struck, you keep fighting. I will keep a tally of your score throughout our bout. If *I* am hit, the same rules apply. *Unless* your strike would be a fatal blow. If this happens, the match is over and you win outright. Avoid fatal mistakes at all costs, because they *will indeed* cost you. Are we clear on the rules?"

"Clear as a Kettlenian crystal buddy." Said Pilet.

"Good... Now..."

Toste takes a defensive posture with his blade pointed down. He brings his feet together and draws a line on the floor with the tip of his rapier. Pilet readies his Dragonflies, holding them blades crossed in front of him, down by his waist. Toste separates his legs in a crouching fashion, draws his blade to his face and points it towards Pilet. He exclaims.

"En Garde!"

In a flash, Toste lunges forward with his fencing foil. But Pilet makes a quick read. He lifts his lead Dragonfly, parrying the foil to his right. This leaves Toste open for a counter attack. As Pilet steps in to deliver a blow with his rear Dragonfly, Toste swiftly draws his parrying dagger with his free hand. Pilet sees this and quickly back steps.

Shit, that's a fast draw. How am I going to counter? Thought Pilet.

"What's wrong King Killer?" Said Toste. "Weren't you going to hit me?"

Pilet furrows his brow. He readies his blades again.

Fwip

Toste lunges with the agility of a huntsman spider, his foil nearly piercing Pilet's nose. Pilet narrowly parries with his rear blade and ducks to gain distance from the foil's dangerous tip. Pilet's lead blade now sits under Toste's striking arm, out of the swordsman's line of sight. Pilet follows up with a rising strike, but Toste draws his parrying knife with his free hand and contorts his body, catching Pilet's blade in the hilt of his dagger.

Klang

With Pilet's lead Dragonfly caught in Toste's rear dagger, and his rear blade still making contact with the foil; Toste unfurls his body and criss-crosses Pilet's arms over each other with finesse. Toste then gives Pilet a bear hug in this vulnerable posture and slips the blade of his foil through the handguards of Pilet's weapons, locking Pilet's arms behind him like a straightjacket. Frustrated, the bound Pilet flails about, unable to free his weapons.

"Shit! What the hell did you do?!" Exclaimed Pilet.

"There are different levels to what we call fighting boy." Said Toste. "And when it comes to these levels, yours and mine are far apart."

Pilet, still struggling to release his blades, trips on his own feet.

Thud

He stumbles and falls on his rear end. Seething in anger, Pilet's eyes begin to glow amethyst. As his temper starts to rise, he looks in the distance to his teacher. Faxion notices, shakes his head and gives him a disapproving glare.

Faxion voices a "Not now" to Pilet. Pilet takes a moment to breathe, his eyes return to normal. He releases the hilts of his Dragonflies, freeing him from the embarrassing trap set by the master swordsman.

"Very good boy, I was beginning to think it was over before it started." Said Toste.

Pilet collects his weapons. He then picks up Toste's foil and hands it to him. Surprised, Toste gratefully accepts the blade.

"Well, I thought I would have to gain this back through crafty footwork."

"Chasing after a guy with just a butterknife, where's the fun in that?" Said Pilet. "Now do your fancy stance again and let's fight."

The two stand across from each other and brandish their weapons. They pause for a moment, waiting to see who will strike first this time. Still and calm, the fighters slowly creep towards each other. Finally, Pilet level changes and swiftly slashes at the knees. Toste nimbly backsteps and ripostes with his foil, stabbing Pilet shallowly in the arm.

Shing *Shlick*

"Hnng!!"

Pilet seethes in pain for a moment, but continues fighting. He rolls forward in another attempt to graze a leg. Toste leaps to avoid the strike and comes down with a downward slash from the sky.

Kshinng kshinng

As Pilet recovers to his knees, he blocks the slash with both of his blades overhead. Pilet catches the foil in the handguard of his left blade and parries it away, exposing Toste's backside. In one fluid motion Pilet moves in to finish with his right, but Toste draws his parrying dagger with unbelievable speed. Toste catches Pilet's blade in the guard of his dagger and twirls himself out of the engagement, delivering a slashing blow to Pilet's cheek on the way out.

Shlick

"Aagh!"

Pilet reeles at the cut caused by the foil. He leaps backwards and touches his face. Scarlet red blood begins to rush down his chin. Pilet revels in the cause of his misfortune.

Why can't I counter? Every time I get close I end up getting punished.

Toste engages Pilet again with a nimble lunge. Pilet parries, and the two begin to dart and slash back and forth in a volley of bladesmanship.

Shing shing shing KSSHH shing shing shing KSSHH

Pilet notices the rear hand of Toste, occasionally motioning towards his parrying knife. Every time Pilet moves as though to counter, Toste's knife hand draws near the blade.

Why doesn't he just hold it in his hand? Why re-sheath the dagger with every parry? It should take too much time... But somehow it doesn't. He's so fast with that parrying draw it's ridiculous.

They continue their deadly dance as some of the other candidates take notice. The furious exchange of metal draws the eyes of onlookers throughout the gymnasium. Suddenly Pilet trips on his hind foot. As he recovers himself mid-fall, Toste sees an opening and pierces directly through Pilet's left shoulder

Shhllick

"AAAGH!"

Pilet hollers in pain. The outburst draws the attention of the weapons testing applicants nearby, as they wince at the sight of the foil straight through his shoulder. In the distance, Max Quinn, (who had just swiftly dispatched his *own* proctor) calls out to Pilet.

"Do not panic, Pilet!" Beckons Max. "It's only a flesh wound, he knows that! Now collect yourself and fight!"

Toste viciously removes his foil from Pilet's shoulder.

Shing

"Aagh! Damn it!" Shouts Pilet. His hand clenches his wound tightly.

Toste responds.

"Your young swordsman friend is right boy. It's merely a flesh wound, if you can't handle that I wonder how you'll fare out there in the real danger."

Again, Pilet's eyes begin to glow. Angered and humiliated, Pilet struggles to compose himself. He knows if he invokes the power of his abilities, he will be disqualified for illegal use of aura. He takes a moment, breathes steadily and relaxes his mind.

The draw, he's doing it on purpose... He thought. *If he had the dagger already drawn I would see it and avoid the idea of countering. But with it holstered I subconsciously believe he's open for attack and keep falling for the same, quick-draw trick. Old man Fax was right, he really is too good. Alright, no more playing around. It's time.*

"Damn Toast, all that butter spreading must've given you some serious blade skill huh?" Said Pilet. "It's only a flesh wound because you're fighting with that skinny toothpick."

Toste's nostrils flare.

"Excuse me? Have you not had enough punishment?! Very well then boy!!"

Pilet anxiously bites his lip.

Ah shit here it comes...

Furious at his lack of respect, Toste begins whipping his foil around at blinding speed. The flexible blade makes it impossible to track in mid air, and produces an ominous whistle in the wind. The tip scratches and cuts the ground around Toste, as he advances toward Pilet. Pilet braces himself and gets ready to engage.

"Nice trick." Said Pilet "What's that for, slicing baguettes? Come on Toasty, gotta do better than that."

With the triggered eyes of a demon, Toste rushes at Pilet. His foil sends an impossible amount of strikes flying throughout the air around him, cutting Pilet mercilessly wherever he cannot cover up. Dowsing Pilet in small, painful scrapes and slashes; Toste loses sight of his purpose to finish his foe. As Pilet endures the vicious onslaught of the master swordsman, he recounts advice from Faxion during their training weeks.

"Pilet, once you reach the weapons fencing portion of the exam, there is a good chance you will meet a Proctor named Toste. If you can, try to make him your opponent."

"His name is Toast?" Said Pilet.

"It's a rarely seen name spelled T.o.s.t.e.

The name means precious gem in the Menanois language, a country far to the south of us. Toste is the son of the late king of Menanois, named "Bu Tear"; commonly mistaken for "Butter" here in Kettlena. His royal father was also a mighty swords master. Now Toste is a perfect gentleman, unless you mistake his name for the breakfast food."

"Hahaha! Yeah, I'd be mad too. Alright but who cares? Why is he so important? What about the other Proctors?"

"Well, Toste is the most skilled swordsman of all the Proctors there, a win over him would surely have an impact on your final score. However, it won't come easy."

"Oooh, alright cool. So I just gotta kick this Toste guy's ass and my score will skyrocket?"

"One could only wish it was so simple... Toste is most likely going to give you a serious thrashing. But I believe you have what it takes to survive against him. His fatal flaw is his temper, which is easily onset by the mistaking of his name. It's an inherited trait from his father, who fell in battle because of it. Pilet, get him angry. And when he lets his guard down, punish him for it. Do this, and the victory will be yours..."

The crowds begin to spectate Pilet and Toste's match yet again, this time reveling at the flurry of blood and metal flying through the air. As

Pilet winces in pain, he notices Toste's right hand is no longer readied by his parrying dagger. The arm is instead up high, providing balance for Toste to continue his whipping flurry of lashes. Another Proctor yells out to Toste.

"Just finish him man, the fight's over!"

"Silence!" Exclaims Toste. "He's not endured what would be a fatal blow yet, and I won't grant one! The boy must learn respect!"

In the moment Toste took to reply to his colleague, Pilet recognized a pattern in his movement. Left swipe across, right diagonal, rising swipe skyward, left diagonal, right swipe across. It's become clear that this is no random pattern, but instead a practiced technique. His mind's eye sees the shape of a six pointed star forming from the foil. He waits for Toste to finish one more starred pattern, and on the final swipe, Pilet catches the foil in the guard of his right Dragonfly.

Cling

Pilet darts in, startling Toste and drawing his balancing arm down to his parrying knife. In that moment, the fight was decided. Toste's right hand sits on his holstered dagger. Pilet's right Dragonfly rests unnervingly against Toste's neck. Speechless and out of breath, Toste stares wide-eyed at his opponent. Pilet stands broodingly, blood trickling down from the cuts all over his body. The crowd gasps, then begins to clamor boisterously.

"KING KILLER! KING KILLER! KING KILLER!"

Pilet looks apologetically at Toste. He lowers his Dragonfly.

"Sorry about your old man." Said Pilet. "You should be proud of your name. People mess mine up all the time, the "T" is silent. I can't get a cup of coffee without the barista yelling "Pee-lot" or some shit. I don't care, my Mom gave me this name. It means a lot to me and if anyone doesn't like it, that's their problem. Oh yeah, and Faxion the Deadeye sends his regards.

Shocked at the events that have taken place, Toste holsters his foil and shakes Pilet's hand.

"Hah, Faxion. That old dog, still looking after me I see. We've been on many a mission together you know!" Said Toste. "The technique you've just witnessed is called the Star of Menanois. It's a trademark flourish of my people. I suppose I overdid it though, didn't I. Thank you Pilet, I've learned a valuable lesson today. I'd bet the spirit of my father looks down in pride at this defeat."

"Your father... Oh you mean "Butter"?" Said Pilet.

Toste's nostrils flare, his brow furrows. He glares at Pilet. Pilet simply looks up, tilts his head and points as if to say, "Think for a second.""

"Hah! You're right boy!" Said Toste. "Thank you for this valuable lesson. Your grade today will reflect it indefinitely."

"Hoh, I'm betting on it buddy." Said Pilet. "I didn't take an ass-whopping like this because I wanted to help *your* sorry ass. Hahahahaha!" Pilet laughs as he walks away. Toste simply shakes his head and inputs his grade into his electronic clipboard.

"Pilet Whydah." Insert score.

"Hmm."

Toste scrolls over the rankings. He stops at "S" rank.

Click

"If to be a Blade you had to beat a Blade, the boy would have his license already. "S" rank it is."

The Master Auracaster

Pilet walks back to the sidelines, now drenched in blood. The medic rushes over as he greets his friends.

"Woah boy! You need some support, STAT!" Said the medic.

"Nah man no need, check this out." Replied Pilet.

He closes his eyes and begins to concentrate. As he opens them, they immediately glow a Violet hue. His body, covered in glowing amethyst patterns, begins to rapidly regenerate cell tissue and heal the cuts instantly. Even the piercing wound in his shoulder miraculously seals itself. Max, Yuuna and Faith watch speechlessly. The medic backs away from Pilet with a puzzled look on his face.

"Never seen that auracast before. Whatever works kid, as long as you're patched up."

He takes his leave. The gang continues their silent stare.

"..."

"Are, are you a demon?" Said Max.

"Hahaha no man, I'm just born this way!" Said Pilet, his voice reverberating with newfound bass. "When I fought the big monkey back home in Chamboree, this started happening out of nowhere. I call it the "Fever Point", because my skin gets really hot before I change."

"That's amazing Pilet!" Said Yuuna. "I had no idea you could do something like that, it's like a super power!"

"You look like an alien..." Said Faith.

"What?!" Said Pilet. "Yeah, well this *ALIEN* could chase down a speeding hovercar! Watch!"

Pilet vanishes in a violet cloud of aura, appearing on the other side of the gymnasium behind a candidate with a large sun hat on. He stealthily peels the hat off of her head and dashes 20 feet away in a flash, planting the hat on an unsuspecting Puerto. Confused, Puerto turns and pulls the hat off of his head. By this point Pilet is back behind the first candidate, tapping her shoulder to turn around. Before she can see him, he vanishes and reappears out of thin air by the Hidden Blades.

"What kind of castery is this..." Muttered a befuddled Max Quinn.

The group watches as the first candidate turns around, notices her hat in the hands of Puerto and rushes towards him in a peeved fit. In the distance you see the innocent Man o' War trying to explain himself, before getting abruptly slapped in the face. The first entrant swiftly takes her hat back and storms off, as Puerto's confused team breaks into laughter at his expense.

"My God, such speed is incredible." Said Max. "It's no wonder you were able to slay that Wurm King, I couldn't even see you move!"

"I guess the world never saw this, considering the video of your fight was taken from a distance by a low quality camera." Said Faith. "Still, I wonder why this happens to you. I've never read about anything like it in any auracast book."

Pilet shuts his eyes and takes a deep breath. On the exhale his skin returns to normal and the glow in his eyes dissipates. He stumbles clumsily onto a nearby chair.

"Are you ok?" Said Faith.

"Yeah I'm good, just a little woozy." Said Pilet. "That form takes muscle fuel to maintain. Fax told me about it, said something about "ATP" whatever that is."

"ATP..." Said Faith. "That's Adenosine triphosphate. It's what your body's cells use as energy to function, *especially* your muscles. Auric tattoos use that to cast in place of your body's stored aura, that's why so many buff "warrior tough guy" types have 'em." Faith scoffs, as she and Yuuna share a condescending eye-roll. "They're too lazy to learn how to cast on their own... Anyway it's no wonder you're so fatigued, this form is probably very new to you."

"On another note, Pilet your fight with Toste was amazing!" Said Yuuna. "Everyone was watching on the edge of their seats, no one could believe you'd beat a Licensed Hired Blade like that. To be honest I barely skidded-by with my skills. I'm not really good with weapons fighting, I just know the bare minimum. And Max! You too, you beat yours so fast! Most of us were just expected to hold our own, not actually *finish* our Proctors."

"Thanks Yuuna." Said Max "My Proctor was a last minute substitute. He was not a swordsmanship specialist in his own right, and there was no way I could let a Sanda warrior be beaten by a non-swordsman. I must say though, his skills were legit and he gave me some trouble. It's no wonder Licensed Hired Blades are respected the world over."

"Yeah thanks." Said Pilet. "I'm not gonna lie, the guy really messed me up for a second. His old man must've really been a serious swordsman to raise a fighter like that. Faith, how'd you do with your sword fight?"

"I did fine, nothing special like you two." Said Faith. "Like my sister I rely more on auracast to fight than anything else, not so much weapons. Well, there is *one* that I fancy, you'll see soon enough. Speaking of auracast, we've got our last challenge up ahead! I think the auracast test is held outside in the courtyard."

The group grabs their gear and begins marching across the gymnasium, passing by cheering bystanders in the bleachers. Pilet holds a hand out and high-five's the whole front row as he passes.

"Thank you thank you! You're far too kind!" Said Pilet.

As the Hidden Blades reach the exit and take their leave, Pilet stops and flexes at the crowd. They adore his spirit and continue to cheer at the tops of their lungs. Pilet peers over to Faxion in the crowd. His mentor offers himt a thumbs up and a devilish smile.

That's it Pilet! Make me look good! The boss man is right here! Thought Faxion.

With his arms folded and a stone-cold expression, Chairman Yang can't help but release a slight grin, amused by the energy of the fiery prospect.

He mutters, "Not bad boy, not bad.".

Pilet points to the crowd and exclaims. "Stay tuned, you ain't seen nothing yet!"

Faith returns for a moment, rolls her eyes and grabs him by the arm. "Hurry up slowpoke!" She proceeds to drag Pilet out of the gymnasium.

As the group exits the densely populated testing grounds, they're greeted by the fresh breeze of the autumn air.

The courtyard, located directly in the center of the Hired Blades HQ building, is massive. Lined with colossal white columns and tranquil oaken benches along the sides. Gray concrete sidewalks form a circle around an immense fountain of an armored warrior, wielding a pistol in one hand and a double edged sword in the other. The fountain's water spouts forth from the tip of the pistol, pointed skyward above its head. Surrounding the warrior lies more water spouts shooting from the ground beneath him into a crystal clear pool below.

The sidewalks branch out from the circle forming curved patterns leading to the edges of the courtyard, and in between these patterns are patches of green grass lined with white and blue orchids.

The Reaper Elite, one of the groups involved in The Lava Bean Cafe scuffle, make their way back to the gymnasium after their auracast exam. As the two teams cross paths, Pilet and Lazlow The Gavel size each other up. Lazlow flashes a cocky smile, scoffing at The King Killer.

"Hmmph, weak." Said Lazlow.

Without verbal retort, Pilet points down towards his hip with a shocked expression. Lazlow peers downwards, seeing Pilet's other hand flipping him the middle finger. He then looks up to see Pilet smiling at him with a deviant, slightly deranged glare.

"Tch, whatever." Muttered Lazlow, continuing his march towards the gymnasium.

Before The Reaper Elites fully walk by, Arturo and Max both reach for the hilts of their respective top swords. They exchange an ever so slight nod of the head, as if to say "I see you.". Both Hachidorinese warrior's hands leave their Lacerates as they go their separate ways.

The Hidden Blades reach the center of the courtyard where the next

Proctor lies in wait. Wearing a simple maroon button-up shirt and khaki pants, he sits cross-legged on the lifted ledge of the fountain's pool. His hands crossed in front of his chest, facing palm up, reveal triangular tattoos with a "3" in the center. As the crew approaches, the Proctor takes a deep breath and opens his eyes, as if exiting a meditative trance.

"Oh, hey there!" Said the Proctor. "I guess you guys are next for auracast testing right? What's your crew's name?"

Pilet replies. "Yo, we're The Hidden Blades."

"Ok cool one sec..." The Proctor pulls out his electronic clipboard. He scrolls through to mark off their attendance. "Ok great. Yeah so I'm Scott, Scott Diliger. Pleasure to make your acquaintance!"

"Wait." Says Faith. "*THEE* Scott Diliger? The *famous archeologist* Scott Diliger!?"

Scott grins, bowing not-so modestly.

"The one and only!" Said Scott. "Glad to know you've heard of me.

Pilet mutters. "I haven't."

"I am not surprised..." Replied Max. He turns to Scott and bows. "It is an honor to meet you Mister Diliger."

"Yeah seriously!" Said Yuuna. "My parents used to talk about you all the time!"

"Oh stop the pleasure is all mine, or the honor? Well whatever. And who are your parents?" Said Scott.

"Lina and Devin Sierro." Said Yuuna.

"Oh..." Said Scott. "Wow so you must be *their* girls! Listen I'm very sorry for what happened, my condolences. They were absolute pioneers of Rok-Senn cultural research. I actually got to work with them a few times, they spoke very highly of you two... Sorry, let me not get carried away. Welcome to the auracast exam! Oh, and it looks like this is it for you guys. It says here you've completed all the other sections for the day. Hope there's gas in the tank for one more!"

"Me and my sister have waited diligently for this portion, this is our forte." Said Faith.

"I'm sure it is." Said Scott. "Your parents were no slouches themselves. Man this is exciting, alright let's see what you've got!"

Scott begins to rub his hands vigorously and inhales deeply. His right hand begins to glow Cerulean, as he taps his chest. "Callous.". His body becomes covered with the translucent aura of the Callous cast. He steps down from the fountain's ledge and takes 8 paces adjacent to The Hidden Blades team. Scott takes a knee and places his palms on the floor. "Killzone." An iridescent dome of aura forms from the earth to the sky, similar to Faxion's entrapping cast against The Piranha gang. The dome surrounds the perimeter of the courtyard, preventing any form of entrance to the area, or any exit...

"Alright guys so here's how this is gonna go." Said Scott. "At this point of the exam you're finally allowed to use your auracast! But there's a catch. Auracast is the ONLY thing permitted. That means you can't use your fists, ranged, or close combat weapons directly on me." Scott motions to Max. "So watch the swords there buddy! Haha. Anyway, you CAN use your weapons as a casting tool if need be, but not to slash my face off. Got it?"

The Hidden Blades collectively nod their heads and take their ready stances.

"Cool cool. Ok. So if any one of you wants the throw in the towel, just say "I concede." It's not recommended if you want to pass but hey, being a Blade's not for everybody right? No shame in that. The battleground is the entirety of the courtyard, even the fountain! Don't worry about going too far, the barrier will make sure you don't. And don't worry about me either." Scott smiles innocently. "I can handle myself. So let loose! Go all out! Because if you don't you're probably screwed. I mean you're screwed anyway, but might as well put your best foot forward right?"

A bead of sweat runs down Faith's forehead. Yuuna gulps.

"Arm yourselves." Said Scott.

Max rests a hand on the hilt of his M7 Lacerate. He takes a crouching posture and fixes his eyes on Scott.

"Ready..."

Faith pulls out her ancient tome and begins to sift through the pages.

"Set..."

Yuuna presses her hands together and closes her eyes. The crystals on her necklace begin to glow.

"..."

After a brief pause, Pilet raises one eyebrow in confusion.

"Is this guy pulling our leg?"

"GO!" Exclaims Scott flourishing an ominous aura between his grasp.

Auracast Exam, Begin!

A serpentine column of water rises from the fountain and surrounds Scott Diliger, responding to his hand movements like a cobra to a snake charmer. Wide eyed at the aquatic arcane threat, the team simultaneously casts "Callous" fearing the worst. Scotts middle and ring finger press to the tip of his thumb forming a mouth in the aquatic beast. His index and pinky point outward, forming protruding eyeballs on the face of the creature, as the water column starts to form into a massive floating slug. As Scott balls this hand into a fist, the slug develops a lump of boiling water behind its head.

Fizzle sizz fizzle sizz

Scott releases his fist, sending a volley of scalding, pressurized water toward his foes.

FWOOOSH *SIZZLE*

Faith holds out the palm of her hand, she reads from her tome. "Frisio!" Frigid air shoots forth in a cone, freezing the water in place like a sculpture. She follows up with an auxiliary cast. "MohGuu." A wicked smokescreen envelops the surrounding area.

Scott stands behind the ice wall, his water slug readied on high alert.

"Not bad Faith, not bad." Said Scott. He waits for a moment, expecting an attack from his peripherals. His left hand cultivates aura and touches his ears. "Earhorn." He's granted arcane hearing as the inside of his ears glow cerulean.

Pitter patter *Pitter patter*.

The sound of an assailant draws near. He hears a faint whisper.

"Scarrya." *Vrrrrrr*

Just then, Faith darts behind Scott with a blade of pure, red hot aura protruding from her fingertips. She slices through the water slug and tries for a surprise attack on Scott, but Scott was prepared. He steps back and reconnects his arcane gastropod, catching Faith inside of it. Her blade dissipates as her hands become preoccupied swimming frantically to escape. Just then; a vibrant, white auric star the size of a beach ball falls from the sky towards Scott, as the voice of Yuuna can be heard.

"Falling Star!" She casts.

"Ooh, you shouldn't've done that." Said Scott.

He begins rolling his fists one over the other, as if punching a speed bag. He then changes the angle of his arms vertically as his water slug begins to rotate at high speed around him. Faith is caught in the middle of the aquatic barrier, as she's spun mercilessly into the star. Just before the Falling Star makes impact, Faith reads another cast.

"Ruug Yah!" She cries, as water enters her lungs.

The Star strikes.

CRASH

Whatever impact the water does not absorb, Faith does. Scott stops spinning the barrier, as it returns to slug form.

Covering her face from the blast, Faith lowers her guard; revealing her body to be completely covered in durable, rainbow scales. She removes her trench coat, also revealing gills along her vibrant neck.

"Wow! The Rainbow Fish of the Rok-Senn, that's extinct!" Said Scott. "So then, that book. It must be an artifact isn't it? No one could master a cast based on a creature whose remains were never found, unless written in aura by an ancient auracaster! We've only seen paintings of the fish, no fossils were ever excavated."

Faith replies. "Glad you appreciate it, but I'm not so sure your slug will share the sentiment."

Rainbow scales that have fallen off of Faith on impact float throughout the water slug, releasing violet residue. The slug makes a sickly face, as it dissipates into an inanimate puddle of water, soaking the ground around it.

"The Rainbow Fish was famous for its aura toxicity, it was even known to toxify the aurafields of fishermen skinning them." Said Faith as she rises from the ground, released from the slug. "Now where was I? Oh yeah... Scarrya!"

Faith presses the fingertips of her right hand together, yet again forming a red hot aura blade. She rushes Toward Scott, slicing and slashing as he dodges and sidesteps. She backs him into the fountain, as he takes a tumble into the pool.

"Now!" Shouts Faith.

Yuuna presses her hands together, cultivates aura and makes a twisting motion to the air in her grasp.

"Dust Devil!" Casts Yuuna.

A twister appears and blows away the smokescreen, revealing Max

Quinn with his Lacerate pointed skyward. Yellow lightning begins to envelope the blade. Scott emerges from the pool, just in time to see this turn of events.

"Interesting." Said Scott. "A wind and star caster, and a traditional Sandacaster from Hachidori. This might be a challenge."

"Raimei!" Casts Max.

He plunges his aura infused Lacerate into the ground, calling forth a lightning storm directly onto the fountain.

BAM *CRRACK* *BOOM*

Lightning completely downpours on the statue as thunder booms throughout the dome. As the water calms and the light show ends, Scott is seen floating in the water like a fried fish. Max, Faith and Yuuna all lower their guard, stunned at the sight of the fearsome auracaster lying lifeless in the thunderstricken fountain.

"Oh, my apologies......" Said Max, stunned by the onslaught of his own technique.

"Max! What did you dooo!!!" Exclaims Yuuna. "You killed Scott Diliger! Why did you do that?!"

"What?! I did not mean to! He... he is a Licensed Hired Blade, I believed he would have an answer for a technique like that!" Said Max frantically.

Pilet emerges from behind a nearby bush.

"Damn Max, you really roasted him!" Said Pilet. "Oh well, hey where's that Blades badge! We're like, 2-0 today against Licensed Blades. At this point we damn well deserve it."

Faith simply facepalms.

Just then, Scott's body begins to shake and shimmy within the water.

"Oh shit." Said Pilet. "Is that the death rattle? Max hit that buster again!"

"Would you shut up for a second?" Snaps Faith. "Wait... Look."

A hand begins to creep out of the chest of Scott.

"AAAH!!" The whole group leaps back in horror.

"Holy shit!" Screams Faith.

"It's an abomination!!" Exclaims Max.

"It's an alien!! It took over Scott's body!! What are we gonna do!!!" Cries Yuuna.

"What the hell?!" Said Pilet. "Is... is this guy having a mutant baby???"

The rest of Scott Diliger's body emerges from the husk of what seems to be a rubber hide. He stands in the fountain pool and tosses his shed skin to them. They step back, mortified and disgusted by the arcane exoskeleton.

"Phew, close call!" Said Scott. He points to the rubber husk. "That's the "ChewyCicada" technique, it's a good cast! Great for electric attacks."

"Uh, yeah... or heart attacks!" Said Yuuna.

"GGood to know." Stuttered Faith.

"Now, shall we continue?" Said Scott, as he raises his palms upwards. Aura emanates from his hands and begins to envelop the warrior statue of the fountain behind him. "Remember, "The battleground is the entirety of the courtyard, even the fountain!". I didn't say that for nothing."

Forgetting the test is not over, The Hidden Blades backstep nimbly and ready themselves.

"Arcane Battery!" Casts Scott.

Water stops flowing from the tip of the statue's pistol, as its eyes begin to flutter and blink.

"Was I hit in the head too hard today?" Said Max. "I must be hallucinating, that statue just blinked."

"Woah. Yeah me too." Said Pilet. He shakes his head and rubs his eyes in disbelief. "Toste must've done more of a number on me than I thought."

The stone statue lowers its pistol from the sky and points it directly towards The Hidden Blades crew.

"Allow me to introduce you to Mr. Gregory Galant, the original Hired Blade. Or, at least his likeness." Said Scott.

"..."

"...Oh... Shit." Said Faith.

"Now, one more time. Let's fight!" Said Scott.

He casts Fleetfoot and swiftly exits the pool. On his way out Scott snaps his fingers, triggering a circle of cerulean glowing patterns on the ground encircling the fountain.

"Have fun with that!" Said Scott.

"Look out! Auric mines!" Said Faith.

But it's too late, as each member of the group gets caught in the blast. They're all sent flying around the courtyard, crashing into the dome barrier and bouncing off onto the freshly cut grass. Pilet, Max and Yuuna's callous cast begins to flake off in certain spots. Many of Faith's rainbow scales chip off and litter the battlefield, revealing her callous cast beneath.

As The Hidden Blades collect themselves, they're greeted by the sound of heavy thudding footsteps shaking the earth beneath them. Gregory Galante's sculpture begins to stomp its way across the battlefield, headed straight for Yuuna. As it draws near, it swings its massive stone sword at her with an overhead slash.

"AAAAAAAHHH!!!!!" She cried.

Yuuna gasps and covers her face with her hands. In an instant, Max darts in front of her with his trusted M7 Lacerate in hand.

Shing *Clang*

The Sanda draws his blade with blinding speed. He blocks the immense stone sword as it descends on him like a meteor.

Crush

The Sculpture leans its opposite forearm into the back of its sword, applying pressure to force Max downward. But the musclebound Max stands his ground, driving his shoulder into the blunted backside of his Lacerate.

Max grunts. "Man... beast or, Hnnnng! God-forsaken creature, the Sanda yield to no one."

The two become locked in a swordsman's game of tug of war. The Sculpture begins to get the better of Max, forcing himself further and further down upon the young warrior. But in an impressive display of strength and resilience; Max plants his back foot, grits his teeth and pushes forward, gaining back some lost ground. The two are neck and neck, neither giving up an inch to each other.

Yuuna shakes her head, waking herself up to the situation at hand. She removes an earthy red crystal from her necklace and holds it clasped between her hands in a praying gesture. She takes a deep breath, and on the exhale her hands begin to glow red. After a few more deep breaths, she opens her hands.

The red stone glows, as it delivers a bolstering aura towards Max. The red aura surges throughout Max's body, giving him arcane strength and vitality. With this newfound power, Max's eyes begin to glow a searing mahogany.

"GRAAAHHH!!!"

He starts to push back the Sculpture, its giant stone feet plowing across the grass as it tries to root itself in protest. As Max continues to push along the statue, its heavy feet anchor too far into the dirt, forcing the Sanda warrior to halt his advance.

Sensing this, Max parries the stone sword downward toward the ground.

Crash

The sword strikes the ground and buries itself deep into the dirt, leaving the statue stuck in place for a moment. Without hesitation, Max follows up with a skyward slash to the face of the behemoth.

Rrrip

His Lacerate rips a massive crack across the nose of the sculpture from ear to ear, however it appears unperturbed by its fresh wound.

"Does nothing harm this monster?" Said Max, holding his Lacerate before him in a defensive posture.

Just then, the pistol arm of the sculpture whips around Max's guard.

SMASH

The butt of the pistol smacks Max in the temple, sending him tumbling 15 feet across the courtyard. He struggles to get up to his hands and knees.

"Uuungh." Riles Max.

With blurred vision, he is able to make out the form of the pistol pointed right at him. The barrel begins to glow cerulean, as the aura Scott's provided to it forms a bullet in the chamber. Dazed and unable to escape, Max watches as this arcane projectile readies to fire. Just then, a familiar voice is heard in the distance.

"Hollowpoint!!"

A violet, soft ball sized bullet of pure concentrated aura rips across the battlefield at dizzying speed.

Vvvrrrrrripppp *CRASH*

The violet aura sphere blasts the pistol arm of the sculpture away from Max, sending the stored bullet whizzing past his head. Max looks on to Pilet standing 30 feet off.

His right arm supporting his left at the mid-forearm level. His left hand is open wide toward the sculpture, revealing a glowing violet palm with smoke rising from it. His eyes fix on the ominous statue with contempt.

"My turn."

He begins to march toward his foe, firing bullet after bullet of aura onto the enemy. Yuuna staggers to her feet.

"Wow Pilet! What an auracast!"

"Take care of Max." Said Pilet. "I'll handle brick face over here."

"Right!" Yuuna replied. She rushes over to Max, casting Mend on his head.

"Uuugh, I cannot let a minor strike like that stop me. Pilet needs help." Said Max.

"Don't worry Max! I'll have you back, hack-and-slashing in a jiffy! Just let Pilet handle it from here."

Across the courtyard, Faith and Scott have been locked in a deadly duel of arcane combat since the auric mine blast.

"Frisio!"

Fwooosh

Faith fires a cone of arctic wind from her palm toward Scott. He rubs his hands together and projects a net of aura, catching the wind and snow and concentrating it into an auric snowball in between his hands. Shockingly, the snowball transmutes itself into an orb of scarlet flame in his grasp. Scott rips the flame apart with his fingers, creating many, smaller flickers of fire. He then holds the tiny flame orbs up to his face and blows them towards Faith like the seeds of a fiery dandelion. As the orbs approach her, Faith reads off another cast from her tome.

"Miragia."

Illusionary copies begin to emanate from Faith, creating a dozen identical doppelgangers scattered throughout her direct vicinity. The copies actively evade the scarlet projectiles, some being struck down in a fiery explosion. The remaining copies all read the tome in unison and drop the palm of their free hand to the floor.

"Oaaknilifo!"

Krrsh krrsh krrsh krrsh

Oak trees begin to rapidly sprout from the ground in a gradually rising line towards Scott. As the rows near him, he nimbly side-steps out of the line of attack. Peripheral branches from the trees grow towards him as he evades, attempting to clothesline him in pursuit.

The copies begin to cast Oaaknilifo in scattered directions, confusing

Scott as to which line is a real row of oaken danger. He continues to strafe and dodge the trees, treating every cast as if it came from the real Faith. Finally, one row of arcane trees grows directly through a line he just evaded, proving that last one to be a fake. Taking Scott off guard, he covers his face with his forearm. But the trees run right through him without touching him. He stands inside the illusionary oaks, confused at the logic of his foe's attack.

"A fake hidden by a fake?" Said Scott.

Just then, something bounces off of the top of his head. He looks down to see one of Faith's rainbow scales on the floor.

"Oh shit."

He looks up to see Faith descending from the sky above him. Her vibrant red Skarrya blade slashes toward his skull. Without a second to lose, Scott shoulder rolls away from the dangerous aura sword. On the end of his roll he leaps into the air and curls his fingers to form rakes. Each finger cultivates small, cerulean claw-like projectiles.

PFEW PFEW PFEW PFEW PFEW

The claws begin to fire at Faith, one after another like heat-seeking arcane missiles. But Faith stands her ground, parrying and slashing down each auric missile with her Skarrya blade. Scott cultivates more aura in his hands and forms a full row of aura claws from each fingernail. The two castors stand across from each other, stoically brandishing their weapon.

"Wow, this is really fun." Said Scott. "Your parents did a great job."

"Thanks." Said Faith. "But they only taught me how to read Rok-Senn text. I've honed my skills to perfection on my own, painstakingly, my whole life. The auracaster giving you a hard time right now is a product of her own design, no one else's."

Scott shrugs his shoulders.

"Well, then." Said Scott. "I stand corrected. *You've* done a great job. Now let's keep going!!"

The two sprint toward each other, arcane weapons in hand, and continue their mystic duel.

Across the battlefield Pilet continues to fire Hollowpoints at the Sculpture from a distance. As the shots continue, Pilets hand starts to get hot.

Singe

"Agh." Groans Pilet, as he pauses from firing to let his palm cool.

The Sculpture takes this moment to compose itself from the barrage of aurafire. It readies its pistol and trains the barrel on Pilet. Just then, Pilet looks up and sees the stone titan aiming straight for him.

"Ah hell... Fleetfoot!" Casts Pilet.

BOOM

The sculpture fires a cerulean bolt as Pilet narrowly darts out of the way. It continues to fire at Pilet, who nimbly evades like an agile fly avoiding capture. Losing sight of the speedy prospect, the stone statue heaves its double edged blade from the dirt and heads for Max and Yuuna.

The two turn their heads at the thunderous sound of its footsteps, wide eyed at the encroaching behemoth stomping toward them. Seeing this, Pilet dashes to their aid in an attempt to move them out of harm's way.

He tries to lift Max's hefty body.

"Hhhng, damn!" Said Pilet. "Max! What the hell is Kenzo feeding you dude?! We gotta move!"

Still groggy from the shot to the head, Max retorts.

"It's all muscle, muscle weighs more than fat! My father says so! Ughhh."

"There's no time for this!" Said Yuuna. She cultivates a platinum glowing aura in her palm.

"Autumn Jetstream!"

A stream of continuous, pressurized air blasts the statue, slowing its advance.

"We've got to get Max out of here. That pistolwhip really did a number on him, I've been casting mend for like five minutes!" Said Yuuna, still blasting the colossus before them.

"I know I know!" Said Pilet. "Shit, ok let's try again."

Pilet gives it another go as he grips Max under his arms and attempts to move him. As the statue draws near, it opts to fire an aura bullet to close the distance.

"Oh crap! We gotta move, Pilet!" Cried Yuuna.

In a moment of desperation, Pilet's eyes glow violet as he enters The "Fever Point". His muscles swell to three times their normal size, as his body becomes covered in purple hair. Yuuna sees this metamorphosis in action as she holds off their stone foe.

What the hell? What... is that? She thought.

With this newfound strength, Pilet lifts Max with ease, throws him over his shoulder and grabs Yuuna's wrist with his other hand, stopping her auracast.

"Let's blow this fruit stand!" Said Pilet in a low, bassy voice.

The three vanish as Gregory Galante's statue fires a steady barrage of aura bullets into the ground they just occupied. Pilet drops them off about 50 feet away behind the fountain as cover. His muscles return to their normal size, as the purple hair recedes back into his skin. His Fever Point rescinds, returning Pilet to his basic state.

"Alright." Said Pilet. "I don't know where your sister and Mister fancy magic guy went, but chances are she can handle herself. And so can I. Try to patch up Max, and when he's better just help out your sis. Someone's gotta hold off this freaking monster while you guys handle the Proctor, or we'll never finish this damn test!"

"Ok Pilet, sounds like a plan." Said Yuuna. "But please, be careful out there ok?"

Pilet cultivates violet aura in his left hand, readying another Hollowpoint. He looks over his shoulder to Yuuna and grins.

"Hah, no promises..."

Shortcoming of the Elder Sierro

Meanwhile, Faith and Scott continue their auric duel. Faith slashes and jabs with her Skarrya blade. Scott Bob's and weaves, dashing forward and raking off patches of rainbow scales with his mystic claws. Parry, riposte, lunge. The two ferociously exchange clanging blows to each other's defenses. Scott's Callous cast holds strong, as Faith's rainbow scales begin to diminish, revealing *her* Callous layer underneath.

"Hah!"

Faith swings her arm wildly for a horizontal slash, but is met on the inside of her elbow with a forearm block by Scott. The block's impact causes Faith's fingers to separate for a moment, causing a reverberating flicker in the Skarrya blade. Noting her moment of vulnerability, Faith leaps back to create distance.

"Hmm." Said Scott. "Well that's interesting..."

Scott releases his Arcane claws in missile form once again.

PFEW PFEW PFEW

As the projectiles close in on her, Faith parries and strikes down each one with precision. But after striking down the last missile, Faith fails to notice Scott on her right flank, as he grasps her wrist above the Skarrya blade. He slides his hand up her forearm and forcibly closes her hand into a fist, causing the Arcane heat blade to vanish.

"Mudmold." Casts Scott.

Auric mud seeps from the pores of Scott's palm, enveloping Faith's hand and hardening into a thick ball. Unable to move her fingers to auracast, Faith begins to flail about frantically. She pulls out of Scott's grasp and stumbles to the floor.

"Shit!" Said Faith. She looks at the ancient tome in her left hand. *How am I going to cast with one hand?! I need to hold the book!* She contemplates.

"Ha, I figured." Said Scott, pacing toward a grounded Faith. "You haven't made a single cast without that book. Well aside from Callous, but that's a "Kettlenian standardized auracast". Even the lowest level castors can learn "KSA" techniques. My guess is you've focused your entire fighting style around casting from that tome. I'm assuming it's written in the blood of a powerful ancient auracastor, and that casting from it preserves your own aura stores. Right?"

Faith's attempts to hide her nerves, but an anxious glance of the eyes from side to side gives it away.

"Yeah, that's it." Said Scott. "Welp, hope you've got some original tricks up your sleeve little lady. Otherwise this might be a short test for you."

Scott draws closer as he points his right hand toward Faith. He cultivates a set of cerulean aura missile claws. A bead of sweat drops down Faith's forehead. She freezes in place, unable to grasp the situation at hand.

"Concede please." Said Scott. "I'm really not looking forward to littering the daughter of my friend with holes, but I am a Hired Blade. No mercy. No hesitation."

Faith struggles to open her mouth, her lips quiver in fear.

"I, I con..., I con-"

Just then a blast of wind hits Scott in the back, sending him flying inches past Faith's head.

"Gaah!" Exclaims Scott, as he soars 30 feet off to the edge of the dome.

Yuuna whizzes by Faith, flying 3 feet above the ground. Her body, surrounded by a thin veil of platinum light. Soaring toward Scott at breakneck speeds, Yuuna's hands clasp together, cultivating her platinum aura into a small, vibrant bead. She pinches the auric bead between her middle finger and thumb.

"Starshot!" She casts.

She flicks the shining bead toward Scott with precision and speed. Scott's eyes widen as the vibrant projectile zooms towards him. On impact, it explodes in a radiant lightshow of combustion.

BOOM *Crackle*

Debris, pebbles and dust fill the air. Yuuna flies back and grabs Faith by the hand.

"Been working hard sis? We were wondering where you went!"

"I could ask you the same thing." Said Faith. "We need to get this thing off of my hand!" She shows Yuuna her Mudmolded fist as they fly to safety.

"Oh wow, that must make casting hard. Especially with you and your tome. But don't worry! I know just the guy to take care of it!" Said Yuuna.

The two reach the fountain, where Max lies seated in a meditative posture.

"Max here got hit really hard by the stone man, so I patched him up and told him to wait here. How're ya feeling Maxy?" Said Yuuna.

"Much better thank you, I'm ready to return to the fray. Oh what is that?" Said Max, pointing to Faith's hardened mud covered hand.

"It's a long story, but I need it off like now. Could you take care of that for me?"

"I'd be happy to. Allow me..."

Max feels the perimeter of the mud ball with his fingertips, checking the density of the object. He pulls a dagger-like blade from its holster behind his waist. The M6 "Gash", a Hachidorinese shortsword similar to that of the Lacerate, and made from the same steel. He holds the Gash close to the mudball, and with dextrous precision, taps it with the blade.

Chink

Surprisingly, the dense mudball cracks straight down the middle. With his palm, Max drives the back of the Gash slightly further into the mudball and twists, splitting it open like a coconut.

"Phew! Thanks Max!" Exclaims Faith, embracing Max with a tight hug.

"The pleasure is all mine! But I believe we have an issue still at hand, no pun intended." Said Max, pointing to a 7 foot sphere of wind filled with debris and rainbow scales headed their way.

Behind the sphere in the distance, Scott grins. His hands glowing with aura.

"Man, you guys sure are tough. This makes me super excited!" Said Scott, directing the sphere with his right hand.

The three stand to their feet and ready themselves for combat.

Across the battlefield, Pilet continues his shootout with the Sculpture. As the stone man fires bullet after cerulean bullet, Pilet darts and dashes side to side. His natural speed mixed with the Fleetfoot cast make him a highly elusive target for any foe.

"Come on block head! That all you got?!" Said Pilet. "My Grandma throws pots at Grandpa better than that! You might look like Gregory Galante, but you sure as shit don't fight like him!! At least I think, or I hope? Whatever, you freaking suck!!"

Pilet becomes overzealous and begins blowing raspberries and taunting his adversary. With every dodge follows a Hollowpoint shot, mixed with a teasing spank to his buttock or an "L" sign on his forehead with his hand.

The Titan continues firing pot shots at Pilet, unphased by his behavior. During his tirade, Pilet trips over a stone while sidestepping at high speed.

Tumble *Thud*

"Aagh!" Shouts Pilet, as he falls head first where the floor meets the dome wall.

The Sculpture fires a shot at him while he's still dazed by the trip.

Zhoom *Fizz*

He lands a direct hit to Pilet's chest. His Callous cast took the brunt of the shot, but was shattered after impact, leaving Pilet with a massive burn across his right pectoral.

"Gaaaahh!!! Aaaagh!!" Shouts Pilet. "Ugh, shit... Damn, that hurts." He touches the burn with his fingertip. "Not good, not good."

Pilet looks up to see the stone man has disappeared. Befuddled, he frantically looks around until his gaze points skyward. Horrified, Pilet sees the Sculpture not but 10 feet away from him, falling from the sky after leaping into the air. The Sculpture raises its leg, looking to stomp Pilet into the earth.

THOOM

As the titan comes crashing down, a massive cloud of dust follows. The cloud fills the air with stones from the shattered concrete sidewalk.

Having narrowly dashed out of harm's way, Pilet crouches behind a nearby bush.

"Nghh."

He clutches his badly burned chest, reeling in pain. He then notices a pain in his ankle, turning to see it bruised and swollen.

"Ugh, Crap. I must've sprained it when I fell. Good thing Fax isn't here, he'd never let me live it down."

Unbeknownst to him, hidden cameras throughout the courtyard broadcast the candidates performance in this portion. Seeing this, Faxion turns to Chairman Yang and smiles.

"He's right you know, I'm going to give him shit for this later." Said Faxion.

"Aren't you worried?" Said Yang. "The boy looks like he's in serious danger, even a speed demon like *him* isn't going very far on an ankle sprain that bad."

"Oh don't worry sir." Said Faxion. "He knows what to do next, I'd be more worried about that statue. Trust me."

"Hmm." Yang turns to view the courtyard monitor, seeing Pilet writhing in pain across the screen. "If you say so."

Back to the courtyard. Pilet takes a deep breath, he closes his eyes as the Sculpture draws near, beginning to peer over the shrubbery in search of his prey. Faxion's definition of an "Ace in the hole" rings throughout his mind.

"Ace in the hole: Any technique used by a Blade that greatly enhances their combat capabilities and/or fighting style. These skills should be used sparingly or as a last resort, due to the heavy strain they tend to put on the user."

Pilet unleashes The Fever Point. His eyes glow violet as his skin reddens to the color of a brick. The veins throughout his body begin to throb as steam pours off of his head. Amethyst patterns radiate throughout his entire body.

Fshhh *Fshhh*

His ankle swelling immediately goes down, as the burn across his chest dissipates into fresh new skin. Pilet exhales, inhales again, exhales, inhales. He begins to breathe rapidly, groaning in the heat given off by his entire body. The Sculpture finally examines the prospect's hiding place as Pilet looks up to meet his gaze.

"... Boo." Said Pilet.

In a flash, Pilet draws his Dragonfly knives and mauls the face of the stone man. Caught off guard, the sculpture staggers backwards. The details of its stone face now completely scraped off and unrecognizable. It surveys the battlefield puzzledly, unable to locate Pilet around the perimeter. Suddenly, it hears the infrared buzz of the Dragonflies' super-heated edges.

Slash

Pilet slices the gun arm clean off of the Sculpture. It looks down at its removed appendage, stands to its feet and begins to flail its sword wildly.

Rip

Another arm is torn from the Titan, as it soars through the air and crashes right into the fountain. It shatters the ledge, causing water to pour out onto the floor of the courtyard. Pilet vanishes and reappears before the Titans eyes, causing it confusion and forcing it to chase after air. It pursues Pilet's afterimage relentlessly, lifting it's leg and stomping out the various mirages left by his speed. Suddenly Pilet appears in its face, standing on its shoulders.

"Rest in peace, Greg."

SHIIIINNGGGG

He crosses his Dragonflies, forming a lethal scissor; and slices the head of the statue clean off. As the head flies upwards and falls to the earth, Pilet swiftly appears beneath it, catching it on his shoulder like a trophy. The body falls to the ground, lifeless and stiff. The Cerulean aura giving it life exits the statue via the headless neck, making its way back to Scott.

"That's right, the archeologist guy's still out there..."

The Torrent V.S. The Hollowpoint

Max, Faith and Yuuna stand before Scott Diliger, exhausted and frustrated.

"Don't you ever run out of aura?!" Said Yuuna.

"It doesn't make any sense." Said Faith. "You've scraped off literally all of my rainbow scales, by now the aura-sapping poison must have taken effect!"

"And now *we're* the ones out of aura." Said Max. "Using the scattered rainbow scales in your wind sphere cast as a weapon, very cunning indeed. I wonder how you would fare as a swordsman…"

"Now is no time for admiration Max!" Said Faith. "How are we gonna fight without auracast, it's an auracast exam! Even I need *a little* aura to trigger a cast from the tome!"

"Ha, check this out." Said Scott. He begins to peel a pair of skin colored gloves from his hands. "These came in handy. After what those pesky scales did to my water slug, I figured they would probably give me a hard time too. So I put these bad boys on when you guys were all groggy from getting blasted by my aura mines."

"What? Skin colored gloves?! Why do you even have those?!?" Said Yuuna.

"I dunno. I got them at the dollar store once, thought they were neat… Sure came in handy!" Said Scott.

"…"

"I hope my father doesn't see me lose like this…" Said Max.

In the bleachers, Kenzo Quinn is scarfing popcorn when he sees his son's predicament on the courtyard monitor. His mouth is left agape at the removal of Scott's skin colored gloves.

"…"

"How crafty!"

Kenzo begins taking notes in a notebook covered in fresh popcorn butter.

Scott cultivates aura in his hands, raising his palms to the sky. A dark cloud appears in the dome, pouring rain down on The Hidden Blades. Scott makes claw gestures with his hands, summoning a giant water tiger with the falling rain behind him. With each raindrop that follows, the tiger absorbs it and becomes larger.

"Well guys." Said Faith. "We tried our best."

"Max, we really appreciate you being with us for this exam." Said Yuuna. "Maybe next time we'll make it..."

"You two may concede." Said Max. He stands in front of them, arms folded with his chin up high. "The Sanda do not yield. I will take whatever punishment this beast is capable of..."

Max balls his right hand into a fist. He drags it across his abdomen and rests it at the hip. The blade of his left palm thrusts downward. The yellow gem on his chest plate pulsates with vigorous energy. A mysterious aura begins to swirl around him on the floor, as his armor almost appears to start organically wriggling and moving.

Phreew *Phreew* *Phreew* *Phreew*

Suddenly, a volley of amethyst Hollowpoint bullets rip through the air. They whizz past Max's ear, shredding into the blue tiger. Just then, Pilet approaches.

"Good shit, Max." Said Pilet, his vocal chords reverberate with newfound bass. "Don't quit when the chips are down!"

"Pilet! Did you beat the rock guy?!" Said Yuuna.

"Oh yeah, I messed 'em up." Said Pilet. He turns to Scott Diliger. "Hey! Famous guy! Get a load of this!!"

Pilet bolsters his right hand with his left. His fingers curl as he charges large amounts of violet aura in his hand. A Hollowpoint the size of a basketball forms in his grasp. Pilet smiles at Scott as he fires the vibrant projectile at the aquatic tiger. It soars through the air.

FFTHOOM! *PFFFFEEEWWWWWW*

The oversized Hollowpoint explodes on impact, instantaneously evaporating half of the aquatic tiger.

"Not too bad man!" Said Scott. "Hollowpoint, that's a novice KSA. Simple but effective!"

"Thanks, now let's get it on!" Exclaimed Pilet, as he vanishes in an instant.

He reappears behind the water tiger, firing shots of hollowpoint in rapid succession.

Pfew Pfew* *Pfew*

Like a chainsaw, the auric bullets tear the beast in half, then in thirds and fifths. But, with the steady rain of Scott's arcane technique, the aquatic feline re-assembles itself and swipes its mighty claws at Pilet.

"GRROOOAAR!" Roars the water tiger.

As they near Pilet the claws freeze into ice; giving them a sharp, solid form. The fiery prospect swiftly evades the strike, firing a counter shot on the way out. The beast and the boy continue their game of cat and mouse tirelessly for several minutes, creating a vortex of purple aura, ice and water throughout the courtyard.

Man, this kid is a one-trick-pony. Thought Scott Diliger. *Doesn't he have another offensive cast? Or does he think he's gonna fry my tiger with a bunch of potshots... And just how much aura does he have?? Most casters have like, 12 Hollowpoints in the tank before they're tapped out...*

Back at the bleachers, Chairman Yang and Faxion discuss the arcane shootout.

"Well I see why you have so much confidence in the boy Fax." Said Chairman Yang. "He's definitely loaded with surprises. But how much damn aura does he have stored up?! I mean you of all people know how much aura Hollowpoint costs to cast. It pulls directly from your body's aura reservoir. It's a bullet of pure, unfiltered aura. Almost always an effective weapon, but not necessarily cost-effective."

"Pilet is an interesting soul sir." Replied Faxion. "He can't stand guns, like rifles and pistols. He simply doesn't have the patience to aim. But I knew that he'd need to have some form of ranged weapon to fall back on for long-distance combat. And for whatever reason, he has immense, nearly endless amounts of stored aura. *Especially* when he enters *that* state, it's almost like his aura replenishes too fast for him to use it all!"

Faxion scratches his chin, watching his pupil at work upon the monitor.

"Now, we both know how Hollowpoint has a slight "homing" characteristic to it. Your mind's eye focuses on a target, locks on and fires for it. The bullet remains slightly trained on its initial prey, and the reliable accuracy ratio tends to make up for the high aura cost. The nature of this cast, mixed with Pilet's massive aurapool made for a no brainer! He's no mystic sharpshooter, but I believe we'll make an arcane cowboy out of him yet!"

"Hmm, what an interesting observation Fax. Interesting indeed... Blows my mind how astute you can be sometimes Deadeye."

With a devilish grin, Faxion rubs his hands together vigorously.

Yes Pilet. Thought Faxion. *Keep making me look good. Daddy's going to have that new hovercar in no time...*

Down by the courtyard, the battlefield is completely drenched by the continuing auracast rain. The area is enveloped by a humid mist, courtesy of Pilet's Hollowpoints striking the arcane tiger with unbridled fervor. As the fog continues to reach across the battlefield, the Arcane tiger soaks up the moisture in the air and restores itself to massive proportions.

"We could do this all day you know." Said Scott.

"No, *I* can." Said Pilet, nimbly cartwheeling away from a tiger strike. "I could do this *all WEEK*. But *you're* eventually gonna run out of aura buddy, and when you do I'm gonna tear you a new asshole!"

"Hah!" Laughs Scott. "You're the most fun I've had in a long time! Alright, you're on. My tiger v.s. your Hollowpoints. Winner takes all!"

Scott Diliger curls his fingers into claws and swipes them furiously through the air, orchestrating the tiger to maul at Pilet with wicked speed. But Pilet's speed effortlessly outpaces the tiger, dancing and side stepping away from the dangerous arcane extremities.

Dodge *Dash* *Roll*

As he evades the furious blows, Pilet begins to direct his aim towards Scott. He lets loose a four-shot flurry at the mystic archaeologist, putting a newfound sense of urgency in his opponent.

PFEW PFEW PFEW PFEW

"Damn, he's too fast for the tiger." Said Scott. "Now he's after me! Better watch my back, playtime is over..."

Scott whirls his hands around and around vertically, his elbows facing the earth and sky. The water tiger transforms into an aquatic shell that encapsulates him, much like the one that entrapped Faith previously.

As the Hollowpoints draw near, Scott balls his hands into vibrating fists of cerulean aura, densely freezing the shell to brace for impact.

Thudthudthudthud

The Hollowpoints crack the ice, but the barrier holds up.

"Hmm. Don't like being the target for a change, do ya?" Said Pilet.

He begins firing shot after shot at Scott Diliger, prompting the Proctor to guard himself in another arcane encasing. The water shell returns, freezing to absorb the blows. Pilet relentlessly continues his volley, but as he does his right hand begins to grow hotter and hotter.

Tss

Shaking his hand from the heat, Pilet pushes forward with his onslaught of auric punishment. With every increasing shot, Scott is forced to put more aura into layering on sheets of protective ice.

"Shit." Said Scott. "How can he keep firing Hollowpoint like that?! If the cost of aura doesn't stop him, the amount of sheer heat that radiates from it should give him third degree burns! What is this kid made out of?!?

Crack crack crack crack

The shots continue to rattle the arcane shell.

"Well regardless, I can't just keep taking fire like this. It's time for a counter attack!"

Scott Diliger keeps his right fist balled up to continue bolstering the shell, while the fingertips of his left hand begin to radiate aura. This bores five holes into the ice shell that send water shooting out towards Pilet like tentacles.

Pilet begins to evade the tentacles while still maintaining his steady rate of Hollowpoint fire. Darting and dashing across the battlefield, Pilet ignores the clear aquatic distraction and focuses his shots on Scott's shell.

"Damn." Said Scott. "I hoped he would bite on the tentacle bait and waste his fire on them, but this kid's persistent! Even under attack from all angles his fire is still trained on me!"

The heat finally starts to get to Pilet, as his aura stores also begin to diminish.

"Gaaah!" Said Pilet. "Don't run out now! I can't run out now! I gotta keep going!!"

Pilet's body begins to vibrate, his violet aura veil grows to enelope him to twice the diameter it was. As if a separate aura factory begins to go to work within him, Pilet finds himself a second wind. He pushes past the heat, past the fatigue onset by his Feverpoint.

"GRRAAAAAGGHHHH!!!!"

In a blinding display of speed and firepower, Pilet moves so fast he creates afterimages all around Scott's ice shell. The mirages rip and tear the barrier to shreds with Hollowpoint casts, gradually growing closer and closer to the caster inside.

"GAAAAAAHHHH!!!" Scott screams, as he's forced to layer on all of his stored aura to defend against the hailstorm of auric fire. But it's not enough.

CRRACKK *Thud thud thud thud*

Finally the ice egg gives way, as several shots creep through and litter Scott's Callous armor with cracks and holes. They hit him with such force that he bursts through the other side of the ice shell and is sent flying several feet away.

"Ungh." Mutters Scott, as he wearily staggers to his feet.

15 feet off, Pilet charges a large Hollowpoint in his palm and readies to fire at his foe.

Pant, pant "You, you got a pretty strong Callous there buddy." Said Pilet, struggling to catch his breath. "But I bet one of these would be enough to crack you open."

He continues charging, his cast grows to a beach-ball level diameter.

The dome of the "Killzone" cast by Scott disintegrates over the courtyard, as he utilizes what's left of the aura to bolster and re-layer his Callous armor.

Damn... Thought Scott. *It's over. If I need to take down the barrier to keep fighting, I know it's done. And what if someone gets hurt by a rogue cast without it up...*

Pilet unfurls his fingers from holding back the massive Hollowpoint, sending it flying right at Scott.

Scott exclaims "I concede!" as the high powered projectile rips through the air toward his head.

Zhoom

He covers his face with his forearm and closes his eyes, bracing for the worst. But after a brief pause, Scott realizes he is unscathed by the blast. The auracast proctor opens his eyes to see Pilet, standing right in front of him with the oversized Hollowpoint grasped tightly in his Arcane grip.

Pilet clenches his hand tightly and shatters the Hollowpoint like a glass bottle.

He caught up to it mid-flight and stopped it from exploding. What kind of monster is this kid... Thought Scott Diliger.

Just then, Pilet's unconscious body falls onto Scott's shoulders. The reddish tinge leaves his skin, as the steam billowing off of his epidermis diminishes. The amethyst colored patterns across his body disappear, alongside the devilish glow in his pupils. Suddenly, every muscle in Pilet's body begins involuntary trembling, his eyes roll to the back of his head, and he begins foaming copiously from the mouth.

Mighty Fleet of The HBA

"Oh woah woah! What the hell?! Dude are you alright?!" Exclaimed Scott, as he gently lays Pilet's shuddering body on the ground. He holds the touchscreen of his large digital watch up to his face. "Get a medic to the courtyard, now!"

Seeing the events of the past few minutes, The Hidden Blades rush to Pilet's aid. Yuuna is the first on the scene.

"Pilet!!!" Said Yuuna. "What's happening to him Scott?!"

"I think he's having a seizure... Just give him space for a minute. Whatever form he took to fight me totally sapped all the energy in his body." Said Scott, laying Pilet down gently while motioning the others away.

After a few moments of convulsing violently on the floor, Pilet's body slowly begins to calm down. He blinks open his eyes and wakes up groggily to the faces of his team members and Scott peering back at him. Yuuna, unsure of Pilet's fate, cries hysterically on Faith's shoulder. Faith and Max look quietly at Pilet with genuine concern on their face.

"Yuuna, or Scott, or Faith. Any one of you really, can't you cast some healing technique on him or something?" Inquires Max.

"It's not like he just got cut open or hit in the head." Replies Faith. "Those injuries we understand and can heal. But some crazy transformation we don't understand yet just made him have a seizure, and that presents a problem."

"Not to mention we're pretty much all out of aura." Replied Scott. "We'll need to wait for a medic for any further assistance, speaking of!"

A Blade Medic runs out to the courtyard with a medical bag in hand.

"We saw the whole thing on the monitors Scott." Says the Medic. "Caffo

Gilwick sent me out here promptly after the candidate fell unconscious." The Medic checks Pilet's eyes with a flashlight. "Yep, he appears to have suffered a grand mal seizure. This candidate must have really outdone himself. He appears to be severely dehydrated too. Wow, we really need to get him some fluids ASAP. I'll be right back with help and a gurney."

"Ok sounds good, thank you." Said Scott.

The Medic runs back to the auditorium for the needed supplies. Slowly coming to, Pilet sits up laboredly.

"Gguys?.. Wwwhat happened??" Slurred Pilet.

"Pilet!" Exclaims the Hidden Blades gang.

"You turned purple again, and beat Scott! You won Pilet!!" Said Max. "But afterwards you passed out and kinda threw up all over the place, it was a very messy sight..."

"And still is..." Said Faith.

Pilet looks down at his vomit covered shirt.

"Ngguuh!! Acckk!!" Pilet swiftly takes his shirt off. But as he does, a surge of pain and soreness drives itself in waves throughout his muscles.

"AAGH" Exclaims Pilet. "Crap, I really did myself in this time... Just like Fax said..."

"PILET!!" Cries Yuuna, as she tackles Pilet with a tight hug. He wheezes in agony as his sore muscles are further compressed. "I waited to hug you till you did something about that throwup on your shirt, but I'M SO GLAD YOU'RE OK!!!"

"Ughh." *Wheeze* "Faith, faith please help. Tell her to stop." Said Pilet in a raspy, agonizing voice.

Faith laughs.

"Hah, yeah alright. Hey sis, calm down he's clearly in a lot of pain."

Yuuna releases Pilet, who immediately plops back down onto the ground in fatigue.

"I'm sorry Pilet..." Said Yuuna, bashfully rubbing the top of one hand with the thumb of the other.

Pilet simply throws up an arm with a thumbs up.

"All good..."

His arm plops back down lifelessly.

"Pilet. What did you mean when you said you "did yourself in this time" like Faxion said?" Said Max. "Does Faxion know more about your condition?"

"Look man. All I know is that when I turn on the Fever Point, I get really tired afterwards. Sometimes I get hungry and thirsty, sometimes I get a little dizzy. This time I knocked myself out so that's a first, but regardless I know the drill at this point. When I hit my Fever Point I can move really fast and have a shit-ton of aura, which is awesome. But no matter what, I feel like garbage once it turns off. Anyway what does it matter, we won!! We passed the damn auracast test!!! Well I did at least, I killed the statue *and* made the proctor quit. But hey you guys did pretty good too!"

"..."

"Fair enough." Said Max reluctantly. "Good for you King Killer."

Faith face palms. Yuuna Cheers Pilet on.

"Great job Pilet! You looked amazing!!" Said Yuuna.

"You certainly did man." Said Scott Diliger. "I'm not gonna lie, you weren't supposed to beat me at all, just survive until everyone conceded or time ran out. Conceding also didn't mean failure, just that your skills were to be graded up until what I'd seen to that point."

"What?!" Said Faith, embarrassed that she almost conceded. "But you said-"

"I said "It's not recommended if you want to pass" but I never said that it meant an automatic fail either." Said Scott. "You were all going to pass with what you'd shown me by the time I hit you with the tornado of your rainbow scales, but then purple boy here had to go full cowboy on me! Which leads me to my next topic, the topic of grading..."

Scott picks up his electronic clipboard.

"There's no questioning it, you guys are all getting an "S" rank. Collectively you've shown excellent teamwork, and everyone knows beating a proctor is like, a sure-fire way to get an "S"."

"WWWHHAAATT!!!" Hollers Pilet. "Why so low on the alphabet?!?! "S" dude, are you serious?!? I should get and "A" or and "+A" or something! And what's this "collectively" bullshit?!? I DID ALL THE WORK?!?!"

Scott looks puzzledly at the others.

"Is he ok?" Said Scott.

"Quiet you fool!" Exclaims Max as he holds Pilet back from staggeredly storming towards Scott. "Just be glad you passed and didn't choke to death on your own vomit, OK?!"

"I'm honestly surprised he knows the alphabet that well." Said Faith. "Pilet, "S" stands for "Super" you dumbass. It's the best grade you could possibly get."

"Ohhh... ok cool. Hey thanks dude." Said Pilet.

"..."

Max lets go of Pilet.

"The seizure must have killed off more brain cells than he could afford." He said.

The Blade Medic returns with a partner Medic, an IV drip and a gurney.

"Alright, where's the injured candidate?" Said the Medic.

"Oh no worries buddy, I'll be fine."

Pilet laboredly stands to his feet, trips on a rock and falls on his face.

"Yeaaah, no. Here take this side and let's wheel him in." Said the Medic to his partner.

The two hoist Pilet onto the gurney and begin to carry him back to the auditorium.

"Hey look guys, I got a moving throne!" Said Pilet, arms folded behind his head in a cozy posture.

The Hidden Blades crew says their goodbyes to Scott Diliger.

"Bye Scott!" Said Yuuna. "It was really cool meeting you!"

"You too Yuuna!" Said Scott. "And don't be a stranger, hey here's my number! Give me that Chatch on your wrist."

"Chatch" is a brand of high-tech cell phone designed to be worn on the wrist. A play on words, the "Chat-Watch" was born 8 years ago; when a clumsy, engineer father of six grew tired of dropping his phone every time one of his kids called.

"Woooww, thanks Scott!" Said Yuuna. She runs over to her sister. "Faith look! I have Scott's Chatch number! Here give him yours!"

"Oh, ok sure!" Said Faith. She digs fervently into her bag in search of her Chatch." Hang on one sec, I take it off before a fight." Faith locates her Chatch and pulls up a screen displaying a QR code. "Here's my code Scott."

"Awesome!" Said Scott. He scans the code, downloading Faith's contact information. "We should keep in touch guys! It really was a pleasure meeting the Sierro sisters. Good luck, I'm sure the four of you will do great during the exam." Scott looks over towards Pilet being carried away. "Especially with that kid on your team..."

"Thanks Scott, it means a lot coming from you!" Said Yuuna.

"Yeah, let's keep in touch!" Said Faith. "Maybe one day we'll work a Blades job together."

"Maybe!" Replied Scott.

Max bows in reverence to Scott.

"It was an honor doing battle with a castor of your caliber, Mr. Diliger." Said Max.

Scott shakes his hand.

"Why thank you man, likewise!"

The group says their goodbyes to Scott Diliger and follows in suit of Pilet back towards the auditorium.

As they enter the gymnasium, the Hidden Blades crew is met with thunderous applause from the spectating crowd.

"King Kil-ler! King Kil-ler! King Kil-ler!" Shouts the audience.

Still being carried in on the stretcher; Pilet sits up, faces the crowd and flexes his biceps.

"You want more!!" Exclaims Pilet. "I told you to stay tuned! Let's gooo!!!"

The crowd stands up and applauds, rooting and cheering for the fiery prospect.

"WOOOHOOO!!"

"Amazing!"

"That kid's got the moves!"

As the crowd dies down, the voice of Exam head Proctor Caffo Gilwick is heard booming over the speakers.

"Good afternoon candidates. The practical portion of the Hired Blades Licensing Exam has now concluded. The teams eligible to continue the exam will be displayed on the auditorium monitors. Those whose names are displayed please report to the airship hangar located due south of the lounge. If you do not see your team's name displayed, please exit via the double doors located at the west wing of the Blades lounge. Thank you for your contribution to the Hired Blades Association."

Inquisitively, The Hidden Blades look up to the monitors to check the outcome of their efforts. As the group scans the names listed, Faxion and Chairman Yang draw near.

"Congratulations candidates." Said Chairman Yang. "A bang-up job by the lot of you."

"Great job gang! Said Faxion. "You guys really took it to the competition, I'm amazed at both the skill and courage of all of you! Allow me to introduce you to Chairman Bernardo Yang, the Commander in chief of the Hired Blades Association. Sir, this is Max Quinn, Faith Sierro, Yuuna Sierro and Pilet Whydah! My sponsored candidates for the exam."

Max introduces himself with his traditional bow. Yuuna and Faith shake his hand, and Pilet reaches in for a handshake, but falls off of his stretcher, landing directly on his face. The Hidden Blades fight back the urge to laugh in his face as the Chairman helps him up to his feet.

"Thanks Chief!" Said Pilet, struggling to stand. "I think I overdid it shooting down your fancy wizard and his big wet cat."

"Haahaha..." Laughs Faxion awkwardly. A bead of sweat drips down the back of the veteran Blade's neck.

Shit. I've been afraid to introduce these two... Ohh Pilet, I hope you don't muck this up. For both of our sakes...

The Chairman glares at Pilet for a moment, clearly passing judgment in his mind.

" ..."

"BAAHAHAHA!!" Bellows the Chairman. He playfully slaps Pilet on the shoulder with his massive, vascular arm. Pilet's sore muscles go limp on impact, sending him tumbling four feet away. "Fax I like this kid! He's a riot! He's a firecracker! He's--"

"He's limp as a wilted petunia." Said Faith.

"Well yeah that too, but what a stud!" Replied Chairman Yang. "Between the 3 second K.O., your duel with Toste and that masterclass against Scott I think we have ourselves the MVP of this year's exam! The only other candidates that come close are that wily archeologist with the green flames, and Lazlow's boy, what was his name again?"

"It's Lazlow Sir." Said Faxion.

"Yes him, what was his son's name?"

"No no, his son's name is Lazlow." Replied Faxion.

"Fax I appointed him Enforcer of The HBA myself, the father's name is Lazlow. Lazlow the Vice."

"Yes yes of course sir, the boy is Lazlow the Gavel." Said Faxion.

"Faxion how rude." Said Chairman Yang. "He's a man not a boy. And he's not Lazlow the Gavel he's Lazlow the Vice! I signed the paperwork on his title!"

"..."

"Yes well..."

Realizing The Chairman has no hope of understanding the situation, Faxion quickly avoids making things worse.

"Oh of course I remember!" He said. "Lazlow the Vice, how foolish of me! Yes I've met his son before I believe his name was..." Faxion looks around pensively. He spots a nearby vase filled with lovely, seasonal fuchsias. "Fuchsia! Fuchsia the... Florist! His son is Fuchsia the Florist."

"Hmm I see. What an interesting name... Well the boy doesn't fight like a florist, but I guess to each their own. Who am I to judge?"

"Aww the Florist!" Said Yuuna "I wish that were my name."

"Hahaha!! I think it fits that toolbag perfectly." Replied Faith.

Pilet's back and ribcage gyrates as he laughs muffledly, with his face to the floor.

"Well just the same." Said Chairman Yang. "Good work today, The Hidden Blades, was it? It seems as though your group is headed for the desert." The Chairman points to the monitor behind them, revealing their team's name listed on the rotating screen.

The group turns to the monitor and rejoices.

"Yes!" Said Max. "Father will be so proud, this marks a big day for the Hachidori."

"Thank God." Said Faith. "I didn't get blown up by an aura star and beat the piss out of a beefy criminal for nothing."

"Yeaaah. Sorry about that." Said Yuuna.

"Good luck to you, go kill some Wurms!" Said Yang.

"Some what? We're doing what?" Said Faith.

"Oops, I've said too much." Replied Yang. "Well, as you were."

The Chairman takes his leave, leaving Faxion to tend to his sponsored group.

"Don't worry about that right now folks. Here, assist me in picking up our peachy headed comrade and let's get to that airship hangar, yeah?" Said Faxion.

Faith grabs Pilet under the armpit and Faxion grabs the other, as the two hoist him up and make their way to the hangar.

They traverse through the crowded auditorium, past the decorated hallway and through the lounge and bar. They approach a wide, navy blue elevator with the symbol of the HBU symbol brandished across the split in the doors. The diamond and the sword behind it literally split down the middle when the doors open. The group walks in.

"The hangar is on the top floor." Said Faxion. "That's floor five. It's loaded with airships that Hired Blades take to do assorted jobs all across Kettlena. Hell, some jobs even require us to travel to different countries and continents!"

Faxion hits the button for the 5th floor. The elevator shuts.

"Why are we headed for the hangar Faxion?" Said Max. "Are we to be brought to a different country for testing??"

"No silly!" Interrupts Yuuna. "The last part of the exam is somewhere outside of Hired Blades HQ, it's the field exam!"

"They want to see how good we are out in the real world." Said Pilet. "I read the emails. We're supposed to be taken on some made-up field mission or something. They wanna test our skills in real time. It's why we signed the death waiver dude. Not everyone comes back alive from this one."

"What they said." Replied Faxion.

"Ahh I see." Said Max. "Fair enough. The Sanda yield to no one. I do not fear death. Only dishonor, to which there is no redemption."

"..."

"Alright, Im going to use you for bait when I run away from some shit that's trying to kill us then..." Said Pilet.

"He's right Max." Said Faith. "I get that you're chivalrous and all, and that's great. But sometimes it's smarter to run and live, and fight another day."

"What she said!" Said Faxion.

"I respect your opinion." Said Max. "But I have my own, and the way of the Sanda is not that of cowardice. We are warriors, not track stars. Running is not my strong suit, fighting is."

"Hmm." Said Faxion. "Fair enough, you can't fault that right?" He leans in to whisper to Pilet. "If the lad has no sense in a pinch, I say use him as bait too. There are some seriously hungry beasties where you're headed. I'll tell his father he died honorably in combat. The Sanda are suckers for that, there will be a plaque in honor of his sacrifice somewhere on Hachidori with a water fountain to collect coins for the family. The Hachidorinese provide for their kin even after death!"

"I'll be there taking selfies with my Chatch." Said Pilet. "You know, Gotta show love and support for the crew."

The two giggle to themselves devilishly whilst Faith, Yuuna and Max converse about their exam thus far. Just then, the 5th floor is reached and the elevator doors slide open. The airship hangar to the Hired blades Headquarters is revealed, showcasing a myriad of beautiful and fierce looking aviation machines.

Airships are utilized by the Hired Blades not only to travel long distances, but also for use as temporary homes. If speed was their aim, the Blades would favor jets and airplanes. But being that the average Blade spends 8 to 10 months out of the year on jobs across Kettlena, a mobile home setting becomes more or less a necessity. A Hired Blade will take a job, reach their destination and spend their nights hovering in the safety of their flying fortresses for whatever the duration of said job may be.

As The Hidden Blades crew exits the elevator, they begin to take note of the lovely airborne vehicles they pass along the way to the hangar's center. They see a massive red and black airship with several floors. The floors are structurally separated by beautiful, shingled roofs that lip upward at the edges. Each level has a balcony and a row of windows for the assorted rooms within.

"Wow, that's gorgeous!" Said Faith. "Someone travels in style!"

"That's the "Crimson Pagoda"." Said Faxion. "She's a personal favorite of the Chairman himself. He had her made by Zardenian royal shipbuilders. Took them two and a half years to get her up and running to his specifications, but there she is! It's a shame too. A lot of serious hardware runs inside of that beauty, but Chairman Yang has only taken her out maybe... Twice?"

"That truly is a shame." Said Faith. "A wonder like that could sail the skies with ease. And the jealousy of passersby, UGH. Sorry, I'm a connoisseur of aviation myself Fax. My parents taught me how to fly them."

"My goodness!" Said Faxion. "Maybe I've found an effective co-pilot!"

As the gang draws closer to their destination, they begin to hear the voice of Caffo Gilwick instructing candidates as to where to stand.

"Alright everyone gather around." Said Caffo. "There's no need to be so formal anymore given most of you left are serious contenders. I'm sure you're pretty thick skinned to have made it this far."

By now Pilet regains a decent amount of strength and can at least walk and stand normally. This allows the team to quickly join the rest of the candidate pool as they see familiar faces in the crowd.

"Hey look, it's the jellyfish guy!" Said Pilet. "What was his name... Puuto?"

"Hahaha!" Yuuna and Max laugh.

"Shhh!" Said Faith. "That's Puerto you idiot, Puerto the Man 'o War. He's the emissary of one of the highest ranking teams so get to know him well. "The Mystic Marauders." They're the team we met at the shooting range. You know, that test you sucked at?"

"Only thing I need to know well is this cutlery!" Said Pilet. He brandishes his Dragonfly long knives. "I'll dice Puerto and his whole posse up in no time if I have to! No mercy from the King Killer!"

"Ugh." Said Faith, palming her face in frustration. "Just listen to the Proctor."

Caffo Gilwick continues his instruction.

"Now again, just for the sake of professionalism. My name is Caffo Gilwick, I am this year's Head Proctor for the 127th Hired Blades Licensing Exam. Those of you here have proven yourselves more than worthy of becoming Licensed Hired Blades... ON PAPER. *However,* A key component to the true determination of a Hired Blade is how they perform under pressure. That is precisely what this final portion of the exam aims to find out. You will now enter the "Field mission" portion of the exam. Now I'm sure you've all read in the email to bring a change of clothes to prepare for dry, hot weather. The reason for this is because your field mission will be taking place in the "Devil's Tongue Desert", a scorching, barren land with very little plant life in sight. For reasons yet undetermined, Devil's Tongue is home to one of the highest populations of "Wurm infected" wildlife in Kettlena. This means many of you will more than likely see combat with The Wurm menace for the first time. While you are not required to engage in combat with the Wurm, it is recommended as your progress in battle will be monitored by the Board of Directors. Each team will be assigned a Dragonfly seeker camera to broadcast your mission for Grand Titanus to spectate."

Caffo pulls a white metallic object from his back pocket, unfurls his closed hand and presses a button on the top. The short, round object transforms into a literal, flying dragonfly shaped camera.

"The Dragonfly seeker is capable of moving at high speeds effortlessly and carries a high resolution lens and microphone. Do not tamper with the Dragonfly seeker or you will risk forfeiting your eligibility for passing the exam. Now, we will leave Hired Blades HQ shortly via The Selena Marie Flagship found behind me.

Caffo Gilwick points behind him, towards a massive silver airship sporting the name "Selena Marie" across the hull. Whirling propellers jut out from every angle of the aircraft, as the massive blimp begins to fill out from the center of the deck.

Once aboard you may spend the rest of your time until arrival as you please, as long as you abstain from violence. When we draw near Devil's Tongue, each team will be given a single map of the desert. You will then be flown via mini-ships by a designated party to a location on the outskirts of Devil's Tongue. Upon landing, you must traverse on foot to your destination, simply marked "The Cool Oasis" on your map. Once there you will be instructed on the next phase of your mission. Finally, there is one very important requirement to be fulfilled in order to continue the exam, once the Cool Oasis has been reached."

Caffo reaches into his coat pocket and pulls out a bag full of dog tags. Each one is nameless with simply the emblem of the Hired Blades Association embroidered onto it.

"One of these blank "HBA dog tags" will be given to each member of your team. Every team is required to bring approximately 8 of these dogtags to the Cool Oasis in order to continue the mission. 7 or less will result in failure and an immediate return to the Flagship Selena Marie. Clearly what this means is that once dropped off, competition is encouraged between each other in order to obtain the required dogtag amount. This is real life combat. No restrictions, no repercussions. I am aware that not all of you may return to us alive from this portion of the exam, and I will not lead you to believe that you will. Good luck to you, and may the five generals guide your blade. Now, please form a single file line onto the ramp."

Caffo begins to guide traffic boarding the Flagship.

As the Hidden Blades approach the line, they're greeted by Kenzo Quinn with a large mutton leg in hand.

"Eat up my boy!" Said Kenzo, handing the mutton to Max with fervor. "This is the biggest day of your life! Let's give them a show! Fight with honor and dignity!"

"Yes father!" Said Max, gnawing at the mutton vigorously.

"Kenzo!" Said Faxion. "What a surprise, joining us on the candidate's journey to Devil's Tongue?"

"You bet your ass Master Blade!" Said Kenzo. "No chance in hell I'd miss my boys adventure to becoming an official Hired Blade! I bought my ticket to board The Selena Marie way in advance!"

"Well stick with me! We'll have loads of fun!" Replied Faxion.

The gang reflects on the events of the day as they ready themselves for what's to come. But are they truly ready for what happens next? What battles and hardships are in store for our would-be mercenaries? Will this airship ride be their last? And what fate awaits the other colorful candidates? Only time will tell as the sun sets on another day over Kettlena...

CHAPTER

FIVE

Tip of The Devil's Tongue

First flagship of the Hired Blades Association; The Selena Marie. Named after the late wife of Gregory Galante, this immense aircraft serves as one of three flagships to represent The Hired Blades during official matters of business. She hovers over the night skies of Grand Titanus, making her way towards the various forests dividing the Capital city and the Devil's Tongue Desert. The squeaking sounds of the many propellers supporting the ship's ascent, lull weary passengers to sleep in their rooms. Dozens of clamoring voices can be heard, littering the packed dining hall. Down several corridors and past the boiler room, Pilet Whydah and Faxion of the Deadeye discuss matters of great importance...

"This bedroom is bullshit Fax." Said Pilet. "The pillows freaking suck dude, they're stiff as a rock... Wait there's literally a rock in this one!" Pilet pulls a jagged piece of amethyst from the pillowcase. "Freaking Yuuna! I told her she took the wrong pillow!" He chucks it across the room.

Faxion ducks as the stone ricochets off of the metal walls and barely misses the back of his head.

"Easy, easy now killer." Said Faxon, picking up the rogue amethyst and tucking it into his pocket for safe keeping. "No one said the barracks of the Selena Marie were all executive suites like mine and Kenzo's. Especially for candidates like yourself, there's simply far too many of you and the cost of exam admission doesn't cover a premier room."

"Wait, executive suite? What do you mean?... You holding out on me Fax?! Come on, switch with me! Here I'll give you like, $50 aurem!" Said Pilet, reaching into his wallet.

"Not in your life kid, I'm getting too old for these springboard mattresses." Said Faxion. "Come now, it'll build character! You're young, and you do that whole fast healing thing. I'm sure a night on a stiff bed won't do you in!"

"Man whatever." Replied Pilet, stuffing the unorganized aurem bills into his back pocket. "That, fast healing thing sure doesn't seem to be doing wonders for my muscles right now. I'm sore as shit from that auracast exam. Gotta hand it to Scott, the guy sure can cast like a warlock."

"He can indeed. You see in terms of skill, Scott Diliger is the #16th-ranked auracastor in the HBA. Your win over him has definitely put you in the eye of both the Board of Directors and your competitors. I'd be sure to watch yourself these next few days Pilet, your fellow candidates are probably wary of your abilities and would love for nothing more than to eliminate you entirely."

"Ha! Let 'em try." Exclaimed Pilet. "I beat two Licensed Blades today, TWO! Only other person I know who beat even one proctor was Mister "Hachidori Wonderboy", and he even said his guy was a last minute fill-in."

"Hachidori who? Oh, Max??" Said Faxion. "Hahaha! Yes he did quite well in the swordsmanship exam didn't he. Well just the same, try not to overdo the "Feverpoint" again yeah? Had the fight not ended when it did, you'd have ended up without an ounce of aura or stamina to continue. You gave us quite a scare with that seizure too. You're of no use to yourself or your team in that state. Now, speaking of... Where is your roommate?"

"I think Max went to the dining hall with his old man. What, do people from Hachidori do nothing but eat and fight?" Said Pilet.

"Sounds like a good time if you ask me!" Said Faxion.

The next room over, the Sierro sisters ready their beds for the night.

"Faith, have you seen my amethyst?" Inquired Yuuna. "I'm trying to make a crystal grid under my bed, but there's no way to finish one without an amethyst! I mean unless I had another purple stone, but I doooont!" Yuuna sniffs her pillow. "And why does my pillow smell like serious B.O.?"

"Hmm, no idea sis." Said Faith, placing her tome meticulously on the nightstand. "Maybe you left it in your socks?"

"I don't wear socks, or barely ever shoes for that matter, you know that! And even if I did, don't you think I'd notice a sharp rock in them pretty quick?" Said Yuuna.

"Oh that's right." Said Faith. "Pretty sure I'm not the only one around here who's noticed your sock-lessness by now. Are those raggedy toes of yours ever getting a pedicure? You should kick the flip-flops and wear a pair of actual shoes every now and again..."

"How dare you, lady! The balls of our feet are our connection to mother Giganus, and the tops of our heads too! Any border between us weakens our connection to her!" Said Yuuna.

"Riiight... I mean, that's a very poetic way of explaining aura cultivation, Yuuna. But aura goes harmlessly right through most matter, until someone transmutes it to cast with. I'm pretty sure a pair of shoes isn't really going to get in the way of that..."

"Well according to The Wind and Star tribe it does!" Said Yuuna. "They're a barrier between me and my precious planet and I won't wear 'um!"

Tch, those friends of hers... Thought Faith. *Wind and Star tribe. They're not even a real tribe! Just a bunch of hippies that loaf around and trip out on freaking cosmic leaf...*

Yuuna crinkles her toes, as her feet begin to shiver.

"Uh, but it is kinda cold in here. Can't you cast something to heat up this room from your tome?"

"Yuuna. This is an ancient manual for Rok-Senn auracast, written with the blood of a powerful auric Priest. It's not a magic AC unit! But... Yes, yes I can. Doesn't mean I will though..."

"You're meeaann!!!!"

About a dozen doors down in the dining hall, groups of candidates accompanied by their sponsors, sit at miscellaneously placed tables. The maroon, satin tablecloths glimmer in the chandelier light. Max and Kenzo Quinn take a seat at a table not far from the food line. Kenzo begins to pour his son a glass of red wine from a bottle placed as a centerpiece.

"You'll need to stay loose Max, the competition is all around us. Here, have some wine!" Said Kenzo.

"Of course father." Said Max. He sips from his glass, wincing at the tart flavor.

Kenzo spots the Enforcer of The Hired Blades Association walking by. He reaches over and tips Max's glass up, forcing him to take large gulps and spilling wine down his neck under his armor.

"Drink like a man boy! We have an important guest!" Said Kenzo.

Gurgle *Glug*

Max chokes on his wine.

Lazlow the Vice draws near with his son, Lazlow the Gavel.

"Kenzo Quinn. It appears this exam is not as exclusive as I thought." Said Lazlow Sr. "And I take it this is your boy?"

"That would be correct." Said Kenzo. "This is my son Max."

Max gasps for breath. His face stained in red from the spilt wine, Max does his best to greet their guests.

Cough *Wheeze*

"Hello sir, I am Max." *Cough* "It is an honor to," *cough* "meet you." Studders Max.

"Erm, yes." Said Lazow Sr. "You as well. So it appears your son has yet to receive his second stripe. My son's associate is of the Fubuki tribe of your island homeland. I hear he received his second degree two years ago. Are you sure it's a wise idea letting your, one-striper take this exam?"

"Nonsense!" Said Kenzo, visibly angered. "Those Fubuki bastards hand out stripes for taking shits without wiping! I could probably get a stripe from the Fubuki for flipping a coin on heads twice in a row! I'll tell you what..." Kenzo pulls an M6 Gash from his magnetic belt and brandishes it to the Kettlenean warriors. "I'd bet my Gash here that my boy would tear this Fubuki, goat's milk drinker to shreds!"

"Father..." Said Max.

"HA! You're on!" Interrupts Lazlow Jr. "Arturo would love to hear this. Hey Sanda kid, you down for a scrap with my boy later? Or are you too scared because he's got more color in his hair than you."

Max glows beet red with frustration. His nostrils flare as he bares his canines.

"How dare you!" Exclaimed Max, slamming the table as he stands to his feet. "The Sanda yield to no one! I'll fight my own battles and challenge my own opponents, thank you very much!" Max takes a breath, composes himself and returns to his seat. "My father was simply stating that should the need arise, I could defend myself quite adequately in a duel with a rival clan. We cannot battle aboard this vessel, it is forbidden. But should we meet on the desert sands, my Lacerate will be anxious to take on any challenger. If your friend is one of them so be it, and don't be surprised if your blood stains the scorching dunes as well..."

"That's enough boys." Said Lazlow Sr. "Like I always say, settle it on the battlefield. Kenzo, fun talking to you as always." He looks down at Kenzo's rounding gut. "Also, the gym is down the hall should you have use for a treadmill. Not sure if they have those where you're from, but I'd suggest you make use of it."

"No need." Said Kenzo. "The Sanda are Warriors, not track stars. We do not run, we fight!"

"Looks like you have to fight just to see your toes." Said Lazlow Jr. "Let's go father, The Reapers are waiting at our table." He turns to Max once more. "See you in the desert, punk."

Max tightly grips his Lacerate, as the two Kettlenean warriors take their leave.

"I do not like them, father." Said Max. "Not one bit."

"You don't need to." Said Kenzo. "But do not let emotions cloud your judgment, boy. A calm mind guides the sword to the target, and an angered one guides it to an early grave."

Max can't help but recount the heated exchange of his father moments previously.

"But father, what of the bet you just made for your prized Gash sword?" Said Max.

"..."

"Boy do as I say not as I do!"

"Yes of course father, my apologies."

Awaited Departure

As the night passes on, weary candidates make their way to their beds for some much needed respite. Bedroom lights all over the Selena Marie begin to peeter out; as the passengers, one by one, wander off to slumber.

The Flagship sails majestically over the lush forests of Crescenta, as the bow brushes past the stars fervently into the night sky. Smokestacks billow from the ship's wide, striped exhaust funnel, rising to greet the moon. The flying behemoth loaded with mercenaries proves a sight to behold for forest villagers from their bedroom windows.

Hours fly by, as the Selena Marie creeps over the tallest trees, passing the highest heights of the hills overlooking Devil's Tongue. The dawn begins to peek over the horizon, guiding the warm rays of the sun to the soft sand of the wispy dunes. The Flagship slows to a floating halt as she reaches the outskirts of her destination.

The Devil's Tongue desert, a dry and barren land. Ruins of the ancient Rok-Senn people scattered miscellaneously throughout. Small terrariums housing cacti and other desert flora hover above the sand, sporting solar powered propellers. Desert villages pepper themselves into the terrain, thriving off of nearby oases and crystal mines.

A snoring Pilet lies disheveled across his sheets. Empty, disheveled bottles of electrolyte sport drinks litter his night stand. Across the room Max covers his head with a pillow, in a desperate attempt to drown out the boisterous slumber of his roommate.

Snore *Growl* Grumble*

The incessant sound of Pilet's labored breathing finally makes Max snap. He lifts the pillow off of his head and chucks it at Pilet.

Poof

Feathers fly across the room. With dark bags stained under his eyes, Max pushes himself up off of the bed and yells.

"Would you be quiet! Your snoring could wake my dead ancestors! How am I to fight tomorrow without a wink of sleep?! Hmm?!?!" Exclaimed Max.

"Ow!" Said Pilet. "Max don't be a dick, I was having an awesome dream about those steak sandwiches from the dining hall last night."

"Yes, well that makes one of us!" Said Max. "At least you had the opportunity to dream, I had nightmares of a Serpent Dragon's vicious roars, only to find out it was a mixture of both your snoring and your stomach growling!"

Knock knock knock

A visitor bangs on the metal door. Pilet and Max halt their exchange to address the guest. As Pilet cleans his trash into an empty bag, Max walks up and opens the door. Faxion, Faith and Yuuna stand outside.

"Greetings Max!" Said Faxion. "Hope you had a good night's rest."

Max rubs his weary eyes.

"As do I..." Replied Max.

"Yo, what up!" Said Pilet, as he chucks a candy bar wrapper into the trash bag from across his bed.

"You are, finally!" Said Yuuna. "We've been waiting like, half an hour for you guys to get ready. We've arrived at Devil's Tongue! Yay!"

"The crew is meeting on the deck in less than ten minutes." Said Faith. "Better hurry up before we miss any further instructions."

"Let's get a move on gentlemen!" Said Faxion. "Today will be the most fun you'll have yet!"

Pilet and Max gather their equipment and join their comrades, as the Hidden Blades crew make their way to the ship's deck.

They exit the barracks via a wide stairwell, decorated with polished fossils and beautifully restored artifacts. The crew marches up several flights of stairs with haste and emerges onto the ship's deck. The hot, dry desert air strikes their skin, creeping briskly into their lungs. They're greeted by the sight of the remaining candidates and their sponsors, standing huddled around the exam proctors in a large, layered semi circle.

Caffo Gilwick, Scott Diliger, Toste, Rexmere and the two marksmanship proctors from the practical exam stand before the crowd. Caffo adjusts his vambraces and presses a button, holding one up to his face. As he fiddles with its touchscreen, a sound emits from the surrounding speakers aboard the deck; followed by a resounding prompt of, "Microphone connected.".

"Good morning candidates." Says Caffo, speaking into his Vambrace. "The beginning of the final portion of your exam is upon us, The "Field Mission". At this moment I would ask that all remaining teams please activate your designated Dragonfly Seeker cameras."

Yuuna pulls a small, white mechanical device out of her handbag and presses a button atop it. The device transforms into the shape of a Dragonfly, fluttering into the air and circling the group. Yuuna giggles as the Seeker begins flying around her inquisitively. It then approaches Pilet, who begins making various crude faces and gestures at it.

"Very good." Said Caffo. "Now In a moment you will be separated by teams and flown to your designated drop points throughout the outskirts of Devil's Tongue. Each team member will be handed a single HBA dogtag. Your primary objective is to reach the Cool Oasis, having obtained a total of 8 HBA dog tags for your team. You must do so by tomorrow at noon, which will be precisely 12:00PM. The oasis acts as a safe zone for candidates and battling for tags is strictly forbidden once there. There are no further rules for this portion, with the exception of following the law as usual. Battles may be fought to the death, but not within the perimeter of civilians or within domestic settings like desert villages."

Lazlow Jr. can be heard conversing with his team.

"Battles can be, "fought to the death" huh? Finally! I can't wait to smash some weakling's skull in."

"Please respect the hovering desert flora." Continued Caffo. "They are set up this way to protect them from the overly abundant Wurm infected wildlife. Your sponsors will be following you from a distance via the drop point aircrafts, their camouflage fields will be engaged to mask your presence from rival teams. Now, any questions?"

The crowd goes silent, as if muted by the unease of their surrounding competition.

"Fair enough. Let's begin!" Said Caffo. He fiddles with the Chatch built into his Vambraces.

Bing

A resounding notification rings throughout some of the Chatches of the crowd. Pilet gets a ring on his.

"Your designated aircraft, as well as the map of Devil's Tongue has been sent to each Team's Emissary. Please promptly make your way to the flight deck in an orderly fashion."

"Oh God. Pilet gets the map?" Said Faith.

"HAH!" Laughs Pilet. "This map is mine! If you want to see, that's gonna be $5 aurem from the lot of you! Individually of course."

"With every passing moment my chances of victory grow slimmer." Said Max. "Why did we make him emissary anyway? We still end up taking the heat for his nonsense..."

"Alright alright already, hold up a sec." Said Pilet, opening the attachment sent by Caffo. "Hidden Blades, light aircraft No.7." That's gotta be us. Fax where is that?"

Faxion hoists his rucksack over his shoulder and makes for the flight deck.

"Number 7 isss…" He licks his index finger and points it to the wind. "That-a-way!"

"Stop being corny, geezer." Said Pilet.

"…Aw…" Pouts Faxion.

The group laughs. They follow Faxion and soon find themselves at the flight deck, directly in front of light aircraft No.7. Kenzo is found lounging against some crates nearby, patiently awaiting their arrival.

"Took you long enough!" Said Kenzo. "Let's hop aboard! The pilot is waiting."

The group swifty boards the aircraft. They're greeted by a Licensed Hired Blade Pilot in a beige jumpsuit.

"Greetings lucky candidates!" Said the Pilot Blade. "I'm Benny, pleased to meet you! I'll be your Pilot for today, and while you're adventuring in the desert I'll keep your good ol'e sponsors company! Speaking of, is that Faxion of the Deadeye I see? Well how bout that! I heard you were raising a crop for the Wurm initiative, but I didn't think I'd be lucky enough to fly your troupe myself! Now sit back and relax candidates, shouldn't be long before your drop point is in sight."

"Oh my, well look who it is!" Said Faxion. "It's been far too long Benny! What a pleasure to have a pilot of your calibur along for the ride." He turns to the group. "Benny here once beat a squadron of five Itedonian terrorists in a dog fight by himself, with one of his thrusters destroyed!"

"Wow!" Exclaimed Yuuna. "Happy to meet you mister Benny! I'm glad we have a Pilot like you to get us there safely."

"Oh stop." Replied Benny. "It's all in a day's work, a Blades gotta do what a Blades gotta do ya know!"

"Yeah, shit." Said Pilet "That's some serious flying dude, I'd probably fly us into a hill of sand without any broken thrusters."

"Aaaaand that's why you shouldn't fly things with us riding in them." Said Yuuna.

"Agreed." Added Max.

The group unanimously buckles in. The engine begins to fire as light aircraft No.7 prepares for liftoff. As it rolls rapidly down the flight deck, the tires begin to gradually rescind.

Vrrrrrrrrrooooooommmmm

The aircraft begins to hover buoyantly; as it pierces its way into the skies above Devil's Tongue, leaving behind its mothership with haste.

"Camouflage engaged!" Said Benny, as he flips a switch to conceal his ship from the rival pilots. The small airship becomes effectively invisible, vanishing without a trace in the desert sky.

"My Lord." Faith touches her hand to the glass window, she turns to Faxion with a somber look on her face. "Fax, imagine if Mom and Dad could see us now..."

He flashes her a meek grin.

"My friend, words could not describe how proud they would be."

Return of The Wurm

Roughly twenty minutes pass by, as light aircraft #7 reaches its destination. The ship lowers on a random dune of sand, without a major landmark in sight. As the camouflaged airship park's itself on the highest point of the dune, the back door opens and lowers itself onto the scorching sand.

"Last stop, Devil's Tongue!" Said Benny. "Good luck candidates, may the five generals guide your blade!"

Faxion and Kenzo stand at the door, arms folded with excited grins on their faces.

"Good luck my boy." Said Kenzo. He playfully beats his son in the chestplate of his armor. "Whether beast or blade, show not mercy nor fear."

"Of course father." Replied Max. "I will return a Licensed Hired Blade, this I promise you."

Kenzo grabs Max and gives him a tight bear hug.

Unngh! Max grunts in pain.

Suddenly, Kenzo's eyes begin to water. His voice noisily cracks and raises in pitch as he tries to speak.

"That's my boy!!!" He wipes the welling tears from his eyes. "And break a leg out there young warriors! You show great promise, and worlds of potential!"

"Thank you mister Kenzo!" Replied Faith.

"Thanks, appreciate it man." Said Pilet. "I'll watch your son for you." Pilet wraps his arm around Max's neck. "Someone's gotta make sure he doesn't end up lizard food, right?"

"Why thank you Pilet!" Said Kenzo. "Fortunately I don't believe the Sanda are very appetizing, too much muscle on us! Hahahahaha!" Kenzo let's loose a bellowing laugh.

Faxion shakes his head amusingly.

"Alright folks listen up." Said Faxion. "The best advice I could give you is to ration your water wisely, the dry heat of this dessert will bake your lungs without you realizing it. Also, try not to exert yourselves. You'll need to save your energy for a fight, you never know when you might end up in one."

Faxion pulls a paper map of the desert from his side pocket, unfurling the disheveled sheet with care.

"Now, we are here." He circles a portion of the outskirts with a red pen. "The best course of action for you guys right now is to head south from here, to this mining town called Giduh." He proceeds to circle Giduh on the map. "Restock on supplies, and kill time waiting for a team to fight. Remember to pace yourselves, and have fun! If you're too stressed, the mind will end you before the dessert gets a chance."

"Thank's Fax, will do." Said Pilet. "Now let's get to it, I'm starting to get jet-lagged."

"Bye guys!" Said Yuuna, as she waves to Kenzo, Faxion and Benny.

Thank you again for the ride Benny." Said Faith, as she and her sister walk down the platform.

Max simply bows and takes his leave.

As Pilet turns to exit the airship, he stops himself for a brief moment; glancing back at Faxion with a look of disbelief.

"I made it pretty far huh?" Said Pilet. "Think I might even touch gold... What do you think?"

Faxion grins and tips his hat.

"I think so too lad." Said Faxion. "I think so too..." After a brief pause, Faxion rolls up his map and whacks Pilet on the shoulder with it. "Now go man! It's getting hot in here and we're wasting the AC! Last thing I need is for Kenzo to start getting swampy!"

"Hahaha! Ok ok! Sheesh."

Pilet scurries down the off ramp and meets the others on the top of the dune.

The ramp steadily rescinds, as the airship begins to slowly take off.

"Knock 'em dead folks!" Shouts Faxion, as the off ramp door closes before him.

The ship once again engages camouflage mode, as it disappears into the desert skies.

"Welp, it's officially go time." Said Pilet. "No telling when danger will find us now."

"It's time to bake in this God forsaken oven is what it's time for." Said Faith, as she removes her jacket and stuffs it into her bag. I've dreaded the thought of this heat since the moment they told us we were going to Devil's Tongue."

"The discomfort is only mental." Said Max. "Take it as an exercise in callusing the mind, Faith. These moments are a gift to strengthen the soul."

"My mind is strong enough, but thank you Max." Said Faith. "It's more so sweat stains and body odor I'm worried about."

"You could borrow some of my essential oils if you're worried about that!" Said Yuuna. "I've got lavender and cedarwood and bergamot... Ooh be careful with the bergamot though, it's a touch phototoxic so this harsh sunlight will make it burn you like a raisin!"

"Thanks sis, I'll keep that in mind." Replied Faith. "Hey, where's Pilet?"

Faith, Yuuna and Max peer Pilet standing at the top of the dune about 20 feet off, shading his eyes with his hand from the sun. He gazes off in the distance, towards the mining town Faxion informed them of.

"Look, it's right there." Said Pilet, pointing at the town of Giduh some miles away. "If we use fleetfoot, I bet we could make it there pretty fast, and the wind would keep us cool from the sun!"

"I would advise against that..." Said Max. "The extended use of fleetfoot so early in the exam could leave us fatigued and aura dupleted, especially in the event of a surprise attack. And just the same, we're not all speedsters like yourself."

"Uuh, I don't think he's listening, Max..." Said Yuuna, watching Pilet stretch his hamstrings and begin to hop in place.

"Pilet don't..." Said Faith, quivering her lip as her eyebrows raise.

"C'mon guys let's race! Last one there buys a round at the pub. FLEETFOOT!!" Casts Pilet, as he bolts swiftly across the desert; kicking up a cloud of dust and sand in his teammates faces.

"AAGH!" Exclaimed Max with a mouth full of sand. "You fool!"

"God damn it! My hair! It's in my hair!" Yelled Faith.

"Pilet you're a jerk!" Cried Yuuna, as she rubs the sand from her eyes. "We gotta catch up to him!" She claps her hands into a prayer posture and begins to cultivate aura. "Kite stream!" Yuuna's body starts to levitate off of the sand, as a gust of auric wind propels her effortlessly toward Giduh.

Cough *Cough* "Amazing!" Said Max, recovering from the sandblasting prior. "So this is the Wind and Star casting style." He pats the dust off his armor. "The Sanda are not much for running, I guess your homeland's KSA will have to do... Fleetfoot!" He casts.

"Hmmpf, my sister the showoff." Said Faith, as she too casts Fleetfoot.

Max and Faith begin their arcane sprint towards their destination, attempting to catch up to their flying ally and nimble Emissary.

The team traverses miles across the desert at top speeds, easily surpassing 100 miles per hour. They pass tumbleweeds and miscellaneous desert wildlife along the way. Floating cacti in solar powered terrariums hover several feet over the hot sands, creating shade beneath them for weary roadrunners and lizards. Pilet, who's about half a mile in the lead, comes upon a group of armadillos with thick, callous-like armor walking across his path.

"Oh, shit shit shit!"

In an attempt to avoid crashing into them, he leaps promptly into the air. But the Arcane buoyancy granted by Fleetfoot lifts him higher than expected, as an unfortunately placed terrarium hovering overhead clotheslines Pilet, sending him tumbling startledly to the ground. As he pulls his head from the sand, Max, Yuuna and Faith close the distance between them. Drawing near, the group can't help but release a unanimous laugh at Pilet's expense.

"Oooh my GODDD!" Exclaims Yuuna, flying to Pilet's aid. "You just got messed UPPP!!" She helps him pull his head from the sand.

Spit *Gag* *Spew*

"UGGH, stupid giant pillbugs! I was trying to be nice and not step on them. And what does it get me?!? Buried alive!"

Wiping tears of laughter from her eyes, Faith retorts.

"Those aren't pillbugs genius, they're Callous armadillos! They're actually the animal that inspired the "Callous" cast."

"Pill bugs that large, that would truly be something wouldn't it." Said Max.

"Yeaaah, that'd be something I'd like to avoid. Ew." Said Yuuna.

As the family of Callous armadillos scurry by, Max spots a deposit of clear, sharp crystals jutting up from the ground.

"Hey Yuuna." Said Max, pointing to the crystals. "You like stones like those ones right?"

GASP

"Woah!!" Exclaimed Yuuna. She runs over to the deposit and yanks a crystal from the formation. "This is Selenite! Or, "desert rose", I was hoping we might find one of these on this mission!! It's super useful!"

"Clearly they think so too." Said Faith, nudging her head toward a nearby quarry of miners.

The toiling miners pick away at the miscellaneous assortments of stones, crystals and minerals. After stumbling about in a delirious haze, Pilet finally regains his composure.

"Ok then, this must be the mine that Giduh is known for. I guess this means we're getting close." He said.

"Hey you, are you ok over there?" Said a miner, as he approaches the group. His body drenched in sweat from a hard morning's work. He takes off his yellow hard hat and scratches his scruffy brown hair. "I'm in charge around here, the name's Cliff. I saw the fall you just took, didn't seem too pleasant. Looked like you were going pretty fast too, thought you were a damn desert cheetah for a second or one of those Giduh Monsters again. They sure have been nasty lately."

"He's ok, we're just passing through." Said Faith.

"Yeah I'm alright dude, sometimes I'm just too fast for my own good. Thanks for asking." Replied Pilet.

"Fair enough." Said the miner. "Just look out around these parts will ya? If you happen to see a group of 3 foot tall spotted lizards, you better run like hell."

"Why is that?" Inquired Max.

"Two words, Giduh monsters. Named after our good old village of Giduh, since they seem to like the mines. They got a poisonous bite and a mean attitude. But they stay away from people, so when we come through to mine for the day they usually clear out. *Sigh* But the past few months they've been getting a lot more nasty, and BIGGER too. They even got these weird purple eyes. Nowadays we're the ones who have to pack up when they come around. A pickaxe ain't enough to whack one of these suckers, not anymore - ah shit!! Look out!!!"

The miner's sentence is cut short by the screeching of a 3 and a half foot long Giduh monster, eyes glowing velvet with a cracked glowing pattern running across its scales. Following behind is a group of about a dozen more, closing in on the miners with haste.

The miners begin to panic.

"No no no!"

"Not this shit again! I told my wife I'd come home safe!"

"Let's move, move, move!!!"

The Giduh monster lunges through the air, right past Faith's ear as it dives toward Cliff.

"Frisio!" Casts Faith, with record speed.

The lizard is frozen solid mid-flight and falls heavily on top of Cliff. Faith's hand comes down from casting as she turns the page to her next cast.

Phew, damn! She opened that book fast as hell. Thought Pilet.

The rookie from Chamboree presses the infrared button on his Dragonfly longknives.

Vrrrrrrrr!

In a blazing flash, he dices the frozen Giduh monster to pieces. Pilet holds out a hand to Cliff and helps him up.

"Get your people out of here, we got this covered." Said Pilet.

"Shit you don't have to ask me twice." Replied Cliff. "Let's go boys!"

But the miners are blocked, surrounded by Giduh monsters on each side.

"Damn it, alright plan B." Said Pilet. "Cliff, keep the guys together in the center behind us." Pilet yells over to his team. "Yo guys! Pick a corner and keep the miners safe!"

"Who made you captain?" Replied Faith.

"I mean, we kinda did..." Said Max.

"Oh... Alright fine. Get ready, here they come." Said Faith, as the Giduhs March forth menacingly.

The Dragonfly seeker camera flutters to a safe distance and zooms in on the action.

Max, Pilet and Faith all cast "Callous", while Yuuna opts for another technique. She clasps her hands.

"Guardian mist!" Casts Yuuna. Her body is enveloped in platinum light, as every pore of her skin starts to emit a powerful, 2 inch stream of air.

The Giduhs begin their advance. Three monsters savagely roar, leaping for Yuuna in a coordinated assault.

"Dustdevil!" She casts.

A tower of gusting wind loosed from the ground, whipping up a cyclone of sand and blasting the Giduhs soaring into the sky. Another sneaks around to her left flank and attempts to bite her arm. But as it tries to clasp its mouth, the powerful air pressure from her Guardian mist does not allow it near her skin.

"Ah ah ah, bad lizard!" Said Yuuna, wagging her index finger at it. "Starshot!" She compresses a shining bead of aura in between her hands and fires it at the monster, exploding it into pieces. "Yuck!"

Meanwhile Max draws a hand to his Lacerate and lies in wait as the Giduh monsters surround him.

"Who is first to die... Hmm?"

A Giduh behind him lunges forth.

Ksshiinng

With blinding speed he draws his blade, spins around and slices the monster in half.

Click

He resheaths his Lacerate before his adversaries' remains hit the ground.

"I'm waiting..."

The rest rush him all at once, throwing caution to the wind.

Kssshhhingshinshingshingshing

With deadly precision, Max cuts down each and every one of them in a rapid whirlwind of swordsmanship. He holds the blade in a guarded stance toward his head for a moment, making sure the area is safe.

Drip *Drip*

The blood cup above the handle fills to the brim, overflowing onto his hand.

"What is the point of this thing if it won't keep my hands clean. Last thing I need is a case of butterfingers mid-swing."

The miners watch on in awe of the degree of skill these young warriors display. As they do so, a rogue Giduh monster sneaks past Faith and snaps at one of the workers.

"Oh no you don't!" Exclaims Faith. "Skarrya!"

The crimson Skarrya blade flows from her fingertips, as she swiftly chops the head off the beast before it reaches the miner.

"My God!! Thanks kid!" He replies.

"Don't thank me yet..." Said Faith, as more Giduhs arrive to cause problems for the young prospects. "Gilazia Shida!" Casts Faith.

Kshh *Kring* *Shhikk*

Her body begins to sprout crystalline glass from every appendage, covering the elder Sierro head-to-toe.

The monsters attack, lunging and leaping with enraged fervor.

"HAH! HIYA!"

Faith slashes down monsters with her Skarrya blade as they leap in, strafing side to side evasively. Any that land a bite have sharp crystal's broken off into their mouths, forcing them to loosen their jaws in agony. One lunges for her face, but she swiftly meets it with a high kick that sends it flying toward Pilet's corner.

As the flying lizard soars in the air toward Pilet, he hears it's cries coming behind him and turns to address the threat.

"Hollowpoint!" He casts.

A vibrant auric Hollowpoint blast fires from his palm. It explodes on contact, obliterating the lizard before it can reach him.

"Hey you! Keep yours to yourself huh?" Said Pilet.

"Oh hush I was only sharing!" Replied Faith.

"She's funny this one." Said Pilet, as he readies his blades for the impending crowd of Giduh monsters. "Come to Papa." Pilet grins as he starts to clang his Dragonfly longknives together.

A monster in the front strikes. It leaps forth from a large rock, but Pilet effortlessly strafes to the side and slashes as its teeth narrowly miss his head. One runs toward his feet, prompting the fiery prospect to leap high into the air. But at the height of his leap, two more Giduhs jump towards him from parallel rocks above. He twirls and contorts his body in the air; evading them both, while hacking and slashing his adversaries in a tornado of cutlery.

Krish *Kshing* *Clang*

As he lands on the ground, Pilet begins to roll around his grounded opponents like one of the armadillos, slashing wildly and cutting off lizard arms and legs in the process.

"You're no match for my armadillo style! I'm having me some sauteed lizard legs tonight!" Exclaims Pilet.

Seeing all this, Cliff turns to one of his workers.

"That one is having too much fun. These folks are something else, a real freaky lot for sure."

During his tirade, Pilet fails to notice a Giduh monster crawling on a rock behind him. He turns to Max and sees the volume of reptile parts scattered around the young Sanda warrior.

"Yo Max, how many you get?"

Max lifts his gaze to see the monster lurking behind Pilet. But rather than warn him, Max pulls out a retractable, state of the art longbow. The M2 Sunshower, it fires beams of pure plasma from three separate compartments on the front of the bow. Max raises his weapon and fires at the Giduh monster. The golden plasma arrow whizzes by Pilet's ear, causing him to duck and roll in frazzled confusion.

He turns around to see the fried Giduh monster, then back to Max with a relieved yet triggered look on his face.

"Watch it!" Exclaimed Pilet. "You trying to kill my ass?!? Couldn't you just say, "Hey dude there's a lizard behind you." Instead of aiming your fancy freaking bow at me or whatever that is?!?"

"You're welcome." Replied Max, grinning mischievously. He retracts his Sunshower bow and affixes it to a compartment on the back of his armor.

"Man these guys are freaking comedians…" Muttered Pilet, collecting his knives from the ground.

The last of the Giduh monsters seem to retreat, as The Hidden Blades gather by the hiding miners; who subsequently thank them for their assistance and point them to the direction of Giduh village.

"Hey, you know what?" Said Cliff. "Why don't you folks hop in the bed of my pickup! There's plenty of space for you all. Can't have you walking the desert any further in this heat. It's the least I could do after all!"

"That sounds great!" Replied Yuuna. "Anything beats trekking across this sweltering mess!"

"Thank you Mister Cliff." Said Max. "We're just happy to have kept your workers safe."

Pilet gives Max a side eye.

"Oh now you're worried about safety..." Muttered Pilet. "Hey, I'm hungry. Do we get to keep these???" He points to all the body parts of the Giduh monsters.

"Oh no, you don't want to eat that son." Said Cliff. "These beasts ain't right, something's wrong with them. Last time one of the guys killed and ate one he ended up in the hospital for a week. Damn near died too."

"I'm assuming these were some of the Wurm infected animals Caffo told us about." Said Faith. "Best to leave them be, God only knows what parasites live within."

"Damn it, what a waste..." Replied Pilet.

As the miners go back to work, Cliff notifies his men that he'll be taking a half day to drive the prospects to Giduh. The Hidden Blades get in his pickup bed and make their way across the desert.

The Village Giduh

Close to an hour passes as the rumbling and soft bumping of the pickup truck lulls the crew to sleep. The sands of Devil's Tongue begin to blend with rows of mud brick, lining the roads of Giduh village. Vibrant yellow flowers fall from Giduh's many Palo verde trees, and litter the streets like a golden blanket. Red and brown brick buildings house the villagers from the harsh rays of the sun. Shops and restaurants line the main street, welcoming tourists and locals alike. Small ponds are dug out into the sides of assorted buildings, Bluegill and red ear sunfish swim curiously through the freshwater.

The truck passes the main gate and enters Giduh, its weathered tires rolling smoothly over the meticulously evened brick.

"Wakey wakey folks, we're here!" Said Cliff.

The Hidden Blades wipe the crust from their eyes, yawning and stretching from their quick sun-nap.

"Damn, I think I got a tan... Either that or I'm definitely going to burn." Said Faith.

"Yeah seriously, how could we forget freaking sunblock." Said Pilet. "I'm gonna be a lobster on live TV. You know, when they put that license in my hand at the winner's circle?"

Cliff lowers the hatch door, as the heroic prospects leap from the truck bed onto the brick road.

"Hey thanks a ton man." Said Pilet. "Saved us a lot of trouble with that ride, I had no idea Giduh was so far from the mines."

"Yes it was an honorable act that you did not have to undertake, we're in your debt." Said Max.

"Oh stop, like I said it was the least I could do." Said Cliff. "Your kindness is much appreciated and there's no way I could let it go unnoticed. Now look." Cliff motions down the road to the many bustling shops and buildings lining the sidewalks. "This here is mainstreet. To your right you got the fish markets, the general store and one of them fancy Lava Bean's or whatever. Then on the right ya got shops for clothes, jewelry, pottery, all that good shit. Oh there's a bakery, and last but not least is mine and the crew's FAVORITE hang out spot. The Laughing Lizard, a badass pub with all the liquor you could hope for."

"Oh sweet, finally something to look forward to." Said Pilet.

"Pilet, aren't you still like... In high school?" Said Yuuna.

"Shh, be quiet!" Whispers Pilet. "I got a fake ID, my age is nobodies damn business!"

"Wait a sec, that's right!" Said Faith. "You were still totally a high schooler, your only what... 18? And Faxion just pulled you out of school? That's allowed??"

"Pssh, are you kidding me?" Said Pilet. "First of all I'm 19, I got left back once. Second, Fax flashed that Hired Blades badge and my principal nearly handed me a diploma on the spot. I guess he was a big fan of Fax's work and found some legal loophole for me to join the Hired Blades before graduating. Not that he wanted me hanging around anyway."

"Wow, one can only wonder the man's accomplishments if a school principal in some random mountain village knows him so well." Said Max.

"Oh for sure, guy's a beast." Said Pilet. "But anyway now that everyone knows my damn business, how old are you guys??"

"Well I just turned 22 last month!" Said Yuuna.

"I'm 26." Said Faith. "But hasn't anyone ever told you not to ask a woman's age? Rude."

"I am 24." Said Max.

"Well, screw you guys I'm drinking anyway!" Said Pilet.

"I'm not your father, do as you wish." Said Max. "But if you're caught I will pretend I don't know you."

"Me neither." Said Faith. "In fact I encourage it, maybe security will find out and start chasing you. I'm sure you could outrun them, but watching you jump into another flying cactus would make my day."

"Ohh poshh." Yuuna puts an arm around Pilet's shoulder. "Pilet this'll be funn. Let's get you DRUNNKKK!"

"HELL yeah, see she gets it!" Said Pilet.

"Oh my God Yuuna." Said Faith. "You're ridiculous as always. Ok, when Yuuna turned 21 her friends found her blacked out behind a trash can at a bar in Miantha. She had an empty martini glass in each hand... And an empty bottle of whiskey in her purse."

"AND a box of vodka chocolates! Muahahahaha!" Said Yuuna.

"She stole those..." Replied Faith.

"Well folks it's just about time I get back to the mine, Lord only knows how much slacking off the boys are up to without me." Said Cliff, hopping back into the front seat of his truck.

"Thanks again Cliff." Said Faith. "Best of luck to you and the crew."

The Hidden Blades wave goodbye to the mining foreman as he drives off into the desert heat.

"So what do we do first?" Said Max. "No one said this mission was to be a trip to the local village. My Lacerate still thirsts for battle."

"Have a little patience Max!" Said Yuuna. "We just gotta get some food n' water before we go back out there. We got really lucky with Cliff and his truck, otherwise we'd probably have started to run low by now."

"Yeah, especially considering this." Said Pilet, holding up an empty, sliced open canteen. "I guess I cut it up when I was rolling around in the sand, killing Wurm lizards. Man, my armadillo style let me down huh. Gotta work on that…"

"Oh shit, Pilet you're really lucky we had Cliff." Said Faith. "You would've definitely shriveled up like a prune without that ride because there's no way I'd have given you mine."

"Well nobodies asking for yours are they!" Replied Pilet. "Freakin', probably has bookworm germs all over it. You can keep that shit."

"Holy Serpent Dragon may we please get past this?" Said Max. "Look Faith, why don't you come with me to the general store? Pilet and Yuuna can go pick out some fish at the market."

"Why that sounds like a wonderful idea Max, I agree." Replied Faith. "You two try not to poison us with your selections, ok? Last time Yuuna cooked fish she almost killed me. Remember sis, pufferfish are a terrible idea."

"Oh boo hiss. It was so cute and pouty! And you didn't die did you? My mendingcast skills are just toooo good!"

Faith facepalms.

"Yeah well I could do without the vomiting and paralysis this time around, just ask the vendor what's edible ok??"

"Damn, at this rate maybe we should just order take out to the oasis." Said Pilet.

"Ha-Ha." Faith snickered.

The group separates, Max and Faith head for the general store while Yuuna and Pilet enter the fish market.

As Pilet and Yuuna walk through the front door of the fish market, they notice the Dragonfly seeker camera has chosen to follow them over Max and Faith. It flutters rapidly around them, sending a constant stream of video to monitors of the Hired Blades board room.

"So this little guy picked us over the others huh?" Said Pilet. "See Yuuna, it's the head honchos. They know the people want to see the most good looking ones on camera."

"Aww Pilet, you think I'm good looking?" Said Yuuna. "It's probably just set to follow the emissary if ever we got separated, but I appreciate the sentiment!"

"Well now let's not get ahead of ourselves ok. I'm the pretty one here, but your personality is LEAGUES above those two sticks in the mud. So I mean in my book that gets you some points right."

"Pilet your so meeean!" Pouts Yuuna. "Who taught you how to talk to a woman you jerk! You'll never get a girlfriend that way!"

"HA! I already have one back home. I'm a King Killer and a lady killer, but I don't wanna brag. Gotta stay humble you know?"

"Oh realllly..... Give me the dirt, what's the details?"

Pilet folds his arms, looking away in a slightly bashful manner.

"Well I mean, we're not official or anything. But she gave me this letter and told me she loves me. That's pretty much the same thing right?"

"Letter?" Replied Yuuna. "Do you have it? Let me see!!"

Pilet fishes through his bag in search of Nivia's love letter, sifting through clothes and gadgets. He nicks his index finger on the unsheathed edge of the bronze, cloud serpent dagger.

shlick

"Ouch! Shit!" Yells Pilet, placing his finger in his mouth. "Here's the damn letter."

He abruptly places it in Yuuna's hands, as she proceeds to scan it up and down.

"..."

"OOOHHH MYYY GODDD!" Exclaims Yuuna. "YOU GUYS ARE SOOOO ADORABLE!"

"Shhh quiet down will you?!" Said Pilet, taking note of several shoppers turning their heads inquisitively at Yuuna's outburst.

"I'm sorry, but this is freaking cute. Pilet what did you say back?!"

"Well, nothing." Replied Pilet. "Two weeks ago, she gave me the letter as I was leaving town with Fax and told me to read it later. Then I forgot to open it until like, yesterday morning before the exam. Haha...Ha..."

"..."

"..."

Yuuna rolls the letter up tightly and begins relentlessly swatting Pilet in the head with it.

Smack *Smack* *Smack*

"Ow what the hell!" Said Pilet. "What'd I do?!"

"WELL IF YOU THOUGHT YOU HAD A GIRLFRIEND BEFORE YOU DEFINITELY DON'T HAVE ONE NOW!!!!!!" Said Yuuna, continuing her spastic assault.

"Chill Yuuna chill! Stop for like two seconds! Why, what's bad about this situation?!" Said Pilet.

"Dummy! She probably thinks you either forgot about her or just don't care!! Honestly Pilet if that were me, I'd already be onto the next guy. I value myself toooo much to put up with that kind of neglect." Replied Yuuna.

"Ok, sooo. I guess I should text her or something?"

Yuuna starts a gradual, slow clap for Pilet.

"Congratulations sir, you did it!" Said Yuuna. "You figured it out all by yourself! Yes silly, you need to text or call her on your Chatch, write to her, send a messenger pigeon or something! Just like creditors, if you ignore the ones you love, eventually they go away forever!"

"Creditors?" Said Pilet. "Wait, Yuuna I don't think that's how it-"

"Hush this isn't about that." Said Yuuna. "Listen we gotta fix this, text her right now."

Yuuna stands with folded arms, her left foot begins incessantly tapping the floor.

Pilet looks at his Chatch. He opens up his contacts and scrolls over Nivia's name.

"..."

After a brief pause he closes his contacts and locks the Chatch's home screen.

"I can't, I just can't." Said Pilet. "I... I'm freakin' scared."

Gasp

"Pilet why??" Said Yuuna.

"I just want to wait until I pass this test. I want to go back home as a Licensed Hired Blade before I talk to anybody from Chamboree. Until I've got that badge, I'm just not doing it. I haven't talked to my grandpa or my grandma or my best friend OR the woman who loves me." Pilet's face starts to become visibly reddened. "I'm not ready yet, I'm not... I'm not good enough yet!"

Yuuna's gaze becomes somber.

"Pilet...I-"

"Nah forget this!" Exclaimed Pilet. "Look, when I get that badge I can go home and know that for once in my life, I did something good! I'll know that I literally amounted to something. I'll be good enough to be together with Nivia, I can go back to my grandparents with pride, I'll find my dad and-"

Pilet begins to choke up. He fights back tears.

"And my dad might want me! He might actually want to stay with me!" Tears begin to flow down Pilet's cheeks. "He's gotta know how cool I am. Yuuna he's gotta know. If he knows he'll want me and he'll stay, he's got to! Why wouldn't he?!"

Not knowing what to say, Yuuna simply embraces Pilet in a warm hug and says.

"I'm sorry. I'm so sorry Pilet. I'm sorry......"

The two stand there, hugging and crying in the middle of the fish market. A foreign vendor woman speaks to them from behind.

"Hey, you gonna buy some fish or no? You buy or you go outside. You scaring the customers! You buy fish to give to your dad, he probably hungry. Probably went to lunch for a long time and got lost. Stop crying and buy fish!"

Still hugging, Pilet and Yuuna pause and turn their heads to look at the vendor woman.

"Do you have any pufferfish?" Said Yuuna.

Pilet turns his gaze to Yuuna with a look of confusion.

"You very stupid girl, pufferfish make you dead." Said the vendor. "But that not my problem, I sell to you for $12 aurem."

"Deal!" Said Yuuna, slapping her money on the counter.

Pilet wipes the tears from his eyes and simply gazes in awe of the transaction in progress.

"...How did you make it to 22 years old..."

Meanwhile, in the general store...

Max and Faith stroll down the aisles in search of supplies to get them to Cool Oasis. As they pass the first aid section Faith begins to pick out some bandages and peroxide.

"You know, we forgot a first aid kit didn't we?" Said Faith. "My sister is actually incredible with healing auracast, but just to be safe we should get one."

"I believe we did forget one, how ill prepared we are." Said Max. "You would think the Proctors would at least set us up with some sort of general pack for this trip, right? I'm not surprised so many people die attempting to become Licensed Hired Blades. I mean as soon as we got here those Giduh monsters tried to make us their lunch."

"I know right? Those things were ugly, and huge! It's always startling to see a creature infected with the Wurm. In Miantha, me and Yuuna would sometimes see Wurm foxes and raccoons. They were bigger than normal, but never that much larger. Once we saw a Wurm bear, holy shit was that scary. It looked kinda like the gorilla Pilet fought in the news, massive and covered in shiny tattoos."

"It appears that the stronger the parasite is, the larger of a host it is capable of overtaking." Said Max. "They're rare on Hachidori, unlike here. I myself have not seen too many infected beasts in my lifetime, save for one Wurm shark while fishing with my father. That was quite a wild catch. Why do you think so little is known of this foe?"

"Well from what I've read, the Wurm melds strongly with the brain of any host it inhabits." Replied Faith. "By doing so it relies on the health of the host to survive. So if the host is killed, most Wurms are so intertwined that they can't escape the body alive. There's also no known way to remove the Wurm safely."

Faith shivers squeamishly.

"When scientists try to remove it from a corpse, the thing seems to freaking evaporate into thin air! So because they vanish without a trace, it's a real problem trying to examine them for further study. It's almost as if the little pests are hiding something...."

"I see..." Said Max. "I wonder, has the Wurm ever infected a human? I've never heard of such a thing, but the thought is assuredly haunting."

"Oh God it's terrifying to imagine." Said Faith. "Humans have a higher intellect than most creatures, which for some reason seems to give us a natural resistance to their infection. Which, thank God for that. The last thing I ever want to imagine is a squirmy Wurm, swimming through my brain!"

"Yes, I do share the sentiment..." Replied Max, as a large jug of water falls from the shelf above him, nailing him on the top of his head. His braided hair whips about as his head snaps forward. "Ouch!" He catches the heavy jug before it hits the ground. "The ghosts of the unfortunate Wurm's prey must be mad that we are talking about them."

"Hahaha!" Laughs Faith. "Stop, don't say that. I'm so scared of ghosts!"

The two carry on, scanning the aisles for assorted goods that could aid them in their journey. After about 10 minutes, they conclude their trip to the general store with a bag full of necessities. As Max and Faith pay and hoist their brown shopping bags from the cashier counter, they start to hear music booming from a distant sound system. The two turn to each other with a puzzled look in their eyes.

"Do you hear what I am hearing?" Said Max.

"Yeahh... What the hell is that?" Said Faith. "It's so loud, it almost sounds like a guitar."

They take their bags and exit through the sliding doors at the front of the general store. As they step outside the sounds of electric instruments become clearer, seemingly coming from the Laughing Lizard bar.

"Yo!" Said Pilet, as he and Yuuna return from the fish market.

The four meet on the brick road outside of the general store.

"What's all that noise about? They do live shows and stuff in Giduh?" Said Pilet.

"I suppose so." Said Max. "Couldn't hurt to check it out. Maybe there are other candidates at the bar, we could challenge them and make headway on this mission."

"If that's the case we had better be on guard." Said Faith. "If there are other candidates, I'm sure they'll be just as eager to take our tags as we are theirs..."

"You guys worry too much!" Replied Yuuna. "It's a show! Let's just go have fun!!"

Faith spots the dead pufferfish peeking out of Yuuna's bag.

"Yuuna... You did not."

"Yeaahh..." Said Pilet. "Sorry, I don't know what's up with her and the pufferfish."

"It's my money and I'll spend it on whatever I want lady!" Retorts Yuuna, guarding her pufferfish tightly. "They're just so freaking cuuute!!"

"UGH, fine." Said Faith. "Just don't cook it this time please."

Clash: The Hidden Blades V.S. The Funk Munkeys!

The Hidden Blades stash their purchased goods away in their rucksacks and make their way to the Laughing Lizard. As they step through the front door, they're bombarded with the sound of electric guitars and percussion drums, and a boisterous, mohawked singer rapping on the microphone.

"Yo, the only thing you gotta know? The munkeys break ground when we gettin' on a flow. Try ta-beat us try ta-see us when you step in through the door, then-ya lights fade out when ya sleepin' on the floor."

As they take their seat at the bar, The Hidden Blades recognize this band standing on stage.

"Oh hey," Said Yuuna, struggling to speak over the music. "isn't that the Funk Munkeys? They were the guys fighting at the Lava bean in HQ!"

"Huh, yeah I guess so." Said Pilet. "Check that out, they're pretty good too."

The Funk Munkeys continue their show while The Hidden Blades enjoy some drinks at the bar, with the exception of Pilet, who's fake ID was clearly exposed by the bartender.

About 20 minutes later the Funk Munkeys rap up their show, prompting the audience to stand up and cheer exuberantly.

"Thank you, thank you!" Said the mohawked singer. "My name's Lukah, and we're The Funk Munkeys!"

The crowd continues their standing ovation.

Follow us on funkmunkeys.com and enter the code "laughinglizard" for some sweet deals on our future gigs. You know, if we don't die taking this Blades exam or whatever."

The mention of their potential death causes the crowd's applause to quickly peeter out; as a random voice in the back can be heard saying, "Oh damn, they goin' die.".

The Funk Munkeys start to put away their instruments, as The Hidden Blades approach them with caution. Except for Pilet, who walks right up to the band and cracks his knuckles.

"Yo." Said Pilet. "Not gonna lie, you guys rocked house. It's a shame we gotta take your tags."

"Pilet!" Exclaimed Yuuna. "Don't be so rude!"

The Funk Munkeys visibly become irate, as Lukah walks up to Pilet and stands right in his face.

"You ain't takin' shit, fool." Said Lukah. His nostrils flare and his brow furrows menacingly.

"Oh I'm takin' 'em, and I'm takin' yours first." Replied Pilet, pushing his forehead against Lukah's.

"Ay, knock it off now." Says the drummer. "You know we're not supposed to be fightin' around civilians. You wanna end up shootin' the bartender in the face by accident?"

"Look, you guys know the drill." Said Faith. "We may not have to fight, but both our teams need those tags. Maybe we could work out a more civilized method of challenging each other."

The drummer stands from his drum seat and walks over to the group.

"The name's Danba, Danba the Witch Doctor. Let's have an arm wrestle. We'll go one on one between the four of us, and each loser gives up their tag."

"You're on!" Exclaimed Yuuna. She spits in her hands and rubs them together, offering Danba a handshake.

Danba's brow raises at Yuuna's eccentricity.

"Uh, dang. You a nasty girl... But ok." He shakes on it.

The first up is the Funk Munkeys guitarist Clint. He sits at the table and plants his elbow down with a thud.

"Who's first, ya know? You're gonna get it, ya know?!" Said Clint.

Faith places her tome inside of her bag and takes a seat at the table.

"I'll start us off." Said Faith as she sits down and clasps hands with Clint. "Try not to disappoint, wouldn't want to lose to a girl in front of your friends."

"I am a girl!" Exclaims Clint.

"What?!" Replied Faith, puzzled by Clint's response.

"Begin!" Said Danba as he swings his hand downward to commence the match.

Still puzzled by Clint's statement, and unaware that the match was about to start, Faith is taken off guard when Clint immediately slams her arm down on the table.

Fwip *Thud*

"HA!" Said Clint. "I told you you were gonna get it, ya know?! And then you got it, ya know?!?! I tricked you. I ain't no girl, don't ya know?!?!"

Frazzled by this turn of events, Faith turns to Danba in protest.

"Hey what gives?! No one said the match was going to start! How was I supposed to know that? And why does he keep saying "Ya know?"?!"

"Clint don't talk very good, none of us really do." Said Danba. "Svenn's mute, I got a thick-ass accent, Lukah got no brain and Clint says "Ya know" a lot. The Funk Munkeys speak through our music, because otherwise our voices may not be heard."

"Wha- yo shut up Danba! I do too have a brain!" Retorts Lukah.

"Well you could'a fooled me, guess you should use it more often." Replied Danba. He turns to Faith. "And sorry for the confusion, next time we'll give ya a three count before startin'. Gotta be ready at all times if you gonna be a Blade, ya know?"

He looks at Clint and they both grin.

"Whatever..." Said Faith, handing Clint her tag and taking her leave.

Max takes a seat next, met by the bassist Svenn.

"Good luck to you." Said Max.

Svenn nods his head, taps his chest and points to Max, as if to say, "And so to you."

Danba begins the count.

"3, 2, 1, Go!"

The two begin their bout. Svenn's vascular arms flex, his biceps taught and puffy. Max holds his ground, his massive triceps bulge and twitch. Their arms begin to quiver as neither one gives up an inch.

"Your strength is admirable." Said Max.

Svenn flips his hair and smirks subtly.

"But not admirable enough! Hnnng!" Said Max as he flexes even harder, pushing Svenns arm past the neutral position.

As the two continue their bout, Svenn is unable to make up the ground lost in the previous exchange. Max pushes further, bringing Svenn's arm dangerously close to the table. But as the struggling Svenn fights to keep his arm up, a single fly begins to buzz around Max's head.

Bzzzz

He attempts to swat it with his free hand.

"Agh, get out of my face you pest. Can't you see I'm busy?!"

The fly continues to pester the young swordsman, buzzing around his ears and eyes, greatly hindering his senses. Pilet begins to laugh at Max's dismay.

"Hahahah" Laughs Pilet. "Should've taken a shower this morning Max, now you're attracting flies like a rotten banana!"

"I did shower this morning!" Replies Max. "Since your incessant snoring wouldn't allow me sleep, I ended up taking a hot bath to help relax. It did not help. Nothing short of earplugs would have helped..."

His distraction offers Svenn the opportunity to gain back some ground, as Max turns to see Svenn getting near the neutral starting position.

"Oh no you don't!" Said Max.

He flexes and brings Svenn's fist back down towards the table. As he does this, he hears the buzzing again but cannot see from where. He ignores it and continues to pressure his enemy.

As the bout continues, Svenn inches closer and closer to the table, unable to recover any space to his strong foe. But suddenly, just as it looks like Max is going to pin Svenn, the fly returns. Swiftly, it flies right over Max's head, in between his eyelashes and lands its tiny feet directly onto the unfortunate swordsman's eyeball.

"............................"

"GAAAAHHH!!!!" Exclaims Max in horror. "I'LL KILL YOU FLY!! WHY HAVE YOU DONE THIS?!?!?!"

"BAAAAHAHAHAHAHAHA!!" Laughs Pilet, hunching over a separate table and smacking it with his hand repeatedly. He turns to Faith and Yuuna. "Looks like one bath wasn't enough to keep the flies away from swampass over here!!!"

Completely surprised and distracted, Max loses his focus as Svenn puts all his strength into a swift, downward pull of his arm. Max's hand is flung back in the confusion and nearly hits the table on his side, but at the last moment he manages to stop Svenn and hover his fist just above the surface. Blinking and tearing up in his left eye, Max's arm quivers as he fights to stay in the bout.

"No no no, *grunt* the Sanda yield to no one!" Said Max, as he musters all of his might to pull back the bassists arm.

In a lastish effort, Max groans as he stands to his feet in a low crouching stance. He drives his hips in the direction of his bicep flexion, and begins martial arts breathing, releasing air from between his teeth in a controlled descent.

KSSSSS *KSSSSS* *KSSSSS*

Unable to match the strength of the young Sanda warrior, Svenn's arm gives out as his muscles fail. Max promptly plants Svenn's hand down on the table, then stands in a meditative posture to calm himself.

Upon losing, a downtrodden Svenn hangs his head in defeat.

"Hey, stop that." Said Max. "You were a worthy opponent my friend, it was a good match!"

Max bows and reaches out for a handshake, as Svenn's eyes light up in glee. The bassist gladly reaches out, shaking hands with his very game opponent. After handing Max his HBA dogtag, Svenn smiles and flips the hair out of his face.

"Mhmm!" Grunts Svenn.

"I hope to hear your music again soon friend." Said Max. "Your band was very good and the crowd loved your energ-"

As Max speaks, the buzzing returns. The same fly whips around Max's ear and lands on his eyeball once more.

"AAAGGGHHHH!" Exclaims Max. "I HATE YOU!!"

Max draws one of his M7 Lacerates and begins slashing at the fly in the air, slicing surprisingly close to it considering he can see through only one eye. The fly takes evasive maneuvers, escaping towards the back of the bar. Max follows suit, hacking and slashing at air along the way.

Pilet drops to the floor in fetal position, writhing in uncontrollable laughter.

"BAAAAHAHAHAHAHAHA!!!!"

"Oh my God relax Pilet." Said Faith. "Poor Max, the guy can't catch a break. At least he won his match."

"That fly be somethin' else huh?" Said Danba. "Maybe it's been a while since he washed his braids, I get that problem sometimes. Anywho, now it's my turn. Let's get on with it."

Danba sits down at the table, lights a cigar and begins to take a puff.

"Who be next, I ain't got all day."

"Meee!" Replied Yuuna, skipping over to the bench to meet Danba.

She takes a seat across from him, clasps hands and says, "You ready tough guy? I'm not going easy!"

"I'm hope you didn't spit in this hand...." Replied Danba.

"I'll start the count." Said Faith. She winks at Yuuna and takes a deep breath.

Inhale

"321go!" Bursts Faith, counting faster than Pilet can run.

Yuuna immediately begins to pressure Danba at the count.

"Woah hey what the hell!" Exclaims Danba. "What kinda countin' was that?"

"Stop complaininnng!" Said Yuuna. "It's not her fault you can't count!"

"I, what? I can count girl! But who counts that fast?!"

Danba, being much larger and stronger than Yuuna, begins to make up for the ground he lost at the speedy count. Yuuna's arm begins to quiver as she fights to keep the advantage. But eventually she ends up back at the neutral position, then slowly creeping towards her side.

"Hnnnng! You won't win, I have a trick!" Said Yuuna, struggling to keep up.

Yunna begins to let Danba take the lead, bringing her hand close to the table.

"Sis, what are you doing?" Said Faith.

"I saw it on TV, you gotta let your opponent think you're losing, then you blow 'em away at the end!"

"..."

"Yuuna, don't you have to be like... Stronger than them for that to work?" Said Pilet. "Like, I've done that with Nivia, just to mess with her..."

"Oh..." Said Yuuna.

As she realizes her folly, she grasps her wrestling hand with the other over Danba's hand in a panic.

"Nooooo! I wanna winnnn!!" Said Yuuna, pulling hilariously with both her hands to survive.

"Sorry kid." Said Danba, as he definitively presses the back of her hand into the table.

"Gaaah!!" Cries Yuuna. After losing, she looks at Danba with a pouty face and begins to whimper. "Please don't take my tag!"

"Whah-hey!" Said Danba. "What be this nonsense. Stop with the faces, you makin' me feel bad! Next time don't give up an advantageous position with silly tricks!"

"Whaaaah!" Said Yuuna. She fake cries while handing Danba her HBA dogtag.

"You a crazy girl you know that?" Said Danba. "You funny though, if you guys want some tickets to our next show let me know. We'll make it happen."

"Oh wow thanks!" Said Yuuna. "I don't feel so bad now, see guys I won in spirit!"

"Could've won for real though, that would've been cool too..." Sneers Pilet. "Now I gotta win back that tag."

"Shut it Pilet." Said Faith. "It's not her fault, he was much bigger than her."

Max returns, out of breath from his tirade against the fly.

Pant *pant*

"The damn pest escaped. *Wheeze* What, what happened." Said Max. "What have I missed?"

"We got free Funk Munkey tickets!" Said Yuuna.

"Oh, wonderful! And who won the last match? Did someone else go yet?"

"Oh don't worry about all that Max." Yuuna replied. "Winners, losers, who cares? We're all winners at heart..."

"I, well... Ok then..." Replied Max befuddled.

Pilet points to Lukah across the room.

"Just me and you left buddy, I want that tag."

"I thought I told you, you ain't getting shit." Replied Lukah.

"Oh I'm getting that tag." Said Pilet. He grins and brushes his buzzed head. "And loser's gotta cut their hair too."

"What? Screw that shit! You don't got any hair to cut!" Replied Lukah.

Pilet laughs.

"Just checking to see if you had any balls. Got my answer."

"Aye, he does too have balls ya know?!" Said Clint. "I seen 'um, they're huge!"

Svenn nods his head vigorously in agreement.

A puzzled expression comes upon Pilet's face. Faith and Yuuna giggle to themselves.

"Oh?" Said Pilet.

"Clint shutup!" Said Lukah. He turns to his opponent. "They just walked in on me on the shitter one time, that's all!"

"Bro bro, don't worry about it. That's between you and the homies, whatever weird shit you're up to." Replied Pilet.

"I don't do any wierd shit! You know what... forget it. Let's go bitch!" Exclaims Lukah, as the two clasp hands.

Danba begins the count.

"3,2,1, Go!"

Pilet and Lukah both flex, vying for control of the center. They grunt and heave, snarling at each other with fully flared nostrils and deeply furrowed brows. The veins between their knuckles protrude as their biceps and forearm flexors vibrate with the intensity of a jackhammer. After about a minute or so of this vicious stalemate, the two realize how evenly matched they are; both having lean, wiry frames. This is where the mental warfare begins.

Hnng "Anyone ever tell you your head looks like a broomstick?!" Said Pilet.

Nghh "You're one to talk, you look like a damn kiwi!" Retorts Lukah. "And what's up with the purple eyes? Contact lenses are for teenage girls. Besides, my kid sister has better looking ones she got from the thrift store!"

"Hey, quit looking at my eyes! Don't be a freaking, freak. You're making me feel weird bro, I might even file workplace harassment!" Retorts Pilet.

The two hotheads continue their back and forth banter, muscles pulsating and quivering under the force of each other's resistance. Realizing this battle is going nowhere, Lukah becomes desperate and shoves the index finger of his free hand into his nose.

"Yo, what the hell?" Said Pilet. "Are you good dude?"

Lukah looks Piket dead in the eye and mutters, "Piss off." and flings a massive booger at Pilet.

"AH!! ARE YOU SERIOUS!!??" Shouts Pilet.

He twists and contorts his body, just enough for the slimy projectile to miss his side. The snot rocket flies past Pilet, over a random barstool and gently lands in Faith's lap.

"..."

"DEAR SWEET GOD!!!" Exclaims Faith in horror. She lunges for

Lukah, but is promptly held back by Max, clutching her tightly by the arm. "I'll kill them both, I don't care!! These idiots have no brains!!!"

"You've got to relax!" Said Max. "Don't interfere. It's not worth it, we need that tag!"

Yuuna is stood high upon the corner of the bar, avoiding her sister like an infectious disease.

"EWWWW" Cried Yuuna. "That's so freaking gross!!!!"

"Oh some help you are!!!" Replied Faith. "Get a rag or something!!! Oh disgusting, it's drooping down!"

Pilet tries to laugh, but is too focused on the opponent at hand. He takes his own free index finger, points it at Lukah, and proceeds to jam it up into his own nose. A long, semi dry strand sticks to Pilet's finger, as he takes aim at his rival.

"Don't you dare punk." Said Lukah.

"Too late bitch." Replied Pilet.

He flicks, sending the booger towards the center of Lukah's forehead. Just in the nick of time, Lukah ducks and avoids the projectile. As it zooms past the brim of Lukah's mohawk, the slimey bullet continues its course and nails Danba on the chin.

"Aaaaaahhhhh!!!!" Exclaimed Danba. He falls to the floor in terror, as if shot in the face by a high powered pistol. "You damn idiot! Watch where you throwin'!' Danba stumbles and trips around until he finds a napkin on a nearby table and wipes the mess from his chin. As he feels the gooey projectile slide off of his face and onto the napkin, a chill and a shiver runs up his spine. "This ain't some shit we signed up for, they said we might die out here, they never said we gonna have to deal wit' this..."

He hears Faith speak from across the table.

"Yours did it first! How does it feel now, hmm???"

Meanwhile, Pilet and Lukah go undistracted, still laser focused on each other. Just then, Lukah sneezes and loses his elbows' traction, allowing Pilet to gain the upper hand.

"Shit!" Said Lukah.

"Oh yeah!, I told you I'm taking that damn tag!!" Said Pilet.

"Only thing you're taking is a huge "L!" Replied Lukah, stomping on Pilet's toes under the table.

"Ow!! My freaking foot!" Said Pilet, immediately losing focus.

In the scramble, Lukah presses his arm against Pilet's enough to drive it directly above the table, Pilet's knuckle side down. Pilet struggles to maintain position, his arm shaking vigorously with muscle failure and fatigue.

"No! No no no!!!" Exclaimed Pilet. "We need that tag!" His eyes begin to glow. The Fever Point begins to engage as he loses conscious control of his emotions. "I need to be a Blade!!! It can't end here!!!"

Pilet's wrestling arm swells to three times its normal size, growing simian-like hair from shoulder to fist. A violet mist begins to emanate from his body.

"Aye!" Said Clint. "Ain't no usin' auracast in an arm wrestle ya know?! That's like cheatin', ya know?!?!?"

"Yeah, why's your boy turning into a gorilla?!" Said Danba.

The Hidden Blades look just as puzzled as The Funk Munkeys.

"I, I don't know..." Said Faith. "He turns purple sometimes, but this is the first we've seen of the monkey arm."

"Not me!" Replied Yuuna. "Pilet did this when we fought Scott's scary statue, during the auracast exam! I thought I was seeing things! While you were busy fighting Scott, me and Pilet were trying to move Max's unconscious body. He was too heavy at first, but right before the statue was gonna squash us Pilet got real big and hairy, picked us both up and brought us to safety in the blink of an eye!"

"How peculiar?!" Said Max. "And as far as cheating, doesn't stepping on your adversaries toes count as interference? Or do you think I was the only one who saw that."

"Well cheating or not, there's no way you're getting this tag!!! GRAAAAH!!" Cries Lukah, mustering all of the strength he has left to offer.

"YES I AM!!!!!" Exclaims Pilet in a fit of rage. He stands to his feet, curls his now mighty bicep and slams Lukah's hand into the table.

CRASH

With this, the whole table collapses, sending Lukah crashing through it with Pilet's immense power. Shards and splinters of wood debris fly through the air, bouncing off of the Blade candidates and bar-goers alike.

"God damn!" Said a random bystander, sipping his beer. "That boy got a hell of a squeeze!'

Another one speaks out. Holy shit! I thought for sure the mohawked kid had it!"

The bartender simply stands there speechless, knowing full well he will be responsible for the mess created by Pilet's overzealousness.

Breathing heavily, Pilet stands above the soundly defeated Lukah with a face of triumph.

"Told ya I'd get that tag."

The whole room becomes quiet.

"... What?" Said Pilet, puzzled by the deafening silence.

"Pilet..." Said Faith. "Look at your arm..."

"Huh?"

He looks down at his right arm, larger than any he's ever seen. Completely covered in dark mauve hair. The typical glowing pattern of his Fever point runs through the back of his forearm. He stands there stunned.

"..."

"What, I... What is this?....." Said Pilet.

The sight of this simian arm calls forth flashbacks of the massive Wurm Gorilla in the center of Chamboree.

"It's just like his..." Muttered Pilet. "Did something happen back then?"

The sound of Lukah spewing wood chips from his mouth can be heard within the wreckage of the table.

Pffft *Pffft*

"Freakin', damn!" Said Lukah, clearing the rest of the wood from around his lips. "That's... Actually kinda cool lookin'. Sure took my ass for a ride."

"Wit' that arm you could be the fifth Funk Munkey!" Laughs Danba. "Just don't be eatin' all our bananas!"

"Tch, funny guy." Said Pilet. He takes a deep breath, and on the exhale deactivates the Fever Point. The overgrown arm begins to rescind in size, retracting the many mauve hairs sprouted along it. "Here bro, sorry for the overkill."

Pilet holds out a hand to Lukah to help him up, Lukah accepts and is hoisted up off of the ground by Pilet.

"All good, I was the one who started dirty boxin'" Said Lukah, as he brushes debris off of his chest. "Take this." He hands Pilet his HBA dogtag. "You were gonna win anyway, at least now our teams are even."

"Thanks dude, it was a close one for sure." Said Pilet as he takes the dogtag, hanging it casually around his neck.

Max, Faith and Yuuna approach Pilet in concern. The white Dragonfly Seeker camera of The Hidden Blades flutters curiously around Pilet's previously transformed arm, then flies discreetly away from the candidate and around the two teams. As it does so, the white Seeker zips by the orange Seeker of The Funk Munkeys. They zoom around each other playfully for a moment before separating to continue recording the action.

"Pilet, do you have any idea what that was just now?" Said Faith. "Yuuna says it's not the first time that's happened, but like, did you notice it last time?"

"What?" Replied Pilet. "That's news to me, this is the first time I've ever seen my arm like that. To be honest, I wouldn't have even noticed if you hadn't pointed it out. It felt so natural, like my arm had been like that all along..."

"Well it definitely hasn't!' Said Yuuna. "Your whole body did that when you picked up Max yesterday. You mean you really didn't notice?"

"Oh shit, really?" Said Pilet. "No, not at all! But... I did feel really tired after that though, and come to think of it..."

Pilet holds his arm up in front of him. His forearm and bicep shake and tremble uncontrollably.

"Well whatever you did, I'm sure glad you did it." Said Max. "Had you not, the three of us might be more liken to pancakes than prospects." Max walks over to Danba the Witchdoctor. He bows and holds out a hand to shake. "It was an honor to do battle with your team, even if only a test of strength."

Danba accepts Max's handshake and bows in response.

"The honor be all mine brotha." Replied Danba. "Please, let's have a few drinks before you go."

As The Hidden Blades and The Funk Munkeys take a seat at the bar stools, they recount the events of the Blades exam thus far, telling stories of pain, triumph, struggle and success. After close to half an hour, the two groups see each other off at the door.

"It was a pleasure meeting you guys." Said Faith. "I hope you do well and we're able to come to more of your shows in the future."

"Ey Thanks." Replied Lukah. "You guys are pretty cool. We got each other's Chatch contacts, hit us up whenever you want tickets and we'll get you in the door."

"Your kindness is greatly appreciated." Said Max. He Pat's the M7 Lacerate on his hip. "Should you ever need an extra blade and an arm to swing it, you have mine. You need only call."

"Wow, thanks! Ya know?" Said Clint. He turns to Svenn and Danba, pointing to Max. "He's a cool guy, ya know?!"

Pilet and Lukah bump fists.

"Let's get together sometime and beat each other up." Said Lukah. "I want a rematch."

"You got it bro." Replied Pilet. "Just don't make me feel bad when you end up 0 and 2."

After exchanging goodbyes, the teams separate and walk opposite directions down the brick roads of Giduh.

Rampage of The Reaper Elite

After taking a stroll through the village, The Hidden Blades decide it's time to continue their quest towards the Cool Oasis. They reach the village gates and take a look back at the humble streets, red brick buildings and yellow trees of Giduh.

"So long Giduh." Said Pilet.

"It was cute, we should come visit some time!" Said Yuuna. "I mean, if you guys ever want to hang out after the exam..."

"Of course!" Said Max. "A friend of The Sanda is a friend for life! We are linked on the branches of time from this day forth."

"Aww Max, that was beautiful." Said Faith.

"I'm down to meet up too." Said Pilet. "Just like Max said, we're stuck to time branches now or whatever. I don't know, just call me on my Chatch whenever you want."

"Hey Pilet." Said Max. "We broke even against The Funk Munkeys. Before we go, don't you think it would be wise to divvy up our extra HBA dog tags to the girls? This way, on the off chance that one of us is attacked and robbed, we only lose one tag as opposed to two."

"Hmm." Said Pilet. "Well there's about a zero percent chance that anyone is peeling these tags off of me without losing a hand, but I see where you're going here. Wouldn't want you two to feel unimportant. Not everyone can be as naturally talented as myself."

Pilet hands Faith his extra dog tag, Max hands Yuuna his.

"Thanks..." Said Faith. She mutters, "Dick." under her breath as she walks away.

"Thanks Max!" Said Yuuna, giving Max a big hug.

"We should get a move on, we've probably got like another 2 hours or so of sunlight left." Said Pilet.

"Ok but this time let's not jump right into Fleetfoot ok?" Said Faith. "We should really conserve our energy, you never know when another group of Giduh monsters is going to pop out."

"Yeah Pilet, and you wouldn't want to trip on any more Callous armadillos either right?" Jabs Yuuna.

"Hahahaha!" laughs everyone but Pilet.

He mutters to himself.

"You're all just jealous I won the race..."

They begin their long journey across the scorching sands. Step by step, the uneven granules shift between their feet. They pass various rock formations hiding small reptiles and scorpions from the harsh rays of the sun. Following the map loaded onto his Chatch, Pilet brings the group past a cluster of hovering terrariums filled with desert cacti. His stomach grumbles horribly.

"Man...." Said Pilet, holding his stomach in lament. "I need to eat. Those cactuses look so juicy right now, and I bet they're so fresh..."

His mouth begins to salivate.

"Don't even think about it." Said Max. "You heard Caffo Gilwick, do not bother the desert flora. They are endangered by the Wurm."

"Yeah yeah I heard him. But c'mon! Literally just one won't hurt."

Pilet casts Fleetfoot granting him Arcane buoyancy. He crouches in preparation to leap toward the terrarium, but is swiftly halted by the strong grip of Max holding his wrist.

"Hey dude, let go!" Exclaims Pilet. "Who made you the exam police?! I just want one!"

He pulls away from Max's hand, shoving Max back a few feet. The whites of both Pilet and Max's eyes turn black, as their pupils and irises glow a bloody crimson.

"Then eat some fruit from the store you fool. Why did we go through the trouble of passing through Giduh if you won't eat what we have?"

"Look, it's hot as all hell out here, and that cactus is fresher and juicier then anything we bought! Now, I'm getting one and that's final. Try to stop me again and I'll kick your ass, pineapple head."

"Hey, cool it!" Said Faith. "Relax guys, what's gotten into the both of you? The last thing we need is fighting amongst ourselves right now. Pilet, don't be an idiot. Just eat a mango or something from the bag."

"Please Pilet, let's all just get along." Said Yuuna, clasping her crystal necklace anxiously. "We were just talking about how we're all good friends now, you don't want to throw that out over some prickly cacti do you?"

Pilet and Max stand face to face, their ghoulish eyes affixed like daggers toward each other. Max puts a hand on his Lacerate as Pilet reaches for his knives.

"Well? Make a move..." Said Max.

"Oh buddy, I'll make three moves before you can pull that toothpick from your hip." Retorts Pilet.

"You'd be surprised." Said Max.

The girls take a step back, unsure of what's to happen next. Faith pulls her tome from the leather satchel across her shoulder and sifts through the pages. Yuuna searches for a stone from her bag.

"Yuuna, get your amethyst. Calm them down ASAP." Said Faith.

Yuuna anxiously rummages her fingers through her stone collection.

"Shit! It's not here! Oh no... I lost it last night, remember?!"

Vrrrr

The infrared buzz of Pilet's Dragonfly longknives cuts through the dry desert air. Max's right hand sits vigilantly at the hilt of his Lacerate. The two young warriors take a low crouching stance, preparing to launch their attack.

"Wait" Said Pilet, peeling the HBA dog tag from around his neck.

"Let's take these off first, wouldn't want to mess my tag up kicking the shit out of you."

He holds the tag out in front of his chest, preparing to toss it to the girls for safe keeping.

"..."

BOOM

An explosion of sand erupting from the ground can be seen far in the distance. In that moment, a hulking, muscular young warrior clad in white armor lunges forth from the sand cloud. His body zooming by with the arcane speed of a bullet, as he closes the gap between the distant sand cloud and the two combative Hidden Blades. The warrior reaches out, attempting to grab the prized dog tag from Pilet's hands.

As he comes but centimeters away from grasping his prize, Pilet's otherworldly reflexes kick in. As if time itself slowed for The King Killer, Pilet pulls the tag just out of the encroaching insurgent's reach. Missing his target, the armor clad warrior's momentum continues, carrying him straight forward into a massive sand dune 30 feet off. Right before impact, he pulls a bulky, white mechanized shield from around his back and drives the edge of it into the sand dune, stopping himself from crashing face-first.

Fwoooosh *CRASH*

The forceful wind from the warrior's speedy assault buffers Max and Pilet.

"What the hell was that?!" Exclaimed Pilet, as his eyes return to a normal, violet hue.

Max shakes his head in confusion. He rubs his eyes vigorously with the top of his first knuckle, clearing the sand from his now neutral brown pupils.

As this is happening, two dark figures emerge from shadows cast behind Faith and Yuuna with daggers drawn. As the assailants ready to strike, Max sees them and yells to the girls.

"Look out! Behind you!"

Startled, Yuuna freezes in place. Seeing this, Faith pushes her sister out of harm's way and dodge rolls the opposite direction, missing a fatal blow by inches. Having missed their attack, the darkened figures shed their shadowy aura-veils. Both adorned in leather armor and compression undergarments. One a man in turquoise; the other, a woman in maroon.

"Dabria, I told you we should have struck another two and a half seconds sooner." Said the turquoise assassin.

"The wind was blowing the sand in their eyes, Asger." Said Dabria. "Two and a half seconds might have lost us our sight advantage."

"Frisio!!" Casts Faith.

A sudden cone of frost erupts from Faith's palm and blasts the stealthy siblings mid-conversation. But as the snow and ice cloud clears up, the twins are nowhere to be seen.

"Guardian mist! Kite stream!" Casts Yuuna. Every pore of her body begins to release a high pressurized aura. Her body levitates six inches off the ground, as a gust of auric wind allows her to glide swiftly to and fro at will.

The twins reappear within the shadow of a nearby rock formation, dusting flakes of frost off of themselves. The maroon assassin picks beneath her fingernails with her dagger, an unphased look glazed across her brow.

"That was a close one, brother." She said, pointing her blade towards Faith. "The bookworm is more fearsome than she looks."

A Frisio cast is instantaneous, just how fast can they retreat into the shadows?!? Thought Faith.

"Thanks for the save sissy. It looks like they're shadow-casters, not surprised since they seem to be all, sneaky-deaky." Said Yuuna.

"Sis get serious, we're in a fight!" Said Faith.

Back where Max and Pilet are standing, a fourth figure drops from behind a floating terrarium. Falling from the sky, Arturo, the Fubuki tribesman of The Reaper Elite lands in front of the two prospects.

"What's with this circus bullshit?!" Exclaims Pilet.

"Ahem." Arturo clears his throat. He turns to Max. "So I hear your father seems to think you'd, what was it? "Tear me to shreds"?"

Max buries his back foot in the sand. A bead of anxious sweat drops down his temple, past his chin and falls to the scorching floor.

"My father believes I'll do what I must to honor the name of the Sanda." He replied. "Your teammate and his father are quite skilled instigators, you should ask them the whole story."

Arturo walks toward them with his hand glued to his sword.

"I'm asking you." He replied. "I don't care what they said or think. They're not the one who's skill is in question. You know the way of our people, this is to be settled before the sun is set. I won't go the whole exam without knowing for certain that I was the best Hachidorinese warrior to grace these sands."

Confused and irritated, Pilet hangs his dog tag back around his neck, then turns to Arturo with contempt.

"Listen dickhead. I don't know what you two are talking about, but if you ate all of the cactuses up there then you're gonna have a lot more to worry about than Max-"

BOOM

Like the sound of a shotgun, Lazlow the Gavel erupts from the desert sands afar. He closes the distance between himself and Pilet in an instant. Pilet swiftly braces his Dragonfly knives to his shoulder, blocking the brunt of the marauder's high speed tackle.

CLANG *Thud*

The mighty shoulder check flings Pilet across the sand, rolling like a tumbleweed until he crashes into a heaping dune.

"WOOO!" Howled Lazlow. "Sent that bitch FLYING!"

Pilet collects himself, spitting out sand and dusting his pants.

"HEY! Who are you calling a bitch?!?!" Exclaimed Pilet. "You want a piece of me?!?!?"

"So you're the one they're calling the King Killer huh?" Said Lazlow. "A scrawny little, peach fuzz headed kid like you killed a Wurm King? I don't believe it, you probably just stabbed it in the back while that old Blade friend of yours did all the work."

"Ok..." Replied Pilet, a more serious drop in his tone of voice. He brandishes his Dragonflies. "Do you want to see how I got that name?..."

"Nah." Said Lazlow, crouching down in a runner's starting position. "Springboard!" He casts. Lazlow's body propels forth yet again at alarming speed. He tackles Pilet, sending the two of them flying off into the distance.

A Deadly Duel of Clans, Sanda V.S. Fubuki

Hovering in the sky above the two clashing teams, the airship housing the sponsors of The Reaper Elite deactivates its camouflage. Aboard the balcony stands the sponsors, and subsequently the parents of The Reapers.

Ingemar and Aslaug Trygve, father and mother to Asger and Dabria; Bernardo Shimo, father of Arturo; and Lazlow The Vice, father to Lazlow The Gavel.

Ingemar Trygve; his hair a dark shade of leafy green, darkened circles under his eyes and a smug, pompous look across his brow. Donning a sleek set of green leather armor similar to his children's, with a green cloth mask covering the bottom half of his face. A straight sword with a violet hilt lies mounted on his back; and a long, red rosewood beaded necklace loosely wraps itself twice around his neck.

His wife Aslaug, a charming and warm glint in her eye. Clad in a stunning teal and gold dress that flows down to her feet, vivid, long teal hair that flows down to her hips and a pair of elegant silver and gold bangles adorning each wrist. She too wears a teal mask over her lower face, concealing from her nose to her lower chin.

Bernardo Shimo, sporting the same set of plated armor as Kenzo and Max, but with azure trim instead of gold. Tall and lanky, Bernardo carries two sheathed swords with blue trim on his hip as well. He stands with his arms folded in contempt, intently looking down on his son as he confronts their rival tribesman.

The sponsors, watching fixedly while their children do battle, lean impatiently over the guard rail.

The voice of Lazlow The Vice bellows across the skies.

"Deadeye I know you're out there!" He cries. "We're all here now! Disengage your damn camo and show yourself, so I can see your face when my son beats your prospect!"

"..."

Zhoom

The camouflage field lowers from Benny's ship, revealing Faxion and Kenzo intently waiting on their balcony. Faxion removes his hat.

"Always a pleasure to see you as well, Lazlow." Replied Faxion. "I hope your son has a backup plan, you know, just in case his Hope's of becoming Licensed don't come to fruition. It's a shame that of all candidates, he had to be the one to meet with Pilet upon these scorching dunes."

"The only shame is that you took a kid out of high school and told him he could make it as a Blade." Said Lazlow. "My son was born and bred for this. He represents everything that a pureblood member of the Kettlenian

Elite army should." He bangs his breastplate with his fist. "Lazlow Don's the alabaster armor with pride, something you know little about."

Faxion smirks.

"Hey there's an idea!" He said. "Send him off to the army again! I'm sure he'll have better luck there than here..."

With Pilet and Lazlow fighting in the distance, Arturo and Max continue their exchange down on the desert sands.

"Come on one-striper," Said Arturo. "I want to see what the Sanda are made of. Won't you show me?"

Max scoffs.

"Fine, just remember it was you who asked for this..."

"Sis, this should be good." Said Asger. "Hey, you two!" He says waving to Faith and Yuuna. "Let's wait a sec, we want to see the Hachidori fight!"

Faith's left eyebrow raises in confusion, she shrugs her shoulders and lifts her palms upward.

"You just tried to kill us!" Said Faith. "Now you want to stop for popcorn and a movie?!"

"Oh stop complaining." Said Dabria, sheathing her dagger. "Look we're unarmed. It's not everyday you get to see two Hachidori hack and slash each other to death. We can kill each other when it's over, and we'll tell Arturo to leave you two to us when he wins."

Faith looks back to Yuuna, who returns her gaze with a concerned nod of the head.

"Meditate while Max is fighting sis." Said Yuuna. "We're gonna need all the aura we can spare..."

Arturo and Max bow to each other. They each remove their swords with the scabbard from their magnetic belts, point them towards each other, and measure the distance between them before re-affixing the weapons to their waist. They stand at range of each other in a crouching position with their drawing hand on the hilt of their blades. Silence befalls the sands of Devil's Tongue, as the young swordsmen await the perfect time to strike.

Above the clouds, Faxion and Kenzo look down on the duel.

"Kenzo, forgive me." Said Faxion. "I'm a bit rusty on Hachidorinese culture. For what reason do warriors from your homeland carry two swords?"

"One's the dueling sword, the other is the drawing sword." Replied Kenzo. "The dueling sword's highly durable, yet not quite as sharp. It's drawn with the knowledge that a bout might take more than one strike."

"I see, and its counterpart?" Said Faxion.

"Ah yes, the drawing sword." Said Kenzo. "It's sharpness knows no match. This blade is drawn with the intent to finish an opponent in one blow. Once drawn, regardless of the outcome, it is immediately resheathed to preserve the edge."

"My oh my, what a very rich combat culture you have." Said Faxion. "I suppose years of duels to the death would naturally yield to such a fighting style."

A tumbleweed rolls by the two young swordsmen as they stand, poised and ready to strike. Silence befalls the area, as the dry air blows sand onto the glinting armor of the hachidorinese warriors. A small lizard runs by, stops at the sight of the statue-esk duel and continues its stride. Finally, after what seems like an eternity, Arturo's eyes begin to water and he can't help but blink them shut to rehydrate. In the moment he does so, Max draws his blade and swipes with blinding speed at the face of the Fubuki duelist. But it was a feint. Arturo draws his own blade the moment he shuts his eye, dips his head back and slashes for Max's ribcage. Foreseeing this deceptive countermeasure, Max contorts his torso just out of harm's way at the very last minute. The two stand with their blades drawn, as their audience looks on, baffled by the blinding speed of the exchange.

"What happened?" Said Yuuna. "I mean, it was so fast!"

"Shh sis." Replied Faith. "Don't mess up Max's concentration."

Max and Arturo take a second to feel their respective targeted regions, making sure they are not cut open. They nod to each other, taking pause to resheath their trusted drawing swords. Unlike the straight edge of Max's Lacerate; the sword of Arturo bears a distinctive serrated edge, with vicious saw-like teeth running down the blade all the way up to the pointed tip. The duelists return to their crouching posture, readying themselves to continue the match.

Max balls his right hand into a fist. He breathes slowly and deeply, exhaling as he drags his fist across his abdomen, sitting it at the hip level. He thrusts the blade of his left palm downard, triggering an abundance of aura to ementate from the yellow gem encrusted in his chest plate.

Arturo balls his left hand into a fist and drags it to his hip in a similar fashion. His back leg straightens out as he bends his front knee, taking a low lunging stance. The blade of his right hand juts out forward in front of him, causing the blue gem on his chest to pulsate with vigorous aura as well.

Suddenly both of their armor sets begin to come to life. They appear to wriggle and move beneath the hard scales that make up the exterior. The pressure of the aura surrounding them begins to shift the scorching sands beneath their feet. After cultivating this aura, they both exclaim in unison.

"MK 2! Release!!!"

Emerging straight from the gems comes dark, gunmetal gray chords liken to muscle fibers. The chords wrap and entwine themselves within every inch of the young warriors bodies, covering them in thick layers of flexible material. The fibers surround them, detailing themselves to the contour of the users muscles. Aura continues to vigorously pulsate throughout the fibers of this new organic armor. For Max, it manifests in the appearance of fierce electrical surges throughout the armor. For Arturo, frost creeps through the fibers, chilling the warm desert air around him. Both of their faces are covered by the fibers, forming a skull shaped helmet with glowing colored strands where the stripes of their hair once lay. The entirety of Max's eyes glow a devilish gold, while Arturo's take the azure hue of an arctic ocean.

On the sidelines Asger beckons to Yuuna and Faith.

"Told you it'd be good." Said Asger.

"Shut up brother." Said Dabria, slapping her brother in the arm. "I'm focused on the fight, this could be over in an instant."

The girls look at each other, back to Asger, and simply shake their heads.

"I can't wait to smash them." said Faith.

Max and Arturo draw their dueling swords. Max's M7 Lacerate glistens in the sun, poised at his opponent and ready to strike. When Arturo pulls his blade the girls eyebrows raise in shock. Like his drawing sword, Arturo's dueling sword yields to a completely serrated edge, different from the Lacerate that Max has made them accustomed to seeing. The M8 Shred, a close cousin to the Lacerate and signature blade of the Fubuki clan. Arturo holds his Shred out towards Max in preparation to continue their battle.

Arturo's voice reverberates beneath the fibrous mask of the helmet.

"Come at me Sanda!!!"

He bolts for Max in an instant, beginning a stunning back and forth of dextrous and skilled swordplay between the two.

Shing *Clang* *Shing* *Clang*

With every slash of their swords, a sharp bolt of pure aura is loosed through the air in said direction, cutting anything in its path.

Faith and Yuuna back up in surprise. In this moment the assassin twins begin to smirk. While the girls are mesmerized by this dazzling display of swordsmanship, Asger and Dabria crouch down onto the ground and focus their aura. They disappear into their own shadows, reappearing behind the sisters with daggers drawn. As they do this, Yuuna looks away from the action and notices the missing Reapers. Without telling her sister, Yuuna clasps her hands in a prayer position. As the twins grow ever closer, they step on a plot of sand behind their prey that begins to glow.

"Detonate!" Casts Yuuna.

"Huh!?" Reacts Faith.

A twister erupts from an auric Windmine set by Yuuna, lifting the twins and blowing them mercilessly into the air.

"AAAAAAAHHHHHHH!!!!!" Exclaimed the assassin siblings, as they're thrust high into the sky.

"Yuuna!" Exclaimed Faith. "You set up mines?! I'm so proud of you!! Now let's get 'em!"

Yuuna giggles.

"Right!"

The Killer and The Gavel

Meanwhile, close to half a mile away...

Tumble *Roll* *Crash*

Pilet and Lazlow end their tumbling tirade, crashing into a raised dune of sand. Lazlow ends up on top of Pilet, holding him pressed down beneath his shield.

"Aagh! Shit! Get off of me!" Exclaims a pinned Pilet in frustration.

"Not before I've had my fun." Said Lazlow, as his shield splits open down the middle. A compartment at the top of the shield houses a small metal gavel with gold trim. Pilet watches in horror as the hulking warrior draws the gavel right before his eyes and raises it high into the air, still pinning his arms tightly beneath the shield.

"I don't know why they call you The King Killer, and I don't care!" Said Lazlow. "But this is why they call me The Gavel!!"

As Lazlow hammers his arm down toward Pilet's head, Pilet thinks fast and readies a Callous cast in response.

"Ah crap, Callous!" He casts.

Thwack

Lazlow brings the gavel down harshly onto Pilet's cheekbone. The blow easily cracks the Callous cast and begins to chip away at the auric coating.

"Nngh, Ugh. Is, is that all you got!!" Said Pilet wearily.

"Hah!" Replies Lazlow, readying another full force swing. "I bet you wish. I'm not stopping until I see brain matter!"

Lazlow brings another massive blow down onto Pilet's forehead, completely shattering the Callous cast across his face.

In a panic, Pilet asks himself what his mentor would do in this situation. He recounts grappling training with Faxion one morning preceding the exam.

"Ok Pilet so now I've passed your hips and I'm on top." Said Faxion, *straddling Pilet in a very compromised position. "From here I can punch you in the face or choke you to death, aaand there's not much you can do about it. So try not to end up here."*

Pilet squirms and struggles to get out.

"OK, great. Good job. What, do I just die now? Is this what grappling is?"

"Relax, this is called a pin, you need to escape. Here look. Pull one of my arms close to your chest."

Pilet pins Faxion's right forearm to his chest at the elbow joint.

"Good, now take your foot and place it behind mine on the same side."

Pilet does so.

"Like this?" Said Pilet.

"Yes! Just like that. Now, I want you to bridge your hips waaay up towards the side of me that you've now pinned down."

"Hnnng!" *Pilet grunts as he bridges his hips up, flipping Faxion over and landing on top.*

"Oh shit, hey I did it!" *Said Pilet.*

"Yes you did!" *Said Faxion.* "Remember, being on the bottom is typically the worst case scenario. But where there's a will there's a way, and there's plenty of nasty stuff we can do from down here too. That's why we train to fight off of our backs. You never know what skills your opponent possesses. Hope for the best, but be prepared for the worst..."

Pilet has a revelation. He sees that Lazlow's right arm is tightly secured to the inside if his own shield, and manages to wriggle his arms out to the side to grab hold of the edges. Securing the shield in place, Pilet puts his foot behind Lazlow's leg on the ground, and waits for him to lift for another strike.

"Well I wish I could say it was nice knowing ya, but really I'll be happier to see you go." Said Lazlow, raising his gavel. "Once you're dead I just need to smash that Bhujanga guy to prove to everyone that I'm the top contender this year!"

But as he raises his arm up high to ready the finishing blow, Pilet bridges his hips and off balances Lazlow's shield, tossing him off and creating space for him to scurry back to his feet. He quickly dashes to his Dragonfly knives which were dropped in the tumble a few feet away, and leaps on top of Lazlow.

"Eat shit!" Exclaims Pilet, driving his Dragonflies down onto Lazlow's head.

But Lazlow blocks them with his alabaster vambraces. The heat of the infrared edges turns the metal a hot orange. But the toughness of the armor holds true, giving Lazlow the time to swing a mighty punch that sends Pilet flying off of him.

THWACK *Tumble* *Roll*

Pilet rolls backwards and nimbly springs to his feet. As Lazlow stands back up, he sheaths his gavel in favor of a two edged sword holstered to his hip.

"Let's go bitch!" Said Lazlow as he dashes toward Pilet, ferociously swinging his sword in a horizontal swipe.

Pilet's nostrils flare as he bares his canines.

"BRING IT!!" He replied.

Pilet darts back in forth deceptively, ducking and dodging the telegraphed swings of his opponent with ease. With each successful evasive maneuver he taunts.

"Where you aiming at? I'm right here! Now I'm here! Who are you fighting right now, the air???"

Lazlow swings another massive horizontal slash, slicing fresh air as Pilet ducks and ends up behind him. He whispers in Lazlow's ear.

"Your Dad's a bitch too."

Somewhere in the sky Faxion can be heard chuckling to himself.

Turning red with rage, Lazlow spins and backhands Pilet away with his massive shield. As Pilet regains his footing, Lazlow points his sword at him and presses a button on the hilt. This causes the blade to split directly down the middle, revealing a taser-like series of live electrical cross sections.

"Ooh, shiny." Said Pilet. "What're you gonna do, poke me with your sparky stick now?"

Lazlow grins. He presses another button directly below the first, sending a cobalt surge of electricity shooting into Pilet's side without warning.

"OooAAAAAGH!!!!" Screams Pilet, the electrical surge rendering him paralyzed. Every muscle in his body spasms uncontrollably, as he drops helplessly to the ground.

Thud

"What, what the hell?! What is this?!"

Pilet lifts his tank top and notices a small electrode stuck with a powerful adhesive strip to his ribs.

"Surprised?" Replied Lazlow. "I stuck you during our little tumble. Never know when you'll get someone who likes to run instead of fight, my "bitch" father taught me that."

Pilet tries to get up, but as he comes to his knees he's met with another crippling surge to the ribcage.

"GAAAH!!!"

"Where do you think you're going huh?" Said Lazlow. "Time to finish what we started."

Lazlow crouches down again, readying to Springboard himself onto Pilet.

"W,why isn't Callous stopping it?" Pilet sees that the electrode was placed beneath the auric veil of his Callous cast, likely before he cast it. "Shit! Are you kidding me?! It just goes right through?!"

As Lazlow springs himself toward Pilet with blinding speed, Pilet manages to come to his knees and dodge roll just barely out of harm's way. Lazlow's momentum continues as he tries to stop himself from crashing into a rock formation dead ahead. As he anchors his shield into the sand to slow his advance, Pilet frantically thinks of a plan to combat this new electrical threat.

"There's no other way, this is going to suck." Said Pilet, as he releases his Callous cast.

The translucent layer of auric armor covering his skin, shatters to pieces and falls to the earth. Pilet takes a deep breath and brings a Dragonfly knife to his side. He begins scraping his own flesh to remove the electrode before his foe can shock him once more.

"AaaAAAGGH!!!" Screams Pilet in agony.

The heated blade of the Dragonfly sears his skin, cauterizing the wound. The foul stench of burning flesh wafts through the air. Pilet peels the electrode off of him, flesh included, and tosses it on the ground between him and Lazlow.

"That tears it!!!" Exclaimed Pilet. "I was just gonna kick the crap out of you before, but now... You're dead!!"

Lazlow collects himself, kneeling down low and readying again for a mighty pounce.

"Nope!" Said Pilet, rushing at a breakneck pace towards Lazlow.

Pilet closes the gap on Lazlow before he can perform another Springboard, and unleashes an unholy, relentless barrage of cuts and slashes on his opponent.

Ksshh Ksshh Ksshh Ksshh Ksshh Ksshh Ksshh Ksshh Kshhiiiinnggg

Lazlow covers up, letting his sturdy alabaster armor take the brunt of the onslaught.

"Your butter knives aren't enough to even scrape the dirt off this armor, dimwit!" Said Lazlow.

"We'll see about that!" Replied Pilet, switching from a hectic, random slash pattern to a buzz-saw like continuous slicing spin. The repetitive, accurate cuts begin to saw into Lazlow's shield, sending sparks flying between the frenzied fighters. During Pilet's tirade, Lazlow discreetly crouches behind his shield and cultivates aura. He readies his signature auracast.

"Springboard!" He casts.

BOOM

The high velocity tackle sticks Pilet to the front of the shield like a moth to a speeding car. As the duo accelerate across the sands, Lazlow slams Pilet into the ground with startling force.

Blegh

Blood and vomit eject from Pilet's mouth from the forceful slam, as Lazlow rolls forward with continuing momentum. Pilet haphazardly scurries to his feet, doubled over in pain. He collects himself, begins to backpedal and cultivates aura in his right hand.

"Hollowpoint!!" He casts.

Pilet fires off a few Hollowpoints in mid-air while leaping backwards in retreat. The force of the shots fired from his palm pushes Pilet further back whilst airborne, increasing the space between him and his foe.

Thud thud thud

The Hollowpoints land flush across Lazlows chestplate, pushing him a few feet back and knocking the wind out of him. Lazlow's brow raises in surprise at the power of his shots.

"So that's the cast that beat Diliger." Said Lazlow. "Maybe now we'll finally start to have some fun. Don't die too quickly on me King Killer."

Pilet back handsprings nimbly with the kinetic force of the hollowpoints.

Shit, I can't keep taking punishment like this. Thought Pilet. He looks up and sees that his evasive measures have brought him back to the colony of floating terrariums. *Hmm.*

Pilet leaps up to a terrarium, clinging to the sides as the dome floats across the sky. Lazlow begins walking to advance to Pilet's position.

Just like I thought, he's not Springboarding up here. That cast would probably send him flying sky-high if he used it to jump.

"You could run across this whole desert." Said Lazlow. "Eventually I'll find you. And when I do I'm taking your tag and your head."

"I'm not running dipshit!" Replied Pilet. "I'm just hungry!" He picks a cactus from the terrarium and tries to remove the spines with his fingers. "Ow. Freaking, literal prick."

"Yeah OK." Said Lazlow. "Well if Hell is as hot as this desert I'm sure there'll be plenty of cactuses for you there. I'll make your life easier and send you off quickly."

"Shut up bitch!" Said Pilet, tossing the cacti at Lazlow's face. "Fight me up here! You won't!"

Lazlow blocks the succulent projectile with his shield. He grins devilishly at Pilet as his shield separates down the center once again. He flips a switch on the interior, revealing the nozzle of a fearsome machine gun protruding from the bottom.

"I don't have to." Said Lazlow. He points the end of the shield towards Pilet in the sky. "Congratulations fool, you're the first one I get to test my new birthday present on. Hope it's not over too fast."

Up in the sky, aboard Benny's airship…

"Oh no…" Said Faxion.

"That thing in the boy's shield," Said Kenzo. "Is that some kind of gun?"

"If that's what I think it is, it's not just a gun." Replied Faxion. "That my friend, is a problem….."

The Arcane Sisters V.S. The Twins from the Shadows

Across the sands, The arcane sisters of The Hidden Blades do battle with the murderous twins.

Yuuna pulls a stone of quartz from her bag. She holds it between her hands at chest level and cultivates aura between her palms. The stone begins to glow, as she tosses it to her sister.

"The quartz is activated sis!" Said Yuuna. "You can cast to your heart's content now!"

"Thanks sis." Said Faith. "Get ready, they're coming down."

The twister of Arcane wind that launched the assassins into the air begins to quell, sending them plummeting to the earth. Asger and Dabria each pull a dagger with a chain attached from a bag on their back.

"Asger!" Exclaimed Dabria mid-fall. "It's time! Blossoming Death Lotus!!"

"Alright, about time we got to show off." Replied Asger.

The two take the end of the chains, to which a small weight is affixed, and toss them dexterously to each other. Each one with the other's chain in hand, and their own blade in the other, begin to cultivate aura into the dagger and chain. Arcane lightning shoots forth from Asger's palm, branching and intertwining throughout Dabria's chain. Dabria's hands release a wicked auric fire, enveloping Asgers chain in an unholy blaze. As the twins are just about to crash into the ground, they blend seamlessly into the shadows cast by their bodies on impact. Their shadow infused bodies safely sink waist deep into the ground like a shallow pool, then shoot back up to their feet in an instant.

"Shadowglide." Cast the twins.

The soles of their feet sink into the shadow cast by their crouched legs, giving them the ability to glide forward along the sands at a breakneck pace. They hold out their chains and rush toward the Sierro sisters.

Dabria closes in on Faith, lunging from the sands with reckless abandon.

"Die bitch!!" Screams Dabria.

The woman assassin swings her dagger with blinding speed at Faith's face. But Faith smoothly leans back, just enough to evade the deadly swipe, as the blade glides just inches past her nose. She feels the slight zap of electricity as the lightning charged chain whizzes by her.

"Hmph." Said Faith, as she slips by Dabria's dagger. "Not today."

Faith's fist creeps under the space between Dabria's face and her dagger, as she smashes her opponent in the mouth with a well-timed counterpunch.

Crrrack

In surprise, Dabria darts to the side to compose herself. As she does so she tugs strongly on her chains, drawing her brother with haste directly towards Faith.

"Callous! Gilazia Shida!" Casts Faith.

First a thin auric layer of Callous armor surrounds Faith's body, followed by sharp, hard crystals forming over it.

"Skarrya." She's casts, drawing her signature arcane blade of fiery aura.

Faith turns the page of her tome with the thumb of the hand holding it and casts "Miragia."

The elder Sierro creates four illusionary copies of herself, each of which plants their feet and points their Skarrya blade at the encroaching assassin brother.

They all speak in unison.

"You asked for this."

As Asger continues his trajectory with his dagger trained on the center Faith, his forehead peels back and his eyes widen at the sight of the razor-sharp crystal covered, fire sword wielding sorceresses.

"Holy shit!" Exclaims Asger.

He throws his chained dagger right past the middle Faith's head. As the dagger whizzes by her, Faith lunges in to swing at Asger's head. Asger flawlessly bends and contorts his torso backwards to avoid the slash, and blends with the shadow of the flying dagger's chain. In an instant he teleports behind the group of copies where his dagger lands in the sand. He retrieves the dagger, yanks the chain to pull his sister to him, and then leaps backwards to gain distance.

"How many auracasts can she do at once?!?" He exclaims.

"Idiot!" Yells Dabria at her brother. She holds her wrist up at him, shaking a bracelet of black onyx crystals wrapped around it. "Remember when we used these to make the other two morons fight each other? Well other people can use stones too! It's the activated quartz necklace! Depending on how much aura was charged into that thing she could cast all day! Take the damn necklace!"

"No wonder!" Said Yuuna, gliding in the air above the twins. "I know Max and Pilet don't always get along, but there was just a different kind of animosity in that moment. Oh by the way... ScatterStar!!"

Yunna points her palms toward the heavens as platinum aura begins to form white hot, shining aura stars in the sky. The stars begin to rain down on the twins from above.

"Now brother!" Cries Dabria. "We need the Blossoming Death Lotus!!"

"Let's do it." Replied Asger, pulling his sister's chain in one hand, and his own dagger in the other towards his chest.

Dabria follows suit, as the two charge their weapons with Fire and Lightning aura. Dabria's fire mixes with Asger's lightning in the space between the two chains, creating a vortex of pure elemental energy.

"Hodejakt clan secret technique!! BLOSSOMING DEATH LOTUS!!!" Cast the twins.

The flaming, electrically charged vortex pours forth bursts of mighty aura, meeting the falling stars head on. Lightning infused fireballs fly haphazardly into the sky, colliding with Yuuna's stars and exploding in a blast of fiery light.

"Holy hell!" Exclaims Yuuna, gliding by her sister. "They're contending with my Scatterstar! That's one of my strongest auracasts!! I can't keep casting at that level, even with the quartz there's only so much aura stored in these!"

"Relax Yuuna." Replied Faith. "First of all, they seem to think that I need this quartz to cast this much at once. That's cute, I haven't even begun to use this baby." Faith brandishes the quartz necklace. "And second of all, if you'd just turn down that costly Guardian mist of yours, or at least stop flying around like that, you'd actually have aura left to fight for once. Then you wouldn't need to rely so heavily on your crystals. But, since you're too scared of a fight as usual, you have to stay like ten feet away from the enemy at all times."

Yuuna looks down in disappointment.

"I know... But now's no time to argue!" Said Yuuna. She pulls out a red jasper stone and activates it, pouring bolstering aura out onto Faith. "Besides, you're the one who's always telling me to stand back! It's not my fault Mom and Dad told you to look out for me before they-" Yuuna pauses. She sniffles, wiping her nose on her sleeve. She tries to choke back tears. "Listen. It looks like their crazy tornado thing is about to peeter out, but so is Scatterstar. Between the strength from the jasper and the extra aura from the quartz these two should be a breeze for you, so go get 'em!"

"Well, thanks sis." Said Faith. "And sorry for digging into you like that, but after this we have to talk. You can't just keep running from the fray like this, what if one day I'm not here to protect you-"

Mid-sentence, a throwing dagger covered in flames bounces off of the real Faith's armored brow. The force chips a portion of the crystals off of her face, revealing the Callous layer beneath. Her mirage copies vanish at the successful blow to the caster.

"We see through your petty illusion." Said Dabria, now sporting an exotic throwing dagger in between each finger."

"That was some cast." Said Asger, rolling up his chain around the dagger and placing it back in his bag. He then draws a one edged, straight sword from a scabbard on his back and points it at Yuuna. "We had to use our family's ace in the hole just to keep it at bay, not bad!"

"Simple minded as always brother, stop being so nice." Replied Dabria. "You're a killer, remember that!"

Aboard the airship of The Reaper Elite's sponsors, the Trygve parents converse on their children's progress.

"Asger God dammit!" Exclaims Ingemar, slamming his palm into the guardrail. "The boy lets his sister dictate everything, and all she wants to do is Death Lotus anything that walks and breathes!" He takes a sip from a mug of coffee brought to him by the pilot. "They keep showing off the family secrets, I'm sick and tired of it."

Aslaug gently leans onto her husband's shoulder, interweaving her arm in his.

"Honey, be easier on the kids. Asger is young, he's been gifted with empathy. I'm sure he's only trying to play nice with his sister."

"Empathy is the curse of an assassin!" Replied Ingemar, pulling away from Aslaug and folding his arms in contempt. "Empathy produces hesitation, hesitation causes mistakes and mistakes lead to failure or even death! An empathetic killer is a dead one... No pun intended." He grabs the guardrail in frustration, bending the metal between his hands with the force of his mighty grip. "If Asger is to be my spear than he'd better prove himself to be better than this. He's a man, he needs to take charge and act like one. I'll not have the feared Death Spear of the Hodejakt be some bleeding heart flower child."

"Your husband is right..." Said Bernardo Shimo, tying his matted dreadlocks tightly into a bun. The four blue stripes intermingle within the brunette, popping with vibrant color. "If your boy is to be a killer, the last thing he needs is habitual kindness. Look at my son." He points to Arturo, viciously slashing at Max with an onslaught of rapid swordsmanship. "He embodies everything the Fubuki represent. His form is fast and ruthless, like the freezing, ice-laden wind of a fierce blizzard. Any chance he gets at a lethal blow will be taken indefinitely, without a second thought. Son or daughter, if you pick up the sword you'd best be prepared to use it. If not, your opponent will."

Aslaug cringes and awkwardly smiles at Bernardo.

"Why thank you Bernardo, I'll be sure to keep that in mind."

Hidden Technique of The Sanda

Ksshh *Shiing* *Jaang* *Shiing* *Gzzsshhh*

The shrieking sound of clanging metal echoes below as the swordsmen of Hachidori do battle. Max and Arturo, slashing back and forth, exchanging blows and parrying strikes. Arturo slices in rapid succession, using his lean frame and slender body to deliver techniques with consistent flowing speed. Max, patiently blocking and defending, delivers a harsh, accurate blow any moment he gets the chance.

Shiing *Pssh* *Kss*

With every strike that is not checked, a gash is put in the muscle fiber-like armor surrounding the young warriors. With every open gash, the armor immediately reconnects itself, interweaving the strong fibers in a complicated network of patterns. Unlike their peers, the Hachidorinese duelists utter not a word to each other, utilizing their full concentration on their opponent at all times.

Shanng *Jinggg* *Kshaah*

The rhythmic battle continues, both fighters lost in a trance of focus and flow.

Suddenly, as Max backsteps a horizontal slash from his opponent, he trips on a hidden stone in the sand.

"Gaah!" Reacts Max.

As he falls back, he smoothly backrolls over his shoulder and back to his feet. But in the moment during his lapse of judgement, Arturo channels some aura into his Shred.

Phrew

He fires a vertical slash that sends a freezing blade of aura slicing through the air towards Max.

Shit Thinks Max as he looks up, not ready for the mighty auric bolt.

He raises his Lacerate just in time, focuses aura into the blade and knocks the arcane slash away, sending it dicing through a floating terrarium in the distance behind him.

Not finished with his auric assault, Arturo rapidly slices and dices into the air, following up his slash with a volley of smaller flying cuts. The vibrant blades of cold fly out inaccurately in Max's general direction, but as they do so Arturo presses his middle and index finger together and focuses his aura. As he does so the Auric slashes begin to change trajectory and home in on Max.

Phreeeeww

The bombardment of flying slashes whizz toward Max, increasing in velocity with each passing inch.

Aware of the nature of Arturo's homing technique, Max waits patiently until the onslaught is right in front of him. As the barrage comes just within arms reach, he swiftly dashes away on a tricky angle, preventing the homing attack from following suit as each cut frosts the scorching sand.

Tss, Tss, Tss, Tss, Tssss

As soon as the last slice has faded, Max looses a savage slash through the air, sending a blindingly fast blade of lightning aura towards Arturo.

Tsooowww

The Fubuki swordsman reflexively turns his body sideways, lending the auric blade the right of way. As Max's bolt passes his opponent, it slices cleanly through a passing desert iguana. The residual electrifying aura seizes the muscles of the unfortunate reptile, spasming the arms and legs uncontrollably.

The two Hachidorinese warriors stand for a moment and glare at one another. They begin to pace methodically parallel to each other, gradually increasing speed from a walk to a run. The racing swordsmen begin to exchange slashing aura bolts, flinging deadly techniques as they sprint alongside each other. Max fires, Arturo blocks, Arturo slashes, Max parries, Max slices, Arturo evades. The deadly run sees the two rising to the highest dune in near sight, fighting to stand atop the uneven edges of the sand.

Suddenly, the yellow stripe running across Max's head begins to glow exceedingly bright, blinding Arturo with its brilliance. As Arturo covers his eyes with his hand, Max sheathes his Lacerate and focuses his aura into the blade.

Wait, is he... Oh no! Thought the dazzled Fubuki.

In an instant, Max slashes in a perfectly vertical arc towards his foe, releasing an incredibly vibrant and expansive wall of lightning across the horizon in a flash.

K K K K K K K K S S S S S S S H H H H H H H K K R A A K K K KOOOOWWWWWWWW

The incredible wall of lightning passes between the two airships, swallowing the sky and stunning the spectators aboard.

"Holy shit!!!" Exclaimed Faxion, clenching the guardrail in shock and surprise. "What the hell are you feeding that boy Kenzo?!?!?!"

Kenzo folds his arms, gazing in admiration of his son's technique as the lightning continues to blaze across the sky. "Discipline and hard work my friend. Discipline and hard work..."

The lightning expands itself as far as the eye can see, passing by other groups of contestants. The Mystic Marauders, exiting a saloon in the far off western town of Helena, see the immense spectacle as it brilliantly flashes through the horizon.

"Puerto, do you see this?!" Exclaims Cornelius, the hulking Kettlenian Elite. He points his massive forearms skyward, his alabaster armor glinting the sun in Puerto's face.

"Aagh, put your arm down Cornelius!" Replied the Marauder's Emissary. As his clumsy companion lowers his hand, Puerto is able to see the spectacle in full effect. "My God... What creature on the planet Giganus has the power to unleash that? Wendy, scope it out."

"Right." Replied Wendy, hoisting her Arcane Pierce over her shoulder. She unpacks a dense metal disc from her satchel, presses a button and tosses it into the air. The disc expands into the size of a sewer lid and levitates via a jet booster underneath, as she hops aboard and flies above the western towns row of small buildings. As she lifts a pair of high tech binoculars to her eyes, she spots Max Quinn, M7 Lacerate in hand, the blade red and smoking with the heat of the electrifying assault.

"Oh wow." Said Wendy. "Puerto, I think it's the Sanda kid from King Killer's team! He looks different though, he's covered in some kind of crazy black metal."

"Are you sure?" Replied Puerto. "If we run into them out here, and he's packin' that kind of heat? Then we've got a problem."

"Oh I'm sure." Said Wendy. "Only those yellow haired guys carry that kind of sword, and his head is covered but there's still this glowing yellow stripe running across the top. Man, it's bright as hell too."

"Don't be such a worry wart, handsome." Said Dunya, flicking her long, silky brunette hair over her shoulder. She puts a hand on Puerto's bicep, pointing to Cornelius. "You've seen what this man can do, there's no firepower on Giganus that can match his.

Cornelius smirks and gives a thumbs up.

"Pure Kettlenian sweat and steel, nothing can stand in Cornelius' way!" Said Cornelius.

"Hah, guess you're right." Said Puerto. "How could I forget." The group begins their walk towards the desert. "I pity anyone who gets in our way. Last time you let loose you put a hole in a mountain..."

Trouble! Onslaught of the ARK Tri-Cannon

Across the desert, Lazlow and Pilet continue their tirade, mocking each other incessantly. Pilet, hanging like a lemur from a terrarium, sticks his tongue out at Lazlow.

"I don't give a shit about your God damn, pea shooter!" Said Pilet. "By the time you pull the trigger I'll have my blade up your ass!"

CCCCCCCCCCCCRRRRRRRRRAAAAAAAAAAACCCCCC CCKKKKKKKKKK

Max's mighty lightning wall passes right in between them like a freight train, flashing the two with brilliant light.

"AAAAAHHH!" Exclaims Pilet in surprise. "WHAT WAS THAT???"

Chk, chk

The sound of a gun cocking can be heard opposite Pilet behind the vivid light wall. As the technique passes, it leaves an endless line of orange, superheated sand crystals in its wake.

Vvvrrrrreeeee

Still in shock, Pilet looks back to his foe who's gun nozzle begins to rotate towards him.

"Ah shi-"

Clangclangclangclangclangclang

The machine gun begins to fire at Pilet relentlessly, cutting through the terrarium like a chainsaw. Pilet nimbly leaps from terrarium to terrarium, narrowly evading the chain of bullets with every passing jump.

"Hey you're not supposed to blast the floating cactus things!" Yells Pilet. "What gives? Are we just breaking all the rules now?"

Lazlow continues to arc his fire through the beautiful hovering flora.

"You decided to jump up there like a baboon with his ass on fire! Don't start crying now just because your stupid plan didnt work. Besides, my Dad's the Enforcer of the HBA. Most I'll get is a slap on the wrist when they pin that badge on me!"

Pilet continues to flip and handspring from terrarium to terrarium, acrobatically flying through the air in a hail of bullets. Seeing that this method is futile for his agile foe, Lazlow flips a switch inside his shield. The machine gun nozzle rescinds back into the shield, as the head of a large laser beam cannon emerges. He does so just in time to catch Pilet mid-flight to a terrarium, aiming and firing at him in an instant.

Pssfeewww

"Woah!" Exclaims Pilet, contorting his body in midair to evade the bright cyan beam.

Kssst

The laser just barely grazes him, singing a line across his chest through his tank top.

As Pilet lands atop another terrarium, Lazlow swings his arm violently, sending the beam haphazardly shooting anywhere he points. With impossible speed, Pilet finds great difficulty tracking the laser beam in the air to evade. He looks to the sky towards Benny's airship.

"I have to use it, there's no other way."

Pilet hides behind a terrarium for a brief moment, taking a deep breath and meditating. As he does so his enemy begins to saw through his cover with his beam.

"Come out King Killer!" Cried Lazlow, slowly cutting through the floating cacti.

As the beam of pure heat nears Pilet's side, the young prospect takes to his Fever Point form, exhaling violet aura and revealing his glowing tattoos. Right before the beam is about to make contact, Pilet disappears, vanishing into thin air.

Fwooshh

Reappearing behind Lazlow in a haze of indigo, Pilet taps the Kettlenian Elite on the shoulder.

"Huh?" Inquires Lazlow, turning to the source of the tap. As he does so, Pilet swipes his Dragonfly knife across Lazlow's face. But as he does so, the hot blade scrapes across a thick layer of Callous armor.

"...Oh right... You can do that too..."

Lazlow grins and switches the nozzle on his shield. A platform of six small missiles surfaces.

"Finally!" Said Lazlow. "That's the true power I wanted to see. Now it's time to turn up the heat!!!"

Lazlow launches a punch at Pilet, who effortlessly back handsprings out of harm's way.

"I knew you would dodge so far away." Said Lazlow, aiming his new nozzle at his foe. "Less is more King Killer, you waste too much movement."

He begins firing missiles at Pilet.

"Hmmph" Pilet scoffs. He disappears just as the missiles reach him, leaving the speedy projectiles targetless in the air. But as he reappears nearby, the missiles instantly follow his movement, tracking him at his superhuman speeds.

"What? How?" Said the swift footed prospect.

He teleports again, even further from his suiters. As he does so, Lazlow continues firing missile after missile. After several more failed attempts at losing the missiles, Pilet finds himself followed by over three dozen tricky projectiles. The missiles start to change trajectory, coming at him from different angles than before. He looks back at the plethora of deadly weapons on his tail, beginning to sweat from nerves.

"How is this happening?!?!?!" Exclaims the feverish Pilet. "Why can't I shake them?! Nothing can outrun me!!"

But as he loses his composure, a missile sneaks in front of him from elsewhere. As he turns to look where he is going, Pilet smashes right into the missile, face first.

PFFOOOWW

The explosion completely decimates Pilet's face, shattering his nose and sending flesh and blood flying everywhere. The wounded Hidden Blade falls to his knees and is instantly bombarded by the hail of enemy fire tracking him.

PFFFFKKKKSSSHHHRRRROOOWWWW

Dust and sand fills the air, leaving a massive crater where the barrage took place. Lazlow walks up and begins coughing as his lungs fill with debris.

At the sight of the scene, Faxion grips the handle of a mug of coffee he's drinking tightly, shattering the cup. Across the sky, Lazlow Sr. smiles arrogantly at his peer.

"Guess the boy should've stayed in school..." Said Lazlow Sr.

"..."

Faxion looks up, revealing cold, expressionless, dead eyes.

"You gave your son an ARK tri-cannon?!" Said Faxion. "Have you any sense at all man?!?"

"What's wrong Deadeye? You sound disappointed." Replied Lazlow.

Kenzo puts a hand on Faxion's arm.

"What is this, "ARK tri-cannon" Faxion?" Said Kenzo.

Faxion takes a breath. He wipes his hand over his face in frustration.

"It's meant to shoot down asteroids that come too close to Giganus... the damn thing belongs on a space colony, not in the hands of a kid!" Faxion cracks his knuckles and glares at Lazlow Sr. "His boy has a weapon capable of leveling a city strapped to his arm, it's completely illegal..."

"Nothing a little finagling at the ARK couldn't fix." Retorts Lazlow Sr. "When the Enforcer of The Hired Blades Association needs a weapon, people give it to him. Perks of the job. Maybe one day you'll be important too, then you'll understand. I wouldn't count on it though."

The triumphant young Kettlenian Elite peers into the dust inquisitively before sheathing his sword.

"Damn, I expected more. Guess you were pretty overhyped yesterday..." Said Lazlow Jr., retracting his ARK tri-cannon into the shield.

Faxion falls silent, removing his hat and holding it to his chest. The words of his arrogant rival echo throughout the halls of his mind.

"The only shame is that you took a kid out of high school and told him he could make it as a Blade."

His chest wells with emotion, the Veteran Blade can only stand there and pray that his protege has not yet left this world.

As the dust clears, blood stains the sands of the newly formed crater. But standing in the center, a torn up, bloodied Pilet folds his arms in contempt. The mangled prospect from Chamboree fires up his Dragonfly knives.

Vrrrrrrr

The scorched and shredded flesh hanging from his face regenerates at an alarming pace. His mouth grows newly cut teeth, replacing those lost from the missile to the face. A brief glint of a fresh coating of Callous armor, glows brilliantly before blending with his skin.

Cough

"Hey, bitch." Said Pilet. "What makes you think that BB gun has any chance of killing me?! The hype is real. I'm the King Killer, and I'm gonna KICK your ass…"

"What?!" Replied Lazlow Jr. "How? That many missiles would kill a damn Serpent Dragon!"

"Open your eyes dipshit, there's more than one crater." Said Pilet, pointing his Dragonflies to several miscellaneous craters surrounding him. "I'm fast, too fast. Yeah I got hit by a few, but most of them blew their load on the sand while I was teleporting around all cool-like. *But this Callous shit is staying up this time, now I see why everyone uses it so much.* He thought.

Lazlow Jr. prepares his ARK tri-cannon once more. He draws his Gavel and gives it a swing.

"YES, THIS IS WHAT I'M TALKING ABOUT!!!!" Howled Lazlow. "LET'S FIGHT PUNK, WINNER IS KING OF THE SAND!!!!!"

Plight of the Spellbound Sisters; The King of the Sands Draws Near

As the two fiery young candidates prepare to continue, Faith is locked in close combat with the assassin twins. Her sister flying around the action, waiting to support.

The elder Sierro, decked out in vibrant, durable crystalline armor; swipes swiftly at her foes with her brilliant Skarrya blade.

Vzzz *Vrrrzzz*

The twins utilize their agility and traditional Hodejakt martial arts to combat their opponent, cutting angles and nimbly evading her strikes. Asger takes the lead, chipping away at Faith's Crystal's with his sword any chance he gets. He bobs and weaves around her Skarrya, counter striking and evading. Dabria fires off a fiery throwing dagger every so often from behind, keeping her eye on Yuuna as well.

Krrss, Krrss

Two flaming daggers bounce off of Faith's hide, further exposing the Callous armor underneath. In response, Faith fires a swift kick to Asger's midsection, causing spittle and blood to fly from his mouth.

Blluggh

The cocktail of bodily fluid sprays the sand. Asger drops his hands to his midsection, tosses his sword into the sand nearby and fades into his own shadow; reappearing within the shadow of the standing sword. As her brother dissolves in retreat, Dabria tosses every flaming throwing dagger she has at Faith in rapid succession. Faith retracts her Skarrya and thrusts her palm to the ground.

"Oaaknilifo!" She casts.

A dense line of palo verde trees emerge from the ground in front of her, protecting her from the onslaught of flaming metal.

"You shouldn't have done that." Said Dabria.

As the flame aura of the blades quickly engulfs the trees, Dabria brings her left palm to her chest, blade of the hand facing forward. Her right palm reaches out towards the burning palo verde, as the flames begin to form the vague image of a massive spined rodent.

"Hell hedgehog!" Casts Dabria, directing the flaming beast with her hands like a puppeteer.

The fiery hedgehog begins to roll towards Faith, increasing in size with every inch it travels. Faith dodges and side steps with every passing attack, her evasive maneuvers becoming more difficult with each centimeter the hedgehog grows. Sensing the urgency of the situation, Yuuna flies out from behind Faith in support.

"Autumn stream!" Casts Yuuna.

A powerful wind tunnel erupts from her hand, blasting the flaming creature and slowing it's momentum. Dabria pours more aura into the technique, locking the two in an arcane showdown. Faith sprints around the auric struggle and makes a break for Dabria with Skarrya in hand, but as she closes the distance, the sound of electricity crackling gives way to concern. As she looks up, the now refreshed Asger drops down on her from the sky with his sword covered in cobalt lightning.

Zzzzzttt *Clang*

As Asger descends, Faith raises her Skarrya just in time to parry his blade away. The two begin a dance of swords, lunging and riposting to and fro at will.

Crackle *Clang* *Tssing*

With every clash of their blades, Faith's blade of pure, concentrated heat aura creates sparks off of Asgers sword, creating a brilliant show of light. Asger's blade continues to find a home across Faith's crystalline husk, but is unable to penetrate the defence of her Callous beneath.

It's no use, her defense is way too strong. Thought Asger. He takes note of the tome held at a safe distance from him in Faith's rear hand. *She keeps casting from that, I wonder what good she would be without it...*

In the midst of the fray, Asger throws a whipping up-kick to Faith's chin, knocking her back in a daze.

"Uuugh" Groans Faith, trying to maintain her composure.

Seeing his opportunity, Asger cultivates aura in his left hand, causing it to turn pitch black. He thrusts his dark arm into his own shadow in the sand. The arm resurfaces beneath the shadow cast by Faith's tome satchel, emerging from her hip.

"What the?!?" Exclaims a dazed Faith in surprise.

Before she can react, Asger's shadowy arm snatches the tome out of her hand and retracts back to him. He pulls his arm from the sand, tome firmly in his grasp.

"I'm guessing you need this?" Said Asger.

"What? NO!!" Screams Faith. "Let go of that!!!!"

Vrrrr *Skreee* *Zhoom*

She swings her Skarrya blade wildly at Asger. The turquoise assassin easily evades her emotionally telegraphed movements. Slipping by her blade, he ducks under a horizontal slash and flawlessly fires a powerful spinning kick into an exposed portion of her lower chest. He twists his heel dexterously on impact, sending extra kinetic force creeping through Faith's hidden layer of Callous.

Fwap

The kick sends Faith staggering back, as her crystalline armor immediately shatters, falling to the ground beneath her. The Callous layer surrounding her releases itself, leaving her completely exposed. She holds her hand up, watching as her Skarrya blade fluctuates and stutters before ultimately dissipating into thin air.

"Hhow, my solar plexus." Stammers Faith, grimacing as she holds her midsection. "Wwhat did you do?!"

"It's in spasm." Replied Asger, tossing Faith's book aside. "You have a great defence, but all I had to do was scrape off some of those center crystals to hit you where it hurts. You're a strong auracaster, you probably know that all your aura flows through the solar plexus. Good luck casting while it's in spasm.

Writhing in pain, Faith involuntarily collapses. Her body hits the ground, the grains of the hot sand rub against her cheeks. She holds her hands to her forehead in defeat, holding back tears.

Asger walks up to her, sword in hand, and pauses. He brandishes the blade, then looks at his fallen opponent. Faith looks up at him, awaiting her fate at the hands of his blade.

"You know, I don't really care too much about this Hired Blade stuff." Said Asger. "My parents made me sign up for this. I honestly hate fighting, I'm just good at it. And the one thing I hate more than fighting is killing..."

He looks back at her, slowly raising his sword for a finishing blow.

"But my old man is watching. Sorry, I can't let him see me be merciful..."

As the pain of the kick begins to lessen, Faith curls up into the fetal position, hiding her satchel from the young Hodejakt's view. She begins reaching in, searching for her standard issue Stinger pistol. Suddenly the gun in question falls to the earth in front of her, out of her reach.

"Looking for that?" Said Asger. "Or what about this." He then tosses her activated quartz necklace.

"I mean come on, I'm an assassin. I literally hide in the shadows. I picked those off of you ages ago."

Faith looks directly at Asger with contempt. Veins bulge across her head, her painful anguish mixed with frustration are apparent.

"Just do it." Said Faith. Her brow furrowed, eyes fixed on her foe like a starving tiger. "Do it so I can haunt your dreams..."

"Alright." Replied Asger. "You asked for this..."

Asger trains the tip of his sword on Faith's neck. He presses his palm into the end of the pommel. But just then, the sound of a fiery explosion shocks the assassin.

FWOOOOOSSSSSHHHHHH

"Asger you idiot!!!" Yells Dabria. "Hurry up! This one has wind, fire is a bad match!!"

In the midst of Faith and Asger's fight, Yuuna has begun to overtake the flaming hedgehog with the power of her Autumn stream. Yuuna's activated quartz necklace glows vibrantly, pouring aura into her technique.

"Grrrraaaaahhhh!!!" Screams Yuuna, unleashing everything she has into her attack.

"Tch" Scoffs Asger. "It's your lucky day." He sheathes his sword, retrieving his dagger and chain. "But not your sister's."

Asger darts off in Yuuna's direction.

"NOO!!!!!" Cries Faith. "YUUNA RUN!!!!!!"

Confused, Yuuna turns at the sound of her sister's voice. As she does, Asger closes enough distance to fade into her shadow before she can see him. He reappears behind her, chain in hand.

"BEHIND YOU!!!!" Cries Faith.

But before Yuuna can turn, Asger begins wrapping her arms and legs in chain, tying her arms behind her back. He tightly pulls the chains together, digging the links into her wrists.

"Aagh!!" Exclaimed Yuuna in pain.

"Finally!!" Shouts Dabria. "Release!" Her arcane hedgehog vanishes, sending it's remaining aura back to her. "Took you long enough, I almost ran out of aura! Now... Hehehe."

"Whatever, I'm here now." Said Asger. "Let's get this over with."

Summoning all of her strength, Faith fights the pain and rises to her knees.

"Let, *pant* let her go!!" Cries Faith. She tries to reach for her Stinger pistol.

"Nope!" Said Dabria, swiftly Shadow Gliding to the elder Sierro. As she closes in on Faith, Dabria draws her chained dagger. She wraps the chain around Faith's neck, dragging her to a tall, peculiar rock formation behind them.

"*Ggggaaghhh*." Faith chokes as the chain tightly burrows into her throat.

Dabria leaps to the top of the tall, slender stone. She holds the chain over the top, hanging her prey mercilessly.

"Brother! Finish her!!" She exclaims.

Asger turns his arms to shadow and burrows both the dagger and the weighted end of the chain deep into the sand, pinning Yuuna helplessly to the desert floor.

"No!" Cries Yuuna. "No please!!"

Asger looks away bashfully, unresponsive to the cries of his helpless foe.

He draws a dagger holstered behind his waist and Shadow glides to the hanging Faith.

"FAITH!!!!!!" Screams Yuuna in distress.

Asger approaches Faith, standing back from her flailing legs as she grasps the chains binding her neck.

"*Ngggh* *Ghhhhhrrrrgghh*" Faith continues to groan as her face turns bright red. Her lips bear an indigo hue, as her blood steadily loses oxygen.

"Hurry up brother! Now's your chance!!" Exclaims Dabria, struggling to hold the weight of the strangling prospect.

Asger holds out his open hand, shielding from Faith's wild kicks. He steadily draws his blade, slowly waiting for the right moment to strike.

Yuuna panics, squirming and wriggling to escape her metal binds. In her efforts she manages to pull the weight end of the chain from the sand, allowing her to fall to one side. With her hands tied behind her, she reaches frenziedly for her bag. As she frantically sifts through the bag's contents, Yuuna's fingers recognise the hand grip of her stinger pistol. She grasps the Stinger, pulls it from the bag and lines the muzzle with a chain link behind her shoulder.

Pssew

She fires a shot. A green bullet of compressed energy breaks the link, freeing her hands from the chain. As Yuuna pulls her hands loose, she aims the Stinger at Asger.

"Please, I don't want to do this!!!" Said Yuuna. "I don't want to hurt you!"

But her cries are unheard, drowned out by the maroon assassin's hollering.

"What's the hold up!! Kill this bitch so we can help the others!!" Yells Dabria.

Asger pauses.

"Sorry..." He said.

Faith holds her hands out in protest, but it's too late.

Ffft fft fft fft fft

Asger begins mercilessly stabbing into her side. Faith's reddened eyes widen in horror, as her ribs begin to pour crimson blood onto the sand.

"NOOOOOO!!!!!" Cries Yuuna in anguish. The sight of her sister being stabbed makes her snap. She begins firing in a frenzy at the Hodejakt twins, missing and shooting the tall stone her sister is hung from.

"Shit!" Exclaimed Dabria. "When did she break loose?!"

Asger melds into the stone's shadow, emerging from his sister's shadow atop the stone. One of Yuuna's shots hits the chain hanging Faith, abruptly dropping the strangling prospect to the floor.

"*Gasp* *Wheeze*" Faith fights to breathe, frantically pulling the chains from around her neck.

Yuuna continues to fire at the twins, hitting the slender stone and chipping pieces from it in the process.

"Callous!" Cast the twins.

The arcane armor protects them momentarily from the fiery projectiles of the Stinger.

"You must not have secured her tightly enough!!!" Said Dabria, ducking and evading Yuuna's shots.

"How is everything my fault?!" Said Asger, dodge rolling to safety. "You never took her Stinger. What, did you think she didn't have one because she's so cast heavy? Every Hired Blade carries a Stinger! You need one to take the exam!! And I'm guessing she still has her Papercut too?!"

Yuuna draws a device, shaped like a small metal bar from her bag. She presses a button, causing an infrared short sword to emerge from an opening at the top.

"GRRRRRAAAAAAAAAAAAAHHHHH!!!!!" Shouts Yuuna, taking flight towards her enemies with Papercut sword in hand.

"Well that answers that." Said Asger.

"Shut, Up!" Replied Dabria. "She's so angry she forgot how good we are at close range. As long as she's not auracasting this should be a walk in the park. Let's get her!"

But as the twins ready their weapons, a shifting can be felt in the sands beneath their feet. The tall stone rises from the desert floor, revealing it to be the stinger of a giant, Devil's Tongue Stone Scorpion. The monster's five sets of eyes glow a fiendish indigo. Its gray, stone-like exoskeleton displays a myriad of vibrant patterns, not unlike the coverings of the gorilla Wurm King of Chamboree. The towering arachnid arises from the desert floor, shaking the sand off of it's stone layered body in the process. A bloodied and half-conscious Faith lay motionless atop the beasts back, unable to grasp the reality of the situation.

"What the hell?!" Said Asger. "That's, is that a Wurm King?!?! Dabria look out!!"

The scorpion lunges it's stone encrusted stinger at Dabria. The maroon assassin sidesteps just in time, as the stinger plunges itself into the sand where she once stood.

The Wurm King pulls it's mighty stinger from the desert floor and bares its pincers to the surrounding candidates. It lets loose an ear shattering screech.

SCREEEEEEEEEEEEEEEEEEEEEEEEEE

A Gash for A Gash/ The Might of The Younger Sierro

Pilet and Lazlow immediately hear the wail of the parasitic titan, as do the ships of their sponsors.

Momentarily distracted by the sound, Pilet's attention is drawn to the scorpion's tirade. He fails to notice the missile launched previously by Lazlow, coming up the rear. The missile nears Pilet, almost making contact before the speedy prospect's reflexes kick in, prompting a swift teleport to safety.

But as he dodges to the right, Lazlow begins to fire his laser beam in the direction of Pilet's evasive maneuver. In response Pilet leaps over the beam like a track hurdle, but his descent is timed by his foe, as Lazlow casts Springboard and catches Pilet right before his feet touch the ground.

Thud *Shhhtttt*

The hulking Kettlenian Elite brings his opponent crashing to the ground beneath him, as they slide across the sand. All in one motion, Lazlow pins Pilet's arms, elbows him harshly in the face and rips the HBA dog tag from around his neck.

"Aagh, No!!!" Exclaims Pilet.

"We'll have to finish this next time King Killer. Why don't you go put that title to good use, otherwise your friends might be bug food. Or you could let them die trying to get this tag back." Lazlow puts Pilet's tag in a compartment in his armor. "But good luck with that."

"GET OFF OF ME!!!!!! NO!!!!" Hollers Pilet in frustration, his body tightly pinned by the much larger Lazlow. In a flash, Pilet's muscles grow three times in size, covered in violet fur.

"Oh?" Said Lazlow. "That's new."

Pilet thrusts Lazlow off of him with his newfound strength. As Lazlow back peddles momentarily, he crouches down to ready a Springboard cast once more.

"Damn, you been workin' out? Where were all these muscles when you needed them before? Welp, hopefully you can use them to pry your friends from that giant freaks pincers. Peace out loser! Springboard!!"

Lazlow bolts across the desert to the aid of the assassin twins.

"Wait!!! Loser?!?!! I ain't no loser!!!!! Get back here with that tag!!!!!!!!"

Pilet stomps his feet in frustration. He bolts after his foe with haste, but the added bulk of his new form slows him considerably, as he watches Lazlow grow further and further away.

"Let's get out of here!" Said Dabria. "We'll have to take some other poor fools dog tags, that thing is way too dangerous to mess around with!"

Yuuna, in shock of the emerging behemoth, flies by the twins to her sister's aid.

"Faith!!!! I'm sorry!!!!! I'm coming!!!!!!!!" Cries Yuuna.

Asger watches Yuuna make her way to her sister, trying desperately to lift her from the back of the Stone scorpion.

"Asger what the hell are you doing?!" Said Dabria. "You're not seriously considering helping them are you?! Are you trying to bring shame to the Hodejakt name?!?!"

"No I... It's just a shame about their tags..." Replied Asger. "It was a hard fight, but all for nothing I suppose."

Just then, Lazlow comes crashing forth onto the scene. The momentum of his mighty Springboard drives him into the Stone scorpion's face with a high speed tackle.

Crrrraaassshh

The powerful bash staggers the beast for a moment, crackling the entire stone layer surrounding its body and sending each and every piece of stone shattering to the floor. The brutal technique exposes the true form of the Wurm Scorpion. A sleek, bronze covered exoskeleton is revealed.

"Hey what's the holdup!" Said Lazlow, holding back the Wurm King with his shield. "You two pajama wearing, hide n' seek playing dipshits done here or what? Let's haul ass." Lazlow holds up Pilet's HBA dog tag. "I got the goods, we got 8 now so let's get to that damn Oasis!"

"Nice!" Said Dabria. "See brother, there's a man that does what has to be done without hesitation. You should take notes."

"Whatever..." Said Asger, reluctantly sheathing his sword and turning to escape.

Before he and Dabria can cast Shadow glide, Lazlow puts his shield around his back and Springboards toward the twins. He grabs one in each arm and proceeds to blast off across the desert at blistering speed.

"Laz what gives! I can walk on my own two feet!" Said Asger.

"I take my compliment back you moron!" Said Dabria. "Put me down or I'll-" Dabria's snarky remark is halted by a gust of wind in her face from the speed of Lazlow's dash.

"You guys take too long." Replied Lazlow, as the three Reapers dash across the sands.

Seeing this take place, a frustrated Pilet picks up the pace, struggling to increase the speed of his large frame.

"Shit, I'm going to kick the crap out of that coward next time!!..."

Meanwhile, atop the highest dune in sight...

After unleashing his mighty wall of lightning, Max scans the dune for his adversary. He walks along the line of superheated glass in the sand, stopping at a large stain of blood where his foe once stood.

"Was the Zen'no Divide so powerful it disintegrated him? No... I know I've never used it in battle before, but this blood pattern suggests he was not hit square..."

Max peers to the side of the dune, seeing a dip in consistency of sand about ten feet below him.

Fsssssst *Kssshing!*

The sand rustles under his feet for but an instant, as Arturo erupts swiftly from within. The hidden Fubuki lands a clean slice across Max's chest, snatching the HBA dog tag from around his neck in the process.

"Gaah!!" Exclaims Max, leaping backwards while drawing his Lacerate chest level. "My tag!!"

Arturo holds the tag out in front of him, gloating in triumph. Blood trickles down his leg, as he turns his back to Max to reveal a massive, singed gash down the back of his shoulder. The Fubuki MK2 armor works tirelessly to reconnect its dense, fibrous stitching.

"I have to say your technique really did a number on me. If I'd moved just a second later, I'm sure I would be in pieces right now. But I've seen this attack before, especially considering your father is known for it. What man from Hachidori doesn't know the Sanda Chief who divided the sea with a single slash, separating an invading Zardenian flagship in two?"

"Tch" Max scoffs. He takes a combative posture, training the blade of his Lacerate on his opponent. "There is more where that came from, this I can assure you."

"Hah! Oh I do hope so-"

Zhooooom

But as Arturo readies his Shred, Lazlow Jr. speeds by, grabbing him by the ankle in the process. The bloodied Fubuki's face drags across the sand, crashing into a school of Callous armadillos along the way.

"Laz you fool!! It was just getting good!!! *Pthew* *Spit* He drew more blood than I did, now he'll think he won!!!!!" Shouts Arturo, struggling to press his face from the floor during their getaway.

"Don't complain, I see you snatched his tag." Said Lazlow, noticing Max's HBA dog tag violently clanging across the desert floor. "That makes you the winner in my book."

"I, well yeah I did... Well either way put me down you alabaster ape! The Fubuki are not track stars, we don't run!"

The Reaper Elite speed away, vanishing like a mirage in the heat of the horizon.

Max stands there, shocked and disappointed at his lapse in judgement. He looks up at his father, as Kenzo draws the M6 Gash from his belt. He holds it up, cultivates aura and passes his hand over the blade.

"Isogu." Kenzo casts.

The blade becomes enveloped in crackling lightning aura. Kenzo then aims it at Lazlow Sr. across the sky.

"Lazlow!" He yells. "A deal's a deal! The sword is yours!"

"No! Damn it!!" Shouts Max. He falls to his knees, plunging his Lacerate into the sand in defeat. "Father... I'm sorry....."

Kenzo tosses the Gash, the aura giving it an arcane accuracy and velocity through the air.

Kshhheeewww *Clang*

The Gash juts forcefully into the wall, inches from Lazlow Sr.'s ear. The Veteran Blade doesn't flinch. He pulls the blade from the wall, brandishing it with a cloth.

"Good man." Replies Lazlow, turning his head into the doorway of his airship. "Pilot! It's time we take our leave. The Reapers are headed due west, follow suit immediately before my son dashes too far off." His gaze turns to Faxion. "And Deadeye... Tough break for the kid. Maybe next year." He whispers to his peers. "But I wouldn't bet on it."

Bernardo and Ingemar laugh, while Aslaug quietly looks down at the Sierro sisters, struggling with the Wurm King.

Poor things... She thought.

Before Faxion can respond, Lazlow's airship takes off at high speed, re-engaging it's camouflage in the process.

"I do despise that man." Said Kenzo. "He's a fool Faxion, you did the right thing showing the boy the way of the Blade. What kind of life does a talented young man like that expect to have in some quaint mountain village, it would be such a waste!"

Faxion takes a seat on the balcony and pulls a cigar from his cargo pocket. He lights it, offering Kenzo one in the process. Kenzo accepts as the two recline over the desert sky.

"Meh, what can you do." Said Faxion. "That's a man with power for you. He can do and say what he pleases, and there's not much one can do to stop him. He will however suffer greatly in life."

"And why is that?" Replied Kenzo."

"He lacks character." Said Faxion. "You see my friend, the measure of a person is not determined by wealth, physical power or political pull. Their true value is determined by the strength of their character. Sadly those who lack the latter seem to compensate by accumulating the former in spades.

He's put all his eggs in a very shallow basket, and one day someone will knock that basket down, scattering those eggs everywhere. I assume the mess that follows will be a very lonely one to clean..."

"Well said man, well said." Said Kenzo, taking a drag of the cigar. He exhales a puff of coarse smoke, reclining himself in the deck chair. "I've no idea what you just said, but well said nonetheless."

After taking another drag, he notices his son kneeling grievously in the sand. Kenzo stands and shouts over the guard rail.

"Getup boy!! What do you think you're doing?! It was only a sword, I can have the Smiths make me one by the time we get back!"

"But Father... Grandpa gave you that Gash..." Mutters Max.

Caught off guard, Faxion interjects. "Kenzo... We're not to speak to our candidates, it's considered interference with the exam-"

"Oh I know it is, but the boy needs to hear it!" Said Kenzo turning to Faxion. "Besides, that troublemaker son of Lazlow all but decimated that "Off-limits" terrarium hover garden, and the clown will probably receive no less than a mild slap on the wrist!"

Faxion's eyebrows raise, lifts his hands and looks the other way. "This is true... Suit yourself."

"Now son, you have to get your ass down there!" Said Kenzo, bellowing to Max from above. "Your allies are rallying without you, did you not hear the cries of a mighty beast but a moment ago? Get a move on! You're representing The Sanda out here, remember it!"

Max stands to his feet. He draws his Lacerate from the sand, wipes the back of the blade in the crook of his elbow and looks up to his father.

"I understand Father, I will restore honor to The Sanda before this trial is finished!" Said Max. He turns in the direction of the monstrous screeching. "Fleetfoot." He casts, as arcane energy lights the soles of his feet. "I will triumph Father, I swear it!"

Kenzo folds his arms, nods to Max and takes a seat to finish his cigar.

"You know, you did a bang-up job raising that one." Said Faxion.

"I simply followed the blueprint set by my own Father." Said Kenzo. "I can take credit for nothing, save being an honest son."

Max bolts across the sand, rushing to his allies' side.

"Why would The Reapers retreat? Were they defeated by the others?

Or have my friends fallen... My God, I'm such a fool for falling into such a petty duel..."

As Max approaches the scene, he sees an oversized Pilet struggling to run across the desert. Recognizing this large, hairy form from The Laughing Lizard saloon, Max closes in on his sluggish teammate with ease.

"Hey." Said Max. "Having trouble with your new look?"

"Ha-ha, *pant* funny guy." Said Pilet. "Hey cool lightning attack earlier, *wheeze* almost took my damn head off with that one. Anyway look! Faith and Yuuna are in trouble! There's a huge freakin' spider or something over there and it looks like even The Reapers wanted nothing to do with it!"

"What?!?" Replied Max. "Is that the cause of the incessant wailing?!"

The two sprint over a high sand dune, the enraged Wurm Scorpion finally in sight.

"See for yourself..." Said Pilet.

Yuuna, still clinging to her downed sister, lets loose small twisters periodically to keep the pincers and stinger of the beast at bay. The monstrous Wurm King struggles to aim at the Sierro sisters atop it's back, unable to see it's foe. Frustrated, the armored beast bucks wildly, sending Faith and Yuuna flying off of it.

"Aaaaagh!!" Cries Yuuna, tumbling across the uneven desert sands. She gets up and flies to her sister right before she hits the ground, breaking her fall just in time.

Thud

"Ugh... Yuuna..." Groans Faith, holding her bloodied side in agony. "The... Tome..."

The scorpion draws near, readying it's stinger to pounce on the vulnerable sisters.

Yuuna holds her sister close, nestling Faith's head into her chest and weeping. She looks up at the ferocious arachnid, wiping her tears and scowling in a terrified rage.

"STAY AWAY FROM HER!!!!!!!!!" She screams at the top of her lungs.

Yuuna grasps her activated Quartz crystal and clasps her hands together at her chest.

FFFFWWWWOOOOOSSSHHH

She becomes enveloped in a vibrant platinum aura, forming a dense, translucent protective orb fifteen feet around the two.

"GUARDIAN QUARTER!!!!!" She casts.

She forcefully pushes her arms out to either side, bolstering the mighty barrier with every ounce of aura she can muster.

KSHH KSHH

The Wurm King strikes the orb, sending both of its pincers and it's scalpel-sharp stinger into the brilliant barrier. But the strength of Yuuna's aura pushes the weapons of the Wurm King out, forcing it away with every inch that it tries to advance.

SCREEEEEEEEEEEEEEEEEEEEEEERR

The beast screeches in frustration.

"GRRRRAAAAAAAAAHHHHHH!!!!" Yuuna screams, as she holds out her technique with all of her might.

Her face beet red, with the veins of her forehead fervently bulging and pulsating; the younger Sierro fights with every fiber of her being to hold back the fearsome creature.

The Scorpion drives its pincers into the orb, attempting to reach far enough in to grasp its wailing foe. As it does so, the powerful wind aura scratches and scrapes the tough hide of either claw. But the beast brushes off the pain, continuing it's reach into the impressive platinum orb. It slowly but surely finagles its open pincers around Yuuna's waist, preparing to close its grip on the windcasting warrior.

"Hollowpoint!"

phffeeeeewww *SMASH*

A powerful violet blast of aura buffers the armored titan in the face, pushing it away from Faith and Yuuna without a moment to spare. As the beast staggers back, it's hide is riddled with a relentless volley of yellow plasma arrows from the sky.

"SCREEEEAAAAAAWWW!!" Screams the beast in horror.

Pilet and Max arrive on the scene, as Max raises his Sunshower bow to the sky and continues his plasmic barrage.

"Yuuna!" Shouts Pilet. "What's going on!? Are you ok?!?"

"It's Faith! She's been stabbed!!" Cried Yuuna. "I tried! I tried to help!! But I couldn't! I just, I just couldn't shoot in time... It's all my fault!" Yuuna wells up in tears, her cheeks rosy and flush.

"Nonono, stop." Said Pilet, rushing to Yuuna's aid as her Guardian Quarter dissipates. "We don't have time for all that. If she can't fight then we need you now." Pilet puts his massive, ape-like hand on her shoulder. "So wake up. If you messed up before you're gonna fix it now, ok?"

Faith struggles to her feet.

"Faith no!" Exclaims Yuuna. "Save your strength!"

"P, Pilet." Mutters Faith. "My...My tome..." Faith points not far off, where Asger tossed her tome aside.

"Got it." Replied Pilet. "Yuuna, get to healing up your sister." He turns to Max, still firing away at the Wurm King. "Max!" He shouts. "Give me 20 seconds."

"Lose the weight and it'd take less!" He replied.

"Shut up I'm trying!"

Max retracts the face of his Sanda armor, the fibrous chords peeling up to behind his ears. He grins to Pilet. "20 seconds it is then."

Pilet scoffs and looks back to Faith. "I'll get the book."

He dashes off as fast as he can, breathing heavily with fatigue. His oversized, fur covered muscles pulsate with fervor, baking in the desert sun.

Round Two; The Hidden Blades V.S. Kuweha The Melter

As Pilet draws ever closer to the Faith's Tome, Yuuna cultivates aura and waves her hands over Faith.

"Overmend." She casts.

Healing aura emanates from her palms, soaking into her sisters wounds and sealing them at an incredibly fast rate. The healing aura courses through her body, mending soft tissue injury around her throat and rib cage.

Gasp

Faith breathes with a new urgency, her body repaired of the damage incurred. She sits up and looks at her sister.

"Yuuna!" Said Faith. "You... You did it!!"

The two look at each other for a moment, the sorrow in Yuuna's eyes all but apparent. Faith embraces her with a firm hug.

"I'm sorry. I'm sorry. I'm so sorry." Said Yuuna.

"No I'm sorry." Said Faith. "I put you in that position, it's my fault." She takes Yuuna's head in her hands and meets her sister's gaze to her own. "We're gonna fight now, ok?"

Sniffle *Hic*

Yuuna wipes the tears from her face. "Right!"

The Wurm King grows ever weary of Max's onslaught, swiping it's massive claw at him while under fire.

Swwiish *Cling*

"Not today beast." Said Max, blocking the mighty blow with his Dueling Lacerate.

But having dropped his bow to block the pincer strike, the volley of arrows comes to a halt, as now the killer arachnid gives way to a furious series of blows to the Hachidori warrior. The Wurm King swipes and slashes at Max with it's pincers, setting its foe up for the deceptive stinger to strike.

Max blocks and parries, as he is pushed back with the force of every technique.

"Good God this creature is dense." Said Max, struggling to hold his footing against the heavy blows.

As he counts to twenty in his head, Max tirelessly battles with the beast, blocking swipe after swipe.

"15, 16, 17!!" Max begins counting aloud.

Pilet reaches Faith's tome, fighting to catch his breath as he approaches.

"Shit this sucks. *Pant* *Pant* Who the hell wants to be this big?! How does that spiky headed douche with the shield do it?!?" He takes a breath, focusing the aura through his entire body. "C'mon, I gotta get control over this... I'm a sitting duck here..." He continues breathing, focusing intently on every fiber of his being.

Fssssssshhhhhhhh

A cloud of steam escapes every pore of his skin, beginning to shrink his muscles back to normal.

Psshpssh *Psshpssh* *Psshpssh*

His muscles vibrate with fatigue, growing leaner and thinner with every breath he takes.

Pwwwsssssshhhhhhhh

Finally, the steam settles revealing a lean, purple-hairless Pilet. His fever point activated in full effect.

"It's cool being strong, but I was built for speed!" Said Pilet, vanishing with tome in hand.

A moment later, He reappears behind Faith and Yuuna; dropping Faith's Tome at her side.

"It's go time." Said Pilet, helping Faith to her feet.

"19, 20!! Pilet where the hell are you!" Exclaimed Max, growing increasingly overwhelmed by the barrage of the Wurm King.

A choice blow sends Max staggering back, tripping over a jagged stone behind him. As Max falls, the Wurm king strategically aims it's tail at the point of his descent, granting Max no time to react. But as the sharp stinger juts forth, Pilet teleports between them, parrying the armored beasts tail to the ground in protest.

"Sorry I'm late." Said Pilet.

"I am not surprised." Replied Max. "Regardless, better late than never!"

"BILIZZAHA!!!"

FWOOOOOOO

A massive orb of cold and snow flies over Pilet and Max, freezing the legs of the Wurm King to it's left.

The two turn and see Faith, open-faced tome in one hand and a floating ball of cold aura in the other.

"Now it's time to play." Said Faith, further casting her frozen storms of cold.

The Wurm King begins to stagger on it's chilled legs, joints locked together. Pilet darts and dashes with blinding speed around the scorpion, hacking away with his Dragonfly knives at the legs and feet when he can.

"Damn this thing is tough!" Said Pilet. "These knives are hot as hell and they're barely putting a scratch on it!"

"Then you just have to hit 'em where it hurts!" Exclaimed Faith, twirling her finger in the air.

"Tiida Craek!!" She casts.

A whip of pure electricity shoots forth from her fingertips, as Faith lashes at the eyes of the Wurm King.

SKKKYYYYEEEEEEEEEEEHHHH

The beast cries in pain.

Kshing *Krshh*

Max begins slashing at the spaces between the joints of the creature, but is unable to penetrate the rough skin in between. Unhappy with the result of his attempts, Max backsteps and fires a bolt of slicing aura from his blade. The slash burns a dent in the armor of the arachnid, leaving a singed mark where it lands.

"I see..." Said Max. He turns to the others. "It appears it's weak to aura!"

"Oh yeah?!?!" Said Pilet, flipping through the air and landing on the Wurm King's back. "Then get a load of this!!"

PFFEW *PFFEW* *PFFEW* *PFFEW* *PFFEW*

Pilet fires a bombardment of Hollowpoints into a single spot on top of his foe. The shots mirror the effect of Max's aura slash, leaving dent after small dent in the surface of the exoskeleton.

"What are you doing?" Said Faith, leaping away from the swiping pincers of the beast. "I said hit 'em where it hurts not where it's most protected!"

"I don't like that rule." Said Pilet, straddling the back of the beast. "It's gonna hurt where I hit 'em. If it's not gonna give me an opening, then I'll make one myself!"

But as Pilet says this, the tail of the beast comes from behind and wraps him tightly, squeezing the life from his lungs.

"Nnnngggggghhh!!!" Gasps Pilet in pain. "Stupid spider!!"

"That's what you get!" Said Faith. "Just hang on. Yuuna!"

"Already on it!" Said Yuuna, flying by her sister.

"Starshot!" Yuuna casts.

She flicks a shining, compressed bullet of aura from between her fingers, landing directly on the tail of the scorpion. The force of the blow spasms the tail, releasing Pilet enough for him to escape. He falls out, sliding on the tail of the beast like a snowboard down a mountainside.

"Hollowpoint!!"

As Pilet descends, he continues to fire mercilessly onto the hull of the Wurm King, leaving as many dents and singe marks as he can.

"Max! Can't you slice this thing with your lightning wall or whatever?!" Said Pilet, as he back handsprings onto the creature's hide yet again.

"That technique has a cooldown time!" Replied Max, parrying the

Wurm King's leg away as it tries to stomp him into the sand. "To use it again so soon would result in seizures not unlike your own!"

"Ugh, damn. Well at least it didn't go to waste. Bet you really jacked up that other swordsman."

"Uuuhh, yes. Would not want to be him right now..." Muttered Max reluctantly.

"Max! Pilet! Stand back!!" Exclaimed Yuuna.

Pilet leaps high into the air, heeding the advice of his ally.

Faith and Yuuna stand side by side, cultivating aura together as they face the Wurm King from afar. They both reach a hand towards the scorpion, gathering aura in the other hand by their chests.

"GRAND AUTUMN BILIZZAHA!!!" They cast in unison.

PWWWWOOOOOOOOOSSSSHHHH

Faith's orb of cold meets Yuuna's stream of pressurized air, creating a massive, unrelenting storm of ice flying towards the Wurm King. Spears of ice and bursts of freezing air blast the entirety of their foe. The ice pierces the openings created by Max and Pilet's techniques, digging into the monster's soft insides.

GRRRRRRRRIIIIIIIIIIIIIIIIIIIIIIIIIIIIIIIIIIIIIIIIIIIIIIIIIIGGGGGGGGHHHHH

The creature wails in anguish, curling its limbs in the harsh cold.

Pilet falls from the sky, landing like a gymnast beside Max.

"Damn. Between your lightning thing and this snowstorm, I gotta come up with a big cool move of my own."

"It is a beautiful thing isn't it." Replied Max. "These two work remarkably well together."

Yuuna turns to Max and Pilet.

"Well of course we do silly! We're sisters!"

Just as it seems the Wurm King has had enough, it's mouth opens widely, spewing a large cloud of acid rivaling the size of the Sierro sisters raging blizzard. As it does so, it reveals a terrifying set of smaller claws inside of it's mouth.

"OH GOD!!" Exclaims Yuuna. "WHAT THE HELL IS THAT?!?!"

"Those are pedipalps sis, it uses them to pinch apart it's food." Replied Faith.

"Holy shit." Said Pilet. "For a second I almost wanted to vomit... Nope... Still do."

"You'll both have to look past it." Said Max. "Adversity like this we will be no stranger to as a Licensed Hired Blade. This is only the beginning of our journey into the vicious unknown!"

"Yeah, ya know Maxy here is right! I ain't scared of no big shiny spider!" Said Pilet.

"It's not a spider you idiot!" Replied Faith.

Wwsssssssssshhhhhhhhh

A peculiar sound comes from the beast, as it's acid spray begins to melt the Grand Autumn Bilizzaha away.

"Uh sis." Said Yuuna, pumping more aura into her technique. "We have a problem..."

"Oh shit!" Said Faith, turning to see the acid fighting back their auric barrage. "No that just won't do, push it back sis!"

The two press forth, imparting more and more aura into their technique to keep the killer arachnid at bay. Max and Pilet join in. As Pilet begins firing Hollowpoints at will, Max charges his Lacerate with an auric lightning and fires it into the beast.

But the scorpion ignores their attacks, focusing on it's spray and forcing it's way closer and closer to the sisters.

"Where did this shit come from?!" Exclaimed Yuuna. "And why is it so powerful?!?!"

"The Devil's Tongue Stone scorpion uses acid spray to dissolve prey, but it can't spray it out to this volume!! Is this the true power of a Wurm King?!?!"

"I don't know what this thing is eating, but it's stomach is definitely not happy with it right now!" Said Pilet. "Hey, dick head! Go puke somewhere else!!"

"This is no time to joke around Pilet!" Said Max. "We have to do something or we're all going to end up like ice cream on a hot summer's sidewalk!!"

The Wurm King grows closer and closer to The Hidden Blades, spewing more and more corrosive acid towards them. With the team on the ropes, it seems as if the end of their exam, and their lives is inevitable...

In the sky, Faxion tightly grips his Arcane Pierce. He swallows nervously, his eyes fixed intently on the mighty scorpion.

"C'mon guys... C'mon..." Muttered Faxion, rocking anxiously in his chair.

Benny engages the autopilot and steps out onto the balcony with Faxion and Kenzo.

"It does not look good does it." Said Kenzo, his arms folded tightly to his chest.

"No, honestly not at all." Said Benny, as Kenzo and Faxion turn to the new voice. "I'm sorry Fax, I was really gunnin' for your crew this year." He puts a hand on Faxion's shoulder. "But I tell you I've seen some real dog fights in my day, and I wouldn't want to be in the fight they're in down there. That beastie's been on The Hired Blades radar for quite a while now, but no one they send has been able to kill the damn thing. I'm sure you've heard the stories of Kuweha, "The Melter". The beast leveled a whole village with it's God damned breath. How could four kids stand a chance."

"Yes I have Benny, yes I have." Replied Faxion. "But never count my crew out. They've done swimmingly so far haven't they, especially given they've just fought the number one team on the roster..."

In the distance, a mysterious figure approaches the fray with haste. A tan skinned man, wearing a green plaid shirt and beige pants. He skates along the sand like a roller blader, the soles of his shoes ablaze with the glow of a mystic, emerald flame. As he nears the top of a particularly high sand dune, the fiery stranger leaps high into the air. He balls his right hand into a fist, emerald flame peeking out from between his sealed fingers. At the peak of his jump, the flaming auracaster releases the contents of his fist, loosing a massive fireball, followed closely by an immensely powerful stream of verdant flame down onto the Wurm King Kuweha.

Fwwwwiiiiisssshhhh *CRASH* *BOOM*

The fireball explodes on impact, roasting the Wurm King's shell at staggeringly high temperatures. The flame engulfs the creature, unrelentingly scorching every inch that it reaches.

SKRRREEEEEEEEEEEHHH

Kuweha screeches, writhing in pain from the auric onslaught. His acid breath pauses momentarily as his hind legs collapse, shaking in pain.

Pfft *Fwishh*

The figure descends from the sky, landing smoothly as his auric flame continues to slide him effortlessly across the sand. A closer look reveals the stranger to be Bhujanga Garuda, solitary teamless candidate of the 127th Hired Blades exam. He skates over to Faith and Yuuna, stopping right in front of them while grasping a white and black stone, wire wrapped onto his necklace.

"Follow my lead." Said Bhujanga, as he cultivates aura into the stone.

The sisters look at each other, then back to him and nod in agreement.

Bhujanga begins waving his arms in circular patterns, leaving trails of green aura in the air.

"Do your combination cast again, but this time pour maybe 66% into it. Trust me." He said.

Bhujanga releases a burst of flame from below his feet, propelling him over Faith and Yuuna, as he back flips in the air and lands directly behind them. He stands in the middle of the two, creating a ball of vigorously pulsating emerald flame between his open palms.

"Sis, do you have enough aura left?" Said Faith.

Yuuna pants in exhaustion.

"I, I think so. I'll make it work, you can count on me sis."

The battle-weary Sierros take note, creating their own elemental spheres of frost and wind. As the two ready their techniques, Kuweha finds its footing and attempts to stand.

"Oh no you don't." Said Max, dashing towards the creature with haste. He slices at the front leg joints of Kuweha, this time successfully separating the beast from it's now singed and battered limbs. Max then swiftly back peddles, leaving the scene clear for the trio of auracasters to unleash their arcane assault.

As Kuweha's severed legs hit the sand, the Wurm King desperately rears its facial claws and readies to spew another wicked cloud of corrosive acid. As it does so, Pilet raises his palm to the beast, charges a basketball-sized Hollowpoint and fires it at the foe.

Ffweeew *BOOM*

The Hollowpoint smashes Kuweha right in the face, shutting his mouth and giving Faith, Yuuna and Bhujanga just enough time to fully charge their auric spheres.

"You guys done yet or what?" Said Pilet, blowing the auric steam off of his hand.

"Release it now!" Exclaims Bhujanga.

Faith and Yuuna point their respective orbs of vigorously churning aura towards Kuweha.

"GRAND AUTUMN BILIZZAHA!!!!" Cry the Sierros.

"KARMIC WAVE!!!" Exclaims Bhujanga.

Bhujanga immediately releases his stored flame into the girls arcane mix, sending a mighty aurora beam of platinum wind, cerulean frost and emerald flame hurtling towards the armored arachnid.

Kssssssshhhhhh *PFFEW*

Kuweha is instantly overtaken by the relentless stream of elemental fury. His hide freezes over, scorches and blows away all at the same time.

SCRRREEEEEEEEEEEEEEE Riles Kuweha in agony.

The frost, wind and fire seamlessly blend to deal perfectly balanced carnage across the Wurm Kings exoskeleton. The verdant fire superheats it's bronze exterior. The ice creeps into its joints, settling into Kuweha's inner flesh. The vicious wind blasts away at the beast, harnessing kinetic energy and ripping shards of bronze from the mangled titan.

Pilet and Max look on in amazement.

"So this is what auracast can really do huh." Said Pilet, arms folded and gaze set intently on the aurora of death. "It's crazy that I've lived my whole life without knowing there were people in the world who could do shit like this..."

"It's truly a sight to behold, Flame working in tandem with Frost and Wind. Such a volatile element is rarely so cooperative with its peers."

The trio of auracasters continue to pour aura into the auric fusion, slowly but surely wasting away at the beast. After a few moments, the shining quartz crystal hanging around Yuuna's necklace begins to dim. She fights to continue to cast, but eventually her wind aura begins to peeter out. As her contribution to the combination dies out, the emerald flame and azure frost dissipate, as the candidates look on to a perfectly decimated Kuweha.

"I'm sorry guys, I've done a lot of casting today and my Quarts ran out." Said Yuuna, grasping her casting hand as it quivers from overuse.

"I don't think you have anything to be worried about." Replied

Bhujanga, grasping his stone necklace to deactivate it's properties. "Not many creatures could have withstood the battering this one just took. I'm sure we've done more than enough to rid the people of Devil's Tongue of this pest."

Faith closes her tome, slides it into her satchel and offers Bhujanga a handshake.

"Thank you for your help, I don't know who you are but we might not have been able to beat that monster without you. Just out of curiosity, how did you manage to aura-fusion your flamecast with wind and frost? As far as I know flame aura hasn't the compatibility to mix too well with either."

Bhujanga pulls a cigar from his back pocket. He cultivates a small amount of vibrant green aura into the tips of his middle finger and thumb, and presses the two together onto the end of the cigar,

Tsssssss

The cigar is lit with an emerald glow. Bhujanga takes a long drag, exhaling am indigo smoke into the air above him.

My Emerald Flame is not as unruly as your typical fire. While most fire burns all that it touches in unkempt aggression, my flame can blend harmoniously with the world around it. It burns only what I will it too."

He then holds aloft his stone necklace, displaying it to Faith and Yuuna. A white stone with black, miscellaneously patterned lines swings back and forth in it's wire wrapping like a pendulum.

"This Howlite then enables me to take my already tame flame, and allow it to coexist with the aura of all other elements and their casters."

"Oh cool!" Said Yuuna. "I knew that was Howlite! It's a calming stone, to sooth fiery emotions. No pun intended, or was it? Muahahaha!"

"You're correct." Said Bhujanga. "Calming the flame allows it to "Play nice" with the other elements. How very knowledgeable you are."

As the three approach the fallen, frosted and roasted stone scorpion, Pilet and Max meet them at the scene.

"Yo!" Said Pilet, walking up to Bhujanga with an outstretched hand. "What's up dude, that was some crazy shit you did just now. I didn't know you could throw down like that. Guess I shouldn't be surprised, seeing as you wanted to take the exam alone and all."

Bhujanga accepts Pilet's gesture, grasping his hand as Pilet pulls him in for one of his unexpected shoulder bumps.

Max deactivates his Sanda MK2 armor, shaking his fatigued body from the strain of the armor's use. Still weary of this mysterious stranger, Max keeps his distance and simply offers Bhujanga a subtle blow.

"Thank you for the aid."

"It's no problem." Replied Bhujanga. "I owe your teammate a drink, but this'll have to do."

Pilet stands atop the head of the now motionless Kuweha, stomping on it until he cracks a damaged portion of shell by his feet.

"Take this you creepy pile of shit! Not so strong now huh?!?"

Faith shakes her head in disapproval.

"Pilet come down from there. We didn't even check to see if it's dead yet."

As irony would have it, the tail of Kuweha begins to lift itself behind Pilet. Bhujanga and the others eyes widen, as the stinger props itself for a fatal strike to the arrogant prospect.

"Yeah take this! And That! And some of this!" Exclaims Pilet, continuing to stamp out the crackling shell.

Finally he stomps too hard and kicks through the exoskeleton, getting his foot firmly caught in between.

"Ow! Damn thing keeps fighting even when it's dead!"

"Uh, Pilet..." Said Max, pointing behind his comrade in shock. "You might want to reconsider that statement..."

"Huh?" Replied Pilet, turning his neck to check behind him.

He sees the stinger trained intently on him.

"OH SHIT!!" Exclaimed Pilet. "You guys all suck!! You didn't kill it enough!!!"

"How is this our fault!?!" Retorts Faith. "You're the genius who decided to go up there and give the thing a headache!"

Max and Faith hop up there and try to pull Pilet's leg from the cracked hide. Bhujanga begins to charge an auric fireball in his hands, while an aura-depleted Yuuna runs to and fro screaming with her hands on her head.

"AAAAAAAHHH!!!" Screams Yuuna. "PILET'S GONNA DIEEE!!!!"

"What?! Yuuna shut up!!!!" Exclaimed Pilet. "I'm not gonna die!! Pull harder damn it!!!

"I'm trying! Stop moving so much, you're just making it harder!" Said Max, yanking as best he can at Pilet's ankle.

"This is hopeless, I need my tome!" Said Faith, frantically reaching for the tome in her satchel. But as she does so, Pilet accidentally knees her in the forehead struggling to free himself.

"Ouch!" Yelps Faith, as the blow makes her drop the tome down onto the sand. "YOU IDIOT!!!"

"Shit." Said Bhujanga, continuing to cultivate verdant fire. "I don't know if I can stop the force of the stingers thrust with flame alone."

Just as the Stinger seems to ready itself to lunge, the deafening sound of a gunshot is heard from afar.

Pheeeww *Crash*

A speeding projectile of pure cobalt light makes impact right into the center of the cracks made by Pilet's previous Hollowpoint barrage. The piercing shot causes a quake across the hull of the Wurm King, knocking pieces of broken shell into the air. The rising stinger falls lifeless to the ground, making one last death rattle before curling into itself tightly. The group looks to the sky as Benny's Jet deactivates it's camouflage. Faxion stands at the edge of the guardrail, Arcane Pierce in hand, with a tinge of smoke escaping the barrel. The Veteran Blade grins from ear to ear, resting the azure rifle onto his shoulder.

"You really are helpless aren't you!" Bellows Faxion in the distance.

The group of candidates looks awestruck.

"Fax!" The Hidden Blades exclaim.

After wriggling his ankle for another moment, Pilet manages to free himself from the hide of the lifeless arachnid.

"Finally." Said Pilet, rubbing his ankle fervently. "Thanks for the assist dude, I was pretty sure this thing was gonna turn me into a keychain with that stinger."

"Faxion I appreciate your aid, but does that not count as illegal assistance of your sponsored candidates?" Said Max. "Were we not to be left to our own abilities for the exam? I would hate to see you reprimanded for your assistance."

"It's no problem Max!" Replied Faxion. "I used my sponsor save, each sponsor gets one chance to bail their candidate's team out! Looks like Pilet just wasted yours! Hahahahaha!"

Pilet grits his teeth and looks to Faxion across the sky.

"Well no one told you to do that old man! Next time save yourself the ammo, I'm surprised you didn't hit US by mistake with the cataracts you're probably forming!"

Faxion loads a clip of rubber bullets into his rifle and fires one into Pilet's arm.

Tchik tchik *Clack*

"You mean like that?" He said.

"OUCH! STOP!" Yelps Pilet, leaping from Kuweha's corpse.

Faxion continues to fire, as Pilet dodges and strafes the bullets with the speed of his Fever point.

"Ha! Keep up the good work guys!" Said Faxion. "Don't let Pilet drag you down now! And Mister Garuda, thank you for your help! Looks like you'll make a fine Blade yet."

Bhujanga gives Faxion a nod, while Benny re-engages the ship's camouflage, flying somewhere into the desert sky.

As the airship vanishes, a mysterious violet aura escapes Kuweha's mouth, enveloping Pilet. Suddenly his body begins to morph, as he becomes covered in bronze armor similar to the fallen stone scorpion's. His chest and back form a bronze protective breastplate. His arms and legs become shielded in a sturdy yet-lightweight exoskeleton, with a rubbery substance protecting his joints. His head forms a sleek, hard, bronze helmet, covering everything but his glowing eyes. Pilet stops and looks at his body in shock. He starts to feel a burning in his wrists and forearms.

"Ow, what's going on?"

He raises his arms as his hands begin to shake. Suddenly, two seven-inch stingers not unlike Kuwaha's emerge from the back of his wrists.

"Woah! What is this?! This is... Cool!"

The others stand motionless in disbelief. Faith picks up her tome and places it back in her satchel.

"Did you see that? The aura escaped the Wurm King when it died, and turned Pilet into that." She said. "Pilet, do you think that has anything to do with your big hairy form?"

"You know, I don't really remember. But now that I think about it... Right after I killed the Gorilla, I was able to move this giant statue that

Fax was stuck underneath. I never really thought about it but maybe the same thing happened then..."

"Maybe you gain powers from the things you kill???" Said Yuuna. "Like some kinda... Battle memory?"

"I'm not sure if that's the case but I do like that name, "Battle Memory"." Added Max.

Pilet takes a deep breath. He focuses intently on every fiber of his being. The armor sheds off of him, falling to the ground with a resounding clang.

"Well, it was getting hot in there anyway."

What a peculiar guy... Thought Bhujanga Garuda.

Mystery of The Emerald Flamecaster

The sun begins to set over the highest dunes, prompting the group to settle in for the night. They traverse back to where their battle with the Reaper Elite first took place, finding their dropped bags and setting up camp under the floating terrarium colony. Faith and Yuuna gather some sticks, as Bhujanga uses them to start a beautiful green fire. As the night falls, the group sits by the fire, roasting marshmallows and recounting the events that have followed thus far. Max takes a rag and starts meticulously wiping his two lacerates.

"So Mr. Bhujanga." He said. "How is your exam coming along, where are you in terms of HBA dog tags..."

The group pauses and falls silent, realizing for the first time that their new friend could quite possibly still be their foe.

Bhujanga reaches into his backpack, as Faith, Pilet and Yuuna each break into a cold sweat wondering what he might pull out. Max's demeanor is unshaken, his gaze stays as stone, fixed readily on Bhujanga as he continues to wipe his blade. The emerald flamecaster pulls a plastic bag, completely filled with HBA dog tags from his backpack. He tosses it on the floor, as several tags fall out onto the sand.

"I've more than satisfied the exam requirement, yourself?" He replied.

Max stops wiping his Lacerate, staring at the engorged bag of dog tags like he's seen a ghost. His peers do the same, eyes widened at the thought of how many candidates have fallen to the Emerald Flame.

"Oh... Well then..." Max turns to his team in shame. "I'm sorry you guys. I've neglected to say it, but my foe got the better of me and took my tag..."

"Shit." Said Pilet. "Same here, I was hoping at least you guys were able to hold onto yours."

"Well we've still got ours!" Said Yuuna. "Although, to be honest I didn't do much to contribute..." Yuuna hangs her head in defeat. She turns to her sister, tears beginning to well up in her eyes. "You were right sis, I really need to get over my fear of hurting people. You... You almost died because I couldn't pull the trigger."

Faith grasps Yuuna in her arms with a tender hug. Yuuna begins to profusely cry into her sister's chest, her sobs deep and visceral.

"Woah woah hey!" Said Pilet, coming over to the sisters. "It's all good Yuuna! You were awesome out there! Here can I give you a hug too?"

Sniff *Hic*

"Of course Pilet!" Said Yuuna, hiding her disheveled face.

Max walks over and puts a hand on Yuuna's back. "May I as well?"

"Mhmm!" She said.

Pilet, Max and Faith conglomerate on Yuuna in a warm group hug. As Bhujanga sits there, awkwardly twiddling his thumbs and looking back and forth. Faith looks at him and silently motions for him to come over. He points at himself, as if confused to who she is communicating to. She smiles and nods while continuing to wave him over. Bhujanga walks over and puts a hand on Yuuna's shoulder.

"Uhh, there there. Don't be sad friend." He said.

"AWW!" Cried Yuuna. "Thanks Bhujanga! *Sniff* You're so kind!! *Sniff* *Hic*"

Faith smiles at Bhujanga and tries not to giggle.

After a brief, uncomfortable moment of group hugging; Bhujanga walks over to his bag of dog tags, picks it up and hands it to Yuuna.

"Here, take as many as you need."

The group pauses.

"Yo... Are you sure?" Said Pilet. "You like, probably went through alot of trouble to get these. Right?"

"Nope." Said Bhujanga. "Most of these candidates were clearly unfit to continue as Hired Blades, so I eliminated them. Wasn't hard at all."

"..."

"Well, thanks Bhujanga. We really appreciate it." Faith nudges Pilet with her elbow and whispers. "Just take the damn tags and give him back his bag before he changes his mind, do you want to get "eliminated"?"

"Chill chill, I know!..." He whispers back.

Pilet takes six tags and hands the bag back to Bhujanga.

"Now we're even, King Killer." Said Bhujanga.

"Yeah, whatever you say man." Replied Pilet. "Whatever you say....."

As the night progresses the group decides it's time to get some rest. Still weary from the long battles that previously ensued, it isn't long before everyone is sound asleep. All except for Bhujanga Garuda, who takes his leave and makes it about twenty paces from the encampment before he hears the sound of a blade being pulled from its sheath.

"Why are you in such a hurry, "friend"?"

Bhujanga turns to the sight of Max Quinn several feet away, Lacerate drawn and rested upon his shoulder. The flamecaster rests his hands on his hips, pulling another cigar from his back pocket and lighting it.

"Impressive that you were able to hear me, over the sound of your boisterous friend." Said Bhujanga.

"The Hachidori are notoriously light sleepers. Rest is the perfect opportunity for the enemy to strike." Replied Max.

In truth, the Hachidori are quite heavy sleepers. While Faith and Yuuna lay well rested, earplugs firmly affixed into their ears, the sound of Pilet's incessant snoring deprives Max of his rest yet again. In short, the young swordsman was never asleep to begin with.

"You never told us. What's your story? Who are you? Where are you from? Why do you hold such a mysterious power? And what reason do you have for "eliminating" so many contestants, only to help us with our foe, and then giving us enough tags to pass? Forgive me for my lack of trust, but I was not born yesterday. Everyone does something for a reason. My reasons are for honor, what are yours?..."

Max readies his fighting posture, preparing to call upon the MK2 Sanda armor.

Bhujanga takes a deep inhale. He releases a mighty cloud of indigo smoke into the air, covering the stars above him.

There's no need for that, please. I've singed the dreams of enough young dreamers today. Do you really want to know?" He said.

Max nods his head.

"Well, I come from a clan of..."

Several feet off, Faith and Yuuna lay cuddled together, staving off the cold. Pilet rolls over in his sleep, revealing a smushed, roasted marshmallow sticking to his left buttock. As a small stone scorpion comes along, picking and probing at the marshmallow, Pilet passes gas directly on it. The scorpion leaps back in shock and prepares to attack, but Pilet releases wind again. The scent becomes too strong, and the scorpion immediately scurries away as fast as it can.

Back to the summit of the flamecaster and the swordsman...

"And that's my story..." Said Bhujanga, taking another drag of his cigar.

"..."

Max falls to his knees and bows in reverence.

"I humbly apologize. I had no idea. Your story is truly heartbreaking."

"It's ok, I understand your distrust." Replied Bhujanga. "Had I been in your position I would share the same level of caution."

Max stands to his feet, he sheaths his Lacerate and shakes Bhujanga's hand.

"Your story is safe with me, a Hachidori's word is bound till death. It is no one's business who you are and where you are from, and I am very sorry for prying."

"Just be safe out there, and take care of your group." Said Bhujanga. "I can tell you have the strongest will of the rest. I can also tell you knew that I would defeat you, and yet you still confronted me. I know very well the look in the eye of someone who knows they are beat, but never have I seen someone who did not crumble nor retreat under the fear it brings. You have the heart of a true warrior. If we ever meet again, I hope you to be my match, for I have yet to find one on the battlefield."

"Agreed." Replied Max.

Bhujanga deeply inhales the last of his cigar, burning it down to the bottom. He steps away from Max and exhales the largest cloud yet, fully enveloping his body in the indigo smoke it brings. The smoke covers him, blackening out his silhouette entirely. In the thick of the smoke, Bhujanga claps his hands, releasing a small burst of green flame within the cloud. As the smoke clears, the Emerald Flamecaster is nowhere to be seen for miles, vanishing somewhere into the desert dunes.

"This world is full of surprises..." Said Max, reaffixing his swords and making his way back to the encampment. "And someday I'll be ready for all of them..."

As the young swordsman walks back to his slumbering allies, he looks up into the dazzling, starry night sky.

"Good luck friend. In this life or the next..."

He takes his place by the fire, lying with his head rested on a mound of sand. As Pilet's snores begin to calm, the young swordsman eventually drifts off into a well-deserved deep sleep. The four aspiring mercenaries lay still, their chests slowly rising and falling with every breath of their slumber. If only they knew of the events to transpire in the coming hours of The 127th Hired Blades exam. Or the changes it will bring........

SIX

Ancient Secrets, Hidden just beneath the Surface

It was a tranquil day in Grand Titanus city. White, fluffy clouds drift through the sky like a migrating herd of mashed potatoes. The traffic runs smoothly, as dino-taxis and hovercar alike share the road, promptly transporting busy city-goers to their various destinations. Dilophosaurus and Majungasaurus effortlessly pull ferry carts of humans across the streets, as the powerful turbines of the many stylish hover cars yield them the right of way. At Grand Titanus Station, a young boy sits on the steps, anxiously awaiting the arrival of his guest. He brushes his buzzed hair between his hands nervously, the spiny bristles prick at his fingertips. Finally, the halting screech of the train can be heard throughout the station. As it comes to a full stop, the screeching ends and is replaced by a resounding boom of steam emerging from the chimney. The conductor speaks.

"Last stop, Grand Titanus Station! Please watch your step exiting the train, and enjoy your stay at the Capital City!"

The boy turns swiftly at the sound of the train doors shooting open. He scans the pedestrians leaving one by one, tirelessly searching for his guest. But as each train-goer exits the cart, the young boy sees no sign of the awaited in question. Finally, the train cart empties, the last of the passengers have emerged, and the onlooker is left in awe. Feeling defeated, he turns away and holds his saddened face in his hands. Disheartened, he leans his chin onto his palms; looking on towards the bustling city streets with a downtrodden frown. Suddenly, a final, unexpected passenger steps out of the train car. As the train doors shut and the metro takes off into the green fields surrounding Grand Titanus City, the last passenger speaks.

"Hey buddy, sorry to keep you waiting. Ready to have fun today?"

The boy's eyes light up. His heart sinks into his bowels.

"...Dad???"

He turns briskly at the stranger's voice, but just as he does so, a sizzling hot goop envelops his face. It covers his eyes and forehead, burning and blinding him.

"Ouch! What is this?! Dad?! Are you still there?"

But as the boy fights to remove the substance, the figure of his father starts to fade away.

"No! Dad, wait!! I have to see you!"

He continues to pull on the goop, crying out in fear and desperation.

"Don't leave again! You can't go! You just got here!!!"

But his cries are in vain, as the silhouette of his father vanishes before his eyes. He shouts boisterously in protest.

"NOOOOOOOOO!!!!!"

Suddenly, Pilet wakes up from his sleep; violently leaping from his sleeping bag. His face, covered in hot, half cooked egg.

"Aaagh!!" He shouts, ripping the egg from his face. "What is this!?"

Faith grasps the handle of a hot skillet in her hand, as Yuuna holds a hand over her mouth in surprise.

"Oh my God Faith you can't even flip eggs right!" Said Yuuna. "Look you totally fried Pilet!"

Faith stands awkwardly over Pilet, hiding the skillet behind her back.

"I have no idea what you're talking about... A Zardenian flare pheasant flew over and shat on him."

"Really? A Flare pheasant? Are we in Zardenia??" Retorts Yuuna. "Do you see any rain forests and fancy, mystical glowing trees around here? Because I don't!"

Max chuckles to himself, his armor spread across his lap. He polishes the jewel in the center with care.

"You know, you have to eat that Pilet." Said Max with a subtle grin.

"Waste not want not, in Hachidori those who do not finish their food do not eat the next day."

Pilet wipes the egg off with a worn tank top and tosses the shirt to the side.

"You guys made me miss him!" Said Pilet. "I was so close..."

"Miss who Pilet?" Said Faith inquisitively.

Coming to the realization that it was all but a dream, Pilet sulks in his sleeping bag.

"My... Never mind. What are you guys doing? And where's Bhujanga?"

"Well we WERE making breakfast, but SOMEBODY doesn't know their own strength! And that's why you woke up as an omelet." Said Yuuna.

"Bhujanga left in the night." Replied Max, gazing off into the distance. "He made not a sound, nor did he say a word to any of us."

"Tch, I'm not surprised. He's good for that sorta thing." Replied Pilet. "Hell I'm more surprised that guy waited til we were all asleep, instead of disappearing like a weirdo when our backs were turned." Pilet gets up and begins packing his belongings. He lifts his Dragonfly knives, gazing into the reflective blades. "Today's the day. Yesterday I let that douchebag get the better of me, but today I'm not settling for anything less than victory..."

"Well said." Replied Max, equipping his freshly polished armor and readying his Lacerates. "I too have something to prove, and I won't rest until I do."

"I'm surprised if you'll ever rest, sleeping next to Pilet." Said Faith. "He snores like an elephant in heat!"

"HAHAHAHAHA!!!"

All but Pilet laugh.

"Yeah yeah, whatever! Are we gonna keep wasting our time talkin'? This "Cool Oasis" isn't gonna go and find itself, and we only got til noon to get there!"

"Ok ok fine." Replied Faith. "So sensitive..."

The Hidden Blades compose themselves, gathering their belongings and putting out the campfire. They clear the area of any trash leftover and ready themselves for departure. Pilet stands at the front of the group and casts Fleetfoot.

"Hey, last one there's a rotten egg." Said Pilet, crouching down into a runner's position.

"But that'd be impossible, Pilet." Replied Yuuna. "We already gave you a facial with the last egg we had!"

"What?! Why you little-"

Zhhooomm!!

Faith and Max take off across the desert, kicking up sand into Pilet's face. Yuuna abruptly follows, casting "Kitestream" and soaring across the arid sky.

"Cough cough, Oh I'm gonna kick all your asses." Said Pilet, gagging on sand and stone.

He blasts off after his team, as The Hidden Blades set off to reach their final destination.

The sun blazes over the Devil's Tongue Desert, sending heatwaves pulsating off of the grainy desert sand. Pilet, Max and Faith dash at dizzying speeds atop the dunes, looking for any sign of water they can find.

"See anything up there?" Said Faith, looking up to her sister in the sky.

"It's hard to say." Replied Yuuna. "There's only so much height I can get casting Kitestream. But nothing yet." However, something suddenly catches her eye; as she cups her hand over her brow to block the sun. "Wait, actually... yeah I do see something! There's water, a big pool of it! And trees! I guess the map on Pilet's Chatch was right!"

"Told ya!" Said Pilet. "I do stuff right sometimes! And you guys thought I would get us lost..."

"What else do you see?" Said Max.

"Well there's a bunch of people there, they're standing around the water and talking. I think... I think I see some of our proctors there!" Yuuna changes trajectory mid-flight. "This way guys!"

The group follows suit, closing in on their destination within minutes. They near the Cool oasis, a large body of water out in the middle of the desert. Palm trees rise high above the outer rim, shading the peach and banana trees beneath. Camels drink from the still water, wagging their tails in delight. About two dozen candidates stand at attention down by the far end of the Oasis, accompanied by an equal number of Licensed Hired Blade proctors. Off to the side of the crowd, Pilet recognizes Toste, twirling his mustache meticulously. The group arrives; as Benny's light airship deactivates its camouflage field, appearing out of thin air behind

The Hidden blades. Faxion, Kenzo and Benny step down from the ship's platform, greeting the team graciously.

"You did it!" Exclaimed Faxion. "Look at that. I didn't doubt you all for a second, even when you looked like bug food! And Max, that lightning wall you casted, what a technique!"

"Thank you Faxion, had it landed flush I may be more accepting of your praise..." Replied Max. He turns to Kenzo in lament. "Father, your prized Gash... I'm sorry I failed you."

Kenzo gently grabs Max's head in his open hands and looks him in the eye.

"Listen boy, a sword is just that, a sword. It is only folded steel. You faced your opponent with honor and pride, and he took your dog tag with deception. And while martial arts is deception, the use of such cowardice during an honorable duel is shameful! It just goes to show the fear that your technique had put into his heart."

He taps Max on the forehead. "Next time be smart, be aware, but do NOT attack yourself after a loss. Through loss comes knowledge, but the presence of remorse is the enemy of such learning. You are to always remember that." He lets go of Max's head and pats him in the shoulder. "Now that being said, what a magnificent Zen'no Divide that was! That's my Max!"

Pilet throws an arm around Max from behind.

"Yeah, I'll say! This guy almost melted my opponent for me! I mean he almost melted me too but hey, I probably could've shook it off."

"Oh my God, Imagine?" Added Yuuna. "I wonder, if Pilet ever gets cut in half while he's in Fever Point, you think each half would grow back and make two Pilets?!"

"Oh I'd certainly hope not." Replied Faith. "One is enough, thank you."

"Agreed." Said Max.

"Yeah? Well... Let's not find out, alright?!" Said Pilet, grimacing while rubbing his midsection squeamishly.

"Fax, I'll be off now." Said Benny "I'm gonna go park the ship with the others around the corner." He turns to the others. "Best of luck to you all! If you keep fighting like you did yesterday, there's not a damn thing in that pyramid that can stand a chance against you!"

Faxion makes a cringy face and motions a finger over his lips to hush Benny.

"Oh whoops! I've said too much. Anyway, have fun out there! Can't wait to see you all standing on the victor's podium."

Benny walks back into the ship, starts the engine and takes off towards the nearby fleet of light aircrafts. As his ship ascends, The Hidden Blades wave him goodbye.

A familiar voice greets the young prospects from behind.

"Good afternoon young mercenaries."

The Hidden Blades turn to see Toste, grinning while twirling his handlebar mustache with care. Pilet's eyes light up at the sight of the swordsmanship proctor.

"Hey! Buddy!" Exclaimed Pilet. "Long time no see! I didn't know the whole lot of you proctors were gonna show up for this... Whatever this is."

"Yes, well we do want to be here in support of the best of the best." Said Toste. "And my God what a stunning display of heart you've all shown in the desert. The Reaper Elite are no slouches in their own right, but when your group met them in battle the whole city roared in anticipation. Every bar in Grand Titanus was filled to the brim with clamoring spectators. What incredible power you all have!"

"Aw, thanks Mr. Toast!" Replied Yuuna. "We did our best, it's actually a little embarrassing that so many people saw me fail. But I'm glad that people still think we did good!"

"You did better than good." Said Faxion. "And you didn't fail! It's true that your opponents may have got the better of you, but did they stay and fight a monstrous Wurm King? No. They ran at the first chance they got. Meanwhile you four courageously rid Devil's Tongue of a beast who's known for eradicating whole villages. The people of the desert can now sleep soundly at night knowing that Kuweha has met his maker."

"Kuwewho?" Said Pilet.

"Kuweha was the name of the Wurm King you bested." Replied Toste. He grins in Faxion's direction. "And thank God you did the job before we were asked to."

Faxion and Toste share a good laugh while the others stand awkwardly in between them. Faxion walks over to Toste and embraces him in a tight hug.

"Ah comrade. I'm glad to see you again!" Said Faxion. "I'm sorry I had to tell the boy how to beat you, but I figured one of these days you had to learn about that temper."

"And I'm glad you did!" Replied Toste. "My father would be proud of the skill the young prospect displayed with a blade." Toste then turns to Pilet. "Now boy, I have something for you..."

"Oh yeah?" Replied Pilet. "Hope it's not another lecture."

Toste unfastens the parrying dagger from around his waist. He holds it up to Pilet, offering it with a bow. Stunned, Pilet looks at Toste with admiration.

"Toste... What? Why?" Said Pilet, accepting the gift hesitantly.

"That dagger gave you a lot of trouble, didn't it?" Toste replied. "May you use it to give trouble to many others, and may it guide you to many more victories."

Pilet silently nods to the Prince of Menanois, tying the leather sheath of the parrying dagger around his waist.

"Well I'm not as quick on the draw, but I'll do my best. You take care of yourself, can't wait for round two."

Toste draws his fencing foil and holds it out to Pilet, who gently clangs the parrying dagger against it in response.

"Here's to round two." Replied Toste.

The Hidden Blades bid farewell to Toste and begin to trek towards the furthest edge of the oasis, where Caffo Gilwick and the other proctors await. As they make their way over, they pass by Bhujanga Garuda and Scott Diliger, locked in a heated arcane sparring match.

Zhooom

Bhujanga launches a jade fireball for Scott's face, as Scott fastens a whip out of water and flails it at the fiery projectile. The water whip lashes into the fireball mid-flight, creating a steam cloud when the two collide.

Fzzzz

Scott then gathers a plethora of floating water spheres around him, launching them at extremely high velocity towards Bhujanga. Bhujanga answers with his own flaming barrage of green fireballs, as the onslaught leaves the area engulfed in a mist of steam. The Hidden Blades get caught in the steam cloud, waving it away and coughing out the perspiration in their lungs.

"Cough cough, Hey say it don't spray it dude!" Said Pilet, wheezing and wiping his steam covered face in the crook of his elbow.

The surrounding steam is pulled in like a vacuum to the space in between Scott's hands, growing larger and larger until forming a sphere twice the size of the learned aquacaster. He holds it stoically above his head, glaring at Bhujanga as his foe readies a fireball of similar size and holds it out to his side. After a tense pause, Scott can't help but release a subtle grin. He tosses the aqua sphere into the oasis, prompting the firecaster to release his Emerald flame.

"You haven't skipped a beat, have you old pal." Said Scott, fixing the ruffled collar of his shirt. "It feels like just yesterday I was assigning you a term paper on the Rok-Senn runic language, and now here you are about to steal my thunder as a Hired Blade."

Bhujanga smirks and rescinds his flames.

"You could've made that paper a bit easier, there wasn't enough coffee in all the fields of Magma Mountain to help me stay awake for it." He replied. "And thanks for the sponsorship by the way. You were right, most of these entrants haven't an idea how even a basic aura fusion works, let alone how to manage their aura without gassing out. It's been pretty sad to see up until this point."

Faith and Yuuna cringe at each other hearing his statement.

"I told you taking the exam was a good idea!" Said Scott. "I could sense your potential a mile away at that dig site last summer. It was a damn shame to see such a talent like yours forced to excavate for such chump change. Such low pay, and even lower respect! Once you're licensed you can tackle as many solo jobs as you like, just don't hesitate to visit your old professor every now and then huh?"

"Thanks, I'll keep that in mind." Replied Bhujanga.

The Hidden Blades leave the duo to their conversation and arrive at the end of the oasis. Caffo Gilwick greets them as they approach their destination, HBA dog tags in hand.

"Good afternoon candidates, do you have the required 8 tags?" He said.

The group hands their tags over to the proctor.

"Good, and just in time too. In a few minutes the next portion of the exam will take place, so just sit tight while we ready the next phase."

Caffo takes his leave, as the group takes a seat on some assorted beach chairs by the water. Several coolers lay scattered throughout, filled with water and refreshments. Along the waterline are tables displaying various assortments of food and snacks for the weary candidates to refuel. As the group eats their fill and recuperates, the rest of the exam candidates converge together by Caffo. Seeing this, Pilet and company join the ranks of candidates and proctors for further instruction.

"Alright candidates." Said Caffo, turning to address the crowd. "This is the final phase of your exam. It's clear that to have made it this far, all who stand before you are the best of the best."

Pilet peers his head out at some of the remaining teams. He notices The Funk Munkeys, The Mystic Marauders, Bhujanga, The Cobalt Killers and The Reaper Elite among several others. Caffo continues.

"What you are about to witness is a recent discovery by The Hired Blades Association's head of the archeology department, Scott Diliger." He motions to Scott. "Scott, if you'd do the honor of debriefing them please."

"Sure." Said Scott, walking to the edge of the water. "Alright guys listen up. The continent of Kettlena is completely jam packed with the ancient ruin sites of the native Rok-Senn people who called it home. Every week archeologists are unearthing a new dig site with more and more ancient knowledge. But these sites are often very dangerous, as the Rok-Senn were crafty auracasters with a knack for setting traps. As Licensed Hired Blades, our knowledge of auracast makes guiding archeologists through these ruins one of our most commonly requested jobs." He looks to Caffo. "Ready?" He said.

Caffo nods. He joins Scott at the water's edge, putting about 15 feet distance between them. They both bring their hands up to chest, fingertips lightly touching. They inhale meditatively, beginning to form a small marble of light between their hands. Faxion taps Pilet on the shoulder.

"Remember this?" He said. "You're no stranger to this technique."

Pilet nods and continues watching, eyes glued inquisitively to the arcane light.

The marble of light grows larger, spanning the size of a beach ball before being compressed back down to a marble like diameter. Both casters exhale roughly and fire the light marble into the oasis.

"Aura Break!" They exclaim.

The projectiles zip through the water, vanishing somewhere into the deep end. The crowd grows silent, as spectators watch and wait for a change in development.

"Uhh, do you think it was a dud?" Said Pilet.

"Shh, watch!" Retorts Faith.

Suddenly, a mysterious light begins to emerge from the center of the oasis. The light travels gracefully over the water and passes Scott and Caffo. It then finds its home in the sand some 50 feet from the water's edge. Scott turns to the spectating crowd and says.

"If I were you, I'd watch your step."

As the words escape his mouth, the ground beneath them begins to tremble. Suddenly, the sand starts to miraculously shift and rise where the aura had touched down.

"Hey what gives, what's going on!" Exclaims Lukah of the Funk Monkeys, tripping on a lifted mound of sand behind him.

"Oooh my." Said Dunya of The Mystic Marauders, as she grasps Puerto's arm for support. "Hold me you strong man!"

"Dunya, get serious! It's just an earthquake... Or something?" Replied Puerto.

Puerto clenches his left fist, raising his hand into the air. The auric tattoo of a jellyfish on the back of his left hand begins to glow fervently a deep indigo. Just then a massive, glowing Man 'O War jellyfish of pure aura takes shape beneath his team's feet. The auric jelly slowly rises from the sand, levitating off of the ground and carrying the Mystic Marauders to safety. The Hodejakt assassin twins can be seen gliding through the shadows of the uneven sand, alongside Bhujanga skating mystically along his Emerald Flame.

"Welp, we'd better get moving!" Said Faxion, readying a fleetfoot cast.

"Faxion, what form of trickery is this?" Said Kenzo, struggling to keep his balance under the seismic activity.

"Oh you'll see in just a moment my friend, until then follow me!" He replied.

Kenzo and The Hidden Blades ready fleetfoot and retreat to safety, leaping and bounding over mysterious stone structures that begin rising from the earth. The Funk Munkeys pass them on the left, flying by on a large, winged tree stump-like platform.

"Ya gotta move faster than that if you wanna be a Blade aye King Killer?!" Jabs Danba the Witchdoctor.

"What? Hey piss off! I'm just slowing down for my crew, that's all!" Pilet replied.

"Oh hi guys!" Said Yuuna, waving at the Funk Munkeys whilst whizzing past in a jetstream.

Thud

A small stone pounds Pilet behind the ear, as Lazlow the Gavel bounds by with his swordsman partner hoisted over his shoulder. He looks back and gives Pilet a devilish smirk, while Arturo angrily beats on his back.

"Laz I swear to God put me down or I'm cutting your head or your hands off or BOTH!!" Exclaims Arturo.

Pilet scoffs, doing his best not to trip on the rapidly changing terrain.

Finally, the crowd seems to get to non-shifting ground as the rumbling grows even louder and more boisterous. As the candidates clear the area and rally together at a safe distance, they watch as an incredibly large pyramid rises from the desert floor. Sand sifts and falls from the time-worn, limestone bricks forming the mighty structure. Many dark, jagged spires jut out from miscellaneous corners and crevices of the pyramid.

Finally, the pyramid stops its ascent with a mighty *CLUNK*, as the foundation sturdies itself into the sand. At the center of the base, a massive stone double-door littered with Rok-Senn runic language appears to be the only entrance to its mysterious halls. As the sand settles, Scott and Caffo approach the entrance, accompanied by Rexmere, the exam's head martial arts proctor. The three stand facing the crowd, postured authoritatively in front of the mysterious double doors. Scott speaks.

"I accidentally stumbled onto this pyramid a few weeks ago while experimenting with auracast by the water." Said Scott. "I found that as I was casting, the reflection of this monstrous structure behind us would fade in and out, and came to the realization that there was a latent aura sealed beneath its depths. Now oddly enough, the pyramid only seems to stay above the surface here for about two days before re-submerging itself. As such I've given it the name of "The Mirage Pyramid", fitting right?"

"Your mission today is to enter the pyramid, safely reach the room at the top, and once there retrieve a pre-placed artifact from a specifically designated table." Said Caffo. "You are to take nothing from this pyramid but the one artifact chosen at the table, and that's one per team, not individually. Once you've chosen your artifact, you will see a green lit button on the wall. This button will open a doorway to the outside, where a light aircraft will be waiting to bring you back to the ground. We've had experts traverse these halls simply to reach the top without triggering the many traps placed inside, and even we don't know the secrets that the pyramid holds. Be wary candidates, as you are about to venture into a completely new ancient ruin. Good luck, and stay sharp. Rexmere, your turn."

Caffo makes way for Rexmere, who takes ten paces from the doorway and begins to hop buoyantly on the balls of his feet.

Rexmere begins throwing punches lightly at the air, shadow boxing while breathing intently. Suddenly, a crimson aura begins to emanate from his muscles, as his punches begin to thrust forth small auric waves of the same shade into the air.

"What the hell is he doing?" Said Pilet. "What, do you have to do a dance for the door to open? If that's the case then I'll just climb to the top from the outside, I've got two left feet and I'm not trying to trip over them in front of everyone."

"It's a technique called "Kinetic chain" Pilet." Replied Faxion. "Martial artists have found that their punches and kicks can pack a wallop with the help of auracast, just give him a second and you'll see what I mean."

After throwing a few more punches, the crimson aura begins to create an arcane binding around Rexmere's fists. It wraps itself around each knuckle, forming a makeshift glove of pure energy. As the wraps congeal, Rexmere crouches, then suddenly explodes towards the double doors.

"HAH, HAH!" He shouts, slamming each door with a mystically charged fist.

KSHEEWWW *FWOOSH*

Each door flies open, as the auric runes written across the front of each begin to glow a golden hue. A jetstream of air follows the force of Rexmere's blows, knocking the doors back violently and blowing his dreadlocks vigorously in the wind. Rexmere stands aside as the airstream subsides, holding a hand out toward the doors.

"You're welcome." He said, leaving the door to join the ranks of his fellow proctors.

"God damn!" Said Pilet. "Alright alright. That was pretty impressive. But I bet I could probably do that if you showed me how."

"Think you can deal with the chronic pain and arthritis that often comes from training Kinetic Chain?" Replied Faxion. "I'm sure Rexmere wakes up in pain every morning. Great power like that comes at a cost..."

"Yeah, you would know Pilet." Said Faith, beginning to act out a standing seizure. "Urgghh, I cast too many Hollowpoints! Now I'm dyinnnggg!!!"

"Yo shut up Faith!" Pilet replied. "I can learn whatever I want to. I'll probably skip that class though..."

Caffo stands at the entrance to the Mirage Pyramid.

"This final phase of the exam is noncompetitive, so no attacking each other ok? The inside of this Pyramid has many rooms and halls, and the way to the top is not easy to find. One team at a time will enter the lobby and choose a hall to traverse, as the next team will wait five minutes before entering. This shouldn't take more than a few hours, but just in case we've set the time limit for 6PM tonight."

Caffo's gaze shifts, denoting a sense of urgency. The Proctor cracks his neck to relieve the tension.

"Of course, being in the Pyramid two days from now when it re-submerges itself could prove quite messy, so I would try not to do that. Take care and defend yourself at all times. Now, who's first? Any volunteers?"

"Yeah, ME!" Said Lazlow Jr., accompanied by his teammates. "We're the best. So naturally, we should go first! Why should I have to wait for these hack jobs?"

"Polish those Hired Blades Badges Caffo." Said Arturo as he walks by. "This won't take very long at all, and I want mine ready as soon as I'm out."

After wiping his sword clean meticulously, Asger gives it a flourish and resheaths it into his back mounted scabbard.

"Guess it can't be helped. I was hoping to have another flakeroll, but since you guys are in such a rush I guess I'll have to take it to go..."

Dabria readies her belt of throwing knives.

"We'll have the quickest time yet, you watch." She says to Caffo.

Caffo rolls his eyes and stands aside for the four to enter.

"Good luck..." He replied. "You'll need it..."

And with that, the members of The Reaper Elite enter the darkness of the

Mirage Pyramid. The group of top-rated candidates stride across the crowd and towards the ancient double doors with haughty pride, a condescending pep in their step as they pass through the darkness. An eerie moment of silence goes by, as the sound of their footsteps begins to peeter out.

"..."

Light, wispy clouds of sand roll through the desert, as the gentle winds howl through the dunes at a harrowing pitch. The audience at the Pyramid's entrance stands erect, in wait of some sign of a struggle or conflict within. With tension in the air so thick a Dragonfly knife could sear through, the company of attendees begins wiping the anxious sweat from their brows.

"AAAAAAGH!!!"

Suddenly a blood curdling scream is heard coming from inside. Many of the candidates jump in response, taken aback by the abrupt, piercing sound. Stunned by the sudden shock, several other candidates trip over their own feet and fall to the floor. As everyone gazes in awe at the darkness between the ancient doorway; a scalp of blonde, spiked hair begins ghoulishly peeking out from behind the corner of one door.

Suddenly, Lazlow fully pokes his head out into the open, a devilish grin strewn across his face.

"Just kidding losers." He said, before strutting insolently back into the darkness.

"Damn idiots..." Said Caffo, holding his heart from beating out of his chest. "Hurry up and get in there!"

"Hahahahaha!" Laugh The Reapers.

Some time goes by, as team after team enters the Pyramid in five minute intervals. Several teams later, Caffo finally calls for Pilet and company.

"Next up, "The Hidden Blades"." Said Caffo, reading from a list on his Chatch vambrace.

"Finally!" Said Pilet. "Let's get in there and beat the hell outta some... Well, whatever's in there!"

"Phew, oh boy." Said Yuuna. "This is kinda scary. It's just like Mom and Dad used to do, right sis? If they could do it, so can we!"

"Damn right!" Replied Faith. "Let's go make them proud. The chance to enter a completely new Rok-Senn ruin, what an amazing opportunity."

"That it is." Said Max. "I cannot wait to see what secrets the ancestors of this continent have in store..."

Kenzo, Faxion and Toste approach the group from behind. Kenzo gives Max an unexpected bear hug, applying great crushing power.

"That's my boy! This is it Max!! This is the end of the road, you go in there and show the world the might of the Sanda!"

"Ugh, Father!" Replied Max, wheezing as the air escapes his lungs. "Ok I will, you're hurting me though."

Faxion removes his hat and holds it to his abdomen, giving the prospects a more serious look.

"Alright guys, this is where it gets serious." He said. "Faith and Yuuna, I'm sure you know all about the Rok-Senn so this is more for Max and Pilet, but listen up. These people were no slouches when it came to auracast, in fact they're the founders of modern auracast itself. The different tribes of the Rok-Senn loved to compete, as well as steal from one another. They would frequently set up these "vaults", where their precious belongings and treasures would be hidden. Of course, in order to reach said treasures, one must first pass the many traps set by the vault's creators."

Faxion glares stoically off towards the Mirage Pyramid."

The Rok-Senn were the best "auric trap" setters in history, able to auracast into inanimate objects, floors, walls, statues, anything really. Be wary of anything and everything you see as out of the ordinary, and even more so of that which seems too normal. Death was never so well hidden in plain sight than in a Rok-Senn ruin."

Toste puts a hand on Pilet's shoulder.

"Hey, don't you go dying on me now." He said. "You still have round two to worry about." Toast grins. "Maybe I'll even show you how to hold those knives proper."

"Ha, don't worry about me Toasty. I'll be alright." Pilet smirks and nods. "And that sounds cool, Fax's idea of teaching is just beating the snot outta me."

Faxion points sarcastically towards Toste.

"What makes you think training with him will be any different??"

They share a brief laugh, as the four ready to take their leave into the perilous ruin. Faith takes the lead, meticulously sifting the pages of her leatherbound Rok-Senn tome. She gives her sister a soft grin, as Yuuna treads dreadfully behind her.

"We'll be ok, I promise." Said Faith.

"I know sis, I know." Replied Yuuna, anxiously rubbing a necklace of amethyst around her neck.

Max falls in line after Yuuna, affixing his Lacerate belt and peering back at his father. Kenzo gives him an affirmative nod and a stoic gaze, lightly beating his armored chest plate once with his fist. Max takes a deep breath, looking back at the Mirage Pyramid whilst gripping the handle of his Drawing Lacerate.

"I'll make you proud." He muttered to himself. "I'll make you all proud..."

Brandishing his Dragonflies, Pilet stares intently into his reflection on the face of the blades. He gazes into his mauve eyes, a stark look of determination glazed across his face.

One last step. He thought. *I just gotta get through this, and then I'll find you. I promise...*

As Pilet approaches the door, he turns back one last time in excitement. He sees Kenzo, standing with his arms folded and his chin up high, giving him a thumbs up. Toste draws his rapier and points it down towards the earth, his other hand behind him as he bows. He then spies Faxion, who smiles deviously and pulls his Stinger pistol from his back pocket.

"Hurry up Pilet!"

He points it toward Pilet, pulls back the slide of the weapon and fires a BB round at Pilet's forehead.

"Ow!!" Exclaimed Pilet. "Alright alright already! I'm going! Shit..."

Pilet enters the double doors right behind Max, holding his stinging forehead in lament.

The four aspiring mercenaries step boldly into the darkness between the two doors, vanishing almost as quickly as they enter. A brand new ruin with untold secrets, filled to the brim with mystery unknown even to The Hired Blades Association. What dangers lie in wait for the would-be Blades? What secrets lie at the heart of this relic of an ancient world? The final test, the last obstacle in the way of joining the illustrious, world renowned Hired Blades Association has finally arrived. Or so one would believe...

ABOUT THE AUTHOR

J.D. Rajotte is a Reiki Master, Licensed Massage Therapist, and Martial Artist of over a decade. Born and raised in the lush, woodsy suburbs of Brentwood, New York; a young J.D. spent many an hour dashing through his backyard with his childhood dog, swinging sticks at his father's neatly-trimmed hedges and daydreaming about epic adventures battling robots, pirates, and ninjas. Enthralled with the world of martial arts, he started training Shaolin Kung Fu at 18, and began learning Brazilian Jiu Jitsu at 25. That same year, J.D. graduated from The New York College of Health Professions as both a Licensed Massage Therapist and a certified Reiki Master; taking with him a wealth of knowledge in both western and eastern medical practice. Suffering an injury that removed him from martial arts competition, J.D. took to writing as a creative outlet. Thus this work was born.

Printed in the United States
by Baker & Taylor Publisher Services